HIS FIRST KI

He was not sorry.

He was not sorry at all.

He looked coldly down at the still face. The man had deserved it. He was a killer. He destroyed deer illegally and laughed. He had threatened another man with death and walked away chuckling. He was the same as the man who had killed Aaron and walked away.

Looking down at the man, his ears ringing with the high, crazy aftersong of the explosions, he had a sudden sense of crisis, of slippage. But it was past and gone before he had a chance to think. His mind cleared and his vision cleared and he saw what it all meant. It all fit, and it was right; it was all true, and set, and irrevocable.

Paul Michelson had realized what it was all about.

THE DEAD OF WINTER

DAVID POYER

THE
DEAD
OF
WINTER

TOR

A TOM DOHERTY ASSOCIATES BOOK

THE DEAD OF WINTER

Copyright © 1988 by David Poyer

First printing: March 1988

A TOR Book

Published by Tom Doherty Associates, Inc.
49 West 24th Street
New York, NY 10010

ISBN: 0-812-50787-8
Can. No.: 0-812-50788-6

Printed in the United States of America

0 9 8 7 6 5 4 3 2 1

For C. L.

Amazing Grace! How sweet the sound
That saved a wretch like me
I once was lost, but now am found
Was blind, but now can see!
                    —John Newton, 1779

ONE

Monday, November Twenty-fourth

THE WINTER THAT YEAR CAME COLD; COLD AND OVERCAST AND gray. It had snowed early that autumn and then frozen and then snowed again, and in late November the season opened colder than anyone in Hemlock County, Pennsylvania, could remember it.

It was on that first day of the hunt, an hour after dawn, that the old man found the body of the boy.

Halvorsen sat by it in the snow for a long time after he knew it was too late to help. Around him, upright on the ridge that ran for miles east and west, waited the white and black trunks of birches, like overexposed negatives, and a few beech and a little way off a stand of small hemlock. The birches stood lifeless and immobile, their winter-nude branches interlocking over the old man's lowered head. Along the whole sweep of hill only the boughs of the hemlocks moved, swaying gently to a chill breath that came up the hollow from the north. Above their tops the sky was gray.

Presently he lifted his head. Two hunters, in flame-orange coats and caps and casually carrying deer rifles, were working slowly along the hill toward him, one above and a little behind the other. The old man hummed a few words of an old hymn, waiting, as the distant orange winked on and off among the trees. When the lead man stopped, he knew they had seen him. At his wave they looked about warily, then came toward where he knelt. The air was so still he could hear the crunch and squeak of their steps long before they reached him.

"What happened?" said the older hunter, looking down at the body.

"Somebody shot him," said Halvorsen.

"Is he dead?" asked the younger hunter. He looked a little scared.

"That's right," said the old man. He looked at the melt edges of the red patch in the snow, at the way it had spread and cooled and at last frozen. "Not long ago, either. If I'd of been a little earlier—or if whoever done it had stayed around to help—"

"What's that he done in the snow there?" said the younger hunter.

Halvorsen had already seen it. A wavering scrape, a semicircle open to the right. The bare hand lay buried at its incompletion. It might, he thought, have been an attempt to get up.

After a few more words the three of them lifted the body. Halvorsen staggered a little under his share of the weight. They carried it, with frequent rests, a quarter mile through the woods to where the two hunters had left their pickup on a partially cleared lease road. They all knew it was futile, but something made them lay the boy gently on the dirty bed of the truck and draw a shroud of cold-stiffened tarpaulin over the fair hair, the closed, tensed eyes, the white blood-drained face. The younger hunter looked around at the silent trees, at the hillside that rose above them. His gaze stopped at the old man's face.

"Let's take him on into town," Halvorsen said quietly.

The pickup burrowed into the snow, tires whining, engine roaring a cloud of white into the still air, then gained traction as it reached frozen clay and swung up onto the rutted snow of the road. In the cab the old man was jostled against the door as they bounced down the hill, skidding at the turns as the road dropped into Mortlock Hollow. There the jolting lessened as the road widened and became straighter. They passed other vehicles, trucks and four-wheel drives, parked off the road among the trees. They saw other men only once; four of them were hoisting the body of an animal into the back of a Jeep. A couple of miles down the hollow the valley opened suddenly and the younger hunter, who was driving, braked at a bullet-punctured stop sign and then pulled out to the left, onto a recently plowed paved road.

They drove into Raymondsville along Route Six.

Ralph H. Sweet had been appointed the county game warden three years before. Or, as he liked people to call him, the game protector. He was Halvorsen's grandson, though the two had never been very close; and when he came into the waiting room of the hospital where three men sat outside the green swinging doors marked EMERGENCY, it was to the old man that he nodded, clearing his throat. "Uh, hi, Racks. What is it? I heard there was something wrong up here."

The two hunters looked up at Sweet. He was the largest man in the room by a considerable margin. Broad-shouldered, in heavy khaki pants and a red lumberjack coat, his face reddening from sudden warmth after the outside air, the warden sat down on the bench opposite the men and took out a pack of filter-tipped cigars. He lit one, the jut of it making his face look older

3

for a moment, and offered the package around. Halvorsen shook his head silently. The older hunter took one. Sweet held his Zippo for him. Halvorsen saw that the flame was steady in the currentless hot air of the room.

"We found a boy laying in the woods, Ralph," the old man said then.

"Who found him? Was it you?"

"That's right."

Sweet looked at the others, but still spoke to Halvorsen. "Tell me what happened."

"I was walking out Mortlock Run," said the old man. He rubbed his stubbled chin with one hand, and his eyes, blue as a far stand of spruce and set deep in a shadowed wrinkling of squint and age, grew a little distant. "Couldn't sleep. Happens sometimes . . . anyhow, lying there before dawn I happened to think today was openin' day. Figured I'd take a walk, see how they were doing down the hollow."

"You used to hunt down there, didn't you?"

"Used to," said Halvorsen, looking at him in the bright fluorescent glare. "Anyhow, that's how I come to find him."

"How is he? Hurt bad?" asked Sweet, looking toward the glass doors. Beyond their square windows, small and spotlessly clean, they could see nothing but white light.

Halvorsen told him. The warden sucked in on the little cigar, grimacing as if it gave him pain. One shoe began tapping against the tile, an expensive-looking brown tassel loafer, wet through from the snow. "Was he dead when you found him? You should have left him there and called me, not brought him in here."

Halvorsen looked at him. After a moment Sweet shook his head and looked toward the two hunters. Up to now they had been silent. "How do you men come into this?" he asked them.

"Maybe we should wait for the police," said the younger one, looking at Sweet's lumberjack coat. "Or the sheriff. We'll talk to them."

"No," said Sweet. He straightened up on the bench and dug one hand into his coat pocket. The badge hung before the men's eyes. "I'm the Game Protector here in Hemlock County. The investigation and disposition of everything having to do with hunting is my responsibility. And that includes accidents." He pinned the carefully polished brass securely to his coat and relit the cigar, which had gone out. "Now, you tell me what you saw."

"We were out near the end of the run there," said the older hunter, taking a drag on his borrowed cigar and glancing nervously at Halvorsen. "Got there about an hour before dawn. Jim and I been going out there a few years now. We work together. Do stand-hunting, mostly. We got us a six-pointer last year. Well, year before last."

"That's a nice size buck."

"Dressed out over a hundred pounds . . . well. We was seeing most of the deer this morning going further along the hill from where we were. There was some shooting from over there too. We didn't see anything where we were but two does. We had a nice stand there but didn't see buck one. And it's too damn cold this year to sit still for long. So Jim he finally says, why not walk over a ways and settle in nearer where the shots were coming from."

The younger man nodded and picked up the story. "So we packed up the guns, had a drink of coffee out of the Thermos, and started still-huntin' along the hill.

"Midway along it we saw this guy"—he looked at Halvorsen—"wavin' to us. We went over. That's when we seen the kid lying there."

"Where exactly was that?" Sweet asked him.

"Mortlock Run, like he said. You know the old pump house to the right of the road, just after the fork?" The warden hesitated, then nodded. "It's about half a mile straight uphill from there. Maybe a hundred yards down from the crest on the south side of Town Hill."

"I can show you if you want, Ralph," said Halvorsen.

"Yeah, thanks, I'll do that on my own. Maybe get some pictures. Was there anyone else around when you found him?"

"No."

"Did you . . . you didn't have a gun on you?"

"No," said Halvorsen evenly. "I don't hunt anymore, Ralph. Remember?"

"What did you see after you came up?" Sweet asked the two hunters.

"The boy was face down in the snow," said the older hunter. He opened his hand jerkily; ash fell from the cigar and made a gray star on the clean tile floor. "His hair was spread out over the snow. Long, blond, shining —pretty—like a girl's, I mean. I thought for a minute it was a girl. This old guy here was sitting beside him. I saw the boy's gun lying off to one side. His arms were stretched out—like this." He lifted his hands up and out. "And one hand 'd kind of scrabbled around some in the snow."

"When we got close we seen the blood," said the younger hunter. "It was all over in the snow. Bright, like when you lung shoot a deer. Just so red."

"Where had he been hit?" Sweet asked, looking at the closed door to the emergency room.

"In the side, kind of around in the back," said the older hunter. "There wasn't a lot of blood there though. Where it was, was by his mouth. He must have coughed it up, and died, all alone there."

"Except for whoever shot him," said Halvorsen. They all looked at him.

Sweet shook his head and aimed smoke at the ceiling. "Jesus. This is the first hunting death I've had. I'll have to get an identification, do the accident report, call his folks, arrange the—"

Halvorsen said, "How do you know it was an accident?"

His grandson raised his eyebrows. "Well, what else could it be? I mean, did you see any tracks or anything?"

"Some."

"What?"

"Well, you know, I didn't look too close. You want to go up there and check them out yourself, I imagine."

"What else did you see?"

"He didn't have a license," said the old man.

"That's right, he didn't," said the older hunter suddenly. "I didn't notice it but now you say it—"

"Kids have been known to shade the law," said Sweet. "Game deputies can't be everywhere. There's no reason to complicate this, Racks." He took a yellow notepad out of his coat. "I need your names. Better let me see your driver's licenses too."

"Will there be trouble?" asked the older man.

"Not from what I've heard so far," said Sweet. "I'll try to find out who did it. But that's pretty hard to do if they don't stay around and give themselves up. It's a hell of a big woods out there."

While he was checking their identifications the green door swung open. A blonde woman came out in a scrub suit. She looked around the room. "Hello, Mr. Halvorsen," she said.

Sweet stood up. "What's his status, doctor?"

7

"The boy? He was dead when your granddad brought him in, warden. I'm sorry."

"In your opinion, was it an accident?"

"Certainly could have been. It was a twelve-gauge shotgun slug. Entered the anterior portion left lung, exited the left chest wall. I'd say he lived for maybe fifteen minutes after being hit. Maybe as long as a half hour. He would have been unconscious most of that time. He died of shock and loss of blood."

"Could he have lived?"

"If he'd been brought right in, I *might* have been able to stabilize him. Even then his chances would have been about fifty–fifty. Wasn't there anyone with him?"

"No one who stayed around," Halvorsen said.

Sweet finished writing, put the pad away, and sighed. "I guess I'd better see him. Have you called Charlie? The coroner?"

"Of course." The woman turned away from them and went back through the doors. Sweet followed her. Halvorsen, after a moment's hesitation, got up and went after them.

The room beyond was even brighter, cleaner, hotter than the waiting room. White partitions sectioned it. Sweet and the doctor were standing in one of the sections, their backs to Halvorsen. The old man walked up behind them, his snow-wet boots going squish-squish across the tiles. They did not turn when he came up and he had to look between them.

The boy lay face up on the gurney. His closed eyes looked relaxed now. Around the smooth, pale face yellow hair curled damply. He looked very young.

"So," the warden said to the doctor, "when are you going to have that drink with me?"

"I'm not."

"Give me a break, babe. How often do I have to—"

"You're here to look at this body, Ralph," said the doctor. "Look at it."

Sweet did. In the fluorescent silence the old man, behind him, could hear him swallow.

"Anything on him?" said the warden at last.

"A wallet," said the doctor, picking it up from a tray. "He's from here in town, on Barnes Street. He's seventeen years old.

"His name was Aaron Michelson."

TWO

Wednesday, November Twenty-sixth

FROM OUTSIDE THE NIGHT-DIMMED WINDOW THE EYES STARED back at him above the neatly-trimmed black beard. They stared; and sometimes, it seemed to him, they accused.

Je m'accuse. . . .

No. It is these hills that are to blame, he thought, looking through the frost-etched window of his office.

The hills ruled this country. They stood always at the edge of vision, walling off the horizon, damming up the sky. They isolated those who lived between them, made them narrow as the huddled, suspicious towns. He knew what they could do. He had grown up among them; although he, in spirit at least, had escaped.

His son had not.

Paul Michelson sat in a comfortable chair at a familiar desk in a warm book-lined room, and shivered.

It had been cold at the funeral. He'd tried to talk to Anne there, after the priest had left. She'd turned away without a word. So he'd stood by the hacked-open earth after she and her husband left, looking down at the box. Behind him the men with the shovels shifted impatiently. They blew on their hands and cursed almost loudly enough for him not to ignore. At last, after some minutes, someone started the engine of the backhoe. He had turned, at that, and stared them down; and they had looked away from him, their eyes had sought the hills, and the man in the cab had killed the engine. It was as if none of them could withstand whatever they had seen in his face.

And now he looked into his own haunted eyes, seeing beyond them only the hills, and thought: Someone out there killed my son.

The campus was covered with snow. Little straight trails had been tramped through the white as the students went to and from classes. West Kittanning State Teachers College was not a large school, though it had a good name in the western part of the state, and now, looking downward, he could make out only a few tiny figures, booted and overcoated, leaning into the wind as they floundered along.

He had hoped Aaron might someday be one of them.

Michelson's office was a ten-by-ten box. On the metal desk in front of him were slanted piles of ungraded papers. Beside them was an empty coffee mug made of pewter and Spanish leather, engraved with his name and the legend Assistant Professor. A stack of textbooks and monographs occupied the rest of the desk. There were books on the floor, also in stacks, and hundreds more on the painted pine shelves that reached from window to door and almost to the ceiling. All of one shelf was filled with bound volumes of professional periodicals in sociology and anthropology. Loose copies of other scholarly and political journals lay on an end table near the closed door.

Seated there, unmoving, Michelson imagined how it had happened.

He had done this over and over in the last two days.

And what he saw, or imagined, had refined and sharpened itself until at last it had become as clear and immediate and real as the bright mirror of memory itself could have made it.

In the scene, the bright mirror, he saw his son not dead but alive. Alert, bright-haired, straight, he was walking in the forest. He carried a pack and bedroll, but his hands were empty, innocent. He was wearing the yellow sweater his father had sent him for his seventeenth birthday, a few weeks before. He paused often, looking up as a squirrel chattered, smiling at the blue electric whir of a jay, bending to examine the bark of a tree. His face was absorbed, intelligent, happy.

For a moment Michelson's lips twitched. He almost smiled. Then, once again, he saw the other figure in the mirror. And in his lap his hands locked white-knuckled into a double fist.

Though the face was unclear he saw plainly the gross body, the brutal jaw, the coarse, short hair. The man shambled through the forest. The neck of a bottle showed at the side pocket of a red-and-black-barred hunting coat.

In his hands he carried a scoped, high-powered rifle.

And Michelson, staring unseeing at the dark window, hands clenched in his lap, watched it all happen again, powerless to halt or alter any of it. He saw his son brush against a bush. It moved, and snow fell from it. On its far side the hunter stopped, swaying, and turned and lifted the rifle to his shoulder with a snarl.

He fired.

Aaron Michelson, shock and pain in his eyes, looked directly toward his father. His hands went to his chest. His lips moved, but words did not carry through the mirror.

He fell.

The hunter came and stood above the body. For a moment he looked frightened, but then his mouth turned cunning. He looked left and right, and then down, at the snow-pillowed face.

He walked off into the woods.

Michelson leaned forward, feeling the edge of the desk sharp in his stomach but welcoming the pain.

Aaron had been independent. He'd had to be. After the separation—God, how small and lost he'd looked at ten—he'd gone with his mother; in those days the courts always decided for the woman. There were visitation rights, sure, but then came that opening in New Haven —sociology slots weren't that easy to find—and four hundred miles was too far to drive for just a weekend. Three years ago Michelson had been able to move back to Pennsylvania, having found this position at West Kittanning; but for most of the boy's childhood, he'd been . . . not there.

The eyes were accusing again.

His son had grown up with Anne's people, up in Hemlock County. Not bad people, Michelson thought. But limited. Closed-minded, conservative, and increasingly hostile to him, especially after Anne remarried. Typical small-town people.

If only he'd been around more, when the boy was growing up. . . .

Alone in his office, Michelson shook his head wearily. His fists rose slowly, pressed into the emptiness of his chest, and he stared at the rows of impotent books with eyes that looked not outward but in, toward an endlessly repetitive private hell.

"A hunting accident," he whispered.

At last the torture was interrupted by a discreet knock.

He glanced toward the door but did not rise. The knob turned slowly, and then he heard the low grind of a seldom-used key.

"Paul?"

It was the department chairman, McKean Connolly. He came hesitantly into the room, a smallish, busy-bearded man with horn-rims. "Paul?" he said again.

"My door was locked."

"I know. Forgive me." Connolly glanced around the little office. "I thought you might be back. I heard about what happened. I'm terribly sorry, Paul. Is there anything I can do for you?"

"No," said Michelson. He had turned and was looking out again, at the swiftly deepening night. Connolly waited, nodded finally, and turned to the door.

"Mac—" Connolly paused. Michelson continued, "I'm sorry." He took a breath and brought his hands above the desk and unlocked them. "Christ. You read —you know about loss reactions, but it—it doesn't seem to make any difference. It's supposed to help to talk about things like this, isn't it? Come back, Mac. Please."

Wordless, Connolly sat in the chair that faced Michelson's desk. He rubbed his hands on his suit trousers, adjusted his glasses, cleared his throat.

"His mother and I couldn't live together," said Michelson, looking out the window again. "And for a long time, while he was growing up, I didn't see very much of him. But still we were close, Mac, real close."

Connolly murmured something inaudible and crossed his legs.

"When I got the news, I . . . I just couldn't believe it. I couldn't internalize it. Someone so young, it didn't seem possible. An old person, your parents, you mourn when they die, but it's comprehensible, it's natural, you expect that someday you'll see them go. But a seventeen-year-old . . . no."

"How did it happen?"

"He was in the woods. Apparently a hunter shot him."

"A hunting accident. That's so damned—"

"No, Mac," said Michelson, interrupting him. He leaned over the desk. "It wasn't a 'hunting accident.' My son didn't hunt. He wouldn't touch a rifle. He's never even owned a cap gun."

"A lot of people hunt up there, Paul. They don't think the way we do about it. It's more or less accepted."

"Not by me, and not by him. I'm his father, Mac, I knew him. We've talked about it. Oh, he loved the woods." Michelson stopped, half lifted his hands to his closed eyes, then jerked them away. "Ah, *God*, it's hard using that past tense.

"He was out there hiking, or camping, maybe. But that's all. And somebody shot him. Accident? That's what that ignorant game warden called it on the phone." He reached toward Connolly as if motioning him closer. "Don't you know what it's like up there, during the season? They shoot at anything that moves. You're from around there, aren't you?"

"Upstate New York," said Connolly, shifting in his chair.

"Then you've seen them. They buy their licenses and head for the woods. It's some kind of reversion for them, some kind of ritual. They call it sport. But it's just killing."

"Well, of course I'm with you on that, Paul. Someday it will be stopped. But—"

"You know, he called me."

"What? Aaron called you?"

"The day before it happened. He wanted me to call

15

back. But I figured it was too late, after I got in from that adult class I do Sundays, and I turned off the machine and it just slipped my mind, and then . . ."

Neither of them said anything for a moment. In the hall, sounding far away through the closed door, the bell rang to release the last class of the day. Suddenly Michelson leaned forward over the desk. "Mac. Do you think I'm a coward?"

"Excuse me?"

"You heard me. Do I have any guts at all? I keep myself in good shape. But I haven't been in a fight since grade school."

"I don't think that's a constructive approach, Paul."

"I've never fought for anything. Never. When I was in school I had a deferment. But I wouldn't have gone anyway. I'd have gone over the border first."

"Weren't you active in the movement? That was a kind of battle, wasn't it?"

Michelson blinked at the smaller man. The movement. And in his mind rose the image of a young face, different, yet still the same, still his own. And with that image came a sick feeling of betrayal, not by another, but the far more bitter taste of betrayal by oneself. "The movement, yeah, but even there . . . Oh, Christ." He covered his face from Connolly's astonished look. "Oh, Mac, damn it, damn them all. There must be something somebody can do."

Connolly sat uncomfortably, murmuring, "Yes, I know," and "I'm very sorry, Paul. Look, if there's anything at all I can do to help—"

"I'd like to find him," said Michelson, forcing his words through his masking hands.

"Who?"

"The one that did it."

16

The chairman reached across the desk and gripped one of Michelson's tensed wrists. The man across from him resisted. He kept his hands before his face as if to deny the sight of a world without what he had lost. Connolly spoke in a low, intense tone. "Listen to me, Paul! I'm sure it was an accident.

"You and I may not hunt. A lot of people don't. But up here, a lot do. They're still good, they're still honest, they just don't understand. No one would intend to kill another human being."

"If he'd stayed to help, Aaron might have lived. Is that an accident, Mac? Or murder?"

Connolly looked helpless. He stood up, edged around the desk, and put an arm around the shoulder of the seated man. "Look, I know it's rough. But if there's anything that can be done, the law will do it. Mourn, yes. But then accept that life has to go on."

"Go on to what?"

Connolly was silent. "No," said Michelson, breathing hard. He revealed his face. "No. I won't accept it."

"What can you do?"

"I can see that someone is punished."

"But who? Are there suspects?"

Michelson laughed bitterly. "That's what I asked the warden—Sweet. Young incompetent. He told me on the phone, when he called to notify me, that he'd investigated and that there was no one to blame. Not the police—he, the *game warden,* had investigated! In one day! You think he's going to find out who did this? He'll put a little check mark in a tally for some state report. That's all Aaron will be, just another statistic. Just another animal shot down in the woods."

"Paul, you're upset. Perhaps we should go over to the dispensary—"

"I don't need a tranquilizer. What I need is justice."

Connolly nodded. He patted Michelson's shoulder once more, then stepped away from the desk. "All right. But do one thing for me. Come out and have a drink with us. That was the last bell. Teresa should be there."

"You don't want to leave me alone, eh?"

"I'm sorry about Aaron, believe me. But there's nothing we can do."

"Maybe that's the trouble."

"What?"

"No one does anything. That's why things like this go on happening."

"Come on." Connolly laughed uneasily. "This doesn't sound like you, Dr. Michelson."

"No. It doesn't. I'm an intellectual, right? A thinker. A man of ideas."

"Come have a drink. It'll do you good."

"Maybe in a little while." Michelson looked at the paper-strewn surface of the desk like a man facing a white wilderness. "But just now, let me alone for a moment, Mac, all right? I need to think some things out."

The long flat-topped ridges that flanked the valley where the college lay were somber edgings to a sapphire sky when Michelson came out of the social sciences building and started across the campus.

It was very cold. Under the globed lamps that starred the half-cleared path his breath glowed. He walked along, head down.

All my life, he was thinking, I have tried to do right. Measured not by the words of a dead book, not by rote or religion, but by what science learned about society. He gave money, sometimes more than he should on the salary of an associate professor. He supported the things he believed in with more than cash: with time —petitions, demonstrations, or when he felt strongly, an article.

Somehow, just now, it seemed futile. Worse. It was half-hearted . . . lukewarm. A man did not oppose evil with placards or signatures or words when it reached out to take those he loved.

Sometimes you had to do more.

He walked along slowly, hunched in his car coat. Under his rubbers the snow squeaked like powdered glass.

Some minutes later he stood irresolute, still undecided, outside the door to the faculty lounge. Laughter and the rattle of ice in glasses came faintly through the wood. In the window of a fire-alarm box he studied the image of a man. The beard lay smoothly trimmed against his cheeks. Above the loosened tie his eyes were shadowed, unreadable.

What would happen if that glass, that mirror of the internal, were shattered? What alarms would sound? What red machines would scream in the night?

As he closed the door behind him the laughter stopped, choked off into a murmur and then silence. Men and women he knew turned, their faces frightened for the first moment, then twisting into assumed sympathy. But their fear was only concealed, and concealed too was relief that it had not happened to them. They would not meet his gaze, but he saw their falsity plainly.

Head down, Michelson crossed the room toward Connolly. Beside the chairman waited a slight young woman in a black peasant skirt and patterned blouse. Her face and mouth were wide, her eyes dark, and her skin as smooth as chamois. She wore pale-pink lipstick and matching turquoise-cut glass earrings an inch square. There was a lavender ribbon in her shoulder-length hair. Gold gleamed at her throat and on her bare arm, smooth links of hammered metal. Her eyes were wide and sad and without guilt or falsity or self-consciousness, and this time he was the first to look away.

"Paul?"

"Hello, Terry."

She moved toward him, then hesitated. "I'm so sorry."

He nodded at the floor. Connolly muttered something, glanced at the two of them, and moved off. She took another step closer and looked up, one hand stretched toward him, palm up, a few inches from his chest. It looked as if she was offering him something, but except for an unlit cigarette her hand was empty.

"Still trying to quit?" he said, looking at her hand.

"Paul, you should have called me," Teresa said.

"Why?"

"We could have gone to the funeral together."

"Not my idea of a fun date." Michelson did not smile.

"Do not joke. I wanted to help." Her hand moved forward another inch and her fingertips brushed his jacket. "Pain is less when it is shared. If you try to build walls around it, around yourself, it will never leave you, and no one will enter—"

"Forget it. I don't want to talk about it," said Michelson. "I tried with Mac. It didn't help."

She was close enough now that he caught her perfume. It was a familiar scent. "Maybe you should try it with someone who loves you."

Her eyes were too deep, too earnest for him; his slipped aside. Her hand was on his arm now, warm.

20

"Paul, have you cried yet for him? Cry with me. Do not lock in that pain. Come with me. We will mourn him together."

He did not have to answer, for at that moment Connolly returned with two glasses. "Paul. Here."

"I don't want liquor."

"We all know how much he meant to you—"

"He was all I had," said Michelson.

He had said it too loudly. Around him the silence, which had been pushed back with chatter while Teresa and he talked, came back in a cold wave. Connolly looked at him wordlessly, unhappily. Teresa's eyes filled with tears and she looked down at her hand, at the cigarette. After a moment the department chairman cleared his throat and glanced around. People began to talk again, hastily, looking away from the three who stood close together. Connolly set the extra glass carefully atop a bookcase.

Michelson looked around the room, and suddenly hated what he saw. He said, "Mac."

"Yes?"

"I can't face a class. I need some time off."

"When do you want it?"

"Right now. Starting tonight."

"Okay. Sure."

He felt Teresa's hand tighten on his arm, then drop away, but he continued speaking to Connolly. "Fred Milner is qualified for the three-hundred-level course. Maybe you'd better take the seniors yourself."

"I'll take care of that. Don't worry about who'll do what. How long will you want?"

"I don't know. A week. Two maybe."

"Just let me know," said Connolly.

"Thanks," he said, and looked for the door. Before he

21

reached it he felt her hand again. He turned impatiently.

On the curve of her cheek a tear was poised to roll downward, clear as glass. She was trying to smile, but her face was full of pain. "Paul—I'll call my department head tonight. I've got two classes, both seminars. I can dismiss them for a week. I'll meet you and we can go away together—wherever you want to go."

"No," he said. Again it was too loud, and again the faces, pale, frightened, afraid of him and of what had happened to him, jerked toward them. He tried to lower his voice. "I'm sorry, Terry. Thanks. But I don't want you along."

Her hand loosened and the dark eyes set; her mouth changed; her hand released him. He heard her draw breath to say something but the door cut it off behind him. He stood in the hall, breathing hard and listening. But not a sound came through to him from all the people on the other side.

Midway across the campus the lonely figure suddenly paused. He looked up at the clouding sky and sniffed at the air. He felt in his pockets.

He turned and headed away from his original destination—the book-lined, televisionless apartment, the single futon—and walked rapidly up a snowed-over path at one end of the campus quadrangle.

Inside the deserted administration building, pocketing his faculty passkey, he halted his hand in its habitual movement toward a light switch. What he had to do could be done in the slight gleams and radiances from the blue bulbs over the exits, the red lights glowing over fire-fighting equipment, the faint parallelograms of yellowed light from the globe lamps of the yard.

The building's air lay cool against his cheek. He

listened to it. It was quiet air, unbreathed, untenanted. He removed his hand from the switch and walked softly down the hall, his rubbers squeaking like gagged mice, and stopped before a paneled door.

NIGHT ADVISOR, said the legend on it. Years before, when a government had swayed and students everywhere cried out against an unreal war, this office had been occupied each night by one of the younger male teachers. It had never been clearly established what he was expected to do at the outbreak of arson and revolution; whether to run, or fight, or face the crazed hordes with pure reason; but the Board had directed that a night guard be maintained, though it had declined to provide funds, and therefore each night for a year after Kent State the lights had burned in this room over a nodding man.

Michelson remembered those years. He had been one of those who marched. Taking out his passkey, he unlocked the door and went inside.

The lamps outside—their light reflected and softened by the snow—lent the interior of the room a silken glow. He moved across the office, striking his shin painfully against an unseen chair but not cursing, not speaking, raised the key again and turned it in the lock of a cabinet on the wall. He leaned close to the rows of shining metal within. The keys jingled, brassy, faint, as his fingers brushed them. He selected one and held it in his hand for a moment, considering, and then turned and went out, closing the door softly behind him.

A few minutes later he used his passkey a fourth time, at the front entrance of one of the oldest buildings on campus, a crenellated brick structure. On either side of him concrete eagles crouched, holding blazoned shields, their four letters faded by time and the night.

Inside he proceeded less confidently. This was only the second time in his three years at West Kittanning that he had been here, and he was unsure of the turns of the halls; also less light came through the narrow, old embrasure windows. He stopped several times, listening to faint clanking sounds, but decided at last that they were from the steam heating, and went on.

He found the room he wanted in the basement. He had been there on his introductory tour, three years before, and it was just as he remembered it. A solid-steel door, barred with iron, it was hinged at one end and held firmly at the other by a padlock. But not just a padlock. This was a laminated-steel Army antiterrorist model, big as a coconut. A speckling of rust had crept over it with the years, but it was still secure.

It snapped obligingly open the first time he tried the key. The bar gave him more trouble. It was much rustier than the lock and it grated and creaked like an alarm as he swung it away from the door.

He grasped the handle and opened the vault. A sigh of cold air came out past him as he felt around for a light switch, the air smelling of grease and oiled metal and time. He found the switch. The single overhead bulb came on and he looked around, blinking in its virulent glare.

He was the first person in here in years. He could see that from the neat, yellowed wrappings, the thick coats of caked, drying grease. The ROTC unit at West Kittanning had closed down long before he arrived, a casualty of a Pentagon-ordered consolidation. But the texts, the training aids, the charts, all had been left here, in reserve for reactivation or war.

And the weapons.

Not that there were many of them. To his left four

pistols hung by their trigger guards from a pegboard. One had been partially disassembled and the parts lay on a small table under the rack. On the far wall, half-concealed by a large exploded-view chart, was a rack of five larger firearms: rifles. A wire ran through their guards and was locked in its turn to a staple driven into the wall.

He crossed the vault—two steps wide—and pulled the chart aside to look at the rifles. He knew little about guns, little more than he had picked up from watching late-night war movies as a child. He was about to reach for one when the chart swung back down. Something on it caught his eye and he held it up to the full light of the bulb. An old smear of grease at one edge had sunk into the paper, making it translucent. He looked at it carefully. A single line of heavy print underlined the diagram: DETAIL STRIPPING. BROWNING AUTOMATIC RIFLE, M1918A2, CAL .30.

He let the chart fall and looked around again. A stack of rain ponchos, green and cracked, covered the remaining wall to the right of the vault door. He pulled them down, the plastic flaking and falling with a crackling hiss.

There was only one of them, alone in its rack. It was larger than the others. He touched it. The metal was cold as death, black, grease-slick.

Finally he reached up. It snagged partway down from the rack. Looking more closely, he saw that it too was wired into place with its own padlocked cable.

Once more he surveyed the room. There, on the table . . . he brought the tool over to the light. Needle-nosed pliers, the kind electricians used, with a cutting edge within the jaws. They failed to cut cleanly at the first try, but he nibbled through the wire and lifted the weapon down, surprised at its solid weight, and carried it to the light.

It was larger, longer, heavier than he had expected. The butt was of dark oil-soaked wood. Ahead of that a squarish massive receiver, topped by a complicated-looking sight, tapered into a bulge-based barrel perhaps two feet long. The foregrip was of the same dark wood. From the bottom of it projected a black metal box that he assumed held the cartridges. All the metal parts were a dull gray-black, coated with some greasy yellowish substance.

He decided that this would do.

He thought of one other need and rummaged about the room till he found squat green metal boxes. He opened one and stared at the magazines. Each was loaded with a row of wickedly pointed cartridges. The right kind? He didn't see any others. He closed the box and hefted it. It was heavy, but he was a big man.

He was also, he told himself in time, an intelligent one. With rag and oil from the table he wiped down each surface he had touched. The light switch, the chart, the locks, the wire, and the pliers. He used the rag when he hung the ponchos back in place, covering the empty rack. When he had done this he looked around the vault. It looked exactly as it had when he'd entered it.

No one had been in here for years. Probably, he thought, the Army itself had forgotten this small college, this obscure vault, these obsolete weapons. He flicked the light off with his elbow (his arms were full) and laid the rifle and the box on the basement floor. He swung the door closed and rasped the bar back into place, wiped it off, snapped the oversized lock closed and wiped that. He looked around the basement then, searching through the dim lines of light that filtered in through the high web-grimed windows, until he found some plastic trash bags. He wrapped the can and the weapon in these.

Michelson sneezed twice, snapping his head forward sharply, and then went up the stairs. The plastic crackled under his arm, shielding from sight, though not from his touch, the cold steel beneath.

Outside, he looked across the campus. Under the silent lights the snow glistened emptily. He laid the bundle behind one of the stone eagles, out of sight, and jingled his car keys in his pocket. He would pick up a few things at his apartment, drive back here for the weapon, then leave.

Briefly, as he turned to go, he remembered a wide face, dark hair, deep brown eyes with tears standing in them. Tears meant for him. Should he call her? Maybe leave a note? Hell, he thought then. Don't involve her. Just go, call her when you get back. It'll probably come to nothing anyway.

Halfway across the state he stopped at a sporting-goods store in Du Bois, open late because of the season, and bought a hunting license.

THREE

Under the buttery light of the kerosene lamp the old brass shone dully, like tired gold.

The old man adjusted his spectacles and leaned forward, turning the cartridge case this way and that in careful age-worn fingers, noting the pitting of age and the razor-thin chamfering of heat-darkened metal at the mouth.

At last he nodded. It was old, but probably still serviceable. He placed the case at the top of the oil-shining cylinder of the reloading ram and pulled the lever. The steel ram rose powerfully, gleaming in the golden light, and the fired primer came free with a tiny sucking sound. With sure hands the old man removed the decapper and screwed in the sizing die. The ram rose once again and when it descended the case reemerged, slick with lubricant. All the patina and corrosion of the years was gone and it gleamed new-minted.

Standing up, stretching, Racks Halvorsen looked about his home.

It was low-ceilinged, dim, and incredibly cluttered. Six inches of daylight seeped through two narrow vents at the very edge of the ceiling, which was of bare unsheathed timber. Through the filmed glass was visible the dried brown of dead grass, pressed like corsages by the snow. The wan daylight and the single coal-oil lamp over the reloading bench lit the room: a table, covered with used dishes and half-empty cans of food; fading, curling magazines ten years out of date; unopened envelopes that might be bills or pension checks; dog-eared western novels with no covers and broken spines; beyond it, a hulking cast-iron woodstove, shimmering with heat, on which simmered a big graniteware coffee-pot; a rack of old books, and another of long objects, wrapped loosely and shapelessly in faded oilcloth. Two doors that led into other rooms were closed against the cold.

The old man saw what he wanted: a red metal can. He crossed the room toward it, limping a little with the stiffness that came with sitting. He stumbled by the table, catching himself at the edge of a fall.

"Dammit, Jessie," he said, without heat. "You know I can't see you under that table."

The dog came out into the light. It was a hound, of medium size, tan and black with a little white on its breast, with long ears and a sway in its back. Its muzzle was grizzled with age. It looked up at him silently, trotted across the room, and curled down near the stove.

Halvorsen plucked the can down from the shelf and examined it under the light from the windows. He nodded.

Crossing to the bench again, settling himself in the chair, he measured out the black grainy powder into an antique scale. After long seconds the lever arm quivered still and he poured the powder into the shell, poised a bullet above its mouth, and ran the ram home a last time. He removed the finished round, wiped it carefully with a piece of rag, and held it under the lamp, squinting to sharpen his sight.

Yes, Halvorsen decided, it looked all right. But there was only one real test for old brass like this.

Dropping the freshly loaded cartridge into the pocket of a coat he took from behind the door, he limped across the cluttered dark room again—the hound following him with her eyes from beside the stove—and took down one of the wrapped bundles. He unswathed it and held the weapon to the light. It was an old government-issue Springfield. On the stock the scratched initials JKH 1918 were still visible.

Limping stiffly to one of the doors, closing it on the suddenly inquisitive muzzle of the bitch, the old man emerged at the top of the stairs, blinking and shivering in the morning air.

He stood in a clearing in the deep woods. The only evidence of man was the open sweep of the road, its ruts still faintly traceable under the snow as it led off past a copse of tall, old snowcapped hemlocks, and disappeared in a sweeping curve down the hill. Behind Halvorsen the rusted tin stack of his stove protruded smoking from a long humped rectangle like an Indian burial mound.

Once, years before, a house had stood here on the crest of the hill, its second story overlooking the whole long sweep of the hollow. Now all that was left was the basement, and over it, covered in winter by the snow and in summer with a tentative creep of weed, were six inches of soot and ash and fire-blackened brick. The clear area between it and the road had once been lawn, garden, when there had been a woman to want lawns and gardens.

But what was left was enough for the old man.

His eyes narrowed against the overcast light, the white monotone glow around him. He lifted his head toward a point distant in the trees. Something caught his eye there and he smiled slowly. After a moment he waved an arm suddenly and the raven started from the trees and cawed cynically twice as it mounted into the sky.

When it was well clear the old man raised his rifle at last. He reached into his pocket and flipped back the bolt. A moment later he fitted it to his shoulder, eyes still fixed on the distant trees.

A deep-throated boom like a cannon shook snow from the hemlocks and jolted the old man's chest. He lowered the gun. As the report rolled back from the surrounding hills, slow and sonorous, diminishing at last into far thunder, he slogged forward. Twenty paces. Fifty. A hundred yards.

The hole, large as his small finger, lay in the upper left quadrant of the four-inch bulls-eye, its edges ragged with paper fibers.

Halvorsen pulled the target down from the post and drew another from inside his coat. The wood behind it was rotten, shattered to splinters with so many holes that, as he pressed the tack into it, it yielded like rubber rather than solid oak. When the new target was hung to his satisfaction, he turned and began plodding back along his own trail toward the house. He was about to go down again, looking forward to the warmth, when the sound of a motor caught his attention. He waited, looking down the road.

A few minutes later a red and white pickup shouldered its way around the bend, through the uncleared snow of the road. The old man watched it. It snorted and dipped, threw snow as a speedboat throws water, and stopped at last opposite him. A large, plain woman in a green cloth coat got out and waved.

"Hello, Alma," said Halvorsen.

"It's cold, isn't it," said his daughter. She reached back into the cab and lifted out a grocery bag. She pushed her way through the snow toward the old man. Behind her the truck idled, venting a pool of fog that expanded slowly in the cold air, creeping along the ground after her. When she reached the old man they both hesitated, and then she turned her red round face sideways to his. The old man leaned forward and kissed her awkwardly, a full inch away from her cheek.

Halvorsen led the way down the steps. They were icy and he went slowly, holding the rifle to his side.

"That Uncle James's old gun?" asked the woman.

"Uh huh."

"I heard it coming up the hill. Surprised it still shoots."

"Shoots good," said the old man. He opened the door. The dog was nowhere in sight. "Good as I can hold anyways. Come on in. I got coffee on the stove."

"I can't stay too long."

She sat at the littered table while he searched for a cup and cranked the hand pump and washed it. The coffee steamed. While she added sugar and slow-flowing yellow condensed milk, he scraped his chair opposite hers. They sat together. The stove whispered to itself with collapsing ash.

"How's things in town?" the old man asked.

"Real busy. Lots of people this year. Fred's doing a real good business at the garage."

"That's good," said Halvorsen.

"You ought to come live in town," said his daughter.

"I like it out here," said the old man. "Anyhow, I get around enough."

"I heard about you finding the boy the other day."

"Ralph tell you?"

"Not Ralph—no." Alma shook her head slowly. "He doesn't come around the station, or the house either. Him and Fred don't get along too good anymore. It's terrible—isn't it?—about the boy, I mean. People don't have any respect for each other anymore."

"I guess not," said the old man.

"And the crimes you read about—it's just terrible. How's Jezebel?"

"She's all right."

"Have you fixed your pants yet?"

"My pants?" The old man looked down at his worn trousers. "Oh . . . no. I'll get to them this week."

"Take them off. I'll do them now."

"Dammit, Alma! I said I'd do them myself!"

"All right, all right, pa."

They sat together for a few minutes longer, and then the woman set down her cup. She had to go home, get some lunch on the table for Fred. She asked the old man to come down and eat with them. It sounded like an invitation made and refused often before. The old man refused again.

When his daughter had left he went to the table and looked into the brown paper bag. She had set it there when she came in and neither of them had looked at it or referred to it. Now he peered into it and reached in and pulled things out. Loaf of bread. Macaroni. Some cans of soup and sausages and beans. A foil pack of Mail Pouch. The local paper. He left the last two items on the table and gathered the other things up and took them into one of the sealed-off rooms. It was small and earth-cold. He put the food on a shelf. As he was about to leave he paused, looking up toward what stood on the topmost shelf, up against the ceiling. A pint bottle, its ornate blue seal unbroken. It would be nice, he thought, to have a swallow of something warming. . . .

He shook his head suddenly and turned and went back into the warm room, firmly shutting the door to his makeshift pantry. He checked the stove and put in two split chunks of beech from the pile in the corner, poured himself some more coffee, and sat down in the chair. After a moment he got up again, found his glasses on the reloading bench, settled down again, and shook out the paper.

Inflation was down slightly, a trainload of something had derailed out in the Midwest . . . his slow blue eyes sifted down the page. Midway to the bottom he stopped and began to read.

HUNTING ACCIDENT VICTIM BURIED

Aaron Vincent Michelson, 17, son of Mrs. Anne Oleksa of Barnes Street, Raymondsville, was buried yesterday in a graveside service at Willow Oaks Cemetery. Michelson was the victim of a fatal hunting accident Monday in Mortlock Run, south of Raymondsville.

Hemlock County Game Protector Ralph H. Sweet said today that no conclusive evidence had come to light, but that his investigation of the accident would continue. "It appears to be a regrettable but completely accidental incident," he told *Century* reporter Sarah Baransky. "Most hunters in our Pennsylvania woods, both local residents and our out-of-town guests, are careful and sportsmanlike individuals. They observe proper firearms-handling procedures and are careful about game identification. But we do have a few

spoilers—"slob hunters"—in our ranks. The
Michelson boy may have been the tragic victim
of one of these. . . .

Halvorsen held the paper, seeing again the inert,
crumpled form on the snow; the boneless earth-tending
weight; the tense dead eyes.

His grandson, he thought, was not much of a "game
protector." The old warden—what was his name?—oh,
yes, Rhine, like the river, had been better, a real hard-
nosed fella. Sometimes out in the woods, with
jacklighters and all, you had to be. Not that Ralph was
soft. It was something else. This newspaper story showed
it. His grandson seemed to be letting the incident slide,
letting it be forgotten, trying to grease it over and get on
with what the local merchants and the City Council saw
as the real business of the county: attracting and catering
to the visiting hunters, the out-of-towners who in one
two-week season paid the bills for the entire year.

Not that there was anything wrong with that either,
the old man reminded himself. If they wanted to hunt, to
come from Buffalo and New York City, from Pittsburgh
and as far away as the South, well, this was prime
country for it, and since the oil was running out the
money they brought in was welcome. Some of the older
local people cursed the "flatlanders." Some of the local
hunters did too. But as long as the outsiders hunted
legally and safely, stayed in season and spent their
dollars in the diners and sporting-goods stores, the
motels and bars, most people in Hemlock County figured they could stand it for two weeks out of the year.

No, that wasn't what he minded. It was something else
nagged at him sometimes about his grandson. He didn't
love the land, the way a warden, or a grandson of Racks

Halvorsen for that matter, ought to. To Ralph it was just a job, a way to get money. A title. *Game protector,* the old man thought, feeling how strange it sounded. As if a plain game warden wasn't worth respect anymore, so you had to call it something different, something fancy.

He sighed. But Ralph was young. Perhaps he would learn. Besides, Halvorsen thought, it's none of my business anymore. He no longer hunted; the deer were not his. He took off his glasses and let the paper sag in his lap.

The boy was right about one thing, though. It was tragic. Death was always tragic, but especially so when it came to the young, to those who did not expect it and had never seen it and had not had time to prepare themselves for it.

Not that dying was easy when you were old. But at least you had thought about it a little. Not out loud, but to yourself, in the sleepless silences of the night. The hours when you felt its slow advance in your joints, in the slackening of your blood, in the way the cold crept in and stayed; in sudden dizziness, and racing heart, and in a score of other slowly gaining accesses of pain and inadequacy; the beachheads of the Destroyer, inside yourself.

The old man reached for the tobacco and bit off a chunk of the black rough-cut. He still had enough of his teeth to chew. Thank the Lord for that, he thought.

Yes, when you were young you didn't think about things like that. You just lived. You lived in youth the way you lived in summer.

Sitting in the chair in the warm, cluttered basement, the old man's jaw slackened. The tobacco bulged in his cheek unchewed.

He remembered summer.

He remembered the rails that used to lead out west of town, along the high cut bank above the Allegheny. In the summer you walked along the hot rails, smelling the fresh creosote on the ties, the heated iron. Waves of heat came up across your face from the white-veined cracked granite bed. You'd look down for lucky stones and loose spikes.

And sometimes you heard, under your feet, the click-click of the joints and looked up to see, far down the valley, the stain of smoke far on the corner of the sky that meant the 2:10 was coming. So you hopped off the rails and sat a little way up the bank and watched it as it crept into view, a tiny black thing far out on the curve where the line carried onto the old timber trestle over the river.

And you watched and listened as gradually it grew nearer, louder, the deep chuffing of the exhaust steam coming first and then through that the clatter of the points and the rattle of the couplings and the battering jangle the coal cars made. And the engine, seen head-on now, black, enormous, powerful beyond imagining, filling the sky with smoke and filling the earth with the pounding of the drivers, and finally as it swept toward you, the pain-filled scream of the whistle, like all the dead in hell crying their sorries to an inattentive God.

Then suddenly it was on you and over you and around you, a steamfarting, ironclattering landslide of hot black metal, and above it all brooding the calm mustached visage of the engineer, three fingers of his reclining arm raised in benignant acknowledgment of your capering shout. Then, in an instant, it seemed, it was gone, past, dwindling, the clamor growing distant and the coke-smoky fog sweeping over you, twisting in slow whorls after the retreating caboose.

Till finally it was gone and there were blackberries and silence again on the hill, the fat buzzing of drowsy yellow-vested bees; and the serene, hot shining strips of steel lay as if no train had ever been there at all, unless you put your ear to them and listened. You knew even then that the rails stretched away as far as the earth extended; there was no end to them; just as there was no end to summer, or to youth. You were a kid and though you knew someday you would ride those rails out of Raymondsville into the World, you would still be a kid then too. Big people were dull and frightened and you could never be like them. And if summer, three months, ninety endless, hot, verdant, and dusty days, lasted forever, then how could you ever live through all the months and years and decades it took to be old?

Halvorsen held the paper, not looking at it, and the smile lingered on his face. Only when he leaned forward to spit did he blink suddenly; and in that moment sixty years were gone; the summer was gone and the boys who had run beside him were gone and the black engines and even the rails they rode on were gone; and everything he was going to be, and then was, and then had been, were gone, gone; nothing was left to him; he was an old man, and it was winter.

FOUR

Thursday, November Twenty-seventh

THE MOTELS WERE ALL FULL.

Their no vacancy signs stained the night orange as he drove across northwestern Pennsylvania. In the bloody light their lots were crowded bumper to tailgate with pickups and Scouts and Jeeps.

When Michelson saw the first Hemlock County sign he slowed. Raymondsville was only a few miles on. Ahead he saw a small assemblage of darkened houses, not even a one-stoplight town, huddled around a yield sign. A cast-iron marker by the side of the road said WELCOME TO BAGLEY CORNERS.

Michelson blinked and shook his head. He was very sleepy.

Past the sign he slowed and on impulse turned in to one of the crowded lots. The Wi-Wan-Chu, a small motel with perhaps fifteen units, was window-dark under the outdoor floods, and its sign too flashed rejection across the chrome and metal of the waiting vehicles. He looked at his watch. It was almost two o'clock.

He pressed the buzzer at the office nonetheless. A few minutes later a sleepy-faced woman came to the door, knotting a wrapper around her. Her voice was faint behind the locked storm door. "No vacancy tonight, mister. Sorry. Didn't you see the sign?"

He tried to smile, remembering how Teresa liked it, how she said it made him more attractive. "I'm sorry to get you up, ma'am, but I've been driving all night. Don't you have anywhere I can lie down?"

She blinked, her eyes on his tie. "Our rooms been reserved for months, sir. This is the hunting season."

"Isn't there anyplace?" He pulled out his billfold. "Even a warm floor?"

"Just a minute," she said, sighing.

When she came back she had galoshes on and an old-style long overcoat, a man's coat, buttoned wrong. The metal tabs on the galoshes jingled as she led him around to the back of the court. At number ten she knocked twice, then unlocked the door. "It's bunk beds," she whispered. "This party just come in from out of state today. There's five of them this year and six beds in the room. It'll be forty dollars."

It was far too much but there was nowhere else and he paid her. She eased the door open on darkness. "Mister Abrams . . ."

"What is it?" said a male voice.

"Got a man lost here. Don't have no place to sleep. Can I bunk him with you men for tonight?"

"I guess so. Close the door, it's cold."

Michelson murmured thanks and slipped inside. When the door closed he stood motionless for a moment in the dark. He heard snoring and smelled beer, tobacco, the stale close stink of sleeping men. "Over to your left," someone muttered. "Top bunk. 'Night."

He blundered into the head-high frame of the bunk, then felt for the top and hauled himself up. It creaked under his weight. His head slammed the ceiling and he cursed in a low voice and then undid his tie and lay back fully clothed. This close to the ceiling the dark air was hot. The abandoned breathing of unconscious men seemed very loud at first. But he was sleepy himself . . .

"Hey, who's that?"

"Come in last night. Didn't have no place to stay. I said they could stick him up there."

"Hey, Vic," said another voice. "Better get movin'. It's five-thirty, be dawn soon. Come on, we missed three days huntin' already."

Michelson rolled to the edge of the bunk and looked down.

Below him four men were sitting on their beds, pulling on woolen socks and shirts and prickly-looking trousers over waffle-knit underwear. Their faces were pale, bleary from sleep, unshaven. They yawned frequently, passing it around from man to man, and cast yearning glances at a slowly filling coffee maker that snorted and rumbled on the floor.

A toilet flushed and a fifth man came in from an adjoining room. He was very large, fat, dark-haired. He scratched his crotch luxuriously and looked at the machine. "Guess it's ready. Get your cups, boys. We got some sweetening too." He went to a suitcase on his bed and pulled out a full bottle of Jacquin's brandy.

"Hey. That'll put hair on your chest."

"Double shot for me, Abe."

Styrofoam cups were produced and the smell of coffee filled the room. In the middle of their enjoyment Michelson, eyeing the bathroom door, swung down from the bunk. He had relieved himself and was splashing water on his face before the mirror when he remembered, for the first time that day, that Aaron was dead.

He leaned forward, watching the eyes in the speckled glass refilling with the same shock and disbelief and terror that they had held when he'd set down the telephone three days before.

When he came back into the room the men looked at him and suddenly the conversation lagged.

"Coffee?" said the big man at last. Without waiting for an answer he poured a full cup and held it out. Michelson looked at it, then at the men. Bearded faces, sallow faces, some obviously hung over. The trash can in the corner was heaped with dozens of empty beer cans.

"You're not here for hunting, are you?" one said. "That coat and all."

Michelson said nothing. He took the coffee from the big man's hand.

"Want a shot of this in it, buddy?"

"No."

"We got plenty. Go on."

"I don't want it."

"All right, all right," said the big man. He splashed more into his own cup.

"You better take it easy, Abe," said another of the men. "You get too damn mean when you drink."

"Screw you . . . you guys ready for breakfast? Mama DeLucci's is open early for hunters."

After they all had left, Michelson, shaking a little in the ebb of the emotion he'd felt facing them, sat on one of the lower bunks and sipped at the bitter brew. Might as well get going, he thought. I won't sleep any more now.

Six-ten, before sunrise, yet the snow-paved streets of Raymondsville were crowded with men and vehicles. Main Street was a wide expanse of rolled snow, glistening under the light of street lamps and headlights. On either side rose one- and two-story brick buildings, dated by the cast-iron cornices and false fronts and ornamentation that had flowered on buildings, like pestilential epiphytes, in the 1880s and '90s. Most of the storefronts were still dark, but from some paths of yellow light slanted out across the sidewalks and lay weakly over mounded snow from which here and there the frosted tops of parking meters emerged like severed heads. There were many sporting-goods stores, all open. Michelson counted five little greasy-spoon restaurants and "cafes," all with windowed signs saying, OPEN FOR HUNTERS 5 A.M. and SEASON HOURS. They were crowded with men in hunting caps.

He decided he did not feel hungry.

His little car danced uneasily on the slicked snow, despite the radials. The other vehicles on the street had no such problems. They pulled around and passed him in the dark between the streetlights, International Scouts and Jeeps and Toyota four-wheel drives, engines loud and aggressive, chains jingling eerily cheerful.

He saw a lone boy standing outside a small store and stopped at the curb for directions to the warden's office. As he pulled away, Michelson looked back. The kid was sixteen, seventeen; near Aaron's age, dark-haired, but with that same air of youth, of mysterious waiting. Behind him, leaning against the pallid brick of the storefront, was a single-barreled shotgun.

The game commission office was in a modern-looking one-story building on a side street. Michelson parked behind it and straightened his tie as he got out, remembering how the woman at the motel had been impressed by it. The office was lit in spite of the early hour. A fortyish woman with smeared orange lipstick looked up from a magazine as he came in. From a back room a radio hissed. "Mr., uh, Sweet—is he in?" he asked her.

"He was up late last night, sir. Can I help you?"

He felt his hands, hidden in the pockets of the car coat, turn into fists. Then his anger retreated as he realized that it might be better for his purposes if the man did not know he was here. Perhaps I can find out something on my own, he thought.

"I wanted to ask some questions about a case."

"Oh. The state police. I wondered, sir—the suit and all—"

He took the gift without reflection or even gratitude, and nodded. "Right. Like to look at your files for the incident on the twenty-fourth."

"The Michelson boy."

He nodded, not trusting his voice. He watched her move about the office, riffle through file folders. She came back holding one. "Here's what we have on it, sir. I don't think Ralph . . . Warden Sweet has had time to type the official report yet. He's just so terribly busy during these two weeks. Checking on the deputies, on the road, stopping at the weigh-in stations . . . these are just his notes on it." Michelson nodded again.

He sat in the chair she offered him and opened the folder. It contained three sheets of yellow notebook paper. Two were filled with scrawled handwriting. The third, water-stained, was a crudely drawn map.

There were also several Polaroid photographs, taken, apparently, in a hospital or morgue. He stared at them.

"Are you all right, sir?"

He grunted. He was not; he wanted to throw up, and the taste of the coffee that the hunter had given him was sour at the back of his throat. Then a little of the disbelief, the numbness, returned.

No. This was not the time for numbness. He was a gentle and caring man, but this was beyond bearing. I've taken many things without fighting, he told himself.

Maybe too many. But I will not take this. Not without looking into it, at least.

"Do you have any coffee around here?" he asked the woman. When she left the room he tucked the yellow sheets inside his coat and closed the file. He left the photographs. He knew he would carry them always, just behind his eyelids, in finer grain and sharper contrast than any lens could print. She came back in just as he took his hand out of his coat. "The coffee's on now, sir. If you'll wait for just a moment—"

"I've got to be going. Sorry."

"The warden will be in soon, I think. Can I give him your name?"

"I'll be back."

Outside the office the cold slid under his unbuttoned coat, making him shiver. The papers crackled as he got behind the wheel again. He drove out of the lot, made a couple of random turns, and found himself on a back street lined with small, shabby houses. He parked and turned on the dome light and took the papers out.

> *Season opened 6:36. Heard call channel 9. To hospital.*
> *Racks fd boy*
> *Aaron Michelson. Lives with mother, stepfather Barnes St*
> *Out hunting first time. Illegal—no permit*
> *Called mother, Oleksa*
> *Called father—West Kittanning state coll*

The second sheet was a description of the wound, apparently copied word for word from a doctor's explanation. He skimmed it, feeling each word like a blow in the stomach, and then went back to the first page. It was easy to make out, even through the misspellings and abbreviations, what the man was saying. All but that one remark: Racks fd boy.

Racks fd boy. What could that mean?

A truck rolled past him on the street, chains jingling. He peered out. The streetlights seemed fainter. A dull gray, like smoky opal, showed in the sky.

It occurred to Michelson that he had some errands to do.

He'd need clothing. The jacket and tie and car coat he had worn up from school had been useful. But they were too conspicuous in this remote and uncouth town, and they were not warm enough. The car coat was good-looking but too thin and the rubbers were completely inadequate. He put the papers and their meaning aside for the moment, drove back to Main Street, and parked near one of the sporting-goods stores. The door shut with a jangle behind him and three plainly dressed men looked at him from around a counter.

"Yes, sir!" one of them said, coming toward him.

"Need some warm clothes. Boots too."

"Well, we sure got 'em. Come on over here. What size you wear? Be a forty-four, forty-six long?"

He bought what the man suggested: long underwear, woolen pants heavy as woven peat, a thick wool shirt, insulated vest, heavy hiking boots, and socks. The only coats in stock that looked warm enough were in the bright hunters' orange. He did not like it but he bought one and took a hat in the same shade. When he saw the total he knew the store owner was overcharging him, ripping him off in his small-town, small-time way, but he didn't care enough to argue. He felt tired. The man examined his charge card. "Michelson, huh? Like that kid they found the other day. You related?"

"No," said Michelson. "No relation."

One of the loungers laughed.

As he signed the slip he had a thought. "Say. What does 'racks' mean?"

"Racks?" The owner made horns with his fingers. The other men laughed. "You serious? Means antlers on a deer. See that mounted head on the wall there? You get a trophy head, have Sonny Fretz mount it for you, you call that a nice set of racks."

That made no sense. "Anything else it could mean?" he asked them.

They looked at one another. "Rifle racks?" said one.

"There's old Racks," said the other.

"There's what?"

"An old guy named Racks. Nickname I guess. Used to be quite a hunter—I heard that years ago he was out west, Canada, all over. But he must be awful old now."

"I think he's dead," said one of the loungers.

"No, he ain't," said the other. He wore a red cap that said NRA: FREEDOM. "I seen him a couple of months ago down at Fred Pankow's station."

Racks fd boy, Michelson was thinking. Racks found boy. That was possible; the word had been capitalized in Sweet's scrawl not because it began a sentence, but because it was a proper name. The phrase made sense that way. And if this "Racks" had found Aaron . . . "How would I find this guy?" he asked them. "Would you have his number?"

"Halvorsen don't have no phone out there," volunteered the man in the hat. "He lives alone with his dog out top of Mortlock Hollow. Had a nice house there once, with all kinds of trophies in it. Mounted heads, shooting trophies. He was a hell of a shot. But that burned down fifteen, twenty years ago. They say it was an accident, when he was drunk. His wife was in it. He never rebuilt."

"This . . . Halvorsen, he's a hunter?"

"I said he *used* to be." The man's eyes sharpened on Michelson. "Not anymore though. He must be pushin' seventy. I heard he's kind of off hunting, but he still shoots some."

"Yeah, that's right," said the owner. "Old crazy Racks. His daughter lives here in town. Married the guy who owns the Texaco station. Second marriage. You see her taking groceries out to Mortlock once in a while."

"I'd like to meet him," said Michelson.

"Well, he lives up on the hill, like Dean said. You take Main Street south, then turn left at the stop sign about half a mile past the Chevy dealers . . . go out that road for six, seven miles, till you come to a fork. Right-hand road goes up the hill sort of in a zigzag. It's pretty rough, but keep on going even if you think you're wrong. His place is right up top of the hill."

"Don't run over the house," said one of the men, and they laughed.

He was picking up his packages when the man with the NRA hat pushed it back and said casually, "Say, buddy, you ain't in town to hunt, are you?"

"No."

"I didn't think so. It don't sound like you like hunters too much."

"That's right," said Michelson. He looked the man in the eye. "I hate the bastards."

He shouldered the coat and walked out, leaving sudden silence behind him.

On the street again, he opened the hatch and dumped his packages in back, completely covering the humped shape under the blanket. He started. He'd forgotten about the thing; had not thought of it once since awakening in the room in the Wi-Wan-Chu. He could not remember, imagine, what had made him take it, bring it all this way with him.

I was really off balance last night, he told himself. No wonder Mac and Teresa were worried about me. Well, I can take it back and no harm done. Certainly no one would miss it for a couple of days. He got in and started the car. Well, he told himself. Racks Halvorsen.

Outside town the hard-packed snow of the street gave way quickly to roads that had once been cleared but which were now swiftly being re-covered with the drifting snow. His small car was high off the ground but it was also light and in the drifts the wheels caught and tried to wrench him off the road.

After the turnoff the going became more difficult still. It was all right, if slippery, till the fork the storekeeper had told him about, but after that the road, if road there really was under an untouched blanket of white, grew narrow and steep. It squirmed back and forth against the face of the hill like a climbing snake. The little car slid and threw snow at each switchback and he grappled, sweating, with the wheel. It was snowing, flakes whirling down out of the gray dawn sky, between the trees that met above the narrowing road, and buffets of wind hacked at the car as he slowed to make a turn. If I get stuck up here, he thought . . . miles from anywhere, on a track no one's traveled for God knows how long . . . he could be here until he froze. He would have turned back, but the road was too narrow. So he went on.

At the very top of the hill the road turned left. He followed it for about a mile, whirring along the crest of a long ridge. From time to time the trees thinned to his left and through the snow-blurred air he could see the rough flanks of the hill falling away; gray rock, the sharp points of stands of pine, the stark black of hardwoods, all foreshortened by height till they looked like smooth meadows far below.

At last he turned a sweeping curve and saw that the road ended ahead in a cleared space of level snow. He let the car drift to a stop, grateful that he could now turn around. He had almost forgotten why he'd come when he saw a thin trickle of brown, of smoke, coming up over the edge of the hill.

Racks?

He left the engine running, buttoned his car coat, and jumped out. His feet sank immediately into a foot and a half of undisturbed snow. It was heavier here on the hilltop than down in the valley, and the clean wind, freighted with more of it, mingled in his nostrils with the scent of woodsmoke as he floundered forward.

There was nothing there.

No house . . . but there was a sort of chimney, and a low humped form. The basement the men had mentioned. Driven by the wind, Michelson circled it, found the stairs, half-filled with drifted snow, went down them and knocked. He waited for a long time, shivering, wishing he'd put on the clothes he'd bought, and then knocked again. The door knocked back, startling him, and he stepped back. It shivered under a series of heavy blows from within, the icicles that fringed it tinkling and singing as they fell. It opened.

"C'mon in," said an old man's voice.

Michelson took off his hat and bent to get through the low door. It was wood, he noticed, of old rough-cut planks closely fitted. He blinked as it closed. He was in sudden darkness, the darkness of an animal's den, noisome and stiflingly hot.

"What you need, mister?"

"Are you Racks Halvorsen?"

"Racks?" From somewhere in the dim came a chuckle. "That's what they used to call me, sure . . . I'm W. T. Halvorsen. Say, you're dressed pretty light for this weather. How about some coffee?"

"Well—"

"Sit down. No, not there, that chair's about done for. Over here by the stove."

Michelson sat where he was directed and looked around. The place was dark and hot and smelled of mildew and canned food and the old man. He looked at the old stove and the split wood beside it, at the dully-glowing kerosene lamp, at the pile of empty tins on the table. He felt slightly sick. The squalor, the abandonment . . . an old man alone like this. He should by all laws of decency and human concern be in a clean, safe, ramped building, with proper care, with other people his own age . . . it was like something out of the nineteenth century.

The old man approached, offering a blue graniteware mug. Michelson looked at the dark stuff and made himself take a sip. Then he took a long swallow, surprised. It was good coffee, thick and hot and deeper somehow than the instant he used at home. He was starting to say so when something poked into his crotch under the table and he almost spilled the liquid on himself.

"Get away, Jess," said the old man sharply.

Michelson peered under the table. The sad brown eyes of an old hound wondered up at him.

"Don't pay any attention to Jezebel. She's just curious; she don't see many strangers. Well, sir," said the old man, sitting down opposite him and looking intently yet politely at him, the yellow light glinting from his half spectacles. "You seem to know of me. What can I do for you? Must be pretty important, comin' up here in dead of winter like this."

Michelson nodded. The cold, the shock of this squalid hole, had almost made him forget for a moment. But this old man had found Aaron; to find the truth, he had to start here. "Yes," he said, clearing his throat. "I'm . . . investigating the case of the boy who was killed three days ago. According to the warden, you were the one who found him."

"You talked to Ralph already, then." Michelson nodded. "The boy . . . that was a terrible thing. He was so damn young. He'd just been left to lay there, bleed to death. He was gone when I found him. I waited till some fellas come along to help me drag him out. But it wasn't any use."

"I'd like to find out more about how it happened."

"Already told the warden what I saw. Just the boy, and then I waited—"

"I know all that. What I want to find out is, who did it."

"Now that's a hard question," said the old man. "Officer . . ."

"McCoy," said Michelson, thinking that again the coat and tie had done it, had impressed the old man; they were so credulous, these people.

"McCoy. Like I said, that's a hard question. I thought that's what Ralph should of been asking. But it's not my place to tell him. He don't take my advice very well. I don't know how you're going to find out much, this late. Or if you ever could. But I'd be glad to help however I can."

"Will you take me there?"

"Where?"

"Where you found him. Where it happened."

"It was down in the hollow," the old man said. "Back where the Whites' lease used to be. They had about sixty wells back there, five-spotted, you know. They used to—well, you don't want to hear about that. But to get to it, you turn around, go down again to the—"

"I want you to come along," said Michelson. "To look at the ground with me."

"Well, I'll do what I can, like I said." Halvorsen went to a corner and began pulling on clothes. He moved slowly, lacing on high old-fashioned boots, snapping suspenders on his worn work trousers, buttoning up a faded red wool coat that looked warm. The last thing he put on was a floppy green hat with ear flaps. A Thunder Oil insignia decorated the peak. He looked at Michelson. "I'm ready."

The outside air was a new shock in his lungs, cold, but welcome after the close hot fetor of the old man's hole. Michelson breathed deeply of it. He turned to see Halvorsen pulling his door shut. "You don't lock it?"

"We don't do that up here," said the old man, looking at him strangely.

Halvorsen directed him as they drove down the hill. From time to time—it was about nine o'clock—they passed cars full of hunters, heading back toward town. Michelson's eyes were drawn by one, a station wagon with New Jersey plates and the carcass of a spike buck draped limply over the hood and tied with cheap yellow polypropylene rope. The men in it waved as the small car went by. Ale cans gleamed in their hands. Neither Michelson nor Halvorsen waved back.

"Waste of good meat," said the old man angrily.

"What's that?"

"Strapping your kill over the engine like that."

"That spoils it?"

"Damned city hunters. That deer wasn't even gutted right."

"I don't imagine they planned to eat it," said Michelson.

"You're right there, I bet you," said the old man. "I never killed nothing I didn't eat. Most of these out-of-towners are probably okay. But I hear stories . . . they say there's some of them come down here out of season, use dogs to drive the deer into 'em. Poachin'. Now, I can't see that."

"No," said Michelson, looking curiously at the old man.

"We're coming up on the turn. At the uphill. Here. Turn right."

At last, on a woods-fringed road that dipped and swayed along the flank of the hill, the old man told him to stop. "We got to walk from here," he said, eyeing Michelson doubtfully. "You sure you're dressed warm enough?"

"It isn't far, is it?"

"Maybe a quarter mile. But them shoes . . ."

"Just a minute." Michelson reached into the back and brought out the new boots. "How about these?"

"That's some better," said the old man.

When he turned the key to let the engine die it was suddenly very quiet. The trees were close around them and the snow was deep and only a little wind moved far back in the woods, making the bare branches rub against each other with little cries. Their breaths mingled and drifted away slowly as they stood together by the car for a moment, the bent old man and the tall younger one. Above them the sky was close and gray and lightless.

"Over that way," said Halvorsen, pointing.

As they entered the woods Michelson's feet felt new and stiff in the boots. Going downhill, they passed a green oil jack with the oval Thunder Oil insignia on it. It was motionless. "Drilled that one myself, thirty years ago," Halvorsen said, nodding at it.

Michelson inspected the thing. It was like a big steel grasshopper, crouched over a bulky motor. Wires led down to it from an overhead line, and at what looked to be the working end a slick-gleaming brass piston led into a pipe in the snow. There was a strong smell of oil.

"You drilled oil wells?"

"Done it all . . . roustabout, driller, tool dresser, lease foreman. Forty years in gas and oil, from Bradford to Coudersport. When I started they were using hickory rods and steam power."

"Is that so," said Michelson. "How much farther?"

"Not too far."

Presently the downhill leveled and then steepened, turning upward. Second-growth maple and beech and pine stood close together, six- and eight-inch trunks dark against the snow. Michelson saw a clearing ahead. The old man stopped so suddenly he bumped into him.

"What is it?"

Halvorsen raised an arm. He looked, and saw nothing. "What is it?" he said again. For some reason he was whispering.

"Hunter," said the old man, his voice low. He looked back. "You're not too safe out here in that tan coat, mister."

"I don't see anyone," he whispered, looking where the old man had pointed. Then, suddenly, he did: an irregular patch of reddish orange, and above it a straight black line that could only be a rifle barrel. Then his eyes made sense of it. The hunter, who was facing away from them, looking downhill, was motionless, and so well concealed by low hummocks of snow that Michelson knew he would never have seen him by himself.

"Come on. We'll go around him this way."

A few minutes later—minutes which passed very slowly for Michelson, feeling as he did dozens of unseen eyes—the old man stopped again. "Here we are," he said.

Michelson looked around him, thinking, So this was it. An ordinary-looking patch of forest, well up on the hillside. A frozen stream. A few birches, sad and naked in the winter light. It was a somber place and as he looked around it he struggled to form his feelings into something he could name, like grief, or regret, or anger, or despair.

"I seen him first over here," said the old man, pushing his way through the snow to a spot not far from the translucent frigidity of the frozen stream. "You can still see it some in the snow . . . lucky it hasn't come down too heavy in the last couple days. Here, away from where they tracked it up. See? This sort of hollow? And over here's where his rifle was laying."

"Why do you say it was his?" said Michelson sharply.

The old man's eyes, blue as faded denim, moved up from the snow to his face, and Michelson thought, Careful, this old bugger is smarter than he looks.

"It was beside him," said the old man.

"What about tracks?" he forced himself to ask.

"Well, let's have a look," Halvorsen said, glancing around the clearing.

"Wait a minute. I've got another question first. What were you doing up here? When you found him?"

The old man shrugged, looking around at the woods.

"I like to get out sometimes. Even if I don't care to hunt."

"It's a hell of a long walk from your place," said Michelson, watching the old man's face.

"I'm a good walker still. But it's not that far. Less than two miles." Halvorsen pointed off to the woods to their left, which were denser, thicker, the trunks merging into a solid wall of gray as they marched uphill. "My place is right up that hill and over into the ridge beyond. We had to come the long way round; roads here stick to the valleys mostly. But if you come over a ridge, walkin', why it isn't far at all."

"Did you have a gun?"

"No, sir," said the old man. "Game deputies find you out here with a gun and no hunting license during the season, that's a fine. On my pension I can't afford no fines."

Michelson studied the open, wrinkled face before him for a moment longer. Something about this old man, his plainness . . . Michelson decided he liked him.

"You want me to look around now?"

"Yes."

The old man moved off. Michelson stayed where he was, feeling the cold numbing his exposed face and hands. He was looking at the slight hollow in the snow. Under it, under the fresh snow that had fallen in the last couple of days, there was a shadow, a layer of darkness under the white.

He could not make himself reach down to it.

Sometime later—it could have been as long as half an hour—he heard the crunch of footsteps behind him, and turned. It was the old man. "Find anything?" he asked.

"Some," said Halvorsen. "This is a popular place for hunters, them that wants to stand-hunt not too far from a road. Like that guy we passed. I saw three stands within rifleshot of here."

"What's a stand?"

"Sort of like a foxhole. You settle in and stay still and wait for the deer to move past you. Most people stand-hunt in these woods. But I don't think the shot came from one of them."

"What do you mean?"

"I mean it didn't come from a stand."

"Where did it come from, then?"

"Uphill, to the left. The way the boy was lying, it looked like the shot came from there. There's a place up there where you have sort of a shot from, but there's some brush in the way."

"You mean somebody in there might have seen movement? And just . . . let go?"

"Except for one thing."

"What's that?"

"It's not that far away."

"Show me."

The place the old man pointed out was a half ring of snow-covered rocks. Faintly, under the dusting of new snow, Michelson could see the long depressions of footsteps. The old man pointed wordlessly downhill. A low stand of weather-stripped brush lay between them and the spot, some twenty yards downhill, where they had just been.

"Can you tell anything?" he asked. The old man's head was bent toward the ground, the bill of the ridiculous green hat shading his eyes. "Can you tell anything about who was here?"

"I'm lookin'," said Halvorsen shortly. He bent and brushed the surface of one of the rocks with his fingers. He brushed the snow away from a small area of the ground. He blew gently on one of the drifted-in tracks. Michelson could see him squinting. He must be far-sighted as hell, he thought.

"Lucky nobody else's hunted here," said Halvorsen at last, straightening up. "But I'm surprised Ralph hasn't —well, there's nobody looked over this ground that I can see. Yeah, I can tell you something. The man who was here was big. Heavier than you. Probably a flatlander, probably from Ohio or New York. He smoked. He used a twelve-gauge shotgun. He was a slob and a bastard."

"How can you tell all that?"

"Well, from the boot prints—a heavy man walks different, sits different. Here, you got a print of where he sat down." Halvorsen outlined with his finger what was, to Michelson's eyes, unmarked snow. He held out his gloved hand. In it were a half-burnt match and an empty shotgun shell.

"Why did you say he was from New York?" said Michelson, looking at the shell.

"Or Ohio. Rifles are illegal for deer up there. Most local people here use the lever actions."

"And a slob?"

"Who else would smoke on a stand, and shoot at something that at twenty yards away he couldn't see good enough to tell was a man?"

Michelson, looking at the ground, remembered his imagined picture of the way Aaron had died. He had been righter than he knew. If only I could find him, he thought. But he would be far away by now. If only that fool of a warden had done his job.

"You okay?" said the old man. The questioning look had come back into his eyes.

"Yeah."

"You want this shell?"

He shook his head. He couldn't bring himself to touch it; it might have been the one. Suddenly he felt his stomach turn. The very trees around him were nauseating, threatening, the old man a twisted dwarf; and all he wanted was to leave, to get back to where it was warm, where there were sane, normal middle-class people who did not know him, who did not have to pretend to sympathize with his crushing weight of loss, of memory, rage, and regret.

"Let's go on back to the car," he said.

As they walked back along their trail Halvorsen abruptly began to talk, as if, Michelson thought, he had just realized he would be alone again soon, and had to practice the art of speech while he had a listener. "I been out here a long time," the old man said, looking around as they pushed through the snow at the spotted trunks of the birches, the gray bulk of the hill rising huge and vague behind them. "Growing up . . . the farm . . . then workin' on timber, and then the leases. I seen a lot. I seen them cut down these woods when they was all hemlock, white pine, black cherry. I seen them come back, aspen and gray birch, maple and oaks, then your beech and birch and even hemlock again here and there. There was bears here when I was a kid. Then they were gone, and then they came back. When I was a boy my uncle killed a wolf. They say there was panthers, too—"

"You hunted them, didn't you?" Michelson said. "They said in town that you hunted."

"You don't think about it twice up here," Halvorsen said, looking up at him. The car came in sight ahead. "You grow up with it. You get the rabbits and the squirrels when you're little and then the deer. Bear, and elk, and turkeys. I went on trips—Canada, Colorado

—once when I was making good money as a foreman after the war, I even went up to Alaska. I had trophies covered the walls of my house."

"What happened?"

The old man did not answer for a while. They trudged along together. "Don't know," he said at last. "I got up one day, after I lost somebody I loved, and the fun was out of it. I remembered how beautiful a live thing is." He shrugged. "Maybe it was just that I was gettin' old. I didn't want to kill anymore, and hunting without killing . . . but them that do, that's their business. Aren't you cold? You're turning sort of white there in the face."

"Yeah," said Michelson. As he tried to unlock the door the key chattered against the metal. "I'll drop you back at your place. Or is there someplace else I can take you?"

"I might go on into town. If it's not out of your way. Where you headed now?"

"I don't know," said Michelson. He looked back at the woods. "I don't know. Maybe nowhere. But I can certainly drop you off in town."

And the old man looked at him keenly, but said nothing.

FIVE

"HEMLOCK COUNTY GAME PROTECTOR'S OFFICE, RALPH Sweet speaking," said the telephone into his ear. "Who's this?"

"Your grampaw."

"Oh, hi, Racks. Did you finally get a phone up there?"

"I'm in town. Down to your step-dad's station."

"Oh. Well—what is it?"

"It's about the Michelson boy. I was just out Mortlock with the guy about it."

There was a pause at the other end. The old man looked across the tool-littered, grease-stained concrete to the lift, where two heavyset men in coveralls stood smoking Camels while oil drained from the car they were working on. From its salt-corroded underside came the slow drip of melting slush. It was stifling in the closed garage and the old man took his cap off and wiped at his face with it as he waited.

"What guy?" Ralph said.

"The fella that's investigating the accident."

"Somebody went out to see you?"

"That's right. This morning."

"And you say you took him out to the scene?"

"That's right," said Halvorsen again.

"Well, who was he?"

"Said his name was McCoy."

"McCoy? Who was he with?"

"Uh . . . I don't exactly recall. I guess he didn't say. Isn't he police? You mean you don't know who he is?"

"I've never even seen him. Mrs. Coyle says he stopped by the office early today, said he was from the state police, but I called Bill Sealey at the barracks and he says he isn't. I wish I knew what agency he's from. Hunting accidents are mine to investigate. Nobody else has any business asking about things like that."

"Anyway," said Halvorsen, "I think you ought to know that he and I found some things up there."

"What things?"

Halvorsen told him. When he was done the line was silent again for a few seconds. "Maybe you should try to find out who was up there with the boy," the old man suggested at last.

"Oh, come on, Racks. Find him from footprints and an empty shell? The woods are full of them. And who really knows if the shot came from there?"

The old man caught the not-so-subtle dismissal, but he tried again. "Ralph, listen. We owe the kid more than that. I'm surprised you didn't see that shell yourself."

"Look, I investigated that accident."

"I didn't see any tracks up there. Except right at the body."

"Damn it, it's the hunting season. I got to cover a thousand square miles of territory. I got eight deputies to supervise. I'm sorry for the kid too, Racks, but nothing we can do will bring him back."

"It might save someone else."

"I agree, I'd like to get that guy—shooting and killing a human in mistake for game, that's five years state prison. But there's just nothing I can do. I'm sorry. I've got to get back on the road."

Halvorsen hung up too, more slowly, and stood in the oil-heavy heated air and looked blankly at a droop-titted spark plug calendar and thought: He's busy. Sure he's busy. But that's part of his job. He shouldn't of shrugged it off, skimped it.

He shouldn't act like I don't know anything.

He stood irresolute. He wanted to call Sweet back, argue, make him do what he wanted. But he knew the boy wouldn't listen. He was young, vain, self-important with the new job. He was educated. And his grandfather?

Only an old man, he thought.

He thanked his son-in-law for the use of the phone. Pankow nodded, shedding ash from the end of his cigarette. Out in the street the cold woke him. Fitting his cap to his head, Halvorsen turned left and walked down Main Street, intending to stop in his daughter's house to get a ride home; but he halted after only a block and looked around him, oppressed by a sudden, nameless fear.

The wind flowed down the street toward him, channeled like creek flood by the flush faces of the buildings, keen and gelid on his face. He lifted his head to it, drawing in the town smells, so different from those of the winter woods; bread from the Italian bakery upstreet, gasoline, the close woolly smell of bundled-up people as they hurried by, passing like city people, neither looking him in the eyes nor saying "hello" or "how are ya." He knew none of them. He looked beyond them up the street. He had grown up here, had known Raymondsville since he was old enough to come into town on Saturdays with his father in the old Ford, and yet this afternoon it felt different, foreign, like a place he had never been before.

Turning his back to the wind, fumbling his collar up

with fingers stiffened by cold and tarnished with age, Halvorsen stepped into the lee of the brick building that had been the City Hall when he was young and now stood derelict, windows open to the wind. He pulled the tobacco from his pocket and bit off a short one and looked down the street, narrowing his eyes.

He did not get into town much anymore. It seemed to change every time he saw it. The old buildings, the brick and stone that the lumber and oil money of the Good-years and Thunners and Whites and Gerroys had built, still stood, most of them; but there were gaps between them now. No longer was Main Street solid with build-ings. Now there were huge holes, leveled areas, and seeing them was like the shock of feeling for a missing tooth. The city tore them down and in the *Century* you would read for a while of private development, depart-ment stores going to come in from Erie or Buffalo; then of Federal housing; then, with a kind of Rotarian de-spair, of municipal parking lots. But somehow the money never came, no matter how much the council spent on studies and receptions and junkets, and the empty blocks lay leveled, covered with snow or dust, as if the town had been bombed out, as if it were conquered and devastated territory.

The building opposite him, for example. It was a pizza den now, garishly painted, a Straub's sign in the window. Yet in straining to reestablish himself in place and time on this windswept street the old man remembered it as a gas station; and before that as a restaurant; and before that, as the county relief office, with eagled windows; and before that, even, a palatial opera house. Yes, there had been opera in Raymondsville once, though that was before his childhood. In the eighties and nineties these gray hills had looked down on splendor. The flooding millions came from a new thing called petroleum. Colonel Drake had first pumped it up seventy miles west of here in 1859. It was greenish gold, the highest grade crude oil in the world. Under those cold gray hills above Raymondsville and Petroleum City the Thunners had found a narrow bed of sandstone, some places a thousand feet down, others as deep as three thousand, all of it spongy with the stuff. Hemlock County oil. And the people came from the crumbling empires of Europe and the towns rose, jerry-built in a night from green timber ripped from the hills, and sparkled briefly with silk hats and satined women and opera here amid the vast cold desolation of the forest.

And young Billy Halvorsen had been part of it. He'd gone to work at thirteen as a slush boy, dipping leather into cans of yellow muck to grease the rod lines that led from the tin-shantied power out to the jacks. Graduated to roustabout in 19 and 28, and worked first at that and later as a driller all over Hemlock and McKean and Potter and Cameron counties. He'd drilled oil wells and gas wells and the five-spots down which you pumped water to drive the oil out. He pulled casings and installed the power and band wheels that drove the rod lines. In the thirties he became a shooter, filling the long sheet-metal casings with gallons of sticky nitro (so delicate it had to be drawn through the woods straw-cushioned in jugs in wagons, the riderless horses trained to follow the man who walked two hundred yards ahead), and lowering them to fracture the sandstone far below with explosions that made the ground thump against the soles of your feet. And in the forties he was a Thunder lease foreman and a field foreman for Penngas and although there were jobs above that, in the head offices, that was as high as W. T. Halvorsen had ever gone.

All that work, all that experience, all that skill; and now he was an old man. He sucked sweet juice from the plug in his cheek and spat between his feet. The brown stain melted into the dirty snow. He did not feel like going home just yet. He liked the aloneness, but sometimes, when he grew afraid, it became hard for a man to take.

He wondered if the Brown Bear was open.

He walked down two streets and saw that the lights were on. He shoved the door open on the music and went in and turned left and even though he knew it was there, had waited in the booths by the door twenty years before and laughed as strangers came face-to-face with it, he still felt a shiver run over his shoulders as he confronted the bear.

He had met it for the first time hunting in the Cassiars with Lew Pearson. It was not a vast bear by Alaskan or Canadian standards, but it was a monster compared to the smaller blacks that populated these forests. It had absorbed four of their .375 Magnum bullets before stopping, as Pearson always put it, "With its paws on our boot laces."

Pearson, Halvorsen remembered, had died in North Africa not long after; but his bear lived on. It towered now just inside the entrance, never growing old, never wearying, free now of the hunger of winter and the heat of summer, purged of all its ursine desires, lusts, and follies: a full seven feet of magnificent taxidermy, its claws raised and massacre shining in its glass eyes. Invariably, when they came face-to-face with it, newcomers to the bar were betrayed by their reflexes into a step backward, raising a chorus of ridicule from the men at the long bar beyond.

The old man patted its muzzle tenderly where the fur was worn and walked on, into the bar.

"Look who's here," said Lucky Rezk from behind the counter.

67

"Hello, Lucky." Halvorsen looked around. Rezk was doing good business. He always did, in season. The dark wood booths were crowded with middle-aged men in hunting caps and boots, drinking beer and whiskey and eating Shooter Specials and the Big Buckburgers that Rezk's wife Roberta made up, half ground chuck, half venison. He walked past them toward the back, where the light was dim. A few men sat there, almost motionless at a little table, their shots of whiskey or mugs of beer before them. As he came up they made room for him, sliding over on the hard old pew seat Rezk's dad had saved when the KKK burned St. Rocco's. He nodded to the old men: Mason Wilson, Jack McKee, Len DeSantis, Charlie Prouper. After a moment Rezk came back from the counter. "Don't see you in here much these days, Racks," he said, looking at the other men's glasses.

"Don't get in town that often."

"Still living out Mortlock?"

"That's right."

"You oughta move into town," said McKee. He was seventy-six and looked every day of it. Halvorsen remembered working for him in '34, '35; he'd been an expert tool dresser. Now his hands were cripple-curled around the beer glass. "I did. Lot easier to get around."

"Where you living now?" Halvorsen asked him.

"Hotel Gerroy. They turnt it into a old folks home. Made it into con—con—"

"Contomomiums," Wilson supplied. Wilson had been in oil for a while, then . . . a lumberman, until he'd lost an arm to one of the big Campbell bandsaws. For twenty years after that he'd run a newsstand near the Odd Fellows Building.

"Condominiums," corrected Rezk, with a bartender's authority. "Racks, what can I get you?"

"I guess coffee."

"Have to wait a while. I just put new on."

"Some pop, then."

"It was the year they wanted to build the airport," McKee said, continuing, Halvorsen supposed, what he'd been saying when he arrived. "Must have been thirty below that winter. I was running night shift for the plant, carryin' broken glass to the furnaces. It was damn cold. Christ! It busted the roads up something awful."

"Them frost heaves will tear a road out by the roots," Wilson said. "That was thirty-seven they wanted to build the airport."

"Thirty-five," said DeSantis.

"No, I remember distinct it was thirty-seven. I remember talking about it to old Dan Thunner himself."

"Bull shit. You never talked to a Thunner in your life."

Halvorsen felt juice gathering in his cheek. He leaned to spit and saw nothing to spit in. "Remember they took it out," said DeSantis to him, in an aside. Halvorsen nodded, feeling silly—there had been no spittoon there for ten years now—and got rid of his chew in a paper napkin.

"I sure as hell did. He come out to my lease one day. But you're right about it being cold. It was so cold that year we had to thaw the lines out with torches 'fore they'd start."

"And snow!" said McKee.

"Nineteen-fifty-five for snow," said Rezk, putting Halvorsen's opened can in front of him. "It was up to my goddamn windows. I had to dig that Hudson of mine out, like to mined for it." He looked at the quarter Halvorsen had laid on the tabletop. "Canned pop's same as draft beer, Racks—fifty cents."

"Fifty cents!"

"I remember," said a low, hoarse, toneless voice. They all turned to look. It was Prouper. He was the oldest man there, maybe the oldest man still ambulant in the town, in the county. He was vein-thin and half-blind and had to hold a finger over a little hole at his neck when he wanted to speak. He had been a machine gunner in the First World War and had been gassed. He was over ninety. They all looked at him, waiting. Up front the jukebox played "Are you ready Yes I'm ready to love you."

"When your dad—"

They waited while the record changed and Charley Pride came on, too loud, and they had all to lean closer to hear:

"Charged a nickel," said Prouper. He took his finger from the silver hole at his collar and looked up at Rezk significantly.

"You get all these flatlanders come in for the season, you jack up your prices," said McKee. "That ain't right, Lucky."

"I never told you bastards," said Rezk, whose face had flushed at Prouper's last words, "but you old guys that sit back here, I give you a dime off everything. Up front they're paying sixty cents each for a small draft and a dollar thirty for a shot. And believe me, it ain't a discount for volume."

The old men did not speak back and when he left, still red-faced, they looked at one another. "Anyway," said DeSantis lamely, "Lucky's right, fifty-five was a bitch."

Halvorsen looked after the stout white-shirted figure of the bartender. He had been in this bar the day Lucky Rezk had been born, and had drunk a glass of needled beer with Tony Rezk to it.

He looked at the other men around the dim table, not following the conversation, instead thinking, as he tipped and nursed the cool can, about them.

All of them were his age, or older. He had known these

men for forty, fifty, some of them sixty years. When he was twelve he'd hunted squirrels and trapped for weasels with Wilson. He'd known DeSantis from his first day of school. He had worked with McKee and he remembered Prouper as seeming old even when he first met him in the mid-thirties. If the buildings, the physical fabric of the town had changed, if this was what disturbed and anachronized him, then these men alone placed him here, anchored him in belonging.

For they seemed to him now—under the time-seamed, life-darkened faces, the skin like fine old leather, the thin age-browned hands—to be the same age they had always been, the age at which he had first met them. Under Wilson's face, like a layer of sandstone deep under hills, he could discern the boy he had trapped with fifty years before. He did not see a crippled, nearly blind old man in McKee, but a hard-fisted, skilled mechanician. DeSantis was even yet the fat boy who drew obscene pictures on the underside of his desk. Only Prouper seemed really old to him, for he had always been old to Halvorsen, and this in a strange way made him much more liable to age.

People don't get old between one another, he thought. Only the young ones make us old. If there weren't any younger people, I wonder maybe we wouldn't get old at all.

"What about it?" repeated DeSantis.

"I'm sorry, Len. What did you say?"

"I'm going on home. Can I drop you off? Or are you stayin' for another pop?"

"No, I'm done," said Halvorsen, draining what remained in the can. "Let's go."

DeSantis had an old Willys, and the wind came sharp through the fabric top. As they drove through town Halvorsen noted the new trucks along the streets, the

71

many men on the cleared sidewalks, the open stores. A heavy season; it would sustain the town's merchants through much of the year. DeSantis drove slowly, as an old man does when he is half-drunk and afraid of speed, and he had plenty of time to look around.

"Town's busy," he said.

"Yeah," said DeSantis. "But wait till antlerless season closes. They'll be rolling up the sidewalks."

Halvorsen nodded. They drove out into the country. DeSantis was going very slow and the big pickups tailgated them and zoomed impatiently around them on blind curves. DeSantis swore at them. "The deer'll wait. They're drivin' too damn fast for this ice."

"They're young," said Halvorsen. He remembered Sweet's unconcealed impatience with an old man's advice.

And suddenly he felt very old. Not that it was bad to be old. It was natural. But he felt discarded and useless, and this was not right. Another car pulled around them, trailing a wave of snow that whirled over their windshield and made DeSantis brake and curse in panic.

"They're young," repeated Halvorsen. "It's their world now. I guess the only thing for guys like us to do, Len, is to get to hell off the roads and find a warm place to die."

After he dropped the old man at the gas station Michelson had driven on, into town, looking for a parking space along the main street. They were all taken up by the hunters, except for those that were buried under huge heaps of snow, still bearing the curving imprints of scraper blades. He found a spot at last on a side street and pulled into it and sat there, the motor running, wondering what to do next.

72

See the game warden, confront him with what he and the old man had found? He had little enthusiasm for that. The man hadn't investigated the site, hadn't even bothered to look twenty yards uphill. Why, in God's name, was it the game warden who did accident investigations? He was no better than another hunter himself. The state police, reactionary and racist though they often were in this state, would at least have done a professional job on an obvious manslaughter.

At last hunger (he remembered belatedly that he had not eaten breakfast, and had missed lunch in his trip out to Mortlock Run) drove him out of the car. He walked for a block or two before he caught sight of a bar/grill sign. They should have sandwiches, he thought, and went in.

The bear startled him so much that he stepped back, involuntarily letting out his breath in a plosive "Ah!" as his hands came up in self-defense. In the dim behind the thing someone laughed. "He's tame," someone called. "He don't eat flatlanders," said another, in a loud, half-drunken voice.

He lowered his hands, feeling his face redden, first with embarrassment, then with a purer, stronger emotion: hatred. He went past the ridiculous stuffed animal, glancing up at the worn fur on its face, and looked for a place to sit. The bar was filled, as were the booths along the side, but three of the men in one waved him over, making room. He nodded to them as he sat down, then picked up the plastic-covered menu and opened it. They took the hint and began to talk around him, discussing where they had hunted during the past three days and where they would hunt the next day, Friday, the fifth day of the season.

His anger grew as he looked down at the clumsily

typed menu. All the sandwiches had cute names—cute, he thought, if you were a hunter. Gunners Delight, Shooters Special, Eight Pointer, even a hamburger made out of ground deer meat.

He felt sick suddenly. He was surrounded by them, submerged in the land they dominated and the subculture that they had formed in these remote towns and valleys. It was uncanny, primitive; he felt as if he had stumbled upon some lost tribe of Neolithic savages. Here was the old glorification of the kill, the celebration naked and unashamed of all the atavistic instincts civilized man had struggled so hard to outgrow.

Even the foods they ate, he thought, bore incantations to aid the magic of the hunt.

He hunched his shoulders. The very smell of the hunters oppressed him. He was moving his legs under him to get up when a fat fellow in an apron stopped at the booth to ask for his order. Hunger came back then in a rush and he looked at the menu again.

"Can I get a salad here? A big salad, with eggs and cheese?"

"Chef's salad? Sure thing."

"And water."

He felt the men with him exchange looks, but they said nothing. He looked off across the room, toward the bar. The place was filled with red wool and orange nylon coats, GMC and Caterpillar and various oil company caps, men in down vests and plaid flannel shirts and heavy snow boots. He glanced down at his own feet. His new leather boots were already salt-whitened by his walking around the town.

"So I said to him, Dwight, give me the old lever-action .32 anytime," one of the men in his booth was saying. "That short barrel, you can't beat it for brush work.

Course, in open country—"

"Then it's a bolt action," another of the men said. "But there's bolt actions you can use in the brush. My brother-in-law, he's got this .270 Savage with a twenty-two-inch barrel on her, and a variable scope, and that gun's just so light and quick pointin' you hate to put it down after one shot."

"Two seventy's a nice cartridge."

"He loads 'em up with 150-grain Speers and that chronographs at three thousand. He says he's got it sighted at two hundred but there's practically no drop out to four."

"Jeez."

"Yeah," said the first man, "but if one of them high-velocity bullets hits a twig it'll blow up. No, give me the old lever-action .32 every time. Or a .44. Tom, what you usin' this year?"

"Same's ever," said a voice that had not spoken before. "Punkin balls."

"Shotgun?"

Michelson turned his head slightly to hear better.

"Uh huh. Remington auto."

"I thought you couldn't use an auto action in this state," said one of the others.

"You can't. I had it altered. It's just like a straight-pull bolt action."

"You ought to get yourself a rifle."

"I don't care," said the shotgun man. Glancing over at him, Michelson saw a small, spare man. Instead of the beers the others were drinking he was stirring sugar into a cup of tan-creamed coffee. "I don't care. I only got the one gun and it works year round. I get rabbits and pheasants in the fall and deer in the winter and this summer I got me a groundhog with it."

"With a shotgun?"

"Yeah, with a slug. It was eatin' my daughter's garden out back of the house, sittin' up there munching on her carrots, and I finally got tired and snuck out of the house and come up on him behind a little rise and got up to about thirty yards from him. Give a whistle and he looks up at me . . . that big old ball just blew him apart. Rags of meat and bloody guts all over. Had to bury him with a hoe. They stink like hell, dead woodchucks."

Michelson felt his stomach contract. The other hunters were silent for a moment too, as if reminded of something that they, in their discussions of actions and velocity and barrel lengths, clean mechanical things, had managed to put out of their minds.

"Well, where we going tomorrow?" said one of the others, ending the pause.

"Let's go south. We spent all last season up around here. Let's go down toward Gasport or Derris."

"Wish we could get into that Kinningmahontawany," said the thin man. He pronounced it "kinny-ma-*hot*'ny." "*Pennsylvania Sportsman* says they's deer three deep in some of them canyons. Specially when it's a cold winter."

"It's that all right," said the first hunter. "But hell, Tom, that's wild country down there. No roads; you can't get in except on foot—the state don't even allow snowmobiles in the Wild Area."

"I was in there once," said the third man. "Nothing but up and downs. Miles of solid woods and once in a while an overgrown Shay right-of-way. Not for me. I paid fifteen thousand for that camper and I like to come back to it at night."

"Near Gasport then?"

"All right."

"Okay by me. Just so's we get an early start."

The three fell to discussing when they would get up and what they would take. Michelson found his salad and water at his elbow—he'd not noticed their arrival, he had been listening so intently—and attacked the lettuce and boiled egg and cheese slices. Their talk faded gradually from the forefront of his attention and he found himself thinking, again, about what had happened, and what he could do.

Could Aaron really have been hunting? He had to admit, at least in the privacy of his mind, that maybe, after all he had heard and seen, it was possible.

Not that he believed it; he didn't; but it was *possible*.

Little by little, after the separation, his son had grown away from him, become less intimately and certainly known. There had been too many years apart. Maybe he *had* decided to go hunting, just once. Just to see what it was like, from youthful curiosity. He tried to put himself in Aaron's place. All his teenaged friends must have hunted. In much of Pennsylvania they even closed the schools for the first day of hunting season. Societal sanction added to peer-group pressure. . . .

But why hadn't he gotten a permit?

And where had the rifle come from? Was it his?

I honestly can't imagine him owning a rifle, Michelson thought. Or even carrying one. And at that, at the image of his son with a gun in his hands, the whole supposition collapsed and was unbelievable again. Unbelievable; yet he *had* been out there. He *had* been hunting. There *had* been a gun. He had to face the facts.

Facts, yes, but why? That was what he couldn't come to terms with. He had always felt his son understood what he'd tried to teach him; respect for life; concern for others, the defenseless, the disadvantaged. Concern and fairness; that was what the world needed, and that was what Paul Michelson had tried to pass on to his students and doubly to his son.

But it hadn't worked. Perhaps I was just away too much when he was growing up, he thought. It hadn't taken; and in his water he tasted the acid of defeat.

Not that I ever told him in so many words not to hunt, he thought. I never imagined that he could want to. No more than I myself would consider killing an animal for sport. It was an act so far outside the framework of values that he had constructed in the course of his life that it would demand a different mind and heart than Paul Michelson's to do it.

In spite of that one attempt . . . that one memory, of his own eyes staring back from the glass in one long moment of betrayal, of self-knowledge . . .

Or, he thought, it could be different.

It could be that he had always chosen nonviolence, not because he was right, but because he was afraid.

He stared into the dark surface of the table, but glanced away, unable to bear the eyes reflected there.

He remembered suddenly, with guilt, the gray weapon that lay outside, under blanket and packages of clothing, in the back of his automobile. It was hard for him to recapture that mood of last night, less than twenty-four hours before. Only in that state of mind, a condition that was alien, frightening, to the man Paul Michelson had always felt himself to be, could he even have picked up a gun.

He was suddenly frightened at what he had done. Frightened, and confused. Why had he brought it here? What had he had in mind? And what was he doing here, in this town, during this season, unbelonging and bewildered and goalless?

"The thing to do," the thin hunter was saying, "is to

get out there and settle in. You got to familiarize yourself with the terrain. You got to understand what goes on, how things move, before you figure out the best way to go in."

"What's that?" he said.

The hunters at the table looked at him, beer glasses half-raised to their mouths, the periaptic sandwiches held in air in an instant of surprised immobility. "Sir?" said the thin hunter.

"Were you talking to me?"

"No."

He nodded. Their dull curious glances fell before something in his. He toyed with the remnants of the salad. What had it been? Something, a current, had passed swift and powerful through him. Some direction or force in him as yet unacknowledged and un-understood. He had felt it last night, in the teachers' lounge; and he had felt it, much stronger, standing beside Aaron's grave. He could still feel it.

And now one of them had told him what to do next.

As he turned over the check and rose to go, saying no words of parting to the others, nor they to him, he saw a familiar line of back: the old man's. He was leaving, turning the corner of the bar by the door, reaching up as he did so to touch the stuffed bear's head. Michelson felt no urge to speak to him. Like the thin hunter, Halvorsen had served his purpose.

He drove slowly out of town, all the way back to the Wi-Wan-Chu. The woman was surprised to see him again. A couple had left unexpectedly and he was able to get a room of his own—small, and at an exorbitant price, but he could sleep alone.

It was still light when he went to bed. It would be dawn all too soon; and he had much to do to ready himself for that angry day.

SIX

Friday, November Twenty-eighth

IN THE NIGHT THE TEMPERATURE HAD FALLEN. MINUS NINE-
TEEN by the sign that flashed in front of the shuttered
bank as he drove by it going west down Main Street. 4:34
A.M., it said, then, SAVE WITH FIRST RAYMONDSVILLE, then
−19° F again.

Michelson was warm in his hunting clothes.

He drove west with no particular place in mind,
following a green Scout through town. He knew very
little of this country, the roads, the names of the hills. He
knew that Route 6 led southwest through Petroleum
City, and that he had come up that way from West
Kittanning, but that was about the extent of his topographic knowledge. I should get a map, he thought,
driving west along a road he did not know, following the
stream that flowed out of the town.

Though it was long before first light on a workday
morning, and the snow was deep under a starless sky,
and it was fifty creaking degrees below freezing, the
roads were crowded. Michelson had to drive cautiously,
for the cars ahead would suddenly brake, giving no
warning, and jerk right or left into uncleared tracks that
led uphill between walls of forest. He had only a second
after the flash of red light to slow, or to steer around

80

them as they turned, his hands tightening on the wheel, fearing a skid on the icy road.

The Wi-Wan-Chu had been lighted, every window bright, and trucks had already been revving out in the lot when he awoke. One of them had been the green Scout. He had followed it out, followed its taillights and Ohio plates, through town; and only now did he lose it as a pickup, chains whining, passed him in a blast of snow. As it went by he saw the black cutouts of the men inside, the silhouettes of their weapons racked in the back-window carriers.

Some ancient rite was going on this dark morning in this dark land. In the winter night each man rose early and dressed in his vestments and left wife and children, accompanied by his eldest sons. They collected their arms, provisions, and gathered with the other adult males.

Then the tribe streamed out, armed and clothed and transported by all the technology and skill and produc-tion of the race, into the chill night of the hills, there to worship at an older and darker altar than any in the huddled churches of the towns.

Only he, among them all, was uninitiated.

As a sociologist, he thought, following alertly behind a white Jeep down the side of a pine-bordered hill, I can put names to it. Male bonding. Brotherhooding. Pack aggression. All the distinctive signs were there: dedicated raiment, animal totems, weapons, blood, exclusion of females. There would be some sort of initiation rite at a boy's first kill, no doubt related symbolically to the sexual act.

It was not that strange, after all; every primitive hunting society had such customs. Thinking of it in familiar jargon should have made him feel more com-fortable. Instead he found himself shivering inside the heated car. Savagery, out here in the night, was not as easy to face as it was to read about.

At last he decided that he'd driven far enough. I don't want to get lost, he told himself. Only see what goes on out here. He followed the Jeep ahead when it turned off up a narrow road. The swing of their lights gleamed off the windows of a darkened house, set back from the main road. The two vehicles passed it, climbing steadily. This road was uncleared, and he could feel his wheels spinning at times, hear the scrape of the underpan on the snow; but the Jeep had broken the trail and the small car had good ground clearance. He kept the pedal down. The road crested after half a mile and then ran along the side of the ridge. Down and to his right he could see a stream of moving lights: the highway. He was above and parallel to it. The vehicle ahead was climbing faster than he could and at last he lost sight of it. He lost the highway lights at the same time and decided he'd better stop. The road was steepening again and he wanted nothing less than to be stuck up here. He pulled to the side of the road and after hesitating for a moment turned the motor and then the lights off.

It was suddenly very black, and very quiet. The wind buffeted the car, making it sway slightly on its springs, jostling him.

Michelson got out.

It was cold. The wind bit at his face and nosed under the flaps of the cap and under the collar of the heavy coat. He lowered his head, blinking at the chill. A faint grayish light was seeping down through the trees to his right, gray with a tinge of orange, the town lights. Not even the loom of the sun yet. He buttoned the collar of the coat and pulled down the cap, then reached inside the car for the keys. They slipped from his gloved fingers and he had to grope for them in the snow. When he had them again he locked the doors and went to the back and raised the hatch.

The rifle was hard under his hands. He threw back the concealing blanket to reveal its long heaviness and slammed the hatch shut. The sound was very loud in the dark.

He stood there for a moment, holding the weapon, and thought. He had clothes; binoculars, the ones he carried in his glove compartment; the license, jauntily official-looking in its little plastic holder, pinned to the back of his orange coat, just as the others wore it.

Yes. He looked just like a hunter. He was ready. I'll go uphill, he thought. That way I can always find my way back.

It was clumsy at first, walking in the heavy boots, the warm but heavy coat, with the long underwear cramping the bending of elbows and knees. The snow crunched reluctantly under his feet. There was a hard crust, and then under that powder for perhaps six inches, and then the iron hardness of the ground. He headed uphill, balancing the rifle in one hand. It was hard to see the trees until he was nose to the trunks, and once he ran into one face-first. He went even more slowly after that. The slope steepened. It was hard going but thanks to jogging, and all the tennis with Teresa that summer, he was still in good shape. So he pushed himself upward, glad of the dark, glad in an obscure way of the piercing air that made his throat ache. It meant that he was alive. Still alive and still seeking, he thought. Still looking. But for what?

And if I find it—will I recognize it?

Just as his thighs began to ache the slope slackened and became a plateau. The trees were scattered here and he was able to walk without watching so closely for them. They seemed smaller, too. Michelson paused for a moment, breathing deeply, and looked back.

He could see nothing. The valley below held a highway, a river, homes, cars, people; but nothing of it showed. The whole wide valley was a pit of dimensionless shadow. No light showed under the immense arch of night overhead. Michelson raised his face to it. He wished there were stars and not this impenetrable overcast. As a boy he'd wanted to be an astronomer, had copied starcharts and maps of lunar craters out of library books, and he knew still a few constellations —Ursa Minor, Orion, Cassiopeia, the Pole Star; the strange fuzzy cluster of the Pleiades, as if the weaker stars had huddled together for warmth. On a clear night he would have felt less lonely.

He turned his back on the valley and walked on.

The plateau ended. It hadn't lasted very long. He could see a little better now and saw the dark hill rising before him again. He was hitching up the binocular strap, getting ready to go on again, when he heard a crunching sound approaching him from the right.

He looked that way, staring into the unrelieved black of the trees, but saw nothing. The steady crunch, crunch went by him off to the left. He made himself relax. It was only another man. There are probably dozens of them up here, all around me, he thought.

There was another plateau after a long climb and he rested there, standing up. It seemed to him that the hill was built in steps. Benches, flat areas, as if the hill too were getting its breath, and then resuming its steady climb. It was getting a little lighter now. Close by he could see the trunks of the trees, like lines of charcoal on the gray paper of the snow.

After a while he went on. It was a steady climb now, the steepest yet. At last he had to sling the rifle, grown wonderfully heavy, over his back, and grasp at branches, claw at rocks half-buried in the snow, to haul himself up. He felt sweat starting under the heavy coat, and breathed harshly, letting the icy air sear deep into his lungs.

Then quite suddenly the ground leveled again and the climb was over; he was at the top. The gray blur of trees stretched level ahead of him. He rested for the space of a minute, bending to knead his thighs through the double layer of thick cloth. Well, here I am, he thought.

He decided to sit down. A rock at the edge of the slope looked convenient and he pushed the snow crust off and lowered himself. East of him a faint suggestion of yellow fogged the air. He slid his sleeve back to uncover his watch. 5:50. Dawn should be along presently. He yawned, missing his morning coffee.

He sat and watched light come to the valley. I might enjoy this, he thought, if the damn rock wasn't so hard. And so cold. He shifted several times, then his buttocks grew numb and he resigned himself to it and simply watched.

There was more to see than he'd expected. From his perch he could see for miles over a broad dropping carpet of blue-gray woods. From this height the tops of the trees looked like sagebrush. Each of the plateaus was visible as a broad band of white, with individual trees tinier and tinier in the distance, yet always perfectly distinct. Raising the binoculars to his eyes, he could see individual branches a mile or more away. The air was that clear, his location that commanding.

He lowered the glasses, and caught a flicker of movement to his left. He examined the tree line where he'd seen it, and saw it again, too distant to make out. He raised the glasses again.

A man was standing beside a tree, aiming a gun at him.

Before he could think or move, the man—dressed in an orange vest over a blue parka, and a red stocking cap—lowered the gun and waved. Michelson held the binoculars on him. The man gazed in his direction, then came walking along the ridge, holding his rifle muzzle-down. He walked right up to Michelson and squatted by the rock. "Sorry if I scared you," he said in a low voice. "The chamber's empty. I use the scope to identify things sometimes."

"I don't like to have guns pointed at me," said Michelson. He heard his voice shake slightly.

"I said I was sorry." The man spread his hands. He was, Michelson estimated, about twenty. A curl of brown hair dangled from under the cap. He looked like one of the freshmen at school. "Hey. Lots of guys do it."

Michelson said nothing.

"This is a nice stand," said the man, looking down the valley. "You seen anything yet?"

"No."

"You stand-hunting? Or just resting?"

"I don't get you," said Michelson.

The boy pointed along the ridge. "I'm still-huntin' —walk slow for a ways, then settle in and wait for 'em to show. Walk faster, it's a drive; stay in one place and wait, like here, it's stand-hunting." His eyes were puzzled. "This must be your first time out."

Michelson nodded. He remembered now that the old man had used that term. "Yes. That's what I'm doing."

"Oh. Well, I don't want to cramp you. I'll go on down the ridge. Good luck."

Michelson looked after him as he left. He did not trust

anyone who pointed a gun at him. The boy moved slowly, making little noise, every step slow and smooth. When he was half-hidden in the trees he stopped and a moment later he had blended in so completely that Michelson could not see him at all. It was as if he had turned into a tree himself.

Somewhere in the distance a shot boomed, the sound echoing dully among the hills. Another followed. Michelson realized that he had been hearing them, distant, occasional rumbles, since just after dawn.

He sat and watched the valley and the slope beneath him, and time passed, and he drifted into reverie.

He had met Anne after he left the movement . . . or that wing of it, anyway. In his welter of self-doubt and depression it had seemed natural to move in with her, and after that, natural and right to go the rest of the way. And of course after the baby (Anne, with his full concurrence, had chosen Lamaze, and though it had hurt her they were glad they had done it the old way, the natural way), he had to think of things like his degree, finding a place to teach. It hadn't lasted long. Michelson now understood that he and Anne had been a mistake. But Aaron had not been a mistake. Michelson remembered the way his son, a tiny piece of himself that would live on past him, had curled into him in sleep; the way he smelled; the way when he was four or five he would say things that illuminated for a moment the whole wonder of life, lost for his father somewhere under the grime and tarnish of time and disappointment.

If only they'd had more time together . . .

He sat for a long time, oblivious to the creeping cold. At last something brought him back and he blinked. Movement at the edge of the woods. More hunters, he thought, and stiffened at the thought of meeting them. It was so peaceful here, so private; some of the quiet of the forest had reached him, and he wanted more of it. He stayed immobile, watching the tree line with narrowed eyes. Perhaps they would not see him, and would go on by.

He almost missed them. They were motionless too. Gray, like the trees, they stood with heads raised to the wind, nostrils open for the scent-laden air, and looked at him.

He stared back, not thinking at all. Somehow, in spite of all logic, he had never expected to see them here.

The deer—bark-gray, pear-shaped bodies nervous on long gracile legs—stared full at him for several seconds. The lead one was not thirty paces distant, so close that he could see the white smoke of its breath. He did not move. His whole being was concentrated in watching.

Finally the lead deer seemed to decide that he was harmless, a part of the rock, for it broke from its rigid wariness and bounded suddenly forward. Still cautious, though, it moved around him in an arc. He could hear the plopping crunch of its hooves in the crust and its hoarse, snuffling breathing. He followed it with his eyes, not daring to turn his head. Two others followed it. When they were past he relaxed, and was beginning to turn back to his view of the valley when another deer appeared at the line of denuded trees and paused, like the first. Michelson froze again. This one was plumper, more maternal-looking somehow, and also less wary. It checked him out quickly and bounded across the clearing behind him in a straight line, disappearing in the same direction as had the others.

Michelson felt it then in the air: the waiting. His side was beginning to cramp with the too-long-continued twist, but he held himself still, watching the spot in the woods where they had all appeared. Their tracks, dark-shadowed in the crisp snow, led away into the recesses of the forest.

At the distant end of them, something moved.

He waited.

In two long, low springs, the buck appeared at the edge of the clearing.

And Michelson saw how it was.

The does—he had not thought it at the time, but now, facing the magnificent foredooming antlers, he realized the other deer had been does—had scouted the clearing and felt it safe to cross. But plainly the buck had doubts. The others did not have as much at stake. For them it was the chance of a fright. For him the innocent clearing was a gauntlet, a trap. The animal paused and sampled the air. To the man, taking the same air in the same instant, it was cold, pure, unscented. Yet the buck seemed unsure. It snuffled and danced swiftly in place, eager to flee, afraid to move.

At the same moment Michelson recollected the rifle that lay across his knees. It had lain there since he sat down and he had forgotten it. Now, very slowly, his hands closed around the stock.

The buck paced nervously, looking away from him, toward the other side of the hill.

Slowly he brought it up. The weight dragged at his arms. He did not know much about guns. He'd fired one exactly once in his life, a .22, when an uncle had taken him out to plink at tin cans. He had been ten years old, too young to know what he was doing or to understand how evil could be embodied in machined metal and fitted wood. Yet now, as he brought the rifle higher, the butt nestled perfectly into his shoulder. The sights, he saw, were low and he brought the long barrel up to steady on the shoulder of the restless animal. The deer, catching that last increment of his motion, stopped dancing, watching him, and crouched its squared-off body lower to the snow.

The sights centered themselves. His finger found the curved hard metal of the trigger. He had the animal, had it . . . just as he realized this something broke in him and the sights dipped and wavered crazily. His arms were shaking. He took a deep breath, remembering at last who and what he was, and that there was a young hunter waiting silently in the woods farther along this same ridge.

Michelson lowered the rifle suddenly. He waved at the deer and gave a low, hoarse, animal shout.

The buck disappeared. One moment it was there, flare-nostriled in astonishment; the next, gone. He could not even have said which way. It had vanished completely, silently, faster than he could have blinked.

He put the rifle back across his knees and tried to steady himself, thinking about what had just happened, how he'd felt. He could not really have fired; he didn't even know how to operate a gun. But the uncertainty persisted. If I had loaded it, he thought; if I were familiar with it—then could he, in that suspended second when the buck danced and the sights lay steady against the gray flank, *could* he have fired?

It was a question Paul Michelson had never expected to have any hesitation in answering. No, he told himself. I could not.

But he no longer felt quite so confident of his own virtue.

He looked down at his hands, and at the gun, which lay long and heavy and dull across his numbed legs.

It had to be simple; the Army had used it. He turned it

over and examined the action. The metal box was obviously for bullets. Magazines, that was what they called them. Then there had to be some way for the cartridges to get from there into . . . he found it, a projection from the left side. He pulled it back experimentally and let it slam forward. There was a powerful spring behind it; the sound of metal meeting metal was loud. Yes, that would have fed a cartridge in. He fingered about looking for a safety, but found nothing clearly identifiable as such. He was still wary of the thing, so he stopped fooling with it and looked down at the valley again.

It was now daylight. The trees were bluish-gray on the hills opposite, growing grayer as they neared him. At the two bench lines below he could see plainly between them. Knowing now how to look for motion, he let his eyes drift over the miles below him. The ache in his legs was returning, but he would not be out here much longer. He had learned, he told himself, something of what he had come out here to find; perhaps even more than he had wanted to know.

Hunting was a seductive vice. No wonder Aaron —only a boy, after all—had partly yielded to its siren call. Even his father had felt its power. Perhaps there was more instinct still in man than Michelson wanted to admit.

And then again, creeping like a thief into his thoughts, came the question: *Why* can't you do it?

Was it really compassion, humanity . . . or was there a less admirable side to his nonviolence?

I can't think about it now, he told himself, desperate to keep some little part of the peace he had sought and found here in the woods. I won't think about it now. It would be so good not to think . . . just to do. Just to act.

When he saw the deer below he was shaking the snow from his boots. He almost let it go. He was done here and it was time to return to where he belonged. Instead, he picked up the glasses for a last look, and pointed them down into the valley.

Four of them were moving along the bench line below. Not a quarter mile away from him, Michelson could see them plainly through the 7×35s. They trotted along rapidly in a strung-out column, moving down the gradual slope of the bench. None of them had antlers. He was watching them just to watch, just to enjoy their animal grace, speed, independence of all man knew and did, when at the very edge of the glasses' field he saw the red figure amid the trees.

The unfolding drama held him, and he steadied the binoculars, propping his elbows on his knees.

The lead deer was nearing the red spot, a little to one side of it. Michelson waited for it to see the man, to break into the leaping run the does had used to cross his clearing. Yet it did not. It trotted on, toward the hunter, and he thought: The wind is wrong. It can't smell—

A report boomed out below him. The lead deer leaped and fell. Michelson's hands tightened on the barrels of the glasses. The deer got up. But he could see the dark patch its flank left on the snow.

Now the deer were running. Bounding, skipping, they scattered like blown leaves, apparently at random. Yet from where he was he could see that once scattered they circled, curving back toward the others in a way that would bring them together again farther along in the original direction of travel.

They might have made it. But another doe, perhaps still confused by the wind, or simply panicked, came circling back too quickly. To Michelson's horror another shot cracked out, echoing up from the tree trunks. Through the binoculars he could see the hunter now, a big man, round in a red-orange coat, working the action of his gun. As Michelson watched, he raised it and fired a third time and the second deer fell. This one lay still and did not rise again.

He watched, eyes screwed into the eyepieces. He did not understand what he had just seen. The man below must have seen that they were does, unless he simply fired at anything that moved. What was he doing down there? A moment later he had part of the answer as the hunter staggered forward toward the fallen deer. He was drunk.

Michelson followed him with the glasses as he approached his kill. The hunter looked slowly around him. He did not look upward, though. After satisfying himself that no one was watching he kicked the dead animal —*only a doe,* his whole body seemed to say—and walked off, reloading his gun.

Michelson lowered his binoculars, shaking with anger.

He loved animals; and this was as callous an act as he had ever seen. The game protector, Sweet, had told him in that fatal call that Aaron's accident was far out of the ordinary; that most hunters were sportsmen. Well, I've seen enough sportsmanship now to last me a long time, he thought.

He became conscious then of something else.

He was not going to let this go by.

Even as he realized it he found himself slinging the glasses, picking up the rifle, and starting down the hill. The action, so suddenly and spontaneously taken, crystallized his intentions. He would act. He would catch up with this man, would get his name. Without a name he was anonymous; as safe as the man who had shot a boy in these woods. That could not happen again. He would get his name and report him to the authorities. This time, as an eyewitness, he could insist on prosecution.

He would make one hunter, at least, pay for his "sport."

He slid rapidly downhill, coming out near where he had first seen the man. The woods looked different when you were in them. They were thicker, less penetrable; more mysterious. He could not see the hunter, but he soon found tracks. The large prints dragged clumsily and wanderingly through the snow. He followed them at a jog-trot, swinging the heaviness of the rifle. He came to where the other had stood to fire, and followed the tracks to the dead animal.

There he stopped. The doe lay sprawled in the snow, already beginning to stiffen. Its eyes were open and glassy. Michelson stared at it; stared, fixed, at the snow beside it.

At the still-steaming patch of bright red blood.

He leaned finally to stroke it. The animal's fur was rough, bristly. He touched its head. There's nothing I can do for you, he thought angrily. Justice meant nothing to the dead.

But it meant a great deal to him, the living.

Trotting on, he followed the trail as it staggered among the trees. The man he tracked seemed incapable of walking a straight line. He could not be moving very fast, even if, as was probably his intent, he wanted to put distance between himself and his illegal kill. At last, at the edge of the slope down, Michelson caught a glimpse of color between the gray trunks.

"Hey!"

The red-orange paused, turned, became, as he jogged closer, a man. He was bundled thickly in clothing but the roundness was of fat too. He carried a pump shotgun. And he was faceless. He stood still, staring at Michelson as he came to a stop a few feet from him.

As he did so Michelson saw that the facelessness was only apparent. The man was masked. He wore a red knit-wool ski hood, and through it, as through the port of a diving suit, his small, suspicious eyes looked out.

"You forgot something," said Michelson, panting from the run.

"What's that?" said the man.

"Your deer."

"I didn't shoot no deer." The man's voice darkened. "What the hell are you talkin' about?"

He swayed slightly as he spoke. Even across ten feet of open snow Michelson could smell the liquor.

"I was up on the ridge," Michelson said. He tapped his binoculars. He felt cool now. He had mastered his anger, and it was burning now with a hot, controlled flame. "I saw the whole thing. You wounded one doe and then killed another."

"Bullshit," said the man, swaying. He sounded uncertain.

"I saw you go up and kick it. Killing it is against the law. But it was that kick that decided me to turn you in." Michelson paused. "What's your name?"

"I ain't gonna tell you my name," said the man, and the uncertain note was gone. "I ain't gonna tell you shit, friend. What I do ain't none of your business."

"You're breaking the law. That makes it my business."

"I don't see no badge. You got a badge to show me?"

I'm not going to be put on the defensive by an oaf like this, Michelson thought. "What's your name?" he said again, louder, in the voice he used when a student got out of hand in class.

"Go to hell," said the man. He hefted the shotgun suggestively, still facing Michelson.

And just that suddenly, with that little motion, Michelson knew that this was the man he wanted.

Heavy. Drunken. The gun was a twelve-gauge shotgun, just like the old man had said. Careless and trigger-happy. And the license on his back had been yellow: an out-of-state tag.

This was the man who had shot Aaron and left him to die.

"You'd better give me your name now," he said.

His own voice sounded different to him. Hollow. Remote. He felt certainty rushing into someplace empty inside him, as if he had been prepared, waiting for this knowledge. As if he had always known what he would have to do; and now he was face to face with it, eye to eye, and once again, as on a hot May night many years before, he knew what had to be done, and was ready to do it; and all that remained was the act.

The fat man, meanwhile, seemed to be smiling under the mask. He too had heard the change in Michelson's voice, and had interpreted it in his own way.

"No way, asshole," he said.

Michelson felt himself stepping forward, felt his free arm come back. The other man was larger and heavier than he was, but he was not thinking of size. He wanted to strike his fist deep into the covered smile, to feel the shock of breaking teeth and smashed bone all the way back to his shoulder.

Instead he found the muzzle of the shotgun pressing into his stomach, holding him away. His arm came up, then stopped, held there suspended as they stared into each other's eyes.

"I'll shoot you like those deer," said the man softly.

"How'd you like to be left lyin' here gut-shot, asshole?"

Michelson looked up at him. The whiskey smell was overpowering. There was a long time when an onlooker might almost have thought them friends, two men standing face-to-face in the middle of the woods, close, silent; and then the fat man gave a little shove with his gun, pushing Michelson back.

They separated. Michelson watched him. His eyes are brown, he thought. The man stepped back one pace, then another. He was at the edge of the slope, about to start down. He looked back at Michelson, smiling even more broadly under the mask. Then he turned and began walking away down the hill.

As he walked, he began to laugh.

For Michelson it was the laugh that broke whatever it was that had held him motionless and wordless for those long seconds. He saw the fat man walking away, staggering off down the slope among the barren trees, as he had walked free once before. No one cared to stop him. No one cared to pursue him or apprehend him for what he had done. The law did not care to prosecute. The warden did not care to investigate.

And now, laughing, he was walking away again. As he had walked away—Michelson saw the act again, the whole scene, as he had seen it in the bright mirror of his imagination so many many times before—as he had walked away from a bright-haired boy, leaving him to bleed to death in the snow.

Had he laughed then?

As he watched, unable to move, the man turned, twenty paces down the slope. He looked upward to where Michelson stood frozen, abeyant, trembling; and he lifted his hand in the gesture of ultimate contempt. "So long, asshole," he called. He turned his back once more, stumbling drunkenly over a log, and then righted himself and took another step downhill.

Michelson raised the rifle. There was no reason in his movement. He was so filled with rage, impotent hatred, inexpressible by any other means he knew, without outlet or redress, that he could not withstand it. He had to make some gesture, even if it was only a gesture, a symbol, or he knew, with absolute clarity and certainty, that he would go insane.

He leveled the gun and pressed the trigger.

The heavy rifle went off, not once, but four or six times, too rapidly for him to hear or count, slamming back into his chest and shoulder and blasting shut his ears. The barrel rose with each slam until it pointed into the trees.

He let go, too startled to think. The gun fired once more, then thudded into the snow and slid a little way downhill. He backed away from it. A thin bluish haze surrounded him for a moment and then drifted away between the trees. The rifle lay in the snow at his feet.

He stared down at it for a moment, rubbing his shoulder.

Only then did he think to look downhill.

When he slid to a stop beside the man, stumbling a little because his legs suddenly offered no support, he could tell that it was no use. Still, he hoped. He held his hand over the man's head, unwilling, somehow, to touch him. The back of the mask had ridden up as he fell, baring a furrowed neck and a ducktail of black greasy hair. On the back of the jacket—the man was lying face downward, arms outstretched, head downslope— Michelson saw two small puncture marks in the cheap nylon fabric.

"It was an accident," he whispered.

He tugged weakly at the man's shoulder. The enormity of what had happened still bewildered him. He was no longer angry or confused. He was simply numb. Maybe, he thought, he's only unconscious. Maybe I can give him first aid . . . then go down the hill, find help, get back here . . .

But first he had to see how badly he was wounded. He mustered his nerve and strength and put both hands under the soft-feeling shoulder under the coat and felt how heavy a body was as he turned him over.

He stood up slowly, looking down at the man's chest and belly. Suddenly he had to leave.

He came back several minutes later, white-faced, feeling the sweat trickle and run under his shirt. He rubbed at his mouth with his sleeve. The rough wool felt comforting and he did it again as he looked at the body. At the face. At the front of the blank orange mask.

Suddenly he had to see. He knelt in the snow and tugged the mask upward, rolling it up over the neck and jaw and then up over the forehead.

The cheeks—the dark hair—something about this face was familiar.

It was Abrams, from the Wi-Wan-Chu.

And then it hit him. Harder than anything had ever hit him in his life, harder than his son's death, for a death was after all not your fault and you did not choose it or acquiesce in it or even accept it, for it happened despite you, it hit him that Abrams had gotten to town the same day he had.

He had killed an innocent man. But even that paled for him, obliterated utterly, as he realized something else.

He was not sorry.

He was not sorry at all.

He looked coldly down at the still face. The man had deserved it. He was a killer. He destroyed deer illegally and laughed. He had threatened another man with death and walked away chuckling. He was *the same as* the man who had killed Aaron and walked away. He was *the same as* that anonymous man; the same as all hunters; they were all the same; and they all, like this man, deserved equally the death and terror they meted out so promiscuously themselves.

Looking down at the man, his ears ringing with the high, crazy aftersong of the explosions, he had a sudden sense of crisis, of slippage. He felt dizzy, unsure for a moment of his footing, as if the tree he leaned against and the mountain he stood on had swayed with a shock from deep within. But it was past and gone before he had a chance to think. His mind cleared and his vision cleared and he saw what it all meant. It all fit, and it was right; it was all true, and set, and irrevocable.

Paul Michelson had realized what it was all about.

SEVEN

"THAT'S ABOUT IT, RALPH," SAID THE CORONER, RUBBING AT his glasses with a piece of tissue paper. Behind him a quiet circle of men, farmers and hunters, stood watching amid the trees. "Please arrange for the deceased to be placed in your truck. Better take him to the Chapel for now, till you can contact the family and determine their wishes for the disposition of the remains."

"Me?" said Sweet, holding a match halfway to a fresh cigar.

The coroner nodded absently, looking back up the hill. Like most country coroners he was a mortician by trade, a thin, rather somber man. His name was Whitecar, like the creek; his family was very old in Hemlock County. He finished polishing his wire-rims and put them on one ear at a time, like an old man, though he was not yet fifty.

"Oh, hell," muttered Sweet. He turned away from the coroner, who stood for only a moment longer and then went off down the hill, and aimed his finger at a man wearing the silver-colored badge of a deputy game protector. "Sam, look alive. Grab a couple of these rubberneckers and carry him down to the truck."

"Who, me?"

"Yeah, you! Move!"

"Okay, okay. What's the hurry, he ain't goin' nowhere."

Their audience nodded and passed that one on in mutters. Sweet glared down the hill and burned tobacco rapidly. When the body was finally in the pickup no one else seemed eager to get in, so the warden drove the green Game Commission truck back toward town alone. From time to time, drawing angrily on the little cigar, he glanced from the freshly ashed and salted road into the rearview mirror. The plastic covering the body whipped in seventy miles an hour of wind. One boot stuck out, not lolling, but rigid. Sweet exhaled raw smoke as he cranked the window down and flipped the butt out. His fingers drummed on the wheel. His eyes lingered on the road ahead, then rose to the hills.

On either side of the speeding truck the ridge lines marched along the road like escorting guards. The afternoon sun struggled weakly behind the overcast, and after glancing up at it Sweet muttered once, "More goddamn snow." The hills looked bare and bald, abandoned and unkempt, like the hair of unloved women. He liked them better in summer. Then they were a thousand shades of green. That, after all, he suddenly remembered, was why he had wanted this job, the reason he took the tests and all the bullshit at the school; because he thought working in the woods would be fun.

What they hadn't told him was that the job of game protector was paperwork for the greater part of the year. Then the season came and you were run raggedy-ass playing cop. Worse yet, it was part-time: the warden drew full pay only in November and December. The salary was commensurately low, and you had to eke it out the best way you could with a regular job.

Ralph hadn't been able to find another job in Raymondsville.

The only advantage to the position, he had gradually realized, was that in the green pickup with the Commission seal on the door he could go anywhere—town or woods, to Harrisburg, across the state line to New York or Ohio. No one looked twice. Cops extended you professional courtesy. Even when another green truck, other men, accompanied it . . .

He had carried some interesting things under that anonymous plastic.

The roads were almost empty. It was midafternoon, and most of the hunters would be back in town. He stopped to drop the "remains," as the coroner called them, at the Charles Whitecar & Sons Memorial Chapel, and then headed in to his office, dreading the afternoon to come.

It was as bad as he feared. Apparently WRVL had gotten the story from one of the spectators and broadcast it, confused as usual, and waiting on Sweet's desk were notes to call the sheriff, the mayor, and the editor of the county newspaper. He reached for the telephone but it rang before he touched it.

"Hemlock County Game Protector's Office. Warden Sweet speaking."

"Hi, Ralph. Bill Sealey, at the barracks. You need us on this one?"

The state police. They would assume responsibility if there was any suspicion that the killing might not have been an accident. Sweet held the phone and shook out a cigar from the pack while he thought.

"Ralph, you there?"

"Yeah, just torchin' a choker. Bill, thanks for the offer, but Charlie certified it accidental. Don't think you need to waste your time."

"Two in one season—that's going to be rough on you."

"Yeah, well, I'll live through it. Look, I got calls to return—"

"Bet you do. So long, Ralph."

The phone rang again as soon as he replaced it. He looked furiously around the office for Mrs. Coyle, but she was nowhere in sight.

"Game Protector's Office."

"Ralph, it's Jerry." The editor. "I heard the news on the radio. Can you give me the details?"

"Can you give me a little time, Jer? I just now got back to the office."

"I don't need much but I need it now, Ralph—I'm holding four inches open on the front page. Who was he? Let's start with that."

He couldn't get the man off the phone for five minutes. When he hung up it rang instantly once again. He heard Mrs. Coyle in the back room making coffee. He went in and got a cup and came back out. The phone was still ringing. As he stared at it the street door opened and two men came in, the mayor and Vince Barnett, the chairman of Hemlock County Recreation, Inc., the local shopkeepers' association. He felt like talking to them even less than to the editor, and so he nodded to them and picked the phone up. "Yeah," he grunted.

"Warden's office?"

"Yeah."

"Hold, please. Long distance from Buffalo."

It was a television station. He looked at the two men. "TV," he said. The mayor did not look pleased. Mrs. Coyle, lipstick smeared and hair hanging forward over her face, came out of the back room carrying the fresh pot and several cups. "Hold on a minute," said Sweet into the phone, and handed the receiver to her. He looked at the two men. The outer door opened again and a woman in a business suit and coat came in, stamping snow from her boots.

"Let's go in the back, Ralph," said the mayor, looking at Mrs. Coyle.

In the back room the smell of coffee lingered. Several chairs were stacked by the sink. Sweet lifted them down and they all sat, he, the mayor, the chairman, and the woman, a city council member who owned a real-estate agency on Main Street. There was a generally sober air.

The mayor spoke first, not looking at anyone. "Ralph, I'm concerned. This is the second death we've had this season, both without anyone identified as the—you know, the uh, perpetuator. The guy that did it."

"Was it an accident, Ralph?" asked Barnett.

"This isn't for general consumption, Vince. But this one was shot twice."

"Twice!" said the woman.

"But that doesn't mean it wasn't an accident. I think it was. I got Charlie Whitecar to go along with that. So there won't be an autopsy, and the sheriff won't be involved. And it's not like he was important: from his ID the guy was an assembly-line worker from Columbus."

"I guess that's a break," said the mayor, "though it's not a nice thing to have to say. Tell me, Ralph, can this be related to the first death? The Michelson boy? Two like this so close together can't be coincidence."

"Sure they can." Sweet took out a cigar and offered them around; the men shook their heads; the woman lit one of her own cigarettes. "Just because they happen close together time-wise doesn't mean they're related. It's the averages you've got to look at.

"Now, listen to this: I checked the accident statistics

after the boy died. He was the first hunting fatality in this county, aside from heart attacks and falling off the backs of vehicles in motion, for eleven years. So now we have two this season, but you could say we were way overdue. We might not have another for five years."

"Hey," said the mayor. "I just thought. The first one was with a shotgun, right? What was this one done with?"

"Some kind of rifle, Charlie said."

"Then they can't be related. Completely coincidental."

"That's a good point, Mr. Mayor," said Sweet with respectful surprise. "I missed that aspect completely. You're pretty sharp today."

"Oh, well."

"I think I understand your concern, sir," the warden went on. "And I think our conclusions agree. My plan is to discourage publicity as much as I can. Keep the lid on and let things cool off."

"That's what we came over to find out." Barnett spoke for the first time. "Ralph, I like your approach to this—especially what you said about statistics. Like it a lot. This is the best hunting country in the state, maybe in the whole country, for whitetail at least. The Association spends a lot of money to get that message to outside hunters. We don't want to give them the false impression that something is out of whack here, that it's dangerous to hunt in Hemlock County."

He had known they'd get around to that sooner or later. "Well, I can sure see your point, Vince," he said as innocently as he could manage.

"We better get over to the *Century* right away, see what Jerry's going to print," said the woman, getting up. "Nice talking to you, Ralph."

"Same here," he said, looking at her legs. A little heavy, he thought, but a possibility if things got desperate.

"I'll go too," said the mayor.

They all left. Sweet sighed and stubbed out his cigar. The pack was empty when he looked for another. He thrust it back into his pocket and pulled blank forms from a file drawer. Hell, he thought then, I can't even touch this till I finish the paperwork on the Michelson case. And those would have to be carefully done. Where had he put the medical notes the doctor had given him? He found the folder but it was empty. He carried it out into the front room.

"Buffalo's still on the line, sir. Channel Ten."

"Tell 'em I left the office."

He stood by the desk as she talked, contemplating the consequences if the second killing was indeed no accident.

It was tricky, all right. If it was murder, then Sealey would take charge of it. And he would do a thorough job of looking into things. Ralph had known him in school: Bill wasn't the smartest cop in the state, but he was conscientious. Untouchable. He was tempted by one thing: if Sealey took it, then the barracks would have to handle all the paperwork.

Offsetting that was the fact that the trooper might consider it part of his job to look into the first death, too, to see if they were related. It was a natural question, even the mayor had asked it, and he was considerably dimmer than Sealey. That would not be so good. Investigations tended to turn up other things than what they set out to find.

No, he thought, I'd better keep hold of it myself.

On the other hand, hunting accidents were worse for

the county's business than homicides. The game protector was paid by the commonwealth of Pennsylvania, not the county, so he had no direct responsibility to people like Barnett or the mayor or the lady realtor; but to continue to work here he had to maintain a certain level of trust. The Game Commission was sensitive to local politics, and if he fouled up he could quickly find himself without a job.

They were a bunch of fogies and oldsters—the locals, not the Game Commission—but he could handle them. As long as their cash registers were ringing they were happy. They had no idea what really went on in this county, in the dark of night, in the deep, wild areas that were legally closed to hunting. Barnett and the mayor would handle the local press and radio. The important thing was to keep the television people out of it. If he could do that everyone would be happy, everyone safe. Today would be hairy, tomorrow less so, and by next week things would be quiet again and he could get the depositions and the coroner's statement and type up the accident report, and that would be it. Oh, and he had better call his boss, the district game superintendent down in Lock Haven, just to let him know.

First, though, a business matter. He picked up the phone when Mrs. Coyle hung up and carried it into the back room. "Long distance," he said. "Chicago, and gave the number." Then, "Hello, Mr. Louis, that you?"

"Who's this?"

"Hey, Ralph Sweet, from Raymondsville."

"Ralph! My favorite huntin' guide. What do you need, buddy?"

"Well, you might have heard we're having a little trouble up here."

"Yeah, I read about the kid got killed. Is it serious?"

"No. No. Just awkward. Unrelated to us, though, and it'll smooth over in a few days. I might be kind of tied up for a while, though."

"Anything that'll hold up the group for Christmas?"

"Uh . . . I don't think so. We're due for some snow, but that should be over by then. No, Christmas looks good. Send me the deposit this week so I can get things started. We'll have a great time."

"Plenty of deer?"

"Always are. Saw an eight-pointer taken yesterday."

"Holy smoke! Okay, thanks for calling, Ralph. Stay in touch."

"I will."

The voice lingered. "This trouble. You're sure it's minor?"

"Yeah, it's minor. I'll take care of it."

"You're sure?"

"Yeah, Mr. Louis, I'm sure."

The line clicked off and he lowered the phone, his face thoughtful. Christmas. There would be men coming to Hemlock County then, wealthy men who would want anonymity, reticence, privacy. They wanted other things too, of course: deer, booze, girls; some things he had to arrange to bring in from outside the county. He'd have to work quickly to get it all for them, get this all quieted down by the end of the season. The phone burred, trying to ring, but he lifted it and replaced it quickly and then lifted it again and held it to his ear, listening to the distant dial tone, thinking.

Another disquieting thought. This McCoy, who had come around asking questions, taking advantage of his grandfather's senility—who was he? Would he be back to sniff around this incident too? Or had he disappeared for good?

For just a moment, standing there with the telephone humming in his ear, Sweet felt events sliding forward, beginning to topple with increasing momentum. Shit happens, he thought. First you made a choice. Maybe you needed cash, saw an opportunity, then met the right people to make it a reality. But then your actions gradually became less free, became not choices at all but obligations: things you had to do just to save yourself. Like making more money just to stay ahead, because your alcoholic grandfather had destroyed everything he owned and you and your mother had nothing to fall back on. Like taking care of people whose curiosity exceeded their wisdom, who pried and found things out they didn't need to know or be concerned about and who threatened to destroy everything just by talking.

He shook his head slowly and reached for a cigar. The pack was still empty and he crumpled it in his fist and rebounded it neatly into the trash can under the sink.

As he dialed the Lock Haven number he had a sudden chilling thought. If the second killing had not been an accident . . . then might it not happen again? The specter of someone out there shooting people, perhaps at random, unknown, faceless . . . no, he told himself, that was impossible. It would endanger everything. He bit at his lip as he waited for the game superintendent's number to ring.

Later that night, an excited man called in from Beaver Fork, nine miles northeast of Raymondsville. The warden was not in the office, and he had told Mrs. Coyle not to give out his number at home. But under the circumstances, she decided that he had better know.

The caller was saying something about another accident.

EIGHT

Saturday, November Twenty-ninth

Cartoons.

Bugs Bunny, dressed as a calico-skirted granny, plants a resounding kiss on the nose of Elmer Fudd. Slowly realization comes. The baby-faced hunter does a triple take, raises a shotgun, and sends a stream of black projectiles winging after the twicky wabbit. Bugs pulls a cast-iron skillet from under his dress and bounces the bullets back at Fudd, who drops the gun and runs. The bullets follow him around corners, making right angles in the air. A loose-lipped, retarded grin signals that Fudd has an idea too. He finds a mirror and holds it up to ward off the stream. The bullets plow through it, shattering the glass. A cloud of smoke, and then Fudd is seen standing up, face blackened, wisps of smoke coming up from his tattered coat.

He shakes his fist at the rabbit impotently.

Teresa del Rosario, slumped as if thrown into one of the soft chairs, stared at the flickering screen.

She was not following the Loony Tune. Her hands were locked under her mouth, fingers paled with pressure. Her tennis shoes lay, kicked off, beside the chair. A

111

cigarette smoldered forgotten beside two lavender-stained stubs in an ashtray. She did not look up when the door opened.

"Anyone watching that? Oh, Teresa. Didn't see you."

"Hello, Mac."

Connolly came into the lounge. Instead of jacket and tie he wore paint-spotted blue jeans and a flannel shirt. He looked at the television, then at her. "What's this? Saturday morning cartoons in the faculty lounge?"

"That's right." She laughed. "I had a thesis to read. Just got done. I didn't think anyone else would be around."

"Classes going all right?"

"Yes, they are, thank you. Would you like some tea? I have hot water."

"Yeah, that'd be good. Mind if I turn the sound down a little?"

Teresa went into the little kitchen. When she came out again a few minutes later they sat facing each other, mugs warm in their hands. "Look," said Connolly at last, scratching at his beard. "I'm sure he'll be okay when he gets back. He just needed some time alone. Don't worry about Paul."

"I am worried about me, Mac."

"Meaning?"

"I love him very much."

"Nothing to worry about there. You're both good people."

"Thank you. But I am not sure that both of us are in love."

Connolly shrugged, looking embarrassed; he sipped his tea. "Hey. He's under a lot of pressure. Don't judge him by what he said to you when he left."

"I am not judging him, Mac. I've known him for

almost a year now. I have felt this . . . this wall he builds around himself. We've been close in some ways. You understand."

Connolly nodded, watching her redden.

"But I have never felt"—she sighed, glanced at the soundless screen where now a cartoon dog was showing a book to a group of figures in space suits—"*intimadad. . . .*"

"Intimate," said Connolly.

"Intimate. Never felt that he was letting me close to the real Paul Michelson. Until—*fue raro,* until Wednesday night."

"That was the real Paul?"

"I think it might have been."

"No. That confused, angry man?" The department chairman shook his head. "Look. I've known Paul since he began teaching with us. He's a gentle, well-balanced individual. But like he said that night, as far as close attachments, his son was all he had."

"He could have had me."

Connolly blinked and looked down at his mug. After a moment he cleared his throat. "Well. Yes. Thanks for the tea, Teresa. I've got to check over some lesson plans, then it's back home to repaint the bedroom. Have a nice weekend—and don't worry. Everything will turn out all right."

"Yes. Good day, Mac."

When he was gone she took another cigarette from her purse, put it in her mouth, and struggled briefly against the desire to light it. She won. Holding it unlit in her lips, she got up and turned the sound up again on the television and clicked through the channels. She hesitated at a movie, then went on; when she found a news program she stopped. After a moment she went slowly back to the chair, lighting the cigarette without thinking, watching the camera as it moved joltingly down the snow-covered street of a small town.

". . . making the third fatality in recent days in this Pennsylvania sportsmen's paradise," the commentator was saying.

"The most recent accident occurred just north of the town of Beaver Fork, a village in the northeast corner of Hemlock County. Discovered by hunters late yesterday afternoon, the body was identified as that of a local man, the assistant manager of an auto-parts store.

"News Ten has ascertained that the death of Joseph Sciortino is the third hunting accident in this area in the six days since the season opened November twenty-fourth. Local sources"—the scene shifted to another town, an office, a handsome man turning away from the camera, face set, filter-tipped cigar tight in his mouth —"are declining comment at the moment, saying only that all three deaths are under investigation. County Game Protector Ralph Sweet has issued a statement, however, saying that there are as yet no grounds for assuming these are other than what he calls 'normal' hunting accidents.

"Ten weather is next, with Ken—"

She sat staring at the screen, not hearing as the weatherman came on, sketching the approach of a front from Canada.

Aaron: he was of course the first of the three. But who was the second? They hadn't said. For a moment she wondered if . . . but no, Paul wouldn't be in danger, even if that was where he had gone. The television had called them all hunting accidents. He would be in the town, not in the woods. She couldn't imagine anyone less likely to be out hunting.

But what was going on up there? First Paul's son, and now two others. She got up, turned the set off, and stood before the window, twisting the bracelet around her wrist. Above the campus, the hills were hard as steel cutouts against a cloudy sky.

Hunting. She knew Paul was almost fanatical about it. That is, against it, she corrected herself. Sometimes she could still hear Latino in her English, though she'd hardly spoken Spanish since she'd arrived at West Kittanning, except in class. Aside from a general fondness for furry animals, Teresa herself had no strong feelings on the subject. There were few hunters in the barrio; she had never thought about it much until she came here for her first teaching job. Here, in the town, she had seen hunters. Not many, not often. She knew that in the northern part of the state there were more, many more; and she vaguely remembered seeing references to Hemlock County and deer in the local paper as she flipped quickly past the sports pages. She had not thought much about it. But something was going on up there now; and Paul was, might be, no, probably was up there, where accidents were happening. . . .

Teresa turned from the window and left the lounge. Crossing the campus to her car, staying on the path to keep her low shoes drier, she suddenly thought, why not go? There was nothing else for her to do today. Nothing Sunday; her next class was Tuesday first period, Seminar in Castilian Literature. I will go up and surprise him, she thought tentatively, testing its sound. He would not want to see her at first. But she could change his mind. She had done it before, in his apartment. In fact she had made the first move toward bed, after their third date, surprising herself. Her mind drifted to that and she smiled. Sometimes she had to laugh; he was comical sometimes; once she had found him wearing bathing trunks under his trousers; bachelorlike, he had run out of clean undershorts. . . .

Assistant professors in foreign languages, untenured, don't make much at small Pennsylvania colleges. Her huge old Chrysler blew one of its worn recaps on the way up to Raymondsville. She stood by it for twenty minutes, shivering, just north of a crossroads called Bagley Corners, before a Ford van, going in the opposite direction, stopped to help. The four men in it, a father and three burly sons, all in hunting red, made short work of her tire change. When she offered them money the father refused gruffly. One of the sons lingered for a moment. She thanked him again firmly and closed the door.

They'd spoken strangely, with a different accent from downstaters. Their clothes and boots were rough. But what Paul had been saying—no, they did not seem like evil men to her.

She got to Raymondsville about three. Driving down the main street, looking for Paul's little car, she was surprised at the size of the town. From the way he had talked about it she'd expected a huddle of log shacks, even tents. She smiled at herself and shook back her hair. Always the City of the Angels colored her thoughts. Just because there were forests, deer, bear, did not mean a wilderness. America was larger than east Los Angeles, larger than all California. But it still seemed strange to her to wake and hear the snow hissing down, to have to "bundle up" (she had loved that phrase when first she heard it) to go outside, to raise her eyes from walking and find always on the edge of her world those strange dark hills, frowning and in a way menacing, hedging in her sight of the sky.

She braked suddenly, skidding around a large van

marked with the call letters of a Pittsburgh station. It was turning, parking in front of a Texaco station. There were few people on the streets. They looked curiously at her from behind the piles of snow, like soldiers from a trench, as she drove slowly by.

¿Adonde va, Teresa? Where would he be, here in the town, looking for the answers to the death of his son? The police station; he would have called there surely. She stopped to ask directions and a few minutes later found City Hall. The man on duty, an unfriendly person not even in uniform, told her the state police barracks was the place for her to ask. She was unfamiliar with the word, but decided not to ask. She drove carefully across town, feeling the nearly bald tires slipping on the polished snow of the street. It was hard driving on snow. Till she had come east she had never seen it.

Again, at the "barracks" (they looked like another office to her), people looked at her curiously and shook their heads. She was told to go to the Game Commission office. But she found it closed and locked, dark inside though it was only four P.M. She stood in the snow outside the door, seeing several film boxes crushed into footprints, and thought. He wasn't here, though he might have been once—say Thursday morning, if he had come straight to the town. But where would he be now? Where could he stay? Did he have any place—

Yes. There were people here who knew him. She looked at the ground. Her mind resisted for a moment, did not want to give up the name. Anne. Anne Michelson, once, but now, Anne—

Oleksa. That was it. Strange name. She found the address in a phone booth and then went looking for the street. Four-thirty, and already it was growing dark. Night comes so soon here, she thought, looking west at the long ridge that sheltered and imprisoned the town.

The sun went down so quickly, silhouetting the topmost trees for a moment as it sank behind them, then suddenly gone, leaving only the immense slanted shadow of the hills. The sky still glowed, but it was as if the light just seeped away, was absorbed and blotted out.

She shivered, wishing suddenly for dry riverbeds and the comforting sweep of freeways.

The snow in the yard of 33 Barnes Street was trampled, slushy, and refrozen. Beside it a little creek had solidified between hand-laid rock walls. A rusty De Soto grille peered from under a hump of snow at the back of the house. The house was tired and shabby, like all the others on the street. Teresa wiped her boots on the mat on the porch, checked the number, and pressed the buzzer. She could hear it deep inside the house. At the third buzz an old woman looked out quickly, lifting a curtain at the window, and then disappeared. Teresa stood waiting, watching her breath frost the glass of the storm door. *Madre de Dios,* cold. The door opened at last, just as she was about to buzz a fourth time. A man in gray work pants and undershirt stared out at her through the glass outer door.

"Is Mrs. Oleksa in, please?"

"She don't want to talk to you," said the man.

"She doesn't . . .? Oh, the newspapers. I am not with them."

"TV?"

"No."

"You're not from around here," stated the man.

"Yes. But it is all right. I am a friend of Paul's."

"Who?"

"Michelson. Paul Michelson."

His look grew even more hostile. She could feel him examining her eyes, her skin, her hair. She suddenly felt her foreignness intensely. Then she thought, I am not foreign. I am as American as they. Whether they realize it or not. The thought stiffened her back a little.

"What do you want her for?"

"Paul has disappeared. I'm worried about him. You must be Mr. Oleksa."

"Yeah," said the man. He glanced behind him. "Well, I'll ask her if she wants to see you. What's the name?"

"Teresa del Rosario."

The interior of the house was cramped, hot, the walls painted in dark colors and the windows shrouded in yellowing old-world lace. Brown fronds of Easter palm curled behind a picture of the Sacred Heart. The old woman she had glimpsed was nowhere to be seen. The man had disappeared too. Teresa sat alone in the parlor, waiting, and decided not to have a cigarette.

"Miss . . . Rosario?"

She rose quickly.

Anne Michelson—no, Oleksa, Teresa reminded herself—was older than she, a thin woman with faded blondish hair. She wore a brown housedress. Standing in the door to the kitchen, she looked beaten and old, except for her startlingly clear, angry blue eyes.

"Jim says you're a friend of Paul's."

"Yes."

"Don't you know what's happened? What do you want here?"

"I've just come to be with him. He should have somebody."

"What do you mean—be with him?" The blue eyes examined her. "He's not here. Why are you looking for him here?"

"He has not been here? You haven't seen him?"

119

Mrs. Oleksa came farther into the room and folded her arms. They were thin under the housedress. Teresa saw that her eyes were swollen, but her voice was cold and self-possessed, withering. She shook her head now. "Not since the funeral. I thought he went back to his school after that."

"He did. But then he left again."

"So what are you? You live with him?"

"No. I'm a teacher too. A friend."

"Paul always liked pretty friends."

"I don't know what you mean."

"You don't sleep with him? I find that hard to believe."

"Mrs. Oleksa," said Teresa, moving toward the door, "if he's not here, I should not stay. I know you feel angry about your son. But I don't think Paul is the one you should feel angry at. Or me."

"She bothering you, Anne?" The man's voice, from somewhere back in the house.

"No. It's all right." Mrs. Oleksa moved between Teresa and the door. "I'm sorry. Sit down. I shouldn't take it out on you; that's true. But it sounds to me like you don't know a lot about Paul Michelson."

They both sat. The parlor furniture was old-fashioned and overstuffed. Two televisions stood against the walls, old cabinet models, both with dusty screens. In the next room Teresa could see a new portable.

"So Paul's back in town."

"Yes, I think so."

"He hasn't been here to see me."

"Oh."

"How long have you known my ex-husband?"

"About a year."

Anne laughed. "I've known him for seventeen. You

learn a lot about a man in that time, a lot that you can't learn in one year."

"You don't like him because of the divorce."

"I don't know what he's told you about me, dear, but I left him; he didn't leave me. No one could live with him. God knows I tried." She smoothed her dress over her legs and her eyes sought the holy picture. "But he wouldn't let me. Jim, now, Jim's no smart-ass college professor, but he's human. Sometimes he's mean but he's open to you, he can be reached. He's a man. Paul's not. He's like a little boy, hiding inside this thick armor of his intellect. It's as if he had some dirty little secret. I used to wonder if he was—you know, queer. But I guess that wasn't it or you wouldn't be here.

"Anyway, I could see the same thing starting to happen to Aaron. I tried to stop it by leaving."

"Did it help?"

Anne Oleksa's eyes closed then, and she let her head sag back onto an antimacassar. "I guess not. Not in the long run. Raymondsville wasn't good for him either. He didn't fit in with the boys here very well. The ideas Paul gave him when he saw him—which wasn't very often —well, they just weren't the sort of things people around here like to hear. Maybe in a college town it would have been different." She recrossed her arms suddenly. "Jim—my husband—he tried, but he couldn't take Paul's place. Aaron loved his real dad. But Paul never even had him over for the summer. Just once in a while, a visit. Just enough to upset him, make him feel that he was different and too good for a place like this. Then he started running with those kids."

"What kids? A gang?"

"A gang? Not really."

"Hunters?"

"Hunters?" Mrs. Oleksa repeated, with some surprise. "No. He didn't hunt. Paul got that across, I suppose. Jim wanted to take him out once after squirrels, but he wouldn't go. Tried to give his stepdad a lecture! And most of the boys around here love to hunt—I know my brothers used to. No. These were smart kids, up at the high school, smart but strange. I remember once they had a demonstration down in front of the Thunder refinery, something about polluting the water. The police cleared them out. There were girls there too."

"Anne?" A woman's voice from the dark rooms behind.

"Just a minute, mother." Mrs. Oleksa got up, her arms still crossed defensively. "But he was a good boy . . . no, I don't know where Paul is. And I can't say I care. I can't really blame him. I feel angry at him but it's just . . . the way things are, I guess. Maybe if I'd stayed with him Aaron would be alive now. Even closed off like that would be better than dead. But I thought I was doing the right thing. I asked God whether it was, and I thought he answered. Now—"

"Anne!"

"I'm coming, Mother!" she called, almost screamed. "You'd better go now," she said to Teresa. "Go find him. Good luck to you. Believe me. Better than I've had. But if I were you, I'd find another 'friend.'"

Out in the now-dark streets, she thought suddenly that it was too late to drive back; she ought to find a place to stay for the night. Driving about the town, she had passed several hotels, small two- and three-story places, and drove back now to the best-looking one, the Antler. She went in, noting the worn carpets, the shabby couches in the lobby. Two men were standing at the desk, arguing with the clerk. They were trying to get a deposit back. The clerk said they were leaving early and so the deposit couldn't be returned. At last the men left, shouting angry threats never to stay there again. The clerk ignored them as he checked Teresa in. "You with the television people?" he asked.

"No."

"It's okay with me if you are. Channel Ten's been here since this morning and they say Four's on its way in too. That's Erie. You want a single or a double?"

"Single."

"How many in the room, please?"

"Just me." She took out her purse; counted out a few bills. She realized she had come without much money.

"Lots of rooms now," said the clerk, shoving across her change. "Lots of hunters leaving. Not so good for business. Some people in town are kind of mad at the TV stations. But that's silly. We're news now."

"Because of the accidents?"

"That's right. Do you have equipment with you, Miss—uh, Ms. del Rosario?"

"I told you, I am not with the television."

"Oh. Sorry."

She stopped on the way to the stairs. "I forgot to ask. Do you have a guest here named Michelson?"

"Michelson? Michelson? No, ma'am."

"Thank you."

"Good night."

"Good night."

In the room she dropped her overnight bag on the bed, opened her purse, lit a cigarette, and began brushing her hair in the mirror.

It was so strange. Where was he? It was as if Paul hadn't been here in town at all. He hadn't seen the police or the state police or even his wife. In all her driving around town she had been watching for his car, and if it was here—were here, she reminded herself, conditional tense—she would probably have seen it; there were not all that many streets. He'd been here for three days now and left no trace. Where was he?

And what was he doing?

Brushing her long dark hair out in swift strokes, holding it out with her head bent, Teresa watched herself in the mirror. Over a pack today, she thought, watching the smoke drift upward. You were supposed to be quitting. She was stubbing this one out half-finished and congratulating herself when a thought occurred to her, something so incredible she gasped out loud.

Was Paul involved in these new accidents?

It was monstrous, impossible, and she felt instantly ashamed for even conceiving of it. He was such a gentle man. Remote, sometimes, his ex-wife was right there, but he cared; as if making up in a way for that remoteness to individuals, he cared about everybody. He is a good man, she told herself fiercely.

But he had been wrong, hadn't he? Hadn't he done the wrong things with his son? He should have been with him more. Or else let him alone to grow up. He should have loved him more, loved the thin woman more —loved me more, she thought.

And if he was here, why was he so hard to find?

Perhaps he had come here and then gone back. She found the telephone and placed the call, hoping. It rang and rang. She visualized the little apartment, the books, the funny Japanese bed on the floor. But the phone rang and rang, emptily, until at last the clerk came back on. She thanked him and hung up and stared at the picture over the bed. A picture of a jumping deer.

He was still here somewhere.

Wrong or not, she decided, I love him. She would be the one to finally break through; she would be on his side no matter what. The resolution strengthened her. She went back to the mirror, lighting a cigarette. But as she brushed again and again, fiercely, as she looked back at herself, her mind still fought a suspicion she was frightened even to name.

Ay, Dios mio, I've got to find him, she thought. *Before something terrible happens.*

NINE

It was not for justice.

Human justice, he knew, was only a compromise based on power; it served those who owned; it had little relation to what *ought* to be. What he was doing was right. But it was not "justice."

Revenge, then?

Perhaps. But not a primitive, personal-feud, Old Testament revenge. He was not doing what he had to do for a personal motive, though he had one. He was doing it for something larger. For the cause of innocence wronged; the cause, in its simplest formulation, of nonviolence to all living creatures, and of peace and tolerance among all sorts of men.

Paul Michelson sat on a stump, deep in the woods, somewhere west of a place his new map called Hantzen Lake. His rifle lay across his knees. With his blaze-orange coat and cap, wool pants, binoculars, the corner of a foil-wrapped sandwich poking from one pocket, he looked the very picture of the deep-woods Pennsylvania hunter.

And in truth, he thought, raising his binoculars to sweep the woods, that is what I am.

And it was easy. That was what was surprising. It was so easy, once he had rid himself, with the catalysis of accident, of the narrow-minded social controls he had internalized.

He wondered if all revolutionaries felt this way.

Michelson now saw quite clearly that his personal value system had been a morass of self-protecting illusions, evolved primarily to let him feel superior to the rest of mankind, while exculpating him from any responsibility for what they did. The failure of his previous attempt to take action, when he had stood with fire in his hand and not been able to throw it, was part of it. Certainly the academic milieu he had spent his adult life within had accentuated it, completing his isolation from what really happened in the world.

My goals were right, he thought. But my methods were inadequate.

The activists—those whom he had opposed within the profession, arguing politely at cocktails that sociology was or should be an objective science, dedicated to research and not to the initiation of action—had been right. You had to act when you knew evil. And once that fact was faced, you had to ensure that your actions were effective. Otherwise they were wasted effort.

Now he knew; and now he was taking action.

It was almost too damned easy. Before dawn he had woken alone in his room and had an early breakfast at Mama DeLucci's and bought one of the wrapped sandwiches at the register to take along for a hunter's lunch. He'd picked up a county map at the sporting-goods store and selected an area well away both from Raymondsville and from Beaver Fork, where he had made his second bag the afternoon before (the second, he had thought, would be harder; instead it was the opposite). Then he'd driven out of town, parked along a lease road with the other vehicles, taken the rifle and an extra magazine of cartridges from the back, and walked up into the woods. An easy fifteen minutes of climbing had put him here, at the base of a ridge. It wasn't as good a vantage point as his first, but he'd seen plenty of tracks on his way up; he knew his quarry was here. All he had to do was wait patiently until conditions were right.

That was all there was to it.

Today, he thought, is Saturday, the sixth day of the season. He had plenty of time. He would proceed deliberately, plan carefully, and make his actions as risk-free as an intelligent man could make them. There were eight days left in the two weeks of the season, and he was in no hurry.

He did not plan to be caught.

Now that everything was all right and he knew what he was going to do, Paul Michelson was at peace. He had left self-doubt behind. There was still a sweet sadness when he thought of Aaron, but it was as if his son had died not five days, but five decades ago. He mourned, but no longer with the knife-sharp bitterness he had felt standing by the snow-swept grave.

What he was doing now would avenge his son, certainly. But it was a more thorough, more radical, more lasting thing that he was really about. What he was doing might mean the end of hunting forever, if he could carry on and avoid exposure or capture. It would cost lives; perhaps even a few who did not wholly deserve to die. But in the long run, and of this he was sure, it would save far more.

He could visualize what would happen as the days passed. The mounting fear in the towns. The rumors, then the headlines. The tale and toll spreading from this remote Pennsylvania corner all over the East, all over the country. And the hunters would fear and the people would take thought. Eventually they would have to close the season, and next year some would ask: Why reopen it? Why take the risk?

It might take several years. But he could continue longer than they could.

There would be some danger to himself, of course. But even if the worst happened, even if he was killed, it would be a worthwhile end, to fall fighting evil with its own weapons. Fighting killing with killing, cruelty with cruelty until, outdone, the bloody hand of the hunter was stayed forever.

He smiled. It was a little like what the Pentagon was always saying about deterrence. But then a shiver suddenly seized him and he thought, if only it wasn't so *cold*.

He stood up and stretched. Above the trees, he didn't know what kind they were, the sky was a cold white-gray. On the light breeze a few small flakes whirled quietly down. Aside from them the forest was still. Michelson sat down again and resumed his watch. Presently a hunter passed him uphill, but he was too far away, a mere distant dot. Michelson waited. He was content to wait, except for the cold. I wait like a tree, he thought. Then for a while he did not think at all, only sat, shivering occasionally.

Later he made out a man coming up the ridge. He checked his rifle. He understood now how to load it, and had figured out yesterday how to fire single shots or bursts. Apparently what had happened was that it had been left loaded, perhaps years ago, when it had been stored. That was why it had gone off. Actually he hadn't speculated that much about it. It had happened and in

doing so shown him what he had to do, and so he
accepted it along with all the other things that had come
to him so suddenly.

The man moved forward steadily as Michelson
watched. On his back he had a blue pack and for a
moment Michelson, not seeing a rifle or shotgun, was
not sure he was a hunter. Then he made out the holster
low on his leg. Fair game, then. The man had not yet
seen him. He was raising the rifle when he saw the
second, a few hundred feet behind the first. There were
two of them, maybe more. He lowered the rifle and the
lead man looked up. They nodded to each other. The
hunter trudged up to Michelson's stump. He had dark
hair long over alert black eyes. He looked Indian. "Hey,"
he said softly to Michelson.

"Hey."

"Cold, ain't it?"

"Sure is."

"Seeing anything?"

"Some. Nothing to shoot at yet though."

The man's eyes were preternaturally penetrating.
Under that look, steady as the breeze that ate hour by
hour into his strength, Michelson felt a squirm of
nervousness. Then he felt annoyed. He was about to ask
the man to move on when the hunter said, "What's
that?"

"What's what?"

"That gun you got. That a Browning?"

"Uh, yeah," said Michelson, looking down at it.

"That's military issue, isn't it?"

"I think so."

The man seemed genuinely interested in the rifle. He
leaned over to look at it more closely. "Jesus. Isn't that
an automatic action?"

"I think so," said Michelson again, feeling the annoyance flicker up. "So what?"

"You must be from out of state," said the young man. "Course, I don't give a shit what you carry, but you better not let a cop see you with that thing. That's illegal as hell in pee-ay."

Michelson remembered a fragment of overheard conversation. "I had it converted," he said, trying to sound confident. "Now it's just like a straight-pull bolt action."

"Oh," said the young man. He looked behind him. The other man, considerably older, also with that same Indian look to him, had almost caught up with them. "Well . . . good luck, man."

The older man joined them, nodded to Michelson, and the hunters walked on together.

Michelson looked after them. He had been ready for long seconds to shoot them both. Maybe I still should, he thought. The young one . . . did he suspect? He would probably remember the gun. Or would he? He watched as they moved slowly up the hollow toward the top of the ridge. He resolved that if the young one looked back at him, even once, he would get up and follow them and take them both. He watched them as they climbed for a long time, using the binoculars, until they were both lost to sight in the cover at the top. Neither of them looked back.

He settled in again to wait. Like the trees he waited silent, motionless. Like a predator, he thought. Like the panthers, the wolves, all the clean beautiful guiltless killers man has banished from the woods, I wait for my prey.

This time he did not wait long.

For Stanley Mizejewski the season was the one bright spot in a long and thoroughly gut-boring Pennsylvania winter.

131

Mizejewski (he pronounced it *Mish*-a-yev-ski, which was wrong, but the old language had died with his grandfather) worked in Pittsburgh, for Carnegie. But he was not in steel. He did not labor stripped to the chest before a night-torching open hearth, his fair skin dripping with sweat. He had a more refined third-generation job. He was a dinosaur duster.

Or so he referred to himself in bars. The women he met there (Stanley, twenty-eight, had not yet married; he lived with his sister Rhea and her husband in an additional room he and Jack built one summer over the garage) always asked:

"What's a dinosaur duster?"

"He's a man that dusts dinosaurs," he would answer.

"You're kidding," they would always say.

"I swear to you," he would say, *using the solemnity of swearing to reach out and take their soft hands in his big muscular ones. Their hands would feel small and timid. "No kidding. That's what I do for a living. I work at the Carnegie, that big marble building over on Forbes. You know?"*

"The art museum?"

"Yeah. Only there's a library and a concert hall and lots of things there. And in one of the wings there's Natural History. You ever been there?"

"I think when I was a kid. In fourth grade."

"Yeah. Well," he would say, *"you remember they got these dinosaur exhibits there. Maybe the best in the world, you know? Right here in Pittsburgh. Diplodocus carnegiei. Tyrannosaurus rex. Great big mothers. Well, I keep them clean. Use brushes and sprays and the hand vacuum. Got to do it up on ladders. Sometimes it's pretty dangerous, if you know what I mean. On those slippery old marble floors and all."*

"Oh, yeah?" they would say as his fingers moved on their hands. The hot ones would squeeze back; that was how he could tell sometimes. Though sometimes it turned out back at the garage that he was wrong. "That's really something," they would say. "They pay you pretty good for that?"

Stanley grinned as he walked up through the woods. Yeah, it was a crazy job all right. When you were talking about it to some chick it was all right. It gave you something to say, a line. But it was dull and kind of dirty, you got sleepy working late at night, and there was always the fear of a fall. Going down sixty feet from the top of the *Diplodocus* skull you could break your neck easy. The guys he worked with had a standing joke. Whoever went first, they would dig him up after a year and wire his bones and put him up in a case as a Cro-Magnon man display.

Homo budweiseriensis, Mizejewski had told them to put on his.

It was dull though, even with the guys to fart around with, but another year was gone and he was off for his two weeks and by God he was going to spend it all out here, away from the city noise and the pavement and the niggers—of which there seemed to be more, and crazier, in the city all the time. He was a little ashamed to use the word nigger, he never said it out loud, but by Christ the way they acted in the neighborhood he found himself thinking more like his old man every year.

Christ, he thought, here I am on vacation and still carrying it all around with me. He felt dismayed with himself. He turned his mind away from the city, his job, the frustrations of his life, and set himself firmly in the crystalline present of the hunt.

He'd missed opening day, always the best day, because

his damn car had crapped out. But he had gotten it fixed at a garage in town and had two good days of hunting so far. Seen plenty deer, mostly doe, but there had been one buck, a four-pointer, gone by too quick for him to get off a shot.

Remembering how that had been, the flash of gray flank, heart-stopping dip of antlers, then the flicker of its flag and silent, graceful disappearance, Stanley thought that he should be ready just in case. He unslung the brand-new Winchester bolt action, his first rifle. He had saved all year to buy it and had fired it only once so far, on the range on the way out here, to sight it in. Before he had always borrowed his brother-in-law's gun. He was proud that this time he had his own and he rubbed the checkering on the stock, admiring the little diamonds, as he fed in gleaming new cartridges out of the white and red box.

Rifle loaded, safety on, he went on up the hollow. The ridge rose ahead like a thundercloud. He had hunted here once last year and passed up a chance at a nice one. He might have hit it, but it was pretty far off. He did not like to shoot unless he was sure he could hit them. He didn't want to take a chance on wounding one, letting it get away from him. It was funny, after all you were out here to kill them, but he didn't like to think of an animal crawling along, suffering, taking hours or days to die. He liked to hit them clean and get it done quickly. If anything ever happened to me, he thought, that's the way I'd want it. Quick. No suffering.

He had been walking steadily up the side of the hollow, head bent. He was still walking like that, thinking again of the women, when he had a funny feeling. Like he was being watched.

And feeling that, Stanley Mizejewski did the worst

thing he could have done. He stopped. He half lifted his rifle. He looked around him.

The first bullet took him in the left side. The second entered a little farther up, went directly through the heart.

And Stanley Mizejewski felt himself turn, looking up at the overcast sky; and it grew bright; and he felt something enormous rushing in on him; and then it was there, and he felt no pain, no pain at all.

When he saw that the man had stopped moving Michelson used the binoculars to search the woods around him, looking carefully between each tree bole. When he was satisfied he picked up the rifle again, feeling the warmth of its barrel through his gloves, and walked to where the man lay. When he was sure the hunter was dead he moved off downhill, still wary. He moved quickly but he did not run. If someone saw him running that would look suspicious. Above all he must blend in; he must never be conspicuous. He got back down to the road, found the car, and threw the rifle in back and covered it with the blanket.

When he was on the main road, a couple of miles from the hollow, he allowed himself to relax. There, he thought. Another one and away clean. Number three. He checked his watch. It was only ten A.M. Should he drive to another spot and try again? Or should he go back to town for lunch? He remembered the sandwich; he had lunch with him. All right then, he thought, I'll stay out here and try again.

It surprised him that he could go about a business like this so calmly, so rationally, so intellectually dispassionate. No blood lust. Not even a great deal of excitement. It made him nervous, certainly, but it was more like a game than anything else. He wondered if this was the way the hunters felt.

He still could not imagine himself killing a deer.

He drove east. Gradually the road contracted, and the country changed, not a lot, but the hills were gentling, becoming more gradual, more rolling. Still, the structure of the land was the same, and the woods did not change at all. The narrowing road turned and twisted on itself, writhing to follow a small frozen-over creek. Uphill and back of the road, old farm buildings, unpainted and abandoned-looking, stood under an icy El Greco sky.

And then the road changed again, leaving behind fields and farmhouses and entering dense woods. The trees thrust against the snowbanked guardrails like an eager crowd. As the car whined upward into a saddle between flat-topped ridges he saw several likely looking areas, occasional empty trucks parked at an angle to the road. The first few did not feel right to him. Also he did not like to park the car on the main road; someone might steal it or run into it while he was in the woods.

At last he passed a cleared patch by the side of the climbing road. Tracks crossed it—apparently several people had turned around in it—and two cars were parked at one side, empty. A bumper sticker on one said, I WILL GIVE UP MY GUN WHEN THEY PRY MY COLD DEAD FINGERS FROM IT. Michelson drove in behind it and stopped and looked at the sticker for a moment.

Perhaps he would meet the man who owned that car.

Half an hour later he was in the woods, on his stand, for the second time that day. He ate the sandwich slowly, relishing the cold egg and thick mayonnaise, almost the consistency of mozzarella. Have to buy a Thermos, he thought. Hot coffee would be good out here.

He looked up from his meal every few minutes to

examine, with his binoculars, a narrow trail that led directly below the overhanging black rock on which he sat.

Ernie Bauer did not think of himself as a hunter. Not for fifty-one weeks of the working year, and not really even for the one week off he allowed himself for deer season.

He was not out for sport, and he would have laughed in his unsmiling bitter way if anyone had called him a sportsman. He was out here because being a farmer in Hemlock County, with two hundred and fifty tilted, stony acres and a worn-out, oil-hungry tractor, was a losing proposition. He was a farmer; decent meat for four kids to grow on was two-fifty, three bucks a pound; dressed out, a solid whitetail buck run eighty to ninety pounds of good-eating venison. Not prime beef, a little wild tasting, but good food. That was two hundred and fifty dollars worth of meat for a layout of ten bucks for the license and maybe a dollar on shells.

Hell, he could remember years he hadn't *made* two hundred and fifty dollars cash. Not that long ago either. And fourty-four wasn't old.

Bauer tramped steadily and heavily through the woods. He was not a skilled hunter. He made too much noise, for one thing. But he hunted like he farmed. During that week he spent nearly every waking hour in the woods, and sooner or later he always scared something up from some patch of underbrush, some mess of second growth or old blowdown. Then he would jerk the old double-barrel J. C. Higgins to his shoulder and let her go. Three ounces of double-ought buckshot generally caught them somewhere and then he would go just as stolidly to work, skinning off the hide with his old Case (hide was worth fifteen dollars, they bought them up the reservation to make the souvenir moccasins they sold, and he sold the antlers too, to people who made knife handles out of them), gutting the carcass before it stiffened up, and then dragging it all back home. It was bloody, sweaty, hard work, but he did not mind it. It was easier than killing a hog.

Last couple of years his oldest, Cecily, had been coming along to help. She was sixteen now, a big solid girl, not pretty, but as the missus said, a good hardworkin' woman that would make a farmer's wife. She kept her mouth shut when she had nothing to say and he liked that. In fact she was a lot like him, and not a man alive could fault that in a daughter. But this year she had a cold, she was home in bed with a tablespoon of ginger brandy every hour, and he had come on out alone.

He sidetracked from the trail to investigate a stand of white pine. Sometimes they sheltered there, just under the lowest brows, in a bed they scooped out of the snow. Bauer bent to look under each tree, the shotgun ready. He saw no deer and went back to the trail.

They're out here, though, he told himself. He had seen them all summer in his garden, eating the lettuce and the tomato plants, rooting up the young onions with their knifelike hooves. The missus threw things at them, he would let the dogs loose sometimes, but then they came at night and in the morning all you found were rows of torn-up earth. Like most of the farmers he knew he had tried fences, first chicken wire and then barbed wire and finally a long loop of electric cattle fencing, but the damn deer were like rabbits, except that the rabbits burrowed and the deer jumped. After a while, he thought, you got so that you didn't care anymore. As the missus said, if you worried about things they bit you twice.

But now was his chance, as he saw it, to get some of his lettuce back.

Holding the old shotgun muzzle-down by his side, Bauer tramped on up the hill. He knew this trail. There were deer tracks on it now, in the snow. He slogged stubbornly along, eyes darting about the woods, looking for where the damn things were hiding this year.

The loud bang made him jump. For a moment he half crouched, confused; and then Ernie Bauer realized that the hiss he had heard overhead had been a bullet. He crouched lower, standing still there on the trail. Hell, he thought, some stupid flatlander took me for a deer.

"Hey!" he shouted. "It's me. I'm a man."

The second shot was closer. It went *whack* into a birch to his right, like an ax hitting hard, knocking off a curling roll of light-gray bark and bending the white wood underneath out like the fat under a hog's hide.

"Goddammit!" screamed Bauer, standing stubbornly upright, though his knees sagged a little under him. "Stop shootin'! It's *Ernie Bauer*!"

A couple of seconds passed and he was straightening up, taking a breath at last, when the third shot struck a yard in front of his boots, opening up a sudden black hole in the snow and spraying him with dirt and dead leaves and stinging bits of rock.

This time, though, he had seen him: seen the man in his red-orange suit, a city guy sure, Bauer himself wore the old red plaid. He was on top of the rock that overlooked the trail, maybe a hundred yards distant and quite a ways above him. Totally enraged, Bauer raised the old shotgun and fired the left-hand barrel into the air. He shook the gun at the distant man, shouting, "Are you blind or deaf, you bastard? What in the hell are you trying to do?"

The man waved.

Bauer, completely disgusted, broke his shotgun and threw the smoking empty shell away and fumbled at his pocket and stuck in another. Damn fool, he thought, walking on, but keeping an eye cocked up at the hill and the man. Costs me seventy cents each for these shells.

He got out of sight of the rock safely, and felt relieved. They ought to have eye tests for some of these guys, he thought.

Ernie Bauer decided to go home, when he was done hunting for the day, by another trail.

When the man was around the corner of the trail, out of sight, Michelson stared down at his rifle. He had been aiming, but the bullets went too high; and then when he tried to correct, too low. He examined the sights carefully and at last saw what he had done wrong. He slid the leaf on the sight up and down. Apparently you had to flip it up if you wanted to aim at long ranges, and there was a sideways adjustment too.

I guess I need practice, he thought. Especially if I try any more long shots like that. Probably he should allow for downhill somehow too. But he had to smile, even though he'd missed. The man had sounded so outraged . . . had shouted out his name, as if that made a difference.

He sat in the same spot for another full hour. No one else came by. No one and nothing passed on the trail or anywhere in sight. The cold crept through wool and cotton and skin and then sliced into his bones.

At last he could stand it no longer and got up, his legs creaky as an old man's, and began a slow walk through the woods. A patrol, trying to glide along, halting often to search the stark white-black circle of woods that, always the same, always different, followed him as he moved. Still-hunting, the man yesterday had called it.

He saw nothing. At last he recalled how most of the hunters had headed into town around lunchtime. He hadn't thought about it before but now he did. It was because of the deer, obviously. They probably holed up somewhere during the bright, dangerous hours of the afternoon. Hours of predators followed the hours of their prey. He remembered that from somewhere, though it had been abstract then, a line in a book that you read for some assignment but never really thought about. Now he saw it as common sense. And since he was a predator too, and his quarry was not abroad in the woods, he too would leave, and return at a better time.

Which he did. Much later that afternoon, after a nap in his car and a good early dinner in Beaver Fork, he scored again on the broad top of one of the ridges overlooking Route 233. As he drove back toward town again in the dimming of evening he felt elated.

No. It was more than elation. He felt immensely powerful, immensely happy, immensely right. Godlike and powerful and above all safe. In the line of cars that moved, taillighted, away before him on the dusking highway, amid the hunters, he was one of the mass, undetectable. He reached for the rearview mirror to see his own eyes. They looked back now with calmness, confidence, and power. There was no reproach at all. No memory.

Behind those calm eyes he moved among men in fatal and impenetrable anonymity, a subtle and omnipotent instrument of right, justice, revenge, and progress.

"We've only begun, my friend," he said aloud, to the eyes.

And driving at thirty-five, just like all the rest, Paul Michelson gripped the wheel and laughed aloud.

TEN

Sunday, November Thirtieth

WHEN HE STEPPED OUTSIDE THE NEXT MORNING, THE OLD MAN knew instantly that everything had changed.

The wind, for one thing. For the past six days, since the season had opened, there had been little wind. The clouds, swollen gray, sullen and dead-looking, had brooded day after day over the long, level tops of the hills. It had been cold, certainly; a static, penetrating, waiting kind of cold; but it had not snowed, beyond a few vagrant flurries.

Sometime during the night just past that had all changed. Now, above the dark rising masses of Town Hill and Groundhog Hill, above Gerroy and Lookout Tower Hill and looming over the shorter lines of Sullivan Hill and Raymonds Hill, across the wide valley where the Allegheny lay coiled like a hibernating blacksnake, the clouds were moving. Northerly winds, he saw. Silent, massive, the churning sky exposed its inner darkness, hid itself, reemerged. The cold that descended from it, the new and deeper chill in the wind told him only one thing by its temperature and its feel and the way it tasted on the back of his tongue: snow.

Halvorsen tucked the paper more tightly beneath his arm and looked back at the snug low mound of his home.

A faint quiver of air over the chimney pipe made the distant pines dance. Downwind, he felt the wash of heat on his face, smelled the tang of the good seasoned birch he had stoked up with that morning before dawn.

At last he turned his back on the house and set off down the path, his back rigid, hands tucked into the old wool coat, the copy of the Raymondsville *Century* tucked tight under his arm.

He had read it that morning—read three of them; Alma had brought him today's and also Friday's and Saturday's in the brown bag with his weekly groceries. After she left he'd cooked himself some breakfast and then read the papers, holding the cold-dampened sheets out so that he could read the fine print, while by the warm stove Jessie worried at the bone from his breakfast pork chop. Her teeth were not so good anymore. She was eleven years old.

And now he was walking into town.

He went along the road stiffly, glancing up from time to time at the clouds. Mostly though he kept his eyes on the ground. He regretted that he did not have a telephone. He had no prejudices against them. He was old enough to consider telephones marvelous inventions. But the company wanted two hundred dollars to extend their lines up the side of Town Hill. So if he needed anything he had to walk damn near four miles, downhill, till the Mortlock Hollow road intersected Route 6 south of town. There, usually, he could hitch a ride in the rest of the way.

The road dipped steeply, walled in on either side by stands of gray-trunked beech and birch and white oak. Halvorsen watched his footing. Under the snow, undisturbed except for the deep-knobbled treads of Alma's truck, the loose gravel and stone of the road was frozen into a slippery surface. So he went warily. He did not want to fall out here. He knew a fall was not good for an old man, even for one who could contemplate a four-mile walk to the highway with equanimity, if not with joy.

The walking was good. Already the steepness was abating, the road turning left for its shallower wandering descent along the side of the frozen-over creek. He could feel his stiffness abating too. He had gone perhaps half a mile already. He took his hands from the deep pockets of the coat and swung his arms, being careful not to drop the newspaper. He had dressed well for the walk, he knew how to dress for cold weather; and now his muscles were warming up and he felt the downhill like ten years gone and he could strike along pretty good, his old Maine boots going crunch-crunch in the snow, his breath a creaking cloud in the air, whirling away before him on the wind that came over the hill behind him and pushed him along, down into the valley.

In the spring, he remembered, there was no pleasanter place than Mortlock Hollow. There was no pleasanter walk than to head on down the mountain and follow the winding rock-shallowed creek down the run toward town. In spring this road was narrow and green-bordered, the yellow clay under its sparse gravel rich with the small lives of plants, insects, small mammals. Along it spring came in May, no, June, for Town and Gerroy and the northern end of Cherry Hill pretty well cut off the sun into the hollow until nine or ten, and then again after five. So that all that lush green of blackberry and thorn, elder and cane, the young trees above the road and the older ones back of them on the hill, all had to live on just seven hours of light. Yet they did; they grew; they flourished in the brief spring and the brief summer and persisted even through the brief fall of the hollow if the creek ran good, as if they and the frogs and the mud wasps that lived in the puddled ruts of the road and the rabbits in the blackberry brambles south of the creek and the deer-gray squirrels that ran the white-oak limbs all knew that the warmth and the light and the green were only an intermission in the chill white silence of the only season that ever really lasted.

And now it was winter again in the hollow, and along the level sterility that was the road the curved ice-preserved bushes were black and lifeless as cast iron. Snow lay between them and on the rough bark of the maples and over the mold of the ephemeral plants. Some would awaken again. But most were gone forever; they had lived swift and green and died in brown resignation, and of them only spores and seedpods remained, deep under the snow, not waiting exactly, but ready. Ready for the sun, ready to be green, no matter how briefly, in their turn.

The snow crunched briskly and regularly under the old man's feet.

He was thinking not about the summer or about the cold, for his activity had driven it back; not gone, but standing off a little, like a dog from a wounded but still dangerous bear; but about what was said in the newspaper he carried tucked under one arm.

About the accidents.

"Rash of Accidents Continues," the *Century* had said. It had not been on the front page, nor in the special season supplement that fattened the county paper in November and early December, full of game tips and articles on turkey diseases and field-dressing diagrams and blocks of ads for markets and gun shops and the local banks. It was on page three. Looking in Friday's and Saturday's he had found it even farther back, on pages four and six. Oh, Racks Halvorsen knew why. And to a degree he even sympathized.

But something had to be done.

He worked it slowly together in his mind as he walked and when an hour later he got to the paved road he had it thought out pretty well.

He did not have to go far along Route 6, a straight-backed old man hiking the edge of the snowplow-cleared center of the road, before a car slowed for him. The occupants were two middle-aged hunters, done for the day after three hours in the woods, and they respected his silence after testing it with a couple of remarks and dropped him off on Main Street pretty near where he wanted to go.

"Ralph in?" he asked the woman at the desk. He could not remember her name.

"He's in back, Mr. Halvorsen. What is it?"

"Wanted to talk to him."

"He's pretty busy."

"You tell him his grandfather walked into town to see him."

The old man looked around for a chair and sat down. He was ready to wait as long as he had to. He saw that she saw this (what *was* her name?) and presently she went into the back room and a moment later young Sweet came out, looking unpleasant—as usual, the old man thought. "Hi," he said, not holding out his hand. "What you got, Racks? I'm awful busy."

"That's what I wanted to talk about," said Halvorsen.

The game protector turned. "Come on back . . . you can talk while I type."

They went into the back room, with the files and the desk and the coffee maker. Halvorsen looked at it after he sat down and Sweet hesitated, looked annoyed, then asked him if he wanted any. The old man held the hot mug in his thawing fingers, seeing the orange lipstick stain on its edge but not saying anything, and watched as the warden settled in again behind the typewriter and began to pick out letters, filling out a green form with carbons behind.

"Don't you got that secretary to do your typing, Ralph?"

"I got to do these myself . . . accident forms . . . what's on your mind?" Sweet frowned at the keyboard.

"Wanted to talk about these accidents."

"That's right, you were the one found the first one, the boy."

"There's been what—four men found dead?"

"Five, counting Michelson. One early this morning."

"Five," Halvorsen repeated. "Ralph, those ain't all accidents."

Without a word Sweet reached into a drawer near him and brought out a mailing envelope. He tossed it to the old man. Halvorsen put down the coffee and opened it, fingers still a little stiff, feeling its heaviness. He shook the contents out into his hand. Like gold nuggets, the pieces of coppery metal, ogival, pointed, were heavier than something so small ought to be. Along their sides ran slanting grooves. The noses were slightly flattened.

"Thirty caliber," said the old man, measuring one of them against his fingernail.

"Uh huh," said his grandson, hunting still for the same letter. "Charlie Whitecar gave me those yesterday. Going to have Sealey send them up to Erie, to the lab there."

"Full metal jacket," said the old man, putting on his glasses from an inside pocket and studying the metal bits. He held one up to the light. "Spitzer point. One-fifty, one-eighty grains. No cannelure. This here's a military bullet, Ralph."

Sweet had stopped typing. He looked up. "What?"

"This come out of Army stock."

"You can tell that by looking at it?"

"Sure. You find any of the brass?"

Sweet reached into the drawer again, and watched the old man turn the blackened empty case over in his blunt fingers. "It's Army sure. Rock Island Arsenal, fifty-five. Fired from an automatic action," said Halvorsen at last. "Tell by this nick at the base, where the ejector dug in."

"What kind of gun was it?"

"Don't know . . . could be several. Ought to be able to tell you that in Erie."

"Automatic actions aren't legal in this state."

Halvorsen shrugged. He handed the empty case and the bullets back. The younger man looked at them and then at him.

"Why are you still calling them accidents?" Halvorsen asked him.

He could see that the question hurt; the boy flushed and looked back at the typewriter. "I don't have any proof they aren't."

"Four . . . no, five, in less than a week?"

"That doesn't prove a thing," said the warden stubbornly. "Statistically it could be. Sure, there could be that many in a season. Hell, there's what, a thousand in the U.S. every year."

"But just in this county? And no one admits doing it?"

Sweet looked stubborn.

Halvorsen looked at him for a moment, then went on to another thing. "Okay, maybe those statistics say it could be. I never studied statistics. What about those bullets? Do they match?"

"What do you mean?"

"Do they match the other ones you got?"

"I don't know. These are the only ones Whitecar gave me."

"Then let's go get the others," said Halvorsen, reaching for his hat. "Let's go over and see him right now."

"Just wait a minute." The warden's face was definitely red. "Are you telling me what to do here, Racks? Because if you are, you sure better know that I'm the game protector for this county and I run this business myself."

"Then why are you still calling things accidental, when they aren't?"

"There are considerations you haven't taken into account."

"If you mean that the mayor and Vince Barnett and the rest of them don't want you to, then I am taking it into account," Halvorsen told him. "You think if you don't, they'll ask the state to fire you."

"Are you saying I'm afraid of that sort of thing?"

They looked at each other for a moment. Halvorsen took his glasses off then. "No," he said, although he knew that he had. "But I'm worried."

"Go on home," said Sweet at last, turning back to the typewriter.

"You ought to call in the state police," said Halvorsen to his back.

"I got to suspect criminal activity before I do that, damn it. And if I do that, I'll have to shut down hunting countywide. Ten thousand hunters'll leave halfway through the season. That's a lot of money driving out of town. Already they're starting to go, just on word of mouth."

"Ralph, even if the paper keeps playing it down, you

can't keep this kind of thing up forever. Are you sure"
—the old man paused, uncertain—"is there something
you're not telling me, Ralph?"

"Damn it, I don't want your advice!" shouted Sweet,
whirling around. "Go home, old man, and let me do my
job!"

Halvorsen blinked. He put the half-empty mug on top
of the file cabinet and got up. The sitting had cooled his
joints and now they were stiff. Sweet stared up at him,
waiting for him to say something, but he merely nodded
thoughtfully and picked up his hat. In the front room the
woman, who must have heard everything, did not look at
him. He remembered her name now but did not say
anything to her. He put on his cap and buttoned his coat
and opened the door and went out.

It was cold outside, on the street. It had begun to snow
at last. From the five and ten he could hear "Jingle
Bells." Christmas in another couple weeks, he thought
vaguely. Have to pick up a toy for Alma.

No. No toys. She was fifty-three now. For Christ's
sake, what was he thinking of. He stood on the street in
the falling snow, listening to "Rudolf the Red-nosed
Reindeer."

The boy shouldn't have said that to him. Go home, old
man. Useless man, used-up, worthless. The funny thing
was that he had taken it, had even felt, for that moment,
old, the way people expected oldsters to be—forgetful,
vacant, impotent.

Racks Halvorsen was not like that and never had been;
and if he was going to be, ever, it was still a long ways
away.

But maybe Ralph's right, he thought then. Maybe
home was the best place for him. Maybe that was the
right thing to do: let the young ones run it their way; let

them do it even when you could see that they were wrong and would hurt themselves and others; not because you couldn't help it, but because you didn't care to interfere anymore. You just didn't care to take the trouble. God, he thought, the cold bites hard. It would be a long winter; the squirrels had seen it coming that fall; he remembered their scampering desperate greed. Or had that been the fall before last?

He stood on the cleared stretch of sidewalk while the snow built white epaulettes on his shoulders.

Yes, he thought, but you can't just walk away from something like this and let them screw it up. It wasn't right. Normally he did not worry too much anymore about right and wrong. There was little he cared to do anymore that was wrong, and doing right took too much planning and energy. But this was definitely a question of right and wrong. He puzzled at it for a while, like Jezebel did when he offered her canned spaghetti, and then shivered suddenly, deeply, and turned and walked up the street.

The Brown Bear was not as full as the last time he had been there. Looking at the booths as he passed them on his way to the back he could see that business was off. Barely half the seats at the bar were filled, and there was little conversation and no laughter among the men who sat in them. Evidently, in spite of the *Century*'s reticence, news, or rather rumor, was getting around among the hunters. Lucky Rezk, behind the bar, waved a rag at him as he passed, and Halvorsen nodded.

The old-timers' table was as usual. DeSantis was there, and Wilson, and McKee. Prouper was nowhere to be seen. "Where's Charlie?" he asked, settling down by DeSantis.

"Heard he had a cold," said Wilson. "They're sick at

all, they won't let 'em out of that place he's in. Could turn bad real easy, the way his lungs are."

"I had the new-monia once," said McKee. "In forty-three. I was drillin' the new wells the Navy funded up on the reservation. Stayed out there once, must of been three, four days. Winter of forty-three. Sleepin' on the ground while the drills were runnin', it got in my lungs. Lew Ziegler takes one look at me when we come in, he says: 'You're goin' right over to Maple Street.' Company paid me a semi-private room, twenty dollars a day."

"I got my check today," said Wilson to Halvorsen in a low voice. His single hand touched his shirt pocket tremulously. "This is my round. You want one?"

"I'll have a cola pop," he said, more or less by reflex, for he really did not want anything cold.

"You're in town a lot these days, Racks," said DeSantis, coughing.

"Come in to see Ralph."

"How are you and him gettin' along?"

Halvorsen shrugged, looking toward the bar. A man was talking to Rezk there, leaning forward over the wet-glistening wood. From this angle the bear, half-turned, appeared to be bending forward to eavesdrop on them.

"No offense, Racks, but I think he's a snot-nosed kid," said DeSantis. "He jumped me about the spotlight on my Jeep. Called it a jacklight. Well, by God, I ain't no poacher, and I got a right to have anything I want on my car."

Halvorsen was barely listening. He was watching the bar, where two more hunters had joined the group around Rezk and the first.

"What's going on up there?" said Wilson, seeing the direction of his gaze.

"Be right back," said Halvorsen.

The group was still larger, six or eight men, when he reached it, but he was able to stand on the edges of it and hear. The man in the center—Halvorsen knew him slightly, Bill something, worked at the glass plant—was telling Rezk and the others about being in the woods out by Triple Band Run, way south of town, when he had, as he put it, "Seen them takin' him off."

"Taking who off?" asked Halvorsen. Heads turned toward him and the man, Bill something, looked toward him, annoyance on his face until he saw who it was.

"The fella that was shot."

"When was that?" said Halvorsen.

"About an hour ago. After I saw him I sure didn't feel like hunting these woods anymore. Maybe the TV guys are right."

Several of the men around him nodded. Rezk looked at Halvorsen. "Did you want something, Racks?"

"No," he said.

"What's the matter? They out of pop?" said Wilson, seeing him come back empty-handed. He had, Halvorsen saw, already tremblingly counted out the dimes and nickels for his drink onto the table.

"I decided I didn't want any," said Halvorsen. He was abruptly filled with pity for Wilson, for the absent Prouper, for all of them. "Save it, Mase. Lucky's busy. You can get me one next time."

He sat down by DeSantis again but did not say anything. He sat there for several minutes, looking down at the scarred dark surface of the table.

He was thinking.

The first killing had been at Mortlock Run. That had been with a shotgun slug, though. He felt somehow that it was different, not necessarily unrelated, but different from the subsequent ones. The others had all been outside the Raymondsville area, though still within the county. He remembered the locations from the short, stereotyped accounts in the back pages of the paper. So-and-so, of such-and-such an age and such-and-such occupation, from place x in state y, had been found dead, presumably as the result of having been taken for game at such-and-such a run or hollow or hill. And reading the paper he could visualize instantly where it had been, for he had seen with his own eyes and trodden with his own boots in fifty years of working and hunting in this land almost every square yard of lease land and hunting territory in Hemlock County.

And now, looking down at the table in a bar, he dipped his finger in the wet ring of DeSantis's beer glass and drew a little outline of the county. Almost square, thirty-five miles on a side, with the little slanted jog of the southern corner snuggling into Potter and Clinton. He put a wet dot near the center for Raymondsville, and another, farther north, for Beaver Fork.

Dotting them in one by one in sequence, he placed the site of each accident on his makeshift map. He sat looking at them, only dimly aware of the looks his cronies were giving him.

There was a pattern, all right.

For one thing, with the exception of the first one, the boy, they took place in pairs. That was pretty evident. Each day saw two accidents, no more than five or seven miles apart.

Looking at the slowly drying spots of beer, he saw another pattern. Each day the location of the killings shifted; from east to west, north to south; and today's . . .

"Racks?"

"What?"

"You, uh, you sure you don't want a drink?"

"No." Halvorsen looked down at the map, pondered for a moment longer, and then wiped it out. He looked across the table, into DeSantis's beer-filmed eyes.

"Len," he said, pushing back his corner of the pew, "come on. I want you to drive me somewhere."

South of town, the old green Willys centered on the crown of the snow-blown road, he remembered something else.

"Turn right up ahead," he said to DeSantis.

"I thought you said you wanted to go down—"

"I do. But I want to stop by my place first. Can you get this thing up my hill?"

"I did it last time, didn't I? Dammit, Racks, I'll get you there. I wish you'd tell me what this is all about."

DeSantis, or rather his old truck, was as good as his word. He stopped it with the front wheels rocked up on the hump of the basement. "Keep her running," said Halvorsen. "I won't be long."

The inside of his hole was dim and warm. Enough of the afternoon light came through the window slits that he did not have to light a lamp. He moved about the room quickly, gathering things from a box here, a shelf there. He looked at the old Springfield, which leaned now in a corner. Yes, that would do. He paused again, searched in a drawer under the bench. No shells for it.

He peered out the window. He could see the slush-caked underside of the Willys, a plume of white smoke trailing across the snow from the end of the tailpipe.

"Hell," muttered Halvorsen. He sat down at the bench. The dies and caseholders were still on the press. He found brass and primers, fumbled for the can. He knew the charge by heart but with the old scale it took long minutes to weigh out a few small heaps of gray-grained powder.

From outside came the nasal honk of the Jeep's horn.

Halvorsen sized and decapped the brass, pressed in fresh primers, and positioned them on the block. Carefully, tapping the folded card he used as a funnel, he filled each case with propellant.

The horn sounded again, and he swore. He was hurrying, but it was not beyond Fatso DeSantis, emboldened with beer, to leave him here. He had only filled three shells but he decided that was enough, he probably wouldn't need them anyway, and he pressed a 150-grain soft-pointed bullet home in each charged case, wiped each with a rag as he finished, and dropped them into the pocket of his trousers. He picked up the rifle and the pack he had prepared and was opening the door when he felt something soft nudging his leg and looked down.

"You want to come along, Jess? You ain't been out in a while."

Together they went up the steps into the cold light outside.

"What happened to you?" said DeSantis.

"Gettin' some things," said Halvorsen, dumping the pack and rifle in back of the seat and holding the door for the dog to jump up after them. DeSantis glanced back at them.

"I thought you didn't hunt anymore."

"I don't."

"What's that? A bolt-action crutch?"

"Let's get going, Len."

DeSantis waited, shrugged when Halvorsen said nothing more, and put the Willys in gear. It went forward and over the hump in the snow, narrowly missing the smoking chimney. "Jesus, Len!" shouted Halvorsen.

"Sorry," giggled DeSantis, wrenching the vehicle back onto the road.

They regained the highway and turned north. Midway to town Halvorsen said, "Where are you going now?"

"Out Route Six."

"The hell you are . . . take the old road, over Sullivan Hill. Then about two miles off the hill there's that turnoff goes over the rise and comes out down Beadle Hollow."

"Are we in a hurry?"

"We sure are."

DeSantis grumbled but took the road he wanted. It was even cleared, for part of the way at least. They came out onto Route Six proper and Halvorsen pointed out the turnoff. They crossed the frozen Allegheny with a clatter of planks laid on an antique iron bridge, one lane wide, that shuddered under the weight.

"Now where?"

"Up the hill."

The going was rougher on this road, almost a trail, but they broke through and were soon winding down the hollow beyond it to meet Whitecar Creek Road. DeSantis turned right on this. They passed very few other cars.

"Now where?"

Where indeed, Halvorsen wondered. The morning's shooting had been near the end of this road, out an unimproved extension of it that ended in Black Hollow. Judging by the pattern he had seen, the man he sought would not be there now; yet he would not be far away. Where would he be . . . farther out, or closer to town?

The white storm of snow, steadily thickening outside the windshield, suggested his answer.

"Turn here," he said, pointing suddenly to the left.

"Where?"

"That lease road."

The Willys whined up it in low gear. Like most of the side roads they had passed this one bore the marks of tires. Hunters had combed, traced, pierced every mile of these woods in the days since the season opened, including the hollow up which this road led, Grafton Run. They jounced past two parked pickups, both empty. "Where are we going?" DeSantis repeated.

Halvorsen frowned, looking ahead, into the snow. "Keep going."

He was proceeding on nothing but feel, instinct. He had felt it before on a trail. Here it was perhaps out of place. But it was all he had to trust.

The Willys had whined, slipped, jounced right by it before he recognized it. Or saw, rather, what it meant, the little car parked a few feet off the lonely road.

"Hold it, Len," he said.

"What?" DeSantis slowed.

"Back up."

The road was too narrow between the trees to turn, but DeSantis fumbled into reverse. Halvorsen told him to stop beside the small car. He got out and looked in the window. Snow had built up an inch deep on the hood; it had been here a couple of hours. It was empty. In back lay a blanket, a couple of cardboard boxes, the kind boots and clothes came in—

And under a fold in the blanket, the corner of a green metal ammunition box.

Halvorsen exhaled. This was it all right. He looked around at the silent woods, the snow-filled air of the hollow. The man—that well dressed, educated-sounding flatlander, with all the questions about the boy—was not very far away now. He went back to the truck.

"Len, listen. I think we found the guy that's been shooting people."

"What?"

"Listen. I'm going to stay here. See this car? It's his. He's got to come back to it. I want you to drive back to town, as fast as you can, and get Ralph. Better get Bill Sealey too. But do it fast—get them all out here as fast as you can."

DeSantis blinked up at him. The beer showed in his empty eyes. "You ain't kidding?"

"No," said Halvorsen. He reached the pack and the old Springfield out of the back. "Come on, Jessie. Down. I'm not, Len. Now get going, before this snow gets too much deeper."

When the sound of the engine had dwindled down the hollow the old man stood still for a moment, looking up at the hills. They were high and stark on three sides of him. The snow in the air, falling steadily, was too thick for him to see their tops.

He's in there, thought Halvorsen, looking up at the hills. And sooner or later he'll come out. I hope they get here before then.

He walked up the hill, the dog floundering behind him, and settled in to wait.

ELEVEN

MICHELSON HAD FELT WONDERFUL, ON A NATURAL HIGH, EVER since the snow had begun to fall.

It had started as a translucent white curtain, drawn across the hills when he was driving east after the morning's hunting. He parked under a stand of trees just off the whitening blacktop and ate the cheese sandwiches slathered with mild mustard and gulped the Thermos of black coffee that was his lunch. He ate rapidly, with relish. It's the hiking, he thought, the excitement, and most of all the cold, clean air.

He grinned, tucking the sandwich wrappings into his litter bag. He felt great.

The morning had gone well. Straight routine. Again he'd gotten out early, well away from town, this time to a place the map called Triple Band Run. After parking he'd headed up into the woods, selected a spot, and settled in to wait. Barely an hour later he had his limit for the morning and was walking rapidly back downhill to his car.

The high had begun then. This, he told himself, was the way to live, on the edge and at risk. How had he doubted himself and played it safe all these years?

After the stop for lunch he finished the short drive to

new territory. Considering the increasingly heavy snow-fall, there was only one turnoff that looked inviting, and he drove up it and parked and hiked uphill again, just as before.

Somewhere, though, he'd made a wrong decision. Or picked a bad spot for a stand, though it seemed as good as any of the others. He waited all afternoon, till the black shadows of the hills lengthened along the floors of the valleys, until the overcast sky began to fade and the wind rose and the flakes, driven into his face, melted and hung like dew in his beard. And he did not see a single man. Plenty of deer; he saw more of them each day, perhaps because his eyes were growing used to the woods. But no hunters. Where had they all gone?

At last he unfolded himself, groaning, from under the tree he'd selected hours before, using the rifle to lever himself upright. He brushed snow from his coat and rubbed melt water from his eyes. No use waiting any longer. It was time to head in.

Walking down the hill, he found a deer trail. Under the new loose snow he could see dozens of tracks. He was examining them, trying to figure out which way the deer were heading, when he remembered suddenly that it was Sunday. Maybe they didn't hunt on Sunday. Then what about the man this morning—was he hunting illegally?

It seemed a reasonable explanation, and his spirits rose again as he neared the bottom of the hollow, anticipating a hot dinner and a long, dreamless night's sleep in his warm room at the Wi-Wan-Chu.

He paused on the slope above his car. The woods were thick here, but through a narrow gap he could see downhill to the bottom of the hollow, to the frozen creek and the road. Perhaps two hundred yards below him a snow hump marked where he had parked his car.

Unslinging the rifle, propping it muzzle-up against a

tree, he reached for his binoculars. He had been careful up to now. He'd bought the paper every day, read about the "accidents." There was no hint of suspicion, incredible as it seemed. He was safe.

I won't get careless, though, he told himself. I want to keep this up for a long, long time.

Adjusting the glasses, he examined the car. It looked just as he had left it. Seemed to be sitting low, as if sunk slightly into the snow. But it was undisturbed. He moved the field of view up and down the hollow from it. Save for the falling snow there was nothing. No other cars were in sight.

He was just beginning to lower the binoculars when he saw it: a slight, almost imperceptible difference somewhere in the trees on the opposite side of the hollow, a little ways above the car. A few days before he might have missed it. He centered the glasses and watched, holding his breath so as not to fog the lenses.

A man was sitting there, half-screened by the trunk of a tree. From this distance his outstretched leg looked like an exposed root. Even at seven magnifications he was hard to see, and Michelson, his eyes tiring in the late-afternoon light, had to lower the glasses and blink before he was sure that it was a human figure there.

I might not go in empty-handed after all, he thought.

He rose and picked up the rifle and started down the trail again. The thick woods, and a dip as he approached the foot of the hill, would conceal his approach. He decided to circle partway around before the forest gave out and try to get close enough unobserved for a shot. Always before I've waited for my quarry to come to me, he thought. Now I've advanced to stalking.

He smiled, feeling his pulse speed up and the forest take on new clarity, new distinctness, as his senses sharpened with the excitement of the hunt.

The snow whispered against the back of his jacket, fell onto his eyelids, formed layers on his shoulders and cap. Like the fingers of ghosts the snow dragged at him, thickening the air, cloaking and quieting his progress around the side of the hollow. He lost sight of the car, located it again, close below him, and paused, looking at it. It was sitting lower, all right. He hoped it hadn't sunk in too deeply for him to rock it out.

He used the binoculars again. The man was still where he had first seen him. He could see no details, only his silhouette. For a moment he had a premonition of trouble. The man was looking straight downhill at his car. Was he waiting for him?

No, Michelson told himself. He can't be. No one suspects me. If they did then this whole hollow would be full of people, cars, police.

But the valley was empty. There was only himself and the other, motionless, waiting, and between them, like an animal staked out for bait, the slowly whitening car. Again he raised the glasses and searched the whole length of the hollow, as far down toward the road as he could see. No. They were alone. But it was getting late, and getting cold. He wanted to get back to town.

He decided to do it from where he was.

It was a long shot, across the hollow, but the other man was about at his height on the hill opposite. I'll have to fire over the car, Michelson thought, over the creek. He moved along the trail till he found a clear space between the trees. The sitting figure remained where it was, not moving.

Michelson sat down in the snow. He set the selector of the rifle for single shots. He looked toward the opposite hill again. Three hundred yards? Two hundred? Say two hundred, he decided. He slid the little bar on the sight to the figure 2 and propped the heavy weapon on his arms.

The man he had missed the day before had taught him to take his time and aim.

He didn't like them to fire back.

The black silhouette wavered in the circle of the rear sight, moving with the throbbing of his heart. He breathed short and fast. Then as he applied pressure to the trigger the sight steadied . . . steadied . . . his finger tightened . . .

The roar filled the hollow. Michelson blinked, recovering from the recoil, and looked over the smoking barrel.

The man was gone.

He seized his glasses. The tree stood alone. A dark patch lay in the snow where the man had been. Hell, he thought. Did I miss him? Or was there really anyone there at all?

Of course there was; he'd seen him. But where had he gone? He examined each tree, each fold of snow-covered land on the hill opposite, each dark side of rock. He saw nothing; nothing at all. He crouched there while sweat broke out under his heavy clothes. It was getting dark. It was getting harder and harder to see.

What had happened to the guy?

At last he decided: he's gone. He's run off. Maybe the land dips down over there like it does here and he went off down it, down the hollow, so that I couldn't see him.

He got up, holding the rifle ready. He saw nothing. Nothing happened. After waiting a few more minutes he began moving down the hill. Then he broke into a trot. He was eager to get to the car, to get away. At the bottom of the hollow the tree cover ended suddenly. He hesitated at its edge, looking across a stretch of open snow to the road, and on the other side of it, its grille toward him, his car.

He paused there, at the edge of the forest, and looked

up at the hills that pent in the hollow. All in shadow now, they stretched off in either direction to the limits of his sight, massive, silent, dreaming under the settling shrouds of blowing snow.

There was no one up there.

He stepped out of the trees and began to jog across the field.

He was not yet halfway across it when the sound came hissing close over his head and the boom of another rifle, fully as loud as his own, came back from the bowl of the hills. Cursing, startled, he did the last few yards in an ungainly sprint, gained the shelter of the car, and flung the muzzle of the automatic rifle over its hood and pointed it up at the mass of the hill and stared along it, panting, eyes darting from tree to tree.

He could see nothing. Yet the other man was up there, not far away. That shot had been close. A yard above his head. Or less.

He stared upward for long seconds, ready to fire at any motion or gleam of color; but none. came. The spaced ranks of denuded trees marched upward against the dimming gray of the hillside, closer together, it seemed, as the hill rose, till at the crest they formed a bristly mass through which he could still see the sky. There seemed no place to hide, no place hidden, on the whole side of the hill. Yet he saw nothing.

Michelson breathed three times deeply and swallowed and felt his heart gradually slow. No. Don't look up there, he told himself. He can't have gone that far. He's still down here somewhere, where the ground has only started to rise. Or maybe he has gone up to the first bench. He let the rifle settle on the hood of the car and took his binoculars and began a close search from where he judged the first bench to be right down to the edge of the woods, about a hundred feet from him, just across the creek.

Nothing. Only the trees, the hills, the gathering dark; the gray wild clouds overhead; the gelid whisper of the snow. Minutes passed. He lowered the glasses.

I have to get out of here, he thought. I can't see him. He can see me—obviously. The best thing to do is just to get out.

Crouching behind the car, he felt in his pockets for the keys. He was easing the door out toward him when, looking downward, he noticed that the front tire on his side was flat. He looked at the rear one. It was flat too. He fell down in the snow and looked under the car.

All the tires were flat. That was why it had seemed so low to the ground.

He looked up at the silent hill. He could feel, some-how, the man's eyes on him.

The other man knew who he was. He had been waiting for him to come back to the car. And he had taken the additional precaution of letting all the air out of his tires.

Michelson's dry lips moved around a curse. He gripped the smooth cold stock of the rifle.

The other, whoever he was, whatever he wanted, had him trapped. He couldn't drive the car a half mile in this condition. Not in this snow. The fact that he wanted to keep him here meant something else, too. The police were probably on their way right now.

Paul Michelson crouched by the car, holding the handle of the half-open door, and thought quickly. He was afraid, but it only stimulated his mind. Should he stay here, and wait for the dark? The other man couldn't shoot in the dark.

No. If he had sent for help they would arrive to find him here, crouching. He could hold them off for a while with the rifle, but he had no illusions about how that would end.

So he could not wait; and he could not drive out. That left him only one thing to do. Walk. These woods were thick, vast, and empty. He could hike out over the hills, find his way to a road somewhere, to one of the five- or ten-house hamlets that lay in the larger hollows. From there he could get out—rent a car, hitch a ride. Back to town? No; it would be better to go all the way back to West Kittanning. Say he'd gotten lost in the woods, couldn't remember where he had left the car.

But if they have the car, they'll know who I am, he thought.

And then he thought, but they won't be able to prove anything by that, will they? Only the gun or a confession would really prove anything.

He debated this with himself for a time, then realized that he was wasting the hour of light that remained to him. Get out now; think later, he ordered himself.

Staying low, behind the metal of the automobile, he swung the door open and crawled inside, tipping the seats forward to give him more protection. He went through the car swiftly. He filled his coat pockets with black magazines of ammunition. He took the map, safety flares from the car's emergency kit, and a package of cheese crackers left over from lunch. There seemed to be nothing else. He checked the glove compartment, raising his head carefully to peer in. Road maps, a pen, a pair of Teresa's sunglasses. He closed it again and looked under the seats. He found a roll of antacid tablets there and took them too.

It seemed that was all. He rested for a moment, sprawled across the floor, and then, driven by the need to escape, wriggled out the door feet-first. He crouched outside and regarded the hill. It loomed over him, its lack of color deepening as the light faded. It was growing dark swiftly now. Dark enough that maybe the other would find it hard to shoot accurately.

Michelson looked across the patch of open snow he had crossed once. Already, in the short period of time he had been at the car, the outlines of his tracks had been blurred by the falling snow. He picked up the rifle and gathered himself, then heaved up and into a sprint, a heavy-footed, sliding, heart-pounding hundred-yard dash in the calf-deep powder. He wondered as he ran, the snow dragging at his feet, whether he would hear the shot before or after he felt the impact of the bullet.

But neither shot nor bullet came and he reached the tree line on the other side of the hollow and kept going, kept running, though his legs were going soft and his breath whistled hastily. Kept running, more slowly now, as pain began in his thighs and the air began to saw at his throat. Kept running till the ground moved upward and the trees were thick and close and finally he slowed, then stopped, sliding to his knees behind the bole of a maple, putting its welcome solidity between him and the hollow. He crouched there, breathing hard. After a while he looked back. He could still make out his car. It looked forlorn, abandoned. He saw that he had left the door open. Snow would get in . . .

Patting his pockets, he drew out the map. It did not show much in the way of topographic features. It was a simple black-on-white handout, showing major streams, towns, the few surfaced roads that threaded the county. He held it close to his face. The nearest roads and towns were north of him. But north lay directly across the hill opposite.

I'm not going that way, he thought.

South there was nothing: a blank area on the map, enclosed by a dotted line. He strained to make out the print. Kinningmahontawany Wild Area, it said. That didn't sound promising either.

Southeast, though, eight or ten miles away it looked like, there would be a creek, and a road along it. Hefner Creek. The road petered out at its southern end, as it crossed the dotted Wild Area boundary, but at its northeastern end it led over into Potter County, toward a small town called Roulette.

Well, I'll gamble on that, he thought, and smiled slightly in the dusk. He folded the map and put it away. I'll try for this Hefner Creek Road. Should be cars along there. When I get to where I can see the road I'll find a likely place and hide or bury the gun and ammunition. I'll hitch a ride into Roulette, or even walk there, if I have to. From there I'll get back to school. They'll probably call me there, if they trace the plates on the car.

But he didn't see how they could prove anything if they couldn't find the gun, and if there were no eyewitnesses. And he was pretty sure there weren't. If they don't come after me, he thought, I'll wait for a couple of weeks, and when the season's over I'll get Teresa to drive me up and I'll get the car. And I'll still have the gun. Or know where it is.

And next year he could do it again. Not in Hemlock County, maybe, but in Potter, or McKean, or Cameron, or even over the border; western New York State was big deer country.

It was too bad he had been interrupted. He wondered who the man was; how he had found out. But it was only a setback, not the end. He would be back next year, every year. He would have a season, just like the hunters did.

All right, he told himself. Let's go. He got up, feeling

naked as his back left the shelter of the tree, and began to walk. He decided to keep moving as long as he could make out the trees in front of him. He hiked steadily up the hill, not looking back.

Later, after dark, he heard, very faint above him, the sound of an aircraft. It did not worry him and he slogged on. It would be blind in the dark and the snow. It would be a long night, and a long hike out to the road after that; but he was confident.

He knew they would never find him.

TWELVE

WHEN SHE STEPPED OUT OF THE HOTEL LATE THAT MORNING, groggy with late-coming sleep, it was already snowing. She paused on the sidewalk outside the Antler and looked up at the clouds, blinking back tears from the knifelike wind, then buried her face in her coat.

She was the only one on the main street. It's Sunday, she realized. Of course there was no one out. At home, her mother made all the family go to Mass early on Sundays. Seeing the Sacred Heart yesterday at Mrs. Oleksa's had made Teresa dream about the blue and white plaster Virgin on the table at home, its paleness a mystic counterpoint to the dark Blessed Martin of Porres in the corner, before whom a candle burned. But even as she recalled the dream, Teresa knew that she would not go to Mass. It was one of many things she had stopped doing in the last year, since she met Paul. Not that he ever said anything against the Church, but . . .

As she walked aimlessly along the narrow cleared paths of the sidewalks, between the piles of dirty snow and the dark shopfronts, the wind whipped at her hair and she thought about him.

Where was he?

Where could she look for him today?

In a diner on Main Street she ordered a cup of tea, then studied the menu. An unshaven man at the counter next to her smiled at her. She ignored him. She lit a cigarette automatically, without thought, and then remembered and put it out.

"Cold morning."

"Excuse me?"

"I said, cold morning. You visitin' in town, good-lookin'?"

She stared at him, realizing only then that she was the sole woman there, that the place didn't look that nice, that in fact most of the men in it were either examining her over their coffee or had done so just before she raised her eyes. She put down the menu, paid quickly for the unfinished tea, and left. She stood outside for a moment, then went to where her car was parked, in a lot in back of the hotel. She cleared snow from the windshield and got in.

She decided to start today at the hospital. Aaron would have been taken there first, and perhaps Paul, thinking this too, would have gone there. It wasn't a great idea, but it was the only one she had at the moment. She started the car, remembering the signs she had seen here and there pointing the way.

At Maple Street she left the Chrysler in the lot and hesitated between the main entrance and the emergency room. At last she decided on the latter. The door gave onto a small room lined with plastic chairs with rusty legs. It was hot after the wind outside. She unbuttoned her coat. Two swinging doors to the room beyond were marked EMERGENCY. After a moment she spotted the button and pressed it. Shortly, steps approached from the other side, a blonde woman in a scrub suit, slightly older than Teresa. She looked tired. "Yes," she said. "What's the trouble?"

"There is no trouble. I just wanted to ask some questions."

"This is the emergency room. The clinic is through the main entrance—"

"Not medical questions. I wanted to see the doctor who saw Aaron Michelson. Last Monday."

"Michelson?" The woman looked uncertain. Then, "Oh, *Michelson*. Of course." She smoothed her hair back, sighed, and sat down opposite Teresa in one of the plastic chairs. "What did you want to know?"

"I wanted to see the doctor who treated him."

"That's me, dear."

"Oh."

"That's all right. It took the town a long time to get used to me, too. But you're not from around here, are you?"

"I'm from West Kittanning. A friend of his father. Have you seen him?"

"The father?"

"Yes."

"I don't believe so. Should I have?"

"He's been in town here for the last few days, but I do not know where."

"Have you tried the police station?"

"Yes."

"Sorry I can't help you. Was there anything else?"

She thought. "Well . . . about Aaron. Paul said it was a hunting accident."

"That's what I thought at the time. But now, after these others . . . I'm not so sure. There were some odd things about it."

"What were they?"

"Do you really want to know?"

"Yes, I do," said Teresa. She reached for her purse.

"You shouldn't smoke those," said the doctor. Teresa

173

halted the cigarette halfway out of the pack, looked at it and slid it back in. She put the purse down as the doctor went on, "Actually, the only detail that disturbed me—and that was only later, after the coroner took the body away—were the wrists. There were slight abrasion on them. Not deep enough to bleed, but you could see where the skin had been rubbed."

"What were they from?"

"I don't know."

"You mean he could have been tied?"

"Not tied, I don't think. Rope leaves a distinctive mark. But they might have been from some sort of restraint. They were faint, though. If they'd been deeper I'd have put them in my report, but as it was I didn' really think anything of them. You can bang your wrists around in a lot of ways out in the woods, I imagine."

"Did you tell anyone?"

"The warden maybe. Ralph Sweet. He was there and if I saw them, he might have. I don't remember if I mentioned it, though. I didn't to anyone else. There was no reason to upset his mother."

"Do you know her?" Teresa asked, not quite knowing what else to say.

"No." The doctor yawned. "Sorry, I'm a little out of it. I was taking a nap on one of the gurneys when you rang. There's been a steady flow in here since the season started. Sprains, minor accidents, they cut themselves gutting those deer—and the DOAs, of course."

"Deeohays?" She did not know that word.

"Dead on arrival."

Teresa reached for her purse again and then stopped herself. "Do you think they are accidents?"

"Not anymore."

"Why not?"

"They're too similar, for one thing. For another, no one stayed to help. A doctor sees a lot of the bad side of people. But one of the good is how few of them will leave the scene of an accident—in this part of the country, anyway. They'll stay and try to help the person they injured. Sometimes you have to push them out of the way to set up the IV." She laughed, then stood up. "I don't think I can tell you anything else. Good luck finding your Mr. Michelson."

"Thanks—doctor."

When she drove past the warden's office this time it was open. Open and packed. Two of the vans were backed up near it, cables and people spilling from their open doors. A frozen-looking group of twenty or so men and women, obviously reporters and interviewers, were standing in the yard. A few townspeople—not many, they barely outnumbered the outsiders—stood around watching, bundled in their heavy coats and boots. The snow drifted down on them all, carried into their rapt faces by the wind. She joined the locals and watched for a few minutes. One of them, a boy of eighteen or so, glanced at her, then away; but she saw his eyes; they were suspicious, hostile.

"Excuse me," she said to him.

"What?"

"What's going on over there? What happened?"

"Over there? That's the game office. They brought in another guy. Another 'accident.'"

"*Another* one?"

He nodded.

"How many does that make?"

"Six, I think."

The boy seemed to lose some of his xenophobia as he

talked. Teresa wondered suddenly if he had known Aaron. He was about the right age. In a town this small . . . she asked him.

"Aaron Michelson? Yeah, I knew him. We were in the same social studies class."

"Was he a good student?"

"I guess so. He was Honor Roll all the time."

"What was he like?"

The boy seemed suddenly to recollect that he was speaking to a stranger; his face renarrowed, reclosed. Suspicion lay always close to the surface, Teresa saw. "Why do you want to know?"

"I am a friend of his father."

"Didn't you know him, then?"

"No. I never met him. You don't have to tell me if you don't want to. I just wanted to find out."

"Well, hey—it's no secret, you could ask any kid in the school. Michelson was weird. Smart, but weird. He always had a lot to say in class. Sometimes he'd argue with the teacher. He had crazy ideas."

"What kind of ideas?"

"He used to talk about women and negroes and stuff. And the environment. And once he said he wasn't going to register when he turned eighteen. Stuff like that. Oh, I thought he was okay, but we were all pretty surprised when we heard he was in a hunting accident."

"Because he did not hunt."

"Right." The boy nodded across the street. "Look. Something's going on."

Something was. The door to the building was open and the reporters were disappearing inside, some of them pulling on the cables that led back to the vans. Through a window she could see a light go on, brilliant and almost green. It looked as if they'd be there for a while.

"What time is it, please?" she asked the boy.

"A little after two."

She had missed both breakfast and lunch, and suddenly she was hungry. I'll find something to eat and come back later, she thought. No hope of talking to the warden, what was his name, Sweet, until these people were gone. When she turned to excuse herself the boy was gone.

She had a heaping dish of spaghetti with meat sauce, garlic bread, salad, and a glass of beer. She had asked for tea but the place, the Brown Bear, didn't have it—in fact the man who took her order looked at her as if she were crazy. It was a heavy, filling meal, but she told herself she deserved it after missing two. That made such good sense she extended the argument to a chunk of hot pie rich with lard-heavy crust and hand-cut, tart apples. This seemed a slightly nicer place than the diner, but here too she was the only woman. Conscious of that, she kept her eyes down over her food and did not look toward the bar when a drunken voice rose in a shout above the murmurs.

"Lucky, damn it, I said gimme another!"

"Cool it, Len. You can barely drive now."

"Barely drive! I just took that Willys straight up Triple Band Run, fella. I got to go see that wet-nosed warden pretty quick now. But let me have another Straub's first."

The voices dropped then and she finished her pie and shortly thereafter walked out, counting her change.

After leaving the restaurant Teresa wandered aimlessly in the wind for a time, looking at the buildings, the few people who hastened by her with barely a sidelong glance. She was trying to place why it felt so foreign to her; foreign to California; foreign even to West Kittanning, where she went sometimes to shop.

It was, she decided at last, knowing that this was not the exact word but as close as she could come, unfriendly. The main street was colorless and cold, brick, stone, wood, all of it old, and more than old—faded, uncared-for, the peeling paint dulled by time and weather to a uniform dull tone like frozen earth. She tried to imagine some of these buildings in a Chicano neighborhood. She could not; or rather, she could imagine the buildings, but there they would be bright with the color and care that gave LA, the better parts, its *vivenza*. But, she thought, perhaps it is better in the summer. Beyond the three-story buildings with the false fronts rose street after street of houses, stepping up the hills on either side of town like would-be escapees. They too were grim, each house weathered, narrowed as if unwilling to touch its neighbors, fiercely protecting its individuality as if saying, each of them, perhaps I am shabby, but I stand alone; I take and give nothing.

She remembered looking down at her own old neighborhood from the air, taking off from LA International on the long flight east. The tiny houses, low, colorful, but above all close, trusting and sharing and depending one on the other.

I would not like to grow up here, she thought. She did not even consider until after she thought it that Aaron had.

When she went past the game office again she saw that she'd been right to delay. The media were gone; the trampled snow of the lot was empty. She knocked twice before a woman jerked the door open impatiently. Teresa stared in disbelief at her lipstick.

"What do you want?"

"I need to see Mr. Sweet, please."

"He already talked to you. Go away." She tried to close the door, but Teresa, surprising herself and the woman too, had her boot in it. They looked at each other.

"I am not with the press. I want to ask him about Aaron Michelson."

"Oh." The woman seemed to see something profound in that; nodding several times, she opened the door wide. "Come in. I'm Donna Coyle. I'll tell Ralph you're here."

"Thank you."

She went into a back room while Teresa bent to scrape snow from her boots. She was still crouched when a moment later a man came out. She froze, looking up at him.

He was the same man she had seen on the news broadcast back at school. She had fleetingly thought him handsome then, even angry and looking away from the camera. Now, face-to-face with him, her eyes moved up his polished loafers to tight khaki trousers, up the casual taper of his body. His face was good-looking too, broad and strong and smiling. Only his eyes were not. They were cool and predatory. She had never seen anyone quite like him. She straightened, looking away from his glance, knowing and hating that she was blushing.

"Yeah?" he said. "You want to come in the back room, miss? I got some coffee there."

"Thank you." She was relieved when he turned his back on her. Those eyes were too cynical, her own reaction to them too unsettling, for her to take much more just then. As she sat down opposite him he lit a filter-tipped cigar and on impulse she took out her first cigarette of the day and he leaned across, holding out the already used paper match, and she felt the familiar explosion deep in her chest, hating it and welcoming the slight sickness and dizziness as comfort at the same time.

"Cream? Sugar?"

"Yes, thank you."

He skated the mug over to her. She looked around, still unwilling to face him. The room was dingy and hot, with a sink, filing cabinets, a small table, a stack of boxes that might have held forms. The walls were a slick yellow streaked with runs where mildew had been scrubbed off.

"Mrs. C. says you're not from the press," he said.

"No. I mean, that is right."

"Why are you asking about the Michelson boy?"

He was direct, all right. She felt nervous and her eyes sought the table. "I am here as a friend of his father, Paul. He's probably been here to see you within the last few days."

"Paul Michelson? I talked to him on the phone the day we picked his son up, but I don't think I've met him. What does he look like?"

"Tall, dark, a dark little beard—"

"McCoy," said Sweet suddenly.

"Excuse me?"

"He was here, yeah. Couple days ago. I didn't see him. He was asking questions about the boy." He stared at her, leaning his chair back till it seemed he must go over backward, the cigar dangling from his lips. "Yeah! Now it makes sense. I wondered who that guy was. Tell me, miss—"

"Del Rosario. Teresa del Rosario."

"Teresa. Pretty name, pretty girl." Sweet smiled, a flash of teeth, then sobered. "Why was he nosing around here, and not using his real name?"

"He didn't use Michelson?"

"Nope. Called himself McCoy."

"I don't know," she said.

"He's from downstate, a teacher or something, isn't he?"

"Yes. Sociology."

"And you?"

"Spanish."

"A friend of his, you said."

He had tipped the chair forward now and was watching her closely. Again she found it hard to meet his eyes. Her gaze kept falling to the cup or the tabletop or her own hands. To cover her discomfort she lit another cigarette from the previous one. Chain smoking now, she thought.

"Yes. A friend. Do you know where I can find him?"

"No idea," said Sweet. "I didn't see him, and I didn't enjoy hearing about somebody skulking around like that. That's not the right way to go at things in this town. If you want to find something out, it's easier and more convenient all around just to go to whoever's in charge. Like you did, coming to me."

"And you would have helped him?"

"Sure. If I'd known what he wanted."

She was watching his hands now. His fingers were short and broad, with a fine coating of brown hair on the back.

"Maybe you can tell me something, Mr. Sweet."

"Hey, we're informal here. Call me Ralph . . . Teresa." He grinned boyishly.

"At the hospital they mentioned some marks on Aaron's wrists."

"Who told you that?"

"The doctor there."

"Oh. Yeah, that's right. Yeah, I saw those when Racks brought him in."

"Racks?"

"An old guy lives out in the woods. My grandfather. He was wandering around out there the first day of hunting season. He found Michelson's body and brought it in with some other hunters." Sweet shrugged. "They shouldn't have bothered with the hospital at all, just taken him right over to the coroner for the death cert."

"What do you think about it?"

"I didn't mention it in my report. It didn't seem germane to the accident, so I let it go."

She nodded. Was there anything else she wanted to ask this man? Yes, there was. "Did you know Aaron?"

"Only slightly. I'd see him sometimes as I drove around town, so I knew who he was. Wore his hair too long. Aside from that, a good-looking kid." He paused. "Anyway, it was too bad it happened. Where are you staying now?"

"The Antler."

"That's not too bad a place. Michelson staying there too?"

"I told you, I'm looking for him."

"Oh, yeah." He grinned again and in spite of herself she smiled back. Then she caught herself and stopped. The space of several heartbeats passed and she thought suddenly, here comes the pass—

"Well, say—you had supper yet? You been to Mama DeLucci's?"

She was silent for a moment, trying to decide how best to say no without hurting his feelings, watching him lean across the table toward her, when someone began shouting in the front room. Sweet cursed and bounded out of the chair. A moment later Mrs. Coyle appeared. Behind her was the fat man Teresa had seen at the Brown Bear, even drunker now; he weaved even as he stood still, and the beer smell rolled off him so thickly that she felt dizzy herself.

"Mr. DeSantis," said the warden, his voice neutral.

"Yeah. I got somethin' to say to you, Sweet."

"If it's about that jacklight, you got ten days to get rid of it. Then you get a summons."

"Screw that. Oh," said DeSantis, bowing drunkenly to Teresa, "sorry, lady. I din't see you. No, this is important. Racks, me and him got you your boy."

"What boy?" Sweet smiled over at her.

"The guy that's been shooting people. Me 'n' Racks got him cornered. He's waitin' up there for him. He wants you and Sealey right now."

"You're drunk, old man," said Sweet, not smiling now.

"Maybe a little . . . high." DeSantis belched and giggled. "But sober enough. C'mon, le's get in gear."

Sweet didn't answer.

"Come on!" The old man tugged at his arm.

"Where, dammit?"

"Grafton Hollow."

"Who is he?"

"He's Racks, Ralph. Your granddad."

"I mean the other guy, DeSantis. You said you saw him."

"Yeah. I mean, no. We din't see him exactly. But he's up there. Racks is waitin' for him at his car."

At the words "his car" Teresa felt a touch of dread. She turned to the chubby, beer-smelling old man, watching him reach out to steady himself on the doorjamb. His cheeks were stubbled gray and there was a ring of dirt around the inside of his green work shirt.

"Why that car?" Sweet asked him, almost drawling. She caught another stab of his eyes, conveying irony, conveying a kind of amused disgust too; sharing it with her. Again she found herself smiling back for a moment before she remembered.

183

"Racks says he knows the guy. He's the tall flatlander that was askin' questions about the first kid—the one he found up Mortlock."

She forgot irony, forgot the warden. "You're wrong," she said, before she even had time to think. "He's wrong. It can't be Paul."

"Your friend?" said Sweet.

"Yes. I mean, it could not be him."

"Why not? You said he was here someplace."

"Maybe . . . it might look like his car. Lots of cars look alike. But Paul could not be involved in something like that."

"People c'n do funny things," said DeSantis.

"Not him."

"Come on, Ralph. He's waitin'. And you know it's almost dark."

"That late?"

"Five o'clock," said Mrs. Coyle.

"Well, look," said Sweet, turning back to Teresa as though talking to her, though his words were for DeSantis, "I got nothing but say-so says he's got any connection with this at all. Just being out in the woods is no crime. Even asking questions isn't a crime. Yet, anyway. Right, miss? If it was, I'd be taking you to jail right now instead of to supper."

She shook her head, unable to think. She didn't want to go anywhere with this man. She wanted to go after him—after Paul—but she wanted to do it alone. Not with anyone else. If he had done something wrong, she could help, she could talk him out of it . . . but no, she was sure he couldn't have. So going after him with someone else couldn't hurt, could it? She decided and looked up. "Look—Mr. Sweet—let's go where he says."

"We got to get the state cops too. He said to have you both come."

"Now wait a minute, both of you. It's dark now. When did you leave the hollow, Len?"

"Just now."

She looked up. "But I saw you in the bar."

"Well—almost now. I was cold, I just stopped for a quick one."

"More likely a quick six-pack." Sweet flashed her, once again, that cynical, sharing, amused look. "You sure you didn't get to drinking and make this all up, Len?"

"Yeah. I'm sure."

"So say it was an hour. It's coming down pretty hard out there. We probably couldn't even get up that road to the hollow again."

"Sure we could."

"I say we couldn't. And I'm the game protector. Look." Sweet moved a step closer to the old man. "There's no rush here. If there really is a killer out there, and Racks is out there like you say, this guy isn't going anywhere without a man on his trail."

"That's the truth," said DeSantis. "Your granddad'll track his ass to hell and back. Sorry." He bowed to Teresa again and almost fell.

"So relax. For tonight anyway. You done what you had to do, you come and told me about it, and I'll take care of it from now on."

"You will?"

"Sure I will."

"Well . . . okay." DeSantis turned his collar up and took an unsteady step toward the door, almost toppling the secretary, who had been standing behind him. "Just remember—it's your grampaw out there."

"I know who's out there," said Sweet, looking at Teresa. The old man went out.

"Donna?"

"Yes, sir?"

"Don't you have something to type?"

When she was gone, he turned to Teresa again, so close now she could see the tiny crinkles under his eyes. He was young—not more than two or three years older than she, she guessed—but his eyes looked older. "How about that supper, now," he said, grinning. "Then later maybe a drink, warm you up a little—"

"No, thank you."

"Come on. You look a little upset." He moved closer and took her arm. He's so big, she thought. So much . . . so powerfully *there*. But she only shook her head again and turned for the outer office, removing her arm from his. This time he did not say anything, but moved back and let her go by.

When Teresa had left, Ralph Sweet, alone now in the inner office, sat down slowly again at the table. He played with a pen for a moment, then lit another cigar. He blew smoke out and leaned back watching it, frowning at the way it complicated the air.

He had the look of a man making a profoundly important decision.

THIRTEEN

Monday, December First

WHEN THE OLD MAN WOKE FOR THE THIRD TIME HE KNEW EVEN before he opened his eyes that it was not far to dawn. Some internal clock, some old instinct, told him that it was time to be up and on the trail.

He wriggled the zipper of the bag down and slid out of it. His movement disturbed a black and brown bundle curled next to him; the dog kicked at him once and woke, raising her muzzle to the air. Halvorsen pulled himself up on the log and reached for his boots. The boughs gave under his stocking feet and the sharp smells of crushed pine and ashes, the smells he had slept within all night, came up. He shivered with the chill air and looked down at his bed.

It had been a long, cold night, but he had slept well. The fallen oak, three feet thick, afforded shelter from the wind. Late in the night he had stripped armfuls of branches from a nearby stand of pines, gathered deadwood, and built in a few minutes a roaring hot fire against the fallen tree. He'd let it burn down after a time, then, growing impatient, stamped out the embers and covered the smoking ground with six inches of the soft, flexible, bluish-green pine needles. Over this, against the fire-smelling bark of the log, he'd spread his old down mummy bag, then slid into it, pulling more boughs over him, and lain there, feeling the warmth of the soil radiating up into his back, until sleep had come. He'd done that twice more in the night, but there was plenty of wood, hacked up into short chunks with his hand ax, and his sleep was hardly interrupted.

So now, stretching, he felt alert, rested, and as fresh, he thought, as a man of his years could expect to feel after a night in the open winter woods.

Around him, between the sparse trees that dotted the wide flat crest of Harrison Hill, the thin gray of first light was seeping down through the overcast. He looked around slowly as he buttoned his coat and pulled on his old rabbit-lined gloves. In the course of the night the snow had continued and over all, over the log, the pine boughs where he had lain, over the few chunks of wood yet unburned, lay a silvery layer of fresh, crisp white. And it was still coming down, not heavily now but steadily, silent and beautiful and steady in the way only Nature, the old man thought suddenly, could be steady, since men could work only in fits and starts and in opposition to one another. Halvorsen thoughtfully rolled up the sleeping bag into a football-sized wad and stuffed it into his pack. Getting up, feeling the stiffness in his legs, he walked several yards downwind and addled the snow, the dog watching him from her nest beside the log.

The old man used the remaining wood to build a small, neat fire. Moving with practiced skill he set snow to boil with coffee and, while waiting, fished around in the pack. He'd had little time to choose, and little, in the chill pantry, to choose from. He had a can of beans, two small tins of cheap sausage, half a pound of foil-wrapped bacon, and some chocolate. He decided on the sausage, opened one tin and ate them slowly. The hound watched his hands attentively as they moved from the can to his mouth and he threw her the last three, then drank the salty juice. The snow had melted by then in the little pan and he had hot strong coffee, flirting the grounds out on the snow.

Breakfast over, he scrubbed the pan out with snow, buried the tin, and restowed everything else in the pack. He pulled the Springfield out from its cache under the log and slung pack and rifle. He looked around for the bitch. She had stretched herself out again on the pine boughs.

"Come on, Jessie," he said. "Got to get a move on."

The dog looked at him. In front of her nose the snowflakes fell hissing into the little fire. Halvorsen kicked snow over it, stretched again and turned.

In front of him, out across the top of the hill, a nearly imperceptible series of shallow blurred impressions led away among the trees. Halvorsen shifted his burdens, glanced back once more at the dog, and started to walk.

He was soon absorbed in the tracking. The prints were all but covered by the fresh fall of the night. An hour later and they would have been gone completely. As it was he had to bend forward at times to see their shadows under the new snow. He hiked along, eager with the morning, following the tracks along the flat crest. At one point, he noticed, they made a sharp correction to the right. The man he was tracking, alone at night in unfamiliar woods, had become unsure of his way. Shortly after that the dog whined behind him and the old man paused, sniffed the air, then moved forward again more cautiously. Shortly after that, a little way down the southern slope of the hill, in a small ravine, he found where the man he tracked had spent the night.

Halvorsen stood still for several minutes, looking around at the remains of a camp.

It was a shambles. Around the edge of the ravine the snow was tracked and trampled, with long furrows showing where heavy objects had been dragged. In the center was a black patch, still smoking slightly. Halvorsen noted the direction of the smoke. The charred hulks of several dead trees lay around the ashy area. Near the patch was a depression in the slushy snow and rooted-up leaves of the ravine floor. Lying near it was a cylindrical red object and a discarded plastic wrapper.

The old man nodded. The man he was tracking had spent a long and miserable night.

The flare was the only thing he did not understand. Perhaps the other had no matches, and had used it to light his fire. That might be it, he thought. And he had burned the campfire all night, lying on the ground beside it, roasting, no doubt, on one side, and freezing on the other. Every few minutes he would have been forced away from the flames to gather more wood. As the night wore on that meant expeditions farther and farther away from the firelit ravine, and a longer way to drag the too-large logs he selected.

It must have been thorough misery. Halvorsen, looking at the remains of his camp, doubted if the other man had enjoyed half an hour of sleep. And then at dawn —doubtless he'd watched it come, red-eyed from smoke, weary from dragging logs—he'd had only a dry snack to eat, and snow to munch.

Halvorsen managed a little pity.

The dog came up and skulked around the smoldering area. She sniffed at the depression in the snow. "Okay, Jessie," he said, not very loud. "Come on. He's somewhere up ahead. You stay behind me, now."

From there on the tracks were clear and crisp. The snow, whispering down in the slight northerly wind, had only dusted the ridges of the sole-prints. The old man moved a bit uphill of the trail and set out again.

He followed them all through the morning. Clear, fresh, they followed the ins and outs of the hill's ravines around its southern end and then dipped gradually down toward the densely wooded saddle between it and the next hill to the south. Halvorsen, moving along steadily and parallel to them, could see that they tended south and east, with the downhill to the saddle exerting a pull. It was fairly rough going along the ravine side of the hill and he moved with care, using the cover of the land whenever he could, moving farther uphill from time to time to get a look at the terrain ahead. The hill's curve and the thick second-growth cover kept him from catching sight of his quarry.

The way the tracks ran was strange. They seemed unable to hold to a fixed direction for long. In the deeper ravines, where the slope of the land ran at an angle to or even parallel with the overall contours of the hill, they lost their way at times, heading in awkward directions for which the man then overcorrected. The trail thus had irregular doglegs in it, going east and west, wasting hundreds of yards of progress. To Halvorsen they were hard to follow. They were different from the deer and bear tracks he was used to. Animals tended to use the terrain, to hold to contour lines around or along a slope, and to pick natural pathways that combined ease of travel with cover and reasonable visibility.

The trail he followed did none of these. The man ahead seemed oblivious to natural obstacles, and did not use the curve and slope of the land. He left contour lines to go deep into ravines and climb out on the other side, an admittedly shorter number of steps, but a much more physically demanding way to travel in rough country. To the old man, slogging along steadily at a moderate pace (which even so began to tell on him as the day wore on), the trail was more difficult to follow than that of a woods-wise man. He simply could not predict it. Only occasionally could he go uphill to the first bench, walk for fifteen minutes or half an hour on the level, and descend to pick up the trail again, the way he would have to catch up on an animal or another woodsman. The man he was following did not know the easy ways to do things, and although his prints were distinct in the snow, he was unpredictable and frustrating to track.

Yet the old man kept on. His legs passed through aching to pain to numbness, his shoulders wearied of the pack and rifle, and his neck and back were tight with climbing hills and slogging through the lees of cover where the snow had drifted in smooth white billows, modeling the sleeping shapes of the hills. The cold ached in his lungs and turned the gray stubble white near his mouth and nose.

And behind him, twenty or fifty yards back, the black and tan hound trotted, short-legged and flap-eared, resigned, using his tracks to lessen the effort of pushing her low-set body through the deepening snow.

Toward noon by the sky, the old man saw the trail turn sharply south, headed definitely now down into the saddle. Here perhaps was a chance to catch up a bit. Halvorsen left the side of the hill as soon as he was sure the new direction was consistent and went downslope in a long diagonal, across and down the shallower lower slopes, trusting that he could intercept the trail somewhere near the bottom of the saddle. Unless there was another radical zig, this time to the east, he felt sure he would run into the tracks, or perhaps even the man himself.

As he worked his way down the hill, the veils of snow that the wind had drawn around him parted for a moment, and he was able to see out and down for a long way—perhaps a mile—and he recognized where he was.

He knew this land. This was gas country, where in the old days he had driven the wells deep through topsoil and clay, sandstone and shale, into the hard porous sands of eastern Hemlock and western Potter counties.

Halvorsen paused. Looking out over it, hearing behind him the panting of the old dog as she caught up, the sighing of the wind overhead, he saw much more than the land. He had listened around the fires to the company geologists and now in his imagination he saw the glaciers that had scoured these valleys, dropping gravel and granite to lie along the ridges of these uniform hills. The subterranean layers of sedimentary rock, undulating like the surface of a pond after the passage of a stone. And over the rock, clay, shale, topsoil, clothing the raw sandstone as skin and fat clothe a young person's bones. And over that, thin and transient to his eyes, was all that was visible: the trees, the snow.

And somewhere out there was a man.

His mind reverted from geology and he frowned at himself, though it did not show on his cold-stiffened face. He had been drifting. That was bad. He shaded his eyes against the snow. It was heavier out here, away from the shelter of the hill, and he felt the pressure of a stronger wind at his back.

He squatted, relishing the change in position, and examined the floor of the saddle, studying it acre by acre. The bitch sat beside him and he glanced at her. She would not be much use on this trail. She hadn't much of a nose anymore, and even if she had, fresh snow wiped out scent almost completely. He thought then of DeSantis. If Len had been believed back in town (a matter of doubt, maybe, considering his condition), Ralph might have had dogs out in the hollow late last night, or at the latest at first light. There were trained dogs at the state police barracks at Petroleum City; not much trouble to drive them down here. Yet obviously the snow had defeated them, covering both tracks and scent.

By the same token—he looked upward at the overcast sky—they might have had planes, or the police helicopter up from Williamsport, if the weather had not turned so bad.

No, Halvorsen decided, he couldn't count on help. Though he could still hope for it.

He looked across the saddle. Opposite him, indistinct through the falling snow though less than two miles away straight-line distance, Storm Hill rose above the five-hundred-foot dip of the saddle. He remembered the way it curved west, like a long comma, its tail curling into Black Hollow. A rutted, damned-near impassable road led up from the hollow to the top of the hill, where, he remembered, one of the old Forest Service lookout towers had once stood. Twenty years before, the last time he had seen it, the timber legs were still there, the tumbled ruins of the tower collapsed between them.

Beyond that hill, southeast of it—west was Whitecar and then Triple Band Run, and the man he tracked would hardly turn back there—was a minor valley, still three or four hundred feet above the general Allegheny base line. It had no name, or none that he recalled at the moment. He had always heard it called simply "Field 23 valley" or "pipeline five." Its eastern slope was dotted with gas wells by the dozen, most of them long fallow, but enough still flowing at reduced rates for Penngas to keep them in service. Across the center of the valley a buried pipeline ran from the wells to the main collection facilities in Pleasant Valley.

And east still of that, farther than he could see since the snow was falling steadily again, turning the distance into a uniform milky white, was another long ripple of hills: Detering, Meade, Selwyn's. These were pierced and drained by the tributaries of Hefner Creek: Jonathan, Shanty House, Coal Run. And Hefner Creek proper beyond them.

That, the old man thought suddenly, is where he is headed: Hefner Road. The man was trying to get away by reaching the road and then hitchhiking, or hijacking, a ride out.

Then only his car would remain as a way to find out who he really was. And it could be rented, or even stolen, the old man thought. For a man who could kill others, not once, in the heat of some mortal but possibly not unjustified passion, but several times—four, five —stealing a car would be nothing.

Beside him the dog whined suddenly, and Halvorsen looked at her. Forcing his stiffened legs to straighten, he got up again and walked on down toward the saddle.

Half an hour later he was deep in the close cover between the two hills. The woods were denser than he recalled them, and younger. In the years since he had seen it last the area must have been clear-cut, and then allowed to grow back naturally. Now it was a tangled, close-set mass of young aspen and gray birch and heavy thorn, and he had to bend low to worm his way through it. It was rough going and he soon regretted the shortcut.

But at last, breathing hard, he moved into a more open part of the woods and was able to look around a little.

The saddle was heavily populated. He could see that from the saplings, from which deer had rubbed the bark, polishing their antlers, and from the frequent clumps of spoor. This was good country for deer. They loved dense second growth; it gave them young trees and cover, food and security. There were rabbits here too. He saw a snowshoe hare, white as a quivering bit of snow, watching him with one dark eye as he paused to shift his rifle to the other shoulder. He looked at it and then at the hound, who looked up at him innocently.

"That's right, Jessie. That's right. Don't see it, then you won't have to chase it."

The dog yawned ostentatiously and sat down in the snow.

Halvorsen shook his head and walked on. The hare held itself panting-rigid under the bush till they were twenty feet away, then streaked for better cover, raising a small puff of snow at each leap.

A few hundred yards on he found the trail. He hadn't gained a minute, nor a foot. The snow was falling more heavily, the north wind blowing hard and cold. The tracks led off in a straight line between the gray trees. He turned slowly and plodded after them.

God, he was tired.

Well, I been hiking steady since sunup, he thought. On the level at first, then downhill into the saddle; that helped some. But the ravines and the brush was murder. He wasn't used anymore to going for hour after hour. He was accustomed to a brisk walk; two hours, say, to roam the hill paths near the house, or to head down the road to town. But not to hiking steadily, under pack and rifle, for the better part of a day. He was too old for that; too old to just keep pushing himself along.

As the man ahead seemed to be doing. He noticed absently that the strides had become longer, the heel marks deeper, as if the man he tracked had speeded up. He matched his stride with the prints. He couldn't stretch that far. The man was bigger than he was. Halvorsen remembered how tall he'd looked when he came into the basement, and how he had looked in the hollow, coming out of the woods toward his car. That rifle of his had looked goddamn big too.

Halvorsen shivered as he remembered how little that shot had missed him by.

And now he was moving along practically at a run. After a full morning's hike, a miserable night spent mostly awake, and who knew how many hours in the woods yesterday. The old man had to respect the other's hardiness.

But then, he thought, it's nothing to him. He's young.

Halvorsen stopped trying to match the strides. He slowed. He would never catch up. All he could do was hang on the trail and hope for something to happen.

Relaxed, moving along more deliberately, the old man felt more comfortable. He had been out here, on the trail in one way or another for so many years of his life, that tracking like this, through deep, snowy, quiet woods, was comforting. It calmed him, gentled him, let him slip back through years and decades to the times when he had tracked game—deer, bear, elk, moose—through these woods, or woods very like these.

Walking along, the old man smiled.

For over thirty years hunting had been his avocation and passion. Each winter, whitetails and sometimes black bear right here in Hemlock County. Knowing the leases and fields and hills as well as he did, the season seldom lasted more than a day for him. He and his working buddies knew where the deer were, and had each staked out "his" bear long before the day for the blacks arrived.

He remembered one year, when he was working for Thunder Oil, must have been around forty-six, when he and Mase Wilson had seen a big cinnamon phase around the test well they were working out on Hantzen Hill, not far from where the lake was now.

They had noticed the deep, splayed-out tracks, near as big as a man's outstretched hand, in the muddy verge of the road they had bulldozed up the backside of the hill, a wild, deep valley full of big old oak and wild cherry, blowdowns and tight little rock pockets full of snakes in summer. Ideal bear country. Anyway, he and Mase had kept their eyes on this bear all summer and into fall. Occasionally they would see it, always from a distance, a squat, slope-shouldered animal. Like all black bears it looked smaller than it really was, ugly-muzzled, with a reddish-brown salting to its coat. It was wary of them, and of the bulldozer especially; when it saw the machine it would instantly turn tail and lump away, in that rolling, fat-assed, deceptively ungraceful run that could pass a horse in the first hundred yards. They only gradually understood that it lived somewhere on the backside of the hill, in some remote pocket of blown-down trunks and thickets and big shelving sandstone ledges.

So anyway, Halvorsen remembered, he and Wilson had waited till first snowfall and taken off work one late October afternoon and gone looking for it. They'd come on a fresh trail just about where they'd expected it. Like most males, "their" bear was putting off hibernating and would stay up as long as it could get something to eat. It was not difficult to track him. Maybe the cold was making the animal dopey, but they had got right up on him, unarmed of course, and crouched and watched for long minutes while it snuffled about, pawing for something under the snow and later ambling off downhill in a lazy, impatient way. They had been close enough to smell the musty odor of its pelt.

And so on the morning of the one-day season that year they had lain at dawn with guns among the lopped-off hemlock and beech tops, around which dozens of rabbits had written shorthand in the snow, and watched the entrance to its den, a shadowy recess under an overhanging stone ledge. They'd watched for about an hour, and then Wilson had crept up and tossed in a snowball.

A growl emerged, but no bear. After a couple more pitches by Wilson, followed by progressively angrier growls, Halvorsen too laid his rifle against a tree and picked up a double handful of snow.

The put-upon animal emerged at last, sleepy, angry, and splotched with white, to be met with a barrage of hard-packed, wet snowballs. He and Wilson had pasted it solidly in the chest and back, the bear dancing clumsily, grunting with each hit, trying to ward off the missiles with its paws. It looked so ridiculous that both he and Mason, breaking into laughter, had forgotten their fear of the bear (for a big black could destroy a man, disembowel him with its claws or break his face with a bite). And they had forgotten about their rifles, guffawing and shouting, until suddenly the bear waggled its head and took a couple of clumsy bounds toward Halvorsen. Then he remembered the gun, all right, but he'd moved forward while throwing and it was several steps behind him; and half laughing, half in sudden terror, Halvorsen had let go with the one hard-packed true-sphered snowball he held, snapped it out fast, and it had exploded on the animal's sensitive nose and the bear, figuring probably that it had been mortally wounded, and deciding suddenly to decamp, turned, cut past Wilson—whose too hastily aimed shot went high, snapping branches above Halvorsen's head and bringing down snow in sodden clumps—and disappeared rolling and bounding along like a big black and rust beach ball down the hill and into a tangle of the beech tops and out of sight.

And after something like that he and Mase could not hunt it anymore, having made an ass of the bear and having been made asses of by the bear in return; and they'd hiked back up Hantzen, telling each other how funny it had been, neither of them admitting to fright although Halvorsen's thighs had been quivering, and they had never told anyone else about it and never bothered that bear again.

Halvorsen hoped that the cinnamon bear, or its great-grandcub, was still back there in the caves and blow-downs back of Hantzen Hill.

These were the memories that lingered, that lasted —the companionships, the funny and unexpected things, rather than the kills and the trophies that it was supposedly all about.

That knowledge had come late. He had saved money and in his thirties and forties gone after bigger, more exotic game—mule deer and blacktail out west, prong-horn in Wyoming, elk and moose and goat in the Cassiar country of Canada, and the one big trip to Alaska. He'd looked forward eagerly to each. But as he grew older a strange thing happened. At each kill, each conclusion of a hunt, he felt more strongly the loss of something precious and wild. At each hunt he spent more and more time and care on the technique, the tracking, passing up not-quite-perfect shots, spending hours hiking alone or with a guide along the sides of sheer mountains or over the broad flat plains, waving with grass almost like the sea he had seen only once in his life, vast and glittering and incredible, beyond the sky-laced mountains above Bristol Bay.

Not that he had turned against hunting, or that he regretted having hunted. It was more complex and deeper than that and he could not quite define how he felt; he had no words for it. Part of it, he felt, was that it was as natural for man to hunt as for the wolf. It was more than food. Its drama called out all that was in man: his animality and precarious enlightenment, his predatory instinct warring with a dawning knowledge of trusteeship, his sense of doom and pity for what lived and suffered and died. In the fever of the hunt he became an animal again; in the kill, a dark side of God; and in the moment after, seeing his handiwork with terror and regret and triumph, he was most fully man, seeing himself lying quivering in the snow.

So he could not regret what he had done, nor could he be proud. It was the way things were and he had lived the best he knew. And finally when he was sixty, after the house was gone, he had killed a buck, a plain Pennsylvania whitetail. Skinning it, he had paused, looking down at its unseeing eyes, and had known then, in that moment of insight into himself and the nature of life as he had lived it and ended it for beings less conscious than himself, that he had caused death for the last time.

Coming back to the present, Racks Halvorsen blinked against the snow and pulled his collar a little tighter and glanced around.

He was moving upward now, out of the valley, having

crossed the saddle and descended in easy increments to the bottom. Now he was headed upward again and southerly, past the long mass of Detering Hill. It was midafternoon. He was tired, his feet were numbed even in the felt-lined boots, and his shoulders and back ached deep down under the weight of pack, and rifle, and the years.

But I'm still on the trail, he thought.

Coincidental with the thought came sudden wariness. He was being absentminded. Plodding along, dreaming, he'd barely bothered to choose cover or try to anticipate the moves of the man he was tracking. He stopped for a moment, looking back along the way he had come, gauging where he had been when the man he was tracking stood here. Yes. He'd been plainly visible, and must have been often during the long descent of the saddle, particularly after coming out of the second growth.

He remembered how deer reacted to being trailed. When they realized it they would stampede off, at speed, and then settle down in cover and wait. Then they would begin to swing back, sniffing at the wind and moving in suspicious semicircles, watching to see if—

Racks Halvorsen dropped to the ground, burying his face in the snow, wriggling deep into it.

A shot ripped overhead, through the man-sized vertical space he had just vacated. A second later another spewed up dirt and snow and dead leaves a few feet from his head.

Halvorsen did not wait for more. He scrambled up into a run, dodging from tree to tree back along his own trail. Jezebel turned with him, plunging through the snow. They did not seem to be moving very fast. A shot whacked into a tree in front of him, sending splinters over the snow. At last he found what he needed, a slight dip in the ground, and tumbled down into it and lay there, arms outstretched, feeling his heart hammer and stop, stutter, hesitate for a terrifying second, and then decide to go on for another year or month or minute. He waited till he was sure he was alive and then put his head up. A fourth shot, wild, came through the trees at his left, and then a long burst, scattering harmlessly over his down-drawn head.

During the burst he had seen a branch sway in a copse ahead. Dead on his trail; if he hadn't felt that instant of warning that sometimes he'd seen deer get, just before a man fired, he would have passed about twenty yards from the waiting man.

The branch shook again. Halvorsen could see the muzzle flashes plainly. It was not a rifle; it was some kind of machine gun.

Halvorsen hoped it was heavy.

Lying there, he burrowed into the pocket of his worn old trousers and found one of the shells. Opening the breech of the Springfield, he inserted it past the cutoff and closed the bolt. He checked the sight, checked that the muzzle was free of snow, and then slid the rifle over the edge of ground and squinched his eyes and sighted very carefully on the branch. He had a good trigger on this rifle, the old two-stage military trigger they used back when accuracy meant more than firepower, and it broke clean and sharp and he called the shot right through the branch at a hundred thirty yards.

A muffled cry came faint against the wind. Halvorsen started to get up but was fired at once more. He slid back down and waited, glad for the chance to rest.

Half an hour went by without further sound or movement from the copse. At last he decided. It took him another half hour to get there, taking advantage of every slant of land, every tree bole, every rock.

There was no one there. Behind a tree he found the print of a sitting man. The branch of pine that had screened him lay snapped off on the snow. Empty brass lay on the slope behind, half-melted into the white by the heat they had retained from firing. A discarded magazine lay beside the prints.

Halvorsen searched the area minutely, but found nothing more. No blood. No evidence of stagger in the footprints that led downhill to the south. He picked up the magazine. Brass glinted deep in it, a last cartridge, jammed there by a weak or broken spring. He slipped it into his coat pocket and looked downhill.

So that's the way it is, he thought wearily.

He sank slowly to his knees beside the broken branch, feeling his fatigue, his fear and inadequacy. Ralph was too late now. There would be no dogs. No helicopters, in the worsening weather that he knew now would be a full winter storm. No hope of help. And the other man was headed south now; south—into the Kinningmahontawany Wild Area. He touched the shattered branch gently. It had all come down to him; to one old man.

If that's the way it has to be.

FOURTEEN

Tuesday, December Second

DURING MONDAY'S LONG TRAMP MICHELSON HAD THOUGHT often about his first night in the woods. He decided he was going about it wrong. A large fire drained his strength more than it replenished him. Worse, it was visible far away; the man he now knew was close behind might creep up on him while he slept.

So on the second night on the trail he had built another fire, using his second flare, but kept it small and screened it within a dense little tangle of scrub pines and boulders. Near it he built a crazy lean-to of sticks, torn-off pine boughs, and armloads of dead needles from under the snow. As the fire made the trees waver and jump in the darkness he crawled in, too tired even to curse his failure to take the blanket from the back of the car. The shelter collapsed on him almost at once; but as he lay under it, too fatigued to get up, he found it didn't matter. It was still warmer than being exposed to the wind.

All night he lay uneasily in this prickly bed, snatching short bursts of unconsciousness. After midnight these grew longer. When he came up groggily for the last time, just before dawn, he felt something hard against his mouth. He worked his arm up and touched it. It was his beard, rimed stiff with ice from his breath.

Now, as it grew light enough to see the trees against a smoky sky, Michelson pushed away the ruins of the lean-to and got up, brushing needles and decaying leaves from his coat, wincing as the cloth of his shirt pulled at the stiffened tear in his side. His feet were numb. His face ached from the frost. He wanted coffee.

He remembered that he had eaten no food for thirty-six hours, save for a package of dry cheese crackers.

In his own apartment, back at school, he would make his own breakfasts. Simple, natural food was what he liked. Organically-grown rolled oats, perhaps, with skim milk and a glass of orange juice. A cheese and mushroom omelet. Nothing heavy, nothing processed or sugary, though if his weight was okay he would permit himself a level teaspoon in each of the two cups of coffee he needed each morning to send him out ready to face a class.

But there was no coffee, and there was no food. He looked at the dead fire and considered his one remaining emergency kit flare. Even if he used it now, leaving no fire for later, there was no way even to boil water.

At last he sighed and picked up a handful of snow. It tasted metallic and melted reluctantly, numbing his tongue, into a tiny swallow of liquid. He couldn't help thinking of what else was in the snow: DDT and PCB and strontium and dioxin . . . but he was very thirsty and he ate all of it, squatting by the ashes and looking anxiously around at the woods as they emerged from blackness into a thin gray parody of morning.

Gnawing on a second handful of snow, he reviewed the situation in his hunger-sharpened mind.

He could not imagine what the old man had seen or heard or perhaps even smelled in that instant when, holding his sights on him, Michelson began squeezing the trigger. He had seen his follower clearly, recognizing him then for the first time as Halvorsen, as the old man dropped clumsily to the snow. Somehow he had sensed the ambush. And then, just when Michelson thought him helpless and pinned down, that single bullet had come through the branches, punching him in the side, knocking up the rifle, passing on under his arm and exploding against the rock behind him with a sound more frightening than the actual impact. For a moment he'd lost control, screamed something, and then he had felt his side and found the hole through coat and shirt and, incredibly, his own flesh. But only a shallow furrow through a fold of fat, opened like a plasticchange-purse. It had touched a rib on the way through, jolting him. But he was all right. As soon as he was sure of that he'd moved out, carefully. He did not care to expose himself again to the old man, to . . . what had they called him . . . oh, yes . . . Racks.

The man who had told him he'd given up hunting, and did not carry a gun.

Now, squatting in the dawn, Michelson pulled his coat open to examine his side. The blood was clotted black in the gray light, binding his handkerchief firmly into the wound. He decided not to remove it; it might begin bleeding again, and he had nothing else for bandages. He left his shirttail out to ease it and zipped up his jacket. He picked up the rifle.

He hefted it in disbelief. It was easily twice as heavy as it had been in the armory five days before. He searched through his coat pockets. He had several full magazines left. He loaded the rifle with one, twenty rounds, and slung it over the shoulder opposite the wound.

He turned and began walking downhill, still thinking.

After he'd slipped away from the copse yesterday afternoon he had hiked along rapidly for about an hour, driven by fear and excitement. Then he had climbed a rise and looked back along the valley with the glasses.

Far behind, dwindled by distance and the long shiplike hulks of the hills, the old man and the dog were moving slowly along his trail.

He had known then that there would be no easy escape.

Now, walking steadily downhill, burdened by the weapon but buoyed by the lightness of his empty stomach, Michelson reviewed the conclusions he had come to during the night.

One. Even leaving the dog out of the picture, he couldn't think of a way to get the old man off his trail. An old hunter like him had probably spent years tracking through woods just like this. So subterfuge was useless; he would not waste time trying to lose him.

Two. He could not follow his original plan: cut cross-country to the road and then go north out of the county. The old man, tracking him, would have only to stop a car and then phone in the alarm. The police would have him before the day was out. Nor would he be able to hide or ditch the gun with Halvorsen's eyes on every step of his trail.

Three, and conclusion from points one and two: the old man had to die.

Swinging loosely now along the side of a hill, looking down on a broad, deserted valley, Michelson reviewed the sentence he had passed and confirmed it. He did so a little unwillingly, for he remembered that he had pitied the old man. But there were other reasons too. There was the hunting. His goal was to end it, to abolish it forever, as in the course of social evolution other evils—slavery, for example—had been abolished through the self-sacrifice of a dedicated few. From his first day in Raymondsville, Racks had been pointed out to him as a hunter of many years and many trophies. The nickname itself was a tribute. For this alone the old man deserved the same fate he had dealt to countless animals.

Perhaps, Michelson reasoned, I killed men who might have been hunting for the first time. Doesn't this man deserve to die far more? Of course he did.

Hunting was evil, and those who hunted were evil as well.

Michelson made sure he understood what he was doing. He felt the need to preserve logic in this. If he did not then he was no more than a lone madman. And above all, he thought, I am not that. I am probably the only truly sane person in these woods.

His fingers moved inside his coat pocket, encountered a small hard cylinder, and unrolled a tablet from it. He chewed glumly on the antacid and walked through the falling snow.

At one period of his life he had cared little for food; and then, not long after, he had cared very much. For a time in California he'd been involved with fasting. There was a minicult of it then, during the year he spent in San Francisco at twenty, in search of something he never found, and he had been a vegetarian for a time and then macrobiotic; and there were days at a time when he drank only water or diluted juice and ate nothing. Once he had gone without food for fifteen days, resuming eating only when he got too dizzy to stand up.

In some ways, he still felt as he had then. He ate meat occasionally, then felt guilty about it. He bought organic foods—grains, juices, preserves, sea salt, stone-ground wheat bread, pure honey—from a little co-op in West Kittanning. He felt privileged and secure sitting down to a meal fixed with his own hands. Visiting the supermarket for perishables he would shudder as he waited in the checkout lines behind the young mothers, looking at what they fed their children: imperishable candy, sugary cereals whose only wholesome ingredient was air, soft drinks spiked with more sugar or with carcinogenic chemical sweeteners, soft bleached bread, "orange" drinks without even the memory of fruit, potted chicken tumors ruddy with sodium nitrite. Thinking of it made the hunger retreat.

But the cold, and the fatigue—they did not retreat.

He plodded down the long slope of the hill's tail, his eyes to the ground.

The snow seemed different this morning. It was more compact, less yielding, as if the night's chill had shaken it into a denser mass. Atop this was two or three inches of fluff, and more new snow fell steadily around him in clumped-together flakes that drove by on the wind and crash-landed, splintering apart, into the downy cover. At each step his boots sank into it and then stopped on the second layer. The regular pace of his steps squeaked like the rotation of an unlubricated shaft. At each step, pain fluttered through his side.

For the fifth time that morning he stopped and looked back. The snow brushed his face lightly, tangled itself in his lashes. He shaded his eyes with a gloved hand and looked back along the hills.

He didn't even need binoculars. The two dots were nearer. Up before dawn, probably; that was the only way the old man could be keeping up with him. But how had he been able to see the trail?

Oh, yes, he thought. The dog.

Michelson stared back at them. He felt pursued, trapped. No, he reminded himself angrily. You're the hunter. Not him. He is the quarry.

He looked about him quickly.

Another stand, another ambush? The old man would be alert now. He still didn't understand how Halvorsen had known he was waiting in the pine copse. And considering his wound, he didn't relish the thought of giving the old man another shot at him.

He looked ahead again, downwind, toward the south, and saw what might be the answer.

An hour or two later he stood above the falls, looking down.

The map was damp from his pocket, frayed and torn, but still legible enough. For some reason he felt better knowing the names of things. This creek—fifty feet across, all but ten or fifteen feet of the middle frozen, actually a small river with the green water dark and swift at its center—was Coal Run, the northern tributary of the Hefner, which it joined several miles downstream. The narrow cut between hills where he stood, where the river bunched its muscles and burst from the mantle of ice in a fifty-foot torrent of spray, was Trestle Crossing. To one side of it a double line of half-rotted pilings stood above the ice.

All right, he thought. He's got to follow me. This is where my tracks lead. All I've got to do is cross here, go downstream a little ways, and then double back fast and find a place that overlooks the crossing.

He knew that this might not be easy. But he had to do it. Gripping the rifle, he trotted down the side of the cut, toward the river.

The ice was solid at first. But a few yards on from the bank it grew rough-surfaced, milky. The spray from the falls, driven downstream by the wind, made the surface treacherous. Even his new waffle-soled boots had little traction. He paused for a moment, standing on the ice, and looked up toward the falls.

The water poured toward him, a bottle-green torrent whose initially smooth, glass-curved surface was quickly torn apart by boulders, churning the falling river into foam and spray. He felt it on his face, numbing his cheeks and caking his beard with a fine frost.

To the left and right of the falls, high as a four-story building, the two hills rose on either side of the gorge. From them evergreens leaned out over the river. And down the gorge, focused by the sides, came the endless deep-throated roar of falling water.

He looked again at the river. Below the fury of the falls it quieted in a wide pool of foam-streaked water, and then flowed on, bound with chains of small bubbles, past where he stood. A gap of twelve or fifteen feet in the middle was clear of ice. Michelson could see the rounded pebbles of the bottom. It was pretty deep. Seven, eight feet, he judged. Far too deep to think of wading, and the water would be freezing cold, kept liquid only by its motion.

Yet he had to get across, and quickly.

He spent a few minutes thinking. He didn't mind the obstacle. It was nice to have a problem that he could attack with his brain. Presently he had a solution. Some hundred feet back in the woods, the water's roar muffled to a sourceless rushing sound, he found what he needed: a fallen tree of medium size, its broken roots reaching upward like despairing arms. He snapped off most of the limbs and tried to do the same with the roots, but they were too tough. When he had it ready he laid the rifle and the binoculars nearby and got his hands under the trunk and lifted, grunting. It came free of the ground reluctantly, dead leaves dropping from its underside. He shouldered his end on up. It was staggeringly heavy, too heavy to carry. But perhaps he could drag it. He walked the crown toward the river, let it drop, then went around to the roots and moved that end. It was like being at the bottom of a refrigerator going up stairs, and he felt himself breaking out in a sweat.

After doing this perhaps thirty times, working the trunk along between the boles of the live trees, he came panting out onto the creek bank again. It was easier here, but the trunk was still awkward. At last he had it as close to the edge as he dared. He didn't trust that milky bubbled ice. He measured the distance with his eye and again looked critically at the tree.

It might reach, he thought.

Leaving the splayed imploring roots at the edge, he got under the crown and sweated it up, up, until the tree tottered upright, resurrected, vertical, for a long moment, and then tilted and gathered velocity and swept downward. It cracked sullenly into the ice at the far side and stuck there, bobbing slightly in the current.

Suddenly remembering, Michelson went back for the glasses and the rifle. He wondered how close the old man was. There was certainly no time to climb back to the crest and look.

He had to cross now.

Putting one foot on the log, he tested it with part of his weight. The roots would keep it from rolling. The trunk itself was not very wide—eight inches, perhaps—but the bark was rough. If I go right now, he thought, before the spray freezes on it, I should have a pretty good chance.

He unslung the rifle and shifted the strap of the binoculars to the opposite side, crisscrossing them on his chest so that neither could come free by accident and unbalance him.

Now. He took a deep breath and stepped up on the near end of the tree and balanced there, one foot in front of the other, arms extended. The log felt solid. But it was damned narrow. I can do it, he thought, if it holds steady.

Here goes, then. He moved out along his makeshift bridge. It felt solid as the earth. He watched his feet, the big, snow-stained, blunt-toed boots, inch slowly along heel-and-toe. He left the dark ice behind and moved out over the bubbly white. All right. Then out over the water, over the swift-running green. He shivered as he looked down into it. The air was colder here. If he fell in, it would be rough trying to climb up from deep water onto crumbling ice. But it was getting wet he feared more. In this cold, and with this wind, a slip could be the end without dry clothes to change to.

No, he told himself. I'm not going to fall in.

He moved slowly out to midstream, instinctively bending his knees under him to steady his weight.

The bottom of the log was under the surface of the water. Looking past his inching feet he saw how the green water rippled around it, making a chuckling sound audible even under the thunder of the falls, so steady that his ears had tuned it out. Drifts of foam shoaled up against the log, then slipped bubble by bubble beneath it and sailed on downstream.

Behind the log—on that downstream side—he could see himself. Smoothed by the lee, the curved plane of the flowing water, underlain by dark bottom, gave him back a subtly distorted yet clear reflection of his down-peering eyes.

He stopped for a moment in midstream, caught by the stare, by the pale beard-shrouded face there under the river. They were bright with fatigue, resolve . . . he bent to look closer, fascinated by them, barely feeling the minute movement of the log beneath his boots. They held him effortlessly, those eyes; they held the power of old memory.

Suddenly Paul Michelson was eighteen again.

He was a sophomore. He had entered early, skipping

his last year of high school with a combined SAT of over 1500. But fairly quickly, in those days of rage, he had graduated from academics to politics. He'd changed almost overnight from small-town boy to radical. And he was not satisfied with words. So that when the Kent State strike began, and even the apathetic marched, he had agreed with the others on the campus committee that more than a march would be necessary now.

He'd been assigned the physics lab, where, as everyone knew, the research was under the direction of Air Force officers.

It had gone well at first, he remembered, teetering on the narrow bridge between past and present. The device was guaranteed foolproof: just gasoline and a rag. As he held it ready, standing there at the corner of the lab, waiting for the campus pigwagon to roll by, he knew that in seconds the interior of the building would be a hell of fire. When the car had passed, he'd pulled the lighter from his pocket and stepped round the corner to the plate-glass front. He saw his reflection raise the bomb, twist the fuse forward, and flick open the lighter.

Then, deeper in the glass, he saw the man within. He was seated in the dark, with the lights off. Just sitting there. He was turned away from the window. He wore a blue uniform cap.

Michelson felt his fingers tighten on the smooth surface of the bottle. They tightened, began presently to shake, and then, gradually, he became aware of someone watching him. A pair of shrouded eyes, deep in the window.

The uniformed man did not move. Now Michelson could see a bottle by his side, a shot glass. Who was he? Why was he here after hours, drinking with the lights off, alone and silent?

It doesn't matter, he told himself fiercely. He is a killer

and he deserves to die. He was raising the lighter again when the eyes asked him: *And what are you?*

He'd stood there for nearly ten minutes before he broke at last and threw the bomb squarely through the eyes, shattering them, and ran.

But he hadn't lit it, and nothing happened. The next day college glaziers replaced the window with reinforced glass. And Paul Michelson was dropped from the committee.

Under his feet the log shifted a little more. Only a little, but it disturbed his balance and he teetered wildly, trying to recover. The sweat broke out anew. His clothes were already wet beneath the heavy coat and he felt the wind under his collar and at his sleeves. He was only halfway across. He held himself rigid, arms outstretched, fighting for balance.

From beyond the hill came the hoarse, quickly stilled baying of a dog.

He couldn't wait. Straightening, he forced his eyes away from the water and took another small shuffle forward. The log moved again.

Now he saw why. The far end of the tree had broken through most of the ice on the opposite bank and was half supported by it, half floating. As his weight came toward it the crown was gradually being forced down. With each step forward it would become less stable.

Sweating, he shuffled forward another couple of inches.

Suddenly it let go. The trunk dipped and began to turn under his feet. The creek came up over it. Feeling his support going, Michelson left the trunk with a spring. He touched briefly with one boot at the half-submerged crown, felt it give way, and fell full length on the jagged crust. His arms scrabbled across it, reaching for the shore. The milky brink shivered and cracked, giving way under his legs. Abrupt cold flooded his boots and he became absolutely still, feeling the fragility of the surface under his stomach and loins. From behind him came a faint grinding sound.

After several seconds he opened his eyes. His feet were already numb. He tried to inchworm forward, toward a root on the far bank, four feet away over the slick ice, but could get no purchase. His gloves slid over the slight waviness, defeated by the greasy film of water.

Behind him the hound bayed again, seeming closer beyond the thunder of the falls.

Michelson watched the snag. That was what he had to concentrate on. It was black, seamed, crooked as the beckoning finger of a crone. He stretched out an arm. His fingers trembled, two and a half feet short.

He pulled off the binoculars. Holding them by the bridge, he tossed the strap toward the snag. He missed eight times but at the ninth try the leather fell over the snag and Michelson gripped the glasses with both hands and pulled himself out and across the ice. As soon as he was free he got to his feet, heedless of the stabbing in his side, and scrambled up the snow-covered bank. He took one look back. The tree trunk had broken away from the ice where he had landed and was going downstream, rolling in the current. As he watched it rounded a bend to the left and disappeared. Good, he thought; no way he'll be able to follow me. The old bastard certainly isn't strong enough to do that by himself.

But he had to make sure. Puffing, the numbness in his legs turning to pain, he half crawled up the hill. It was steep but not too high and as soon as he felt able he began to run, zigzagging between the trees, till he reached the top. He leaned against a trunk there, unable to go on, and panted and spat for a couple of minutes while his breathing slowed. Then, not rested but at least less exhausted, he moved cautiously toward the creek side of the hill.

As he came out above the crossing the tree cover ended and he found himself at a natural overlook, a hundred feet above the falls. He was able to see far up- and downriver.

The old man was not in sight yet. Michelson moved back into the trees and lay down, unslinging the rifle. This time I've got him, he thought. From the elevation he could watch Halvorsen's every step along the far side of the creek, and could take him at the crossing, from cover, with a clear shot from above. He was so close that he could see his own footprints plainly at the far side above the falls. His tracks were alone. He wriggled his toes inside the wet leather of the boots. The old man had not yet come. He checked the rifle and set it for single shots. Firing downhill, he reminded himself, he'd have to aim a little low.

Now he had only to wait.

Time dragged past. The dog bayed occasionally to his left, somewhere in the woods. He stared toward the sound but saw nothing amid the trees, nothing along the bank of the river. How far back were they? He was reaching down to untie his boots when something moved on the opposite hill.

He froze. Only his eyes moved, searching across the ravine, above the waterfall. His tracks waited for the old man's to join them. Minutes passed. His feet grew numb again. He wondered if they were frostbitten. His stomach rumbled and his side ached with dull insistence. Still he kept his eyes on his tracks, glancing occasionally upstream. At last he let his eyes slide up the opposite hill.

A man was moving very slowly down it among the Even as he watched the distant figure stopped and, immobile, melted suddenly into the hundreds of gray trunks.

And suddenly Michelson was suffused with the heat of wasted pains. His arms began to tremble. He waited, nonetheless, still as one of the rocks beside him, until the distant figure moved again, before he began crawling backward, away from the open lip of the hill.

The old man had not followed his trail. Instead he'd swerved left, away from the creek, and climbed the flank of the eastern hill under the screen of the woods. He was now coming out near its top, across from Michelson, all right, but well above him, and with much better cover.

He had not followed the trail; he had not been tricked.

Under the trees again, he sat on the snow, shaking. Halvorsen had anticipated his actions again. How? What extra sense did this squalid old man possess? And what about the dog, baying disconsolately from upstream, well back on the trail?

Of course, he thought; the old man tied it up back there. Or more likely just commanded it to stay till he whistled it up. It was crying because it had been left behind. As the old man had known it would. And known that he, the quarry, hearing it, would not expect its owner to be almost on him.

He felt cold, and not only from the freezing water in his boots. For the first time he felt himself overmatched.

Michelson sat and wondered what to do for a long time. At last, resignation in the slump of his shoulders, he stood up.

One thing remains, he thought. And that is speed. In spite of all his exertions, his wound, his hunger, he could still travel faster. Halvorsen was an old man, after all. He saw again the sunken cheeks, the gray stubble.

I'll just outwalk him, Michelson thought.

I'll outwalk him till he's too far back to bother me or

stop me. I'll gain so many miles on him that when I finally come out on the other side of this—what was it called—Kinningmahontawany, quite a mouthful—when I come out on the eastern edge, not at the Hefner but many miles farther south, I'll be long gone before the old man, moving more slowly, comes out behind me. Along the way I'll figure out something to do with the rifle. As a last resort, he thought, I can chop a hole in the ice and drop it in a creek.

He was resourceful. The save with the binocular straps proved that, he told himself. A less intelligent man might not have thought of that. And even if he hadn't outthought the old man, he'd seen him on the ridge in time to get away.

Feeling slightly better, he took out the map again. It would be a long trek, probably over rough country. The hills seemed to grow steeper and the forest wilder the deeper into this deserted land he went. But that was good, too; there had been no other hunters since he had left his car; he was alone with the old man. Even the low gray sky, the constant snow, was on his side; no matter what was happening back in town—and he did wonder about that from time to time—it could not affect what happened here, even to the extent of sending out an aircraft to search for them. If he could shake the old man, he was free to escape.

And I'll do it, he promised himself.

He would get free. Next year, though, he would return. And then he would make no mistakes. He would study his quarry and his terrain and fit himself for it. Then he would even things up with this uncanny old man, with all the hunters, all the killers.

Gripping the rifle firmly, Michelson began to jog rapidly down the hill.

FIFTEEN

HER UNDERTHINGS WERE DRY. ONE BY ONE SHE PULLED THE lacy panties, the delicate bras down from the shower rod, folded them, and aligned them neatly in the suitcase. Her slips went in next, and then her other clothes: blouses, skirts, slacks, stockings.

Snapping the bag shut, Teresa glanced around the worn little room. She felt angry and unhappy. Her expression became even less pleased as she reached for her purse and thumbed through the billfold. Only eight dollars left and some change, barely enough for breakfast and gas back to West Kittanning. The whole weekend wasted here and I still haven't found him, she thought angrily. Only wasted my time with a lot of stupid, unfriendly people . . .

Well, this afternoon she would be back at school, in front of her Castilian class, and everything (except for Paul) would be normal again. And then I'll just have to wait, she thought. He's got to come back sometime. When he did it might be bad for a while, but then everything would be all right again.

She succeeded in not thinking consciously about the possibility that he might be in the woods. But something of it came through in the nervous way she rubbed her bracelet. Leaving the suitcase on the bed, she locked the room and went downstairs to check out.

The lobby was empty. There was no one behind the desk. A fresh newspaper, still damp from its morning embedment in snow, lay on the marble-topped counter. The dining room, past the desk, was empty too. Teresa frowned. She'd planned on breakfast here before leaving, but the tables were bare and there was no one at the grill. She went out to the lobby again and was about to open the door to the street when the headline caught her eye.

"Oh, no," she said. She picked up the paper and sat in one of the worn, dusty chairs, dating no doubt from the eighteen eighties, and looked closely at the front page of the Raymondsville *Century* for Tuesday, December 2. Outlook: Continued Snow.

NEW VICTIM FOUND IN HANTZEN AREA

The remains of a Pittsburgh man were found today west of Hantzen Lake by a Kendall well-service team out of Bradford. The victim appeared to be in his late twenties.

Identified as Stanley Mizejewski, of 3031 Bougeot Lane, Pittsburgh, the remains were found by James T. Romanelli and William Pendergast about two hundred yards from the top of a saddle west of the lake. The body was almost covered with snow, Pendergast said, making it likely that it had been there several days.

Charles Whitecar, the county coroner, arrived on the scene shortly after the discovery was reported, but declined to comment on how long it might have remained undiscovered.

This brings the total of deaths in Hemlock County since November twenty-eight to at least six. Local hunters are speculating that there might be more, as yet unreported.

A sidelight on the latest slaying was contributed by Ernest L. Bauer, a Hantzen farmer, who told reporters Sunday that he had been fired at the day before while hunting in the general area where Mizejewski was eventually found.

County officials, who earlier felt that the first deaths were accidents, are now taking the view that all were murders and all the work of a single assailant. Accordingly, direction of search and investigation efforts has been assumed by the State Police, operating from the Beaver Fork barracks. Sergeant William Sealey said today that search efforts would probably be fruitless until more information became available. Also, he said, current record snowfalls limit air searches, which would normally be flown. All other measures, he added, were being taken, and additional Civil Air Patrol aircraft and police help were being requested from Commonwealth authorities. "As soon as the weather begins to break, an intensive search will begin," Sealey said.

He also advised all hunters in Hemlock and neighboring counties to travel in groups.

The latest victim was a native of Pittsburgh, employed by the Carnegie Institute in its Department of Paleontology. . . .

Dios mio, she thought, lowering the page and looking out through the doors of the hotel. Her eyes rose without thought, over the snow of the street, over the shabby shops opposite, to where the hills loomed gray and dim in the falling snow. *What is happening out there?*

Filled with unease, she left the paper on the still-deserted desk and went out, pulling a kerchief over her hair. The air was bitter, colder than the day before. She scuffed carefully over the frozen slush of the sidewalks, walking aimlessly for a time, and then paused at an alleyway to put her back to the wind and light her first cigarette of the day. Puffing it into the cold she thought: I've got to eat.

The streets were empty. By the sign in front of the bank she saw that it was nine A.M., yet the town seemed deserted. The restaurants and sporting-goods stores she passed were closed, dark, and she went several blocks, almost to the end of Main Street, before she found a hash-and-egg short-order open.

One of the TV vans was parked in front of it. As she came up she saw the now-familiar cables. She thought nothing of them until she stepped around the van, crossing the street toward the greasy spoon, and looked up to find herself being focused on by a man holding a portable video camera. Her instinctive turn away brought her face-to-face with a woman holding a microphone. For a moment the three of them stood in silence, their breaths drifting away in a single cloud.

"Here's someone. Maybe she'll talk with us."

"Hello, miss. Channel Ten, Buffalo, for national rebroadcast. Do you mind if we ask you some questions? It's about the deaths."

She couldn't just go on; the man and woman were between her and the diner. They looked at her so hopefully that she hesitated, then nodded.

"How do people here in Raymondsville feel about the tragedies?"

"I do not know. I don't live here."

"You're a visitor?"

"Yes."

"A visiting hunter?" The woman sounded dubious.

"No."

"Well, perhaps . . . do you have friends here who hunt? Are you concerned about them?"

"I don't know anyone who hunts. Please let me by."

"One more question, please. We haven't been able to get many people here to talk with us. How do you feel about hunting? Are you against it?" The woman held the microphone close to her lips.

"I don't know anything about it," said Teresa. "I do not have an opinion."

"Oh, let her go. She won't say anything either," the cameraman said. The light went out and they turned from her, looking away up the street. She went past quickly and into the diner. Inside, four townspeople were watching the interviewers through the window. The counterman poured her coffee without being asked, while saying to the others, "Anyway, it's all blown up out of proportion, is what I say. It's on national news now I heard. I figure they'll get the guy eventually. Some nut from out of town. But meanwhile, us here—we're the guys that suffer." He glanced at her as if to solicit her agreement, and she nodded, her eyes down, filled still with the shame and fear she had felt when that eye of millions had suddenly opened and blinked and turned toward her.

"Oh, you were out," said the desk clerk as she came in. "I was ringing your room. You had a call about twenty minutes ago."

"A call? Who was it?"

"She said she'd call back. Didn't leave a name."

"It was a woman?" She was intensely disappointed. For a moment she had thought it might be him.

The clerk nodded. He pulled out a pad of receipts. "Oh, yeah. If you're staying on, we need your payment today, Miss del Rosario."

Teresa looked toward the stairs. What woman would be calling her here? And why? She had missed what the desk clerk said and turned back to him. "I'm sorry—?"

"I said, we require payment on the room. Are you checking out today?"

"You—" she paused; "You don't take credit cards, do you?"

"Not unless they're local. What kind do you have?"

She showed him and he shook his head. "Sorry. We only take the ones from Bucktail Bank."

"Yes, I plan to leave today, but not till checkout time."

While he totaled the bill she investigated her purse again. After her breakfast, and including a quarter she remembered under the seat, there was just enough to get her back to the campus, considering the way the Chrysler burned gas. A light blinked behind the desk and the clerk turned toward her, holding out a receiver.

"Hello?" she said, hoping even then that he was mistaken, that Paul had somehow found out she was here.

"Miss del Rosario?"

"Yes. Who's this?"

"This is Anne Oleksa."

"Oh. Yes."

"Look," the distant brittle voice said, then paused; Teresa heard murmurs in the background; someone said clearly, "Yes." Then Paul's ex-wife came back on.

"Look. I have someone here who wants to see you."

"Paul?"

"No. Not Paul. A girl—a friend of Aaron's."

"Oh. Well, put her on."

"She doesn't want to use the phone. She wants to come and talk to you. Can she?"

"It is important?"

"I don't know if it's 'important.'" Mrs. Oleksa's voice vibrated alarmingly. "I'm just telling you! You were asking about Aaron. Do you want to see her or not?"

"If she can come over here before noon, all right," said Teresa. "I have to leave then. What is her name?"

"Mary. Her name's Mary. And she'll be right over."

Mary was a small girl, thin and pale, with long darkish-brown hair and a face as placid as a coma victim's. She had a tattoo of a cross and the name Chris on her left arm. She sat silently on Teresa's bed for several minutes after she took her coat off, jogging her foot in a nervous way. She looked about fourteen.

"Did you have something to tell me?" Teresa prompted at last.

"I guess so. Maybe."

"Is it about Aaron? His mother said you were a friend of his."

"Yeah. Sort of."

Teresa waited. After a moment the girl looked up at her. The placid surface of her eyes rippled, just for a moment, and she saw that underneath the calm was terror. "Say . . . would you have a choker on you?"

"A what?"

"A butt."

"Oh. Yes, I think I have a couple left in this pack."

She lit one too. The girl leaned back a little on the bed,

227

took a deep drag and hung on to it grimly. She stole another look at Teresa. "Mrs. Oleksa says you're Ari's dad's lover."

"I suppose that's . . . that's right."

"And you don't live around here."

"I don't look like I am from here, do I?"

"You don't talk like it either," said the girl. "What are you, exactly? If it's okay to ask. Are you Mexican, or what?"

"Chicana. From California."

"Oh, California, wow."

"It's not that 'wow' when you grow up there."

"It's got to be better than Raymondsville," said Mary.

Teresa waited, smiling, and the girl glanced at her again, inhaled again, coughed. "Well . . . you're waiting for me to talk. Okay, I just needed to think a minute. Okay. It's about Ari."

"Go on."

"He and me and some other guys at school, we were in a sort of club. I guess he really started it. We called it 'Life Friends.' We made the name up ourselves."

"A school club?"

"Yeah. I mean, no. It wasn't for school. It was kind of like Greenpeace. You know? Preservationists. For saving whales and other animals and stuff."

Teresa nodded. "Aaron was active in your club?"

"He *started* it, I said."

"I see."

"Actually there was only four of us. Him, and me, and Karen, and Beth."

Teresa waited. The girl was growing more nervous, or allowing more of what was there to show. Her free hand wandered about, picking at the coverlet. "Anyway . . . Ari was real mad at the way people were around town here. Hunting and all. He said, it was maybe okay to hunt for food, if you really needed it. But around here it's all done for money. They advertise and get people in here for the deer, sportsmen, and it's all a business. He didn't like that. We had a demonstration about it. And we had an article in the school paper. He wrote it. He was real smart; Ari was real smart."

"A demonstration?"

"Just the four of us. With signs, out front of one of the gun stores. They made us leave. Would they do that in California, do you think? Just come out of the store and tell you to leave or the cops would be there?"

"I don't know. Probably."

"Anyway, it made Ari real mad. But then he found out something. There's poaching going on."

"Poaching?"

"Don't you know . . . ? It's like jacklighting."

"No," said Teresa, a little confused. "I don't know anything about hunting. What are you talking about?"

"Well, like this. Poaching is shooting deer without a license, or at night with lights, or out of season, or like that. A lot of guys joke about doing it for fun sometimes. But Ari said there's more going on than that. He said somebody is bringing in rich flatlanders—that's out-of-town hunters, from the city—in big bunches, taking them out to the places you're not supposed to hunt in."

"And that's illegal?"

"Sure," said Mary. "Out of season, in the Wild Area? Sure it's illegal. That's why it's poaching."

Just that suddenly, Teresa understood. Paul had been right. Aaron had been against hunting. And somehow he had found out, searched out or stumbled on, something illegal going on out in the silent woods.

And for that, he had died.

"Yes," she said softly, "I understand now. Aaron —Ari—did he tell you who was doing it?"

"Running the business? No. I was the only one he told at all, I think. Him and me—we was kind of close." She looked at the cigarette solemnly and rolled over to stub it out. She looked squarely at Teresa. "He said he knew, though, and was going to tell his dad. He wasn't going to the police or anything. He figured they knew already and got paid off or something. He thought his dad would know what to do. He talked about his dad a lot. He really admired him."

"I know."

"But he didn't get to tell him, I guess."

"Somebody else found out first."

"I guess so," said the girl. She brushed the straight mousy hair back and Teresa saw one tear. "Anyhow —now you know. Nobody else does. I couldn't even tell his mom. Do you think you can help? He cared about this so much—"

Teresa found herself stroking the girl's hair. Mary's head was in her lap, the girl was crying openly now, the toughness cracked open. Teresa stroked her head and murmured to her softly. It did not matter that Mary could not possibly understand the Spanish. She was young and she had lost, probably for the first time, someone she loved. There was nothing to say, nothing to do but to hold her for a time and rock her.

At last the sobbing ebbed and Mary sat up, knuckling her eyes, and tried to smile.

"Better now?"

"I guess. I'm sorry."

"Don't be. I'm glad you came."

"I couldn't tell anybody here in town. They might be part of it. You know, it's not anybody off the street doing things like this. It's got to be somebody important, or they'd stop it."

"I didn't think of that, but you are right."

"It's not me. That's what Ari said. He was a lot smarter. Hard to be friends with sometimes, but him and me done okay."

"I know."

"You knew him? His mom said—"

"No. But his dad's the same way."

"You understand then." She got up, sniffled, then wiped her eyes and threw her hair back. She looked at herself in the mirror. "Jeez. Like the girl who backed into a airplane propeller."

"What?"

"Disaster."

"I don't think I understand, if that is a joke. But you look fine."

"You'll help, won't you?"

"Yes. I'm not sure how yet. But I will do all I can."

"You have to promise you won't tell anybody here or outside that it was me. Who let you know."

"No. I promise."

The girl turned from the mirror. She looked placid again, the way she had when she came in; calm, young, a little vacant. Perhaps it's a disguise, Teresa found herself thinking. She had seen that look before here. It must not be an easy life for a woman in Hemlock County.

As she was thinking that, the door closed. The girl was gone.

Teresa looked at the ashtray blankly and lit another cigarette, her last. Have to get some more, she thought.

And now, she asked herself, drawing in the smoke, what are you going to do? She had no money and so could not stay; yet neither could she leave, not now, not knowing this. What if tomorrow or the day after Paul came walking down the street, tall and spare, a smile for her hidden in his beard? He'd have to know. Someone would have to be here to tell him.

Her eyes slid slowly down her arm to the heavy hammered links of the bracelet. After all, she thought, was it not he who gave it to me?

Her arm felt oddly light, naked, as she left the little coin-jewelry-and-pawn shop a half hour later. At the hotel she paid for another night and bought a pack of cigarettes from the machine in the lobby. No more after these, she thought, but without much conviction; she had said it too often in the last week. She had a big dinner, getting down the free rolls, the salad, dessert. She ate all she could hold; there wouldn't be enough for three meals every day.

She was sitting in her room that evening, watching an old movie on the black and white Sylvania, her hair in a towel after the shower and her old bathrobe wrapped around her against the drafts, when someone knocked heavily on her door. She had the chain half-off, sure it was Paul at last, before she thought *better be sure* and slid it back again. Through the crack she could see someone out there, someone about his height; her heart began to pound; but the hallway was too dark to be sure. "Yes?" she said, her voice sounding high-pitched. "Who is there?"

"It's me."

The voice sent a slight chill through her even before she recognized it. She felt disappointed, yet not unhappy; on second thought, even a little glad; she had grown bored being alone. "It's . . . oh, Mr. Sweet. I couldn't see who you were out there."

"Can I come in?"

"It's late. Is it . . . what do you want?"

He didn't answer, only stood there in the darkened hallway, waiting to be let in. Annoyed, but hoping he had news, she pulled the chain off and opened the door, tightening the bathrobe around her waist.

The warden filled the little room like a suite of furniture. His size altered its scale; from comfortable, cozy, it became almost oppressively small. She stood by the still-open door, watching as he paced to the bureau and turned back. He carries himself well, she thought. He wore the same rough-looking but probably expensive plaid coat, unbuttoned over the badge. When his eyes met hers she had the same sensation she had had in his office: of attraction, but also a slight repulsion.

He reached out and took the door from her hands and closed it.

"What do you want?" she repeated, feeling that she sounded a little stupid. She could feel herself blushing too, and she tucked her bathrobe closer at the neck and sat down on the bed. "Please sit down, warden. Did you do what that Mr. DeSantis said? Did you go after your grandfather?"

"Couldn't. Snowin' too hard. We lost the trail."

He spoke sharply, angrily, but in a subdued voice. He glared at her as he spoke, then looked quickly around the room as if searching for something. She waited, feeling apprehension prickle her skin; she was naked under the damp robe. She wished the room lights were brighter, but there was only the single cheap forty-watt desk lamp, heavily shaded, and the violet flicker of the television. The corners were draped with shadow and seemed to move toward the two of them as Sweet stood balanced in the middle of the room, hesitating for the space of perhaps three breaths, and then began suddenly to pace again, glancing at Teresa each time he turned by the foot of the bed.

"What's wrong?"

"What's wrong? Everything's wrong. They've taken it all out of my hands. Sealey's got the investigation now."

"Please be calm. Isn't that normal?"

"Normal? Maybe it is. But I don't care for it. Jesus, they keep these rooms hot enough, don't they?"

He stripped off the coat and flung it onto the chair. Underneath it a blue flannel shirt outlined his chest. At his waist she saw something long; a hunting knife in a leather sheath. She found suddenly that her hands were trembling, that it was hard to breathe, that she dared not take her eyes from him.

He had to go, right now, before things went too far. She took a deep breath and sat up. "Did you want me for something, Mr. Sweet?"

"Uh. No, nothing special. I just wanted to talk. Not many people in this town you can just talk to."

There, he was smiling now; that had been the right thing to say. She leaned back again against the pillow, feeling relieved. He was still talking. "And I was . . . you know, thinking about you, Teresa. Hoped I'd see you again, after meeting you at the office." She said nothing. "So I thought I'd come on up and see if you were still here," he finished, stopping and smiling easily, directly down at her. "Have you found out anything? I understand you've been doing some looking around on your own."

She thought for a moment of telling him about Mary's visit, about what Aaron had found. The game warden would have to be told, certainly, about any illegal hunting. But there would be time for that later; right now it might be best to wait. Perhaps it was still possible to find Paul, to help him somehow, at least let him know why Aaron had died. She still couldn't believe he had anything to do with the hunters' deaths. It had to be coincidence, as the warden himself had told the reporters. Paul Michelson, the man who cared so much for others, who had passed nonviolence on to his son like a knight his sword, was not a man who could kill.

I have to keep believing that of him, she thought. At least until I see him again.

As she thought this she was following Sweet with her eyes. He had crossed to the window and was peering out into the darkness, looking down on the main street.

She could feel something off balance, some tension in him tonight. He was angry, perhaps frightened. She didn't understand it. She didn't like it, or him; he was too rough, too pushy-confident, he had none of the gentleness she found most attractive in men. Yet although she didn't like him, she could still admit that perhaps even because of that dangerousness he interested her. Something that, in spite of the circumstances and how she knew she ought to feel, made her watch him, fearful that he might stay, but disappointed and a little lonely if he were to go just yet. So that when he pulled himself away from the window with a sudden movement and came to the bed and without word or warning sat down beside her, she stiffened but did not gasp or speak.

"Still friggin' snowing," he muttered, looking toward the dark square of glass. The television flickered, spoke on in tiny muted voices. He lit a cigar, then held the match for her as she reached for her purse. She sucked at the tobacco in relief. It steadied her and she lifted its tip from his flame, conscious suddenly of her breasts—her mother's generousness that her father had joked about, that when she was young, Teresa had watched men's eyes admiring in the street—against the fabric of the robe. But when he reached out to touch her she instantly pushed his hand away, almost burning him.

"Don't do that, Mr. Sweet. Leave my room now."

At that he shifted closer on the bed, leaning over her, and she tried to move farther back and found herself against the headboard. "I told you, I do not want you here!"

"What? You don't want me?"

"No."

"Bullshit," he said, and gave her that boyish, cynical, amused grin she remembered from the office. "You knew when you let me in we'd end up in the sack. I could tell it that first second, when you looked at me and couldn't look away." He pushed her hand aside; the bathrobe came open and she gasped and pulled at it, but his hand was already inside, hard and cold. "You don't have to play that little-girl game with me. I hear you Mex babes are hot. I bet you want me more than I want you."

"No. I don't." But her voice was shaking. "Leave. Please. Leave right now."

"What'll you do if I don't? Scream?"

"Yes."

He paused then, leaning over her, and grinned. "I bet you would. I think maybe you just need to be warmed up a bit." His hand left her breast and unbuttoned his shirt pocket, reached inside, tossed something onto the night table. She looked toward it; a plastic packet, white powder.

"I don't want—"

He was suddenly atop her, no longer smiling, his weight too great for her to struggle against, pinning and pressing her down with his hand over her mouth. She fought to breathe. His face was scratchy and smelled of cigars and alcohol. Her fists struck his back with sodden thumps. She tried to turn her face away, needing air, and couldn't. At last she tried to bite, and he lifted part of his hand so she could draw a quick short breath through her nose. In that moment Sweet laid his fist alongside her cheek, pressing the knuckles into her painfully. He let up a little more with his hand and into her ear he said, "You make a noise, bitch, and I'll cut your face off."

"Don't—"

"You won't scream. You all want it like this."

"Go away, " she whispered. "I do not want you here."

"You were hot for me the minute you saw me. Here, take this thing off."

Without air it was hard to struggle. She was afraid, terribly afraid. She fought him half-conscious, as in the night terrors where she knew horror approached, knew she slept, but could neither move nor wake. The memory of Paul dimmed and blended into this heaviness close over her, the rough hand moving hungrily under her robe into her naked warmth. She could not yet understand that this was happening to her. His lips were rough and smelled sickeningly of whiskey. She had thought him attractive, but that did not mean she wanted this. She gasped and twisted and tried then really to scream as his knee and then his hand went between her legs. His hand tightened on her mouth and nose and she fought and thrashed till terror and shock and lack of air numbed her and she lay limp and helpless as the weight shifted above her, poised itself with a grunt, and then drove downward.

She opened her eyes once to the twisted cloth of his shirt, the close smell of him. He was muttering above her as he moved. "Hot," he muttered. "Really nice . . . you love it. You want it. And here it comes."

Under his weight she screamed over and over without breath or sound.

SIXTEEN

Wednesday, December Third

IT WAS THE FOURTH DAY OF THE STORM.

Over the ridges, over the hill-hedged towns, the clouds rolled like many fathoms of murky sea. The snow fell from them in sporadic hour-long bursts, leaving half an inch or an inch each time. People did not bother with clearing it. The temperature was at minus twenty-four, a record low. They knew that more snow was coming. Much more; and very soon.

Far from those narrow towns, in an empty valley of the Kinningmahontawany, the old man dragged himself southward, mile by mile.

Racks Halvorsen had spent his life at heavy work, often in the cold. During the war, when men were scarce, he had put in fourteen and often sixteen hours a day at the fields, dragging equipment up hills because there were no spare parts for the tractors, hauling pipe through dense forest to open new wells, falling asleep on his feet with ropes in his hands. He had been tired before. But never as tired as this.

He hiked slowly along the floor of the valley in an unthinking fog. Each step was an effort. The deep, yielding snow was powdery with the cold, yet as he lifted each boot it clung, wearying his thighs and making the air bite in his throat and lungs. The old Springfield, carried for so long now that it seemed less a physical burden than an unconfessed sin, a weight less on his shoulders than on his soul, dragged him to the side at every step. The pack was light in comparison. He had eaten the chocolate, the sausage, the beans. Only two strips of fatty bacon remained, that and his mummy bag and the hand ax and matches.

Even his clothes, his coat, shirt, boots, the heavy trousers, he felt as a separate and terrible carapace of weight.

He lifted his foot again and moved his aging body after it.

Behind him, panting, floundered the old bitch. A brown-stained crust of ice caked her steaming muzzle. A white coating of snow burdened her paws and back and drooping tail. Her sides heaved as she paused and jumped forward, gathered herself and sprang again, trying to go over what was to her neck-deep snow rather than bulldoze through it with her chest.

All the long valley was silent, except for the labored sounds of their breathing.

"Ho, Jessie," said the old man at last. The dog hesitated in the midst of gathering herself for another leap. She looked up at him and whined softly.

"Let's sit down and rest a second," he said.

They were at the edge of the river. A stand of pines came down to it from the skirts of the bordering hills. The icy beach was strewn with irregular flat-topped rocks the size of hassocks, of settees, of small automobiles. He let himself down on one amid the trees, sighing, and let the pack and rifle slide into the snow. The dog curled up at his feet, rolling her eyes toward the creek.

Halvorsen sat on the rock, feeling the slow movement of his blood and the shallow fluttering of his heart. He tipped his head back and rolled it against stiffened muscles. He put his hands to his hips and stretched and heard his spine pop.

He felt tired and old and hungry, and he was afraid he could not go on much longer. Head tilted back, he gazed up through the interlaced branches of the evergreens. Absently he noted the five long needles in each cluster. Bluish-green. White pine, he thought.

He sat up suddenly and reached into his pack.

The ax was still sharp enough to peel the scaly outer bark off in curling strips. Under it the inner layer was white, slightly glossy, redolent. Halvorsen scraped off a handful and applied it to his mouth. It was sweet but hard to chew. He knew it was better if you boiled it but he did not feel like building a fire here. After the first handful the taste got to him and the stuff stuck in his throat, but he knew he needed it. When he had eaten all he could force down, he tilted his head forward again and sighed. His eyes turned toward the river, drawn by the dark rippling of the unfrozen ribbon in its center. After the pine he wanted water, but he was too exhausted to get up and get it.

In a minute, he told himself. He raised his head and looked around.

He knew this river well, and knew well this unpeopled valley, set between high-forested ridges.

He knew the Kinningmahontawany from decades past, from generations ago. In a way he had grown up here, had passed from child to man in these fastnesses, once peopled, or at least worked, by womanless hard-driven men, foreign-tongued and hard-muscled.

His hand dropped to caress the dog's head.

In the autumn of one of those faraway yet crystalline years—1926? 1928?—he had left the farm for the first time and spent the fall and the winter in these woods, trapping.

He let his eyes sag closed, and that simply saw a September afternoon, lit with the quiet light of over half a century gone. The farmhouse yard. His father, deliberate-moving, almost dumb in English, but voluble in the deep, rich language of the old country. And there before him, its owner leaning on the running board, the strange black vehicle in which Mr. Amos McKittrack traveled was drawn up steaming by the pump.

Halvorsen remembered McKittrack as a small, stocky fellow, heavily bearded, the white snowfall under his chin curled and tobacco-streaked as if his lips were rusting. He wore clean, faded work clothes. McKittrack was profanely courteous to his father, near wordless in front of his mother, and a little sharp to the awestruck boy. He was a trapper; had been pulling fisher and marten, skunk, fox, beaver, bear, and wildcat out of the depths of the Pennsylvania woods for fifty-some years. Now, he told Halvorsen's dad, he was getting along a little; could maybe use some winter help with his lines.

And then both men turned and looked at the boy, who whooped with delight at the prospect of exchanging farm chores for a spell of trapping along the Kinningmahontawany.

They'd driven south along the rutted-up logging roads, while McKittrack inveighed with poetic blasphemy against the Campbells' clear-cutting. Halvorsen remembered his awe at seeing miles of hills stripped naked, ruined and pitiful under the autumn sun, their sides scarred with snaking skids and the slanted slashes of the Shay engines' right-of-way. McKittrack told him that what he was seeing was the final ruin of the land; that where the massive hemlocks fell no tree might ever grow again, and for certain none as beautiful, as darkly and broodingly majestic.

The boy had nodded, listening; and the old man, now, nodded to himself again; the old trapper had been right.

They'd left the Model T at a crossroads store east of a jackleg sawmill at the bottom of Hog Hollow. For four days man and boy pressed south along Blue Creek to the river. McKittrack had a small cabin there, built on a meadow overlooking a bend of the Kinningmahontawany, and they sawed out the sweet-smelling hemlock logs to make it big enough for two.

Through that fall and all through the winter they trapped. The boy learned to lay Oneida Jumps and Victors and Newhouses, learned to boil them in the liquor the old man made from the hemlock boughs and walnut hulls to keep them from rust and take away the man-smell. He learned to nest and clog them so that an animal, once taken, could not maim itself and escape, nor work its way free. They had a line of two hundred traps, checking them in a crude skiff McKittrack dragged out from its hiding place in a bog. The old man showed him how to build log deadfalls, cheaper than steel traps and easier than carrying them, and they stretched and dried mink and fox and fisher and marten. In the winter evenings the old man would lounge by the cabin fire and the boy would lie and listen to stories of panther and bear, of the days when all the northwest of Pennsylvania was primeval forest, when the first trappers to penetrate the country had woken at their campfires to see looking down at them the quiet, remote faces of Indians.

Halvorsen, sitting on the freezing rock with the taste of pine still on the back of his tongue, could almost smell the savory stew the old man made from rabbits they trapped. He saw the way the hemlocks, long gone now except in the deepest, most remote valleys of the Wild Area, made the woods shadowy and awesome like the sun-pierced nave of a great church. He remembered the vigor of youth, the way McKittrack laughed sadly at him as he ran up the hillsides in sheer boyish energy, leaving the white-bearded trapper laboring behind.

And now he could barely keep on himself.

He shook his head angrily, coming back from memory. He was damned lucky, he told himself. He could still walk, get around, do for himself. Look at McKee, hands crippled, confined to his old-folks hotel. Or at Charley Prouper, emaciated, almost blind with sheer age, with his ruined lungs and weird pipy voice.

Or worse yet, and he felt fear to think of it, at Judge Wiesel, senile and paralyzed though he was only a year or two over sixty. He had no wish to end like that, incontinent and whimpering. If I don't come through this, he told himself silently, at least I won't come to that. So it's not all bad. Is it. He looked down at the dog.

"Let's go, Jessie," he said.

He moved slowly along the river. The track was hours old but still plain. The man he followed was not all that far ahead. Perhaps the cold, the hunger, were getting to him too.

He wondered about the man he had tracked so far.

He was the one who had asked him about the Michelson accident. Large man, bearded, well dressed, though since then he had changed to hunting clothes. So in that sense Halvorsen knew who he was; he had talked to him, could pick him out of a crowd. But who was he? What was his reason for murdering men in the woods?

Some sort of revenge? Yet that made no sense. You took revenge on one man. Yet five had died. Five that he knew about. There might be more, lying stiff and silent in overlooked snarls of brush, under the snow.

Could he simply be killing hunters at random? That didn't make much sense. There's no reason in that, Halvorsen told himself, plodding along.

Of course he could be nuts, the old man thought. But he didn't act crazy. Halvorsen thought of madmen as lunatics, people who saw visions or identified themselves as Napoleon. But the man he tracked, though no woodsman, was strong, clever, determined, capable of learning and even of laying traps.

Such as the one the day before, at Trestle Crossing. He set it up real good, Halvorsen thought. Only one thing saved me. Moving head up, senses alert since that first ambush at the copse, he'd seen three does coming down the north face of Britten Hill. Trotting rapidly, not frightened, just moving out of an area a possible enemy —such as a man—was entering. It wasn't a certain sign, but it alerted him, and he commanded Jess to stay and swung wide of the creek to the east and went up the slope of South Meade to where it overlooked the falls.

From there he'd seen the other, lying on the lip of the hill opposite. The orange of his coat stood out like fire. It was too late by then to do as he should have done at first, gone right on up to the crest, but he tried nonetheless to gain a position overlooking him.

But the other had seen him, inferred what he meant to do, and backed off, moving fast down over the hill. Halvorsen had watched him go, almost at a run, envying his strength and youth.

He himself had crossed the creek farther down at a ford he knew. He'd gotten his boots wet, but he waterproofed them every autumn and his socks were not even dampened.

Young and strong as the other was, and he had kept up a fast pace south along the river for all of yesterday and much of this morning, he seemed to be tiring. The old man knew the signs of wounding or fatigue in an animal's trail, and he saw them now in these footprints. In the beginning they had followed a straight line, moving over rather than around hills and ravines. Now they tended to follow the terrain, letting the land dictate to them, avoiding climbs and succumbing to downhills. The once regular tracks of a strong man were taking on the peculiar fumbling slide of otter tracks; and sometimes he could see a long groove in the snow, like a muskrat's tail in mud, which he figured to be the dragging butt of the rifle. The man he followed was weakening—whether from hunger, or fatigue, or the long-delayed effects of a wound, the old man had no way of knowing.

Whatever it is, thought Halvorsen, he's still stronger than I am.

After a long time the bitch whined softly behind him. He turned to see her squat by a bush, staling a smoking dribble into the snow. He waited patiently till the dog was done, then looked up at the sky. The sun was nowhere in evidence. The gray-dead ceiling of cloud told him nothing of time, and he cut no shadow from the diffuse light. Yet it must be midafternoon. The dog came up and stood by his leg, pressing against him, shivering.

"You hungry, babe?" he asked her.

As the hound tossed back her strip of the pink and white meat, Halvorsen squatted silently and chewed at the last one. All he could taste was the salt. The fat revolted him, but he made himself swallow it. In cold weather there was nothing like grease to keep you warm.

A smudge of white moved across the snow on the opposite bank. The dog finished the bacon and looked toward it. Halvorsen remembered the way McKittrack made spring pole snares for them, small saplings bent with a loop of fish line for the noose, and a bit of apple

for bait. He might do that, and . . . but no. He could not
stop, and he would not be back this way, whatever
happened . . .

He woke with a guilty start. The sky looked the same;
only a little darker. He got up immediately, angry at
himself. No matter how old he was, damn it, he had to
stay with a hot trail. If the man he tracked got away,
others would die—perhaps many others. He would stay
on the trail, or he was no woodsman worthy of the name.

He prodded the sleeping bitch with his boot, stood up;
and almost fell as dizziness struck him. He had to sit
down again and close his eyes for a few minutes before
he could pick up the pack and rifle and move out once
more.

A mile farther on he found several spent cartridge
cases scattered in the snow. He cast around, but found
only laurel bushes, the snow around them thick with
stippled ribbons of rabbit tracks. He moved on.

Several times during that long afternoon the dizziness
came again. When it did he would stagger to the verge of
the river, drop to his knees on the ice, and dip up a
handful of water to rub into his wooden face. Its chill set
him blinking and coughing, and after a few minutes he
would force himself to his feet once more and go on.

Once he found the imprint of a body. A man had
fallen full length on the snow, arms outstretched. Like
the snow angels children made, lying on their backs and
moving their arms up and down, leaving the reliefs of
seraphim on their lawns. This print was fresh, its edges
undisturbed by the wind; but the man who made it was
not in sight.

Still, the old man felt that he was getting closer. He
made himself move more cautiously. He trailed now
from the edge of the forest that flanked the creek,
slipping from tree to tree and freezing sometimes to

search the riverbank ahead, looking for motion or color or the outline of a man.

At one point he paused for a long time. A jagged yet oddly regular mass shadowed a bend ahead, where the river dropped several feet. He squinted at it for a long time before he remembered. It was the old Goldman mill, a two-story lumber building with piers of mortared river stone to take the axle of the big wheel. He had never seen it in operation, he was not *that* old, but he remembered exploring its crumbling interior while fishing on the river the fall they laid the gas line. Once it must have been big business, but that had been over a hundred years before. Racks waited, watching it expectantly, but he saw no motion and after a time he stepped out from cover and walked up the creek toward it, the dog following at his heels with slight hungry whimpers.

"Shut up, Jess," he said absently.

The old mill would be a good place to spend the night. Shelter from the wind, and from the heavy snow that the clouds were readying themselves to loose.

Just in time, he realized the other would think so too.

The tracks were indeed headed that way. Although he could not see far ahead along the trail, for the land rose a little and then dipped before the mill, he felt sure that a building, even a ruined one, would appeal to a town man after four days in the open. He crouched a little behind the rise of the land and turned uphill, moving obliquely away from the murmur of the river.

In half an hour his circle was almost complete. He was behind and inland of the mill. He had moved within the cover of the woods the whole way, and took advantage of a hill once too, though he was too tired to climb it to its crest.

Now he crouched again at the edge of the forest, a hundred yards from the shadow of the mill. As he did so a coldness touched his neck, and he looked up.

It had begun to snow again. Heavily, this time, as if above the clouds dumptrucks of the stuff were being upended. It was suddenly hard to see. But that's good, he told himself. It'll give me some protection crossing this field. He tightened the straps of his pack and unslung his rifle. He took a deep breath, feeling snowflakes transient on the warmth of his tongue, and stepped out from under the trees.

It was no dash. He was far beyond even the impulse to run. Instead he slogged forward, maybe a little faster than he had slogged through the woods. Beside him the dog whined suddenly. "Hush up, Jessie," he said to her, keeping his voice low, though in the cushioned air it seemed impossible for a word to travel more than a dozen yards.

Nothing happened. He saw nothing, no movement, and though he expected each moment the crack of a shot, none came. He fetched up against the weathered stone foundation, near its northeastern corner. He leaned against it to catch his breath, looking up at the age-darkened walls of the abandoned building.

It was just as he remembered it from years back. Goldman, whoever he was, had built well; the foundations, ten feet high, were still strong, though time and freezing water had burst the gray mortar from between the river-smoothed rocks. Above the foundation much of the timber structure still stood. Leaning back, Halvorsen could see that this side was largely open to the weather, with only a few cracked boards still clinging to the adze-hewn beams that held up the roof. The other three walls were almost intact, pierced only by the empty sockets of windows a century innocent of glass. Much of the roof was whole, if leaky. The main flooring was still in place, although, as he recalled it, in a bad state; in places only a rusty hand-forged nail kept whole sections from plunging down into the capacious and gloomy basement.

Holding the Springfield, the old man slipped around the corner. At the back entrance a flight of snow-covered stone steps led up to the main floor. There were no footmarks on the steps. But then, the old man thought, if he'd come down the river side he'd of gone in the main entrance, up front. He paused, and then went up the stairs. He went slowly, waiting after each step for some sound from the building's interior. Behind him the bitch panted loudly. He shushed her with his hand and the hound, trained to that movement, fell silent.

The door at the top of the steps was long gone. Halvorsen stepped up to its empty frame and stopped, letting his eyes adjust to the gloom.

Inside the hundred-foot length of the old mill the main floor was littered with slowly rusting iron. Boilers, tanks, the massive pyramid-toothed cogs the vanished wheel had once driven. They lay along either wall, laid there long ago for shipment; but they had never gone. It had never been economic to cart their flaking tons miles overland or upriver, without road or rails, to be melted for scrap. So here they sat, still waiting, rusting with the sad patience of old things. Faint light and a few flakes of snow filtered down through the holed roof. The air lay quiet in the aisle of the dead machines.

Down it, at the far end of the mill, he saw the man.

He was sitting near the main door, half-concealed behind a stack of iron beams. His back was to Halvorsen. His right hand lay upon the rifle, which had been laid beside him on the sagging floor. He did not move for the full minute during which the old man watched him from outside the door.

He's watching the river, the old man thought.

Another trap, but a poor one. Again Halvorsen wondered if the other was wounded, or sick. Certainly a
young man like this should have been able to outwalk
him. He was Racks Halvorsen, true; but he was also very
old.

Perhaps, he thought, I can finish this up right now.

With infinite care he extended his boot through the
empty jamb and onto the ancient flooring. This section
looked sound, but sight was an inadequate test. Ounce
by ounce he increased the pressure on his extended foot.
Only a slight rasping sound, not even a squeak, came up
from the boards. He put his full weight on the leg and
stepped inside.

It was very dark.

Not waiting for his eyes to further accommodate
themselves—the other man could turn around at any
moment—he began to slide forward, keeping weight on
both feet. Maybe I won't have to shoot him, he thought.
If I can get close enough, I can call out. Keep him from
reaching for it. Yes. And then . . .

Holding his rifle ready, he was moving slowly toward
the other man's immobile back, eighty, seventy, sixty
feet away, when Halvorsen recollected that his Springfield was not loaded.

He felt terror, and rage. He had crept all through the
circle, had crossed the field, and waited for breath; had
listened and planned; yet never once had he thought of
loading. Motionless, hardly daring to breathe in the utter
stillness, he cursed his old man's memory.

Damn you, Halvorsen, he thought. Less than fifty feet,
an easy stone's throw, separated them inside the ruined
building. The slightest sound would turn his quarry's

head. He couldn't bluff with an empty rifle. If the bluff failed—and he had no way of predicting what this man might do—he would be dead.

Silently, moving by millimeters, he tipped the rifle barrel upward and slid the bolt open. Sweating, he lowered his arm, very carefully, lest the cloth of his sleeve sing against his side. With infinite care and deliberation he lowered his fingers into his trouser pocket.

There was no cartridge there.

Halvorsen felt his ears move in horror. He thought quickly: did I put it in the coat? No. He never put loose cartridges there because on the trail they might clink and in his trousers the thick wool coat over them muffled any sound.

So that the single round, last of the three he had hurriedly loaded, was not in his coat. The other trousers pocket? No, he remembered clearly, his pocketknife was there. The lost cartridge could only be in this pocket. He pushed his hand in deeper, to the very depth and corner of it, and felt one gloved finger slip through a hole.

Oh, no, said the old man to himself.

He stared still at the immobile silhouette. He had not taken his eyes off him since he had come through the door and in all that time the man had not moved at all. Halvorsen reckoned the chances of his moving backward and then out of the mill, down the steps, back to the woods, all without making a sound. They were not good. The unreliable flooring might creak. It was still as death in the dark hall. He imagined he could hear the air sighing through the crystalline branches of the single snowflakes that came down from the light-speckled dimness of the high-pitched roof. The chuckle of the river around the ruined piers outside was almost loud.

Unnoticed, as he groped in his pocket, the muzzle of the old rifle had drifted downward. Now, as he still hesitated, it passed a downward angle of eighty degrees, pointing at the warped timbers of the floor.

The opened bolt began to slide forward.

He saw it begin to move, and made as if to grab for it, but his left hand was still deep in the pocket; and he tried with the other to bring the muzzle back up, but it was too late. He could see that it was too late. He closed his eyes. The sliding bolt met the edge of the chamber with a tiny, tiny, just audible but terribly definite *click*.

The man looked around at the sound. For the length of a second his eyes locked with the old man's. Halvorsen, rooted to the spot, was so close that he could see his pupils widen.

"You," said the man.

As he spoke Halvorsen saw the eyes flicker down from his face to the weapon he carried; and suddenly the hand was moving, the other man turning, lifting the great dark length of the automatic rifle; and Halvorsen, still frozen as completely and immovably as the rusting masses of iron on either side, saw it climbing up to find him, wavering as it climbed, and the man's hand reaching forward for the trigger; and he knew that this was the last image he would ever see, knew that the last breath he would ever take was even then in his lungs.

There was the quick scrabble of something across the warped floor behind him then; and something tan and black moved between the two men, across the fifty feet of sagging, splitting wooden floor.

Jezebel slipped once, rolled, yapping, but was up again and into a growling leap when the rifle began to fire. The bullets twisted the dog in midair, passing through her to claw and smash at the plank walls, sending showers of splinters and blue smoke and sound into the still air. There was a sodden thump then, and the old dog jerked at the man's feet and then relaxed.

Halvorsen turned and ran for the backdoor.

Though he waited for it there was no firing behind him as he ran slipping down the steps. He missed the last two. His feet turned on the icy stone and he fell. He lay on the snow, full of the agonized emptiness that comes with having the wind knocked out of you.

Then at last he did hear a sound, and he looked upward.

The hunter stood at the open wall, looking down at him calmly. The old man looked back. He was unable to breathe, unable to speak, even to ask for his life. He made a weakly rejecting motion with his hand, half-imploring, half-defiant.

The man above him raised his gun, took a step backward to aim better around the wall, and disappeared. Halvorsen stared. He had simply vanished, like a magic-show illusion. A moment later a terrific crashing clatter sounded from within the stone foundations of the basement.

Gasping, the old man got a little of his breath back. When he found that he could move his legs he got to his feet and began to stagger toward the woods, whooping for breath. Behind him he heard a second crash. His legs moved faster. He was halfway across the field. The snow, falling ever more heavily, had already almost covered the two sets of tracks that crossed it; one set, a man's; the other, the narrow, belly-dragging trail of a weary dog. He sobbed into the slow wind of his passage. Snow curtained the edges of his sight.

At last, after a time that might have been measured in years, he reached the edge of the woods. The oaken trunks were like castings of gray iron. He went on between them until he could stagger no more and fell crumpled into the snow, fingers curling into it like claws. Air tore at his throat. His heart hesitated, fluttered, like a strange live thing struggling inside his chest. He was safe from the gun, but he knew himself still to be on the edge of death.

At last, after several minutes, his strained heart gained a little and after a final, terrifying triple throb settled into something close to a normal beat. He lay face downward for a time after that, feeling his life as a fragile wire run through the middle of his chest.

At last he sat up and looked around.

Behind him the squared hulk of the old mill was invisible in the white pall. He got up slowly, finding that his pack was still on his back and the rifle still in his hands. He had to hammer at his fingers with his closed fist to relax them from the stock. He looked back toward the mill. Nothing showed.

He turned then and began walking away from the creek, going back farther into the woods, at first along the trail by which he had come in. At one place he stopped. Near the side of his footprints, shielded from the falling snow by the lee of an elm, was a yellow deep-melted place where the dog had staled. Halvorsen looked at it, and then walked on.

An hour later, just at the falling of the dark, he looked back from the crest of a low hill. Far back along his trail, vaguely draped and then revealed by the shifting veils of the storm, he could make out at times a tiny black figure. It limped. It moved slowly. Yet surely and unswervingly it followed the line of dragging footprints that the old man saw with sudden terror ended at his own trembling legs.

SEVENTEEN

Thursday, December Fourth

HE DID NOT THINK THE LEG WAS BROKEN, THOUGH IT HURT, making his mouth tighten with each limping step. It was the knee. He remembered hearing something inside his head, hearing it tear, even in the midst of the crash.

Michelson bent forward into the snow, into the press of wind, and glared up the long hillside for the retreating form of the old man. Halvorsen was exhausted. Michelson could see that in the way the dot of black ahead wavered from side to side as it slowly climbed.

He remembered the old man's face.

Sitting in the door of the mill, watching the river, he had been almost asleep. Sleep came too easily; even now, lurching forward through knee-deep drift, he was not entirely sure he was awake. Almost asleep; but awake enough to hear from behind him, from the rear of the mill, the tiny sound of the old man working his rifle. He had turned, and they had looked full into each other's eyes.

He remembered the fanaticism in Halvorsen's face. The look of narrow, alert, focused hate. The way the old man faced him, unmoving, with those eyes with nothing human in them, and had started to raise his gun. And then the dog.

Michelson felt bad about the dog.

He'd gone up to see about it later. After lying dazed for a time in the wreck of the flooring, tangled and half-covered in shattered musty-smelling boards, he had pieced himself together and hobbled back up to the main floor, avoiding the ten-foot gap where it had given way under him. The knee felt loose, wrong, but it hadn't hurt then. Aside from that he had a few cuts, a nail scrape on his face, and the wound in his side had opened again, making his shirt smooth with blood. He was still shaken from the fall, the feeling of dropping into nothing, waiting to hit; the old anthropoid terror of the drop. He was still angry at having the final and satisfying end of the long chase at hand, and losing it by blind chance.

His terror and rage had ebbed as he bent over the heap of fur. The dog's eyes were open and glassy. Dead. He touched the harsh snow-granuled hair of its head. Close up he could see tiny things milling at the edges of the open eyes. As his hand approached they spanged off into the cold, into death.

It was a plain, old, mixed-breed hound, the one that had poked its nose curiously into his crotch that first day in Raymondsville. He smoothed its back gently. The flesh was already chill. He felt tears burn and cleared his throat, looking away from it. I didn't have time to think, he told himself. Looking at it now, huddled, old, incredibly small, it seemed impossible that it had ever looked menacing. Yet for a moment it had, scrabbling toward him across the dark boards, yellow teeth unsheathed of black gum, its growl and fierce eyes menacing his throat.

In some ways, Michelson thought, holding his hand still on the dog's head, even the commonest, most worn, most shabby animal is better than most people.

Sitting there, his hand slowly scratching the cooling

fur, he had realized that the old man was his to dispose of.

Halvorsen had stood there behind him for who knew how long; and he had not fired. A man like that wouldn't have waited. And again, Michelson thought, even after I saw him, the dog gave him another chance. And still he didn't shoot.

There was only one possible conclusion: he hadn't because he couldn't. No question of moral inhibition; the man was an old hunter. No. Either his rifle was broken or he had no ammunition. Michelson recalled that during the whole pursuit the old man had only fired two shots: one at the car, and one at the copse.

So that was the most likely explanation: he was out of ammunition.

Then why, he asked himself, stroking the dead hound, had Halvorsen trailed him so far? Why had he entered the mill at all? That was a puzzle. Perhaps he'd hoped to club him. Or use a knife. To think of doing it like that took courage. But that the old man had. Courage and cunning and endurance; the way he stuck to a trail proved that.

But now he was helpless, and they both knew it. So now, Michelson thought, dragging his numbed feet, his throbbing leg forward through the snow, returning again to the single immediate present, now I again am the hunter; and he, the hunted. And soon the old man would be held accountable for tracking him all these days and nights, and for forcing him into this fastness, and for the hunger, and for the cold, and for the blood.

Paul Michelson brushed snow from his eyelids and beard and limped forward. It must have dropped four inches today alone, he thought. We've got two, two and a half feet here easy. And it's still coming down.

About him the snow dropped heavily, steadily, borne down on a cold ten-mile-an-hour wind. His legs plunged deep into drifts at each step. Around him the trees opened out to either side. Between them drifted spots of brightness that slid away when he tried to focus on them. His watch said ten A.M., though the hour seemed too early, or too late, as if only a filtered and vitiated daylight could reach this land.

Today was the day after the incident at the mill. The night before he had sheltered between massive black rocks, lighting a fire with his last flare. Greedy for warmth, he'd built it high and taken off his coat and stretched and sunned himself before the snapping white-hot blaze. But later, when he woke, the fire was only dull coals, and the rest of the night passed in the familiarly miserable way of the last three. Perhaps he was a little warmer. His side was tender; he wondered if the warmth was fever. If so maybe it was not a bad thing. But certainly it meant that he could not go on much longer like this.

With luck, though, this would be the last day.

The knee was a greater handicap than the side. On wakening that morning he'd cried out. In the night his leg had swollen, stiffened, until now the joint was a puffy mass of inflamed tissue; he could hardly bend it. He walked all the first hour with a scream locked behind his teeth. He kept falling, and each time it felt better to lie and rest in the soft, soft snow. At last he broke a Y-shaped crutch from a tree, and essayed hobbling with this. It helped, but the irregular motion set the binoculars thudding on his tender side. He ditched them by the trail. Another pound less to carry.

And now he moved slowly, painfully, burning with a kind of dull beastlike hatred, through the snow. The rifle crouched on his back like a heavy animal. He was hungry and his feet were numb and dead inside his boots, which he had not taken off for days. He was afraid to take them off now, afraid of what he might find. His side was a constant ache and the knee was agony at each swing of the makeshift crutch and his head seemed light, seemed to want to drift off between the trees somewhere and leave the rest of him behind.

And the snow whirled steadily down.

Near noon he caught a glimpse of the old man. They had made perhaps two miles since dawn and he could see that, slow as he was, he was catching up. The uphill hurt. It was torture to lift his weight with an injured joint. He felt that he could do better on a downhill, when they came to one, or even on a level, where he could find some sort of rhythm.

But, he thought, this deep snow would make it hard even then.

As he thought this a movement caught his eye amid the trees to his left and he glanced up. Some large animal stood there. He was unslinging the rifle, staring at it and thinking already of hot red meat, when he blinked and realized he had never seen it. There had been nothing there.

For a moment he wondered: am I going mad?

No; it was only fatigue. Fatigue and sleeplessness and hunger and cold, and a touch of fever. He told himself this several times and at last felt that he believed it.

He hitched the rifle, his Sisyphean burden, back to his shoulder and went on again, limping slowly in the wandering track the old man had left. The breath of the falling snow filled his mouth and nose. From time to time he rubbed his cheeks. They seemed to be joining his feet and hands in dying numbness, in the slow secession of the extremities. Not without pain, not without reluctance did the blood retreat. But slowly, steadily, he could feel the cold gaining dominion in him. Terror and apathy gradually occupied his mind during the long waning of the morning. At times he saw things. At times he slid waking into a dream; and only because the dream was without pain did he know it was not reality.

And with each retreat he grew less willing to return to reality, to the frozen silence of the woods.

He knew what was happening and he tried to resist. He felt that it was not his body that was failing but his will. Enraged, he beat at his leg with the crutch, struck himself in the face and then in the side; laughed aloud. He stood still and stared around at the trees, the clouds, and above them, barely visible through the snow (though he could feel them looking down on him), the ever-present, all-dominating hills.

He did not belong here.

Even as he thought it he smiled at the banality of the thought.

For that was the true horror of it; there was nowhere you belonged, nowhere you could go. No one who cared for you. Not your parents, who cared for what you were once, a small dependent evocation of their instincts. Not your lovers, who cared for an illusion they wove from their own desires, who would recoil with disgust if they realized what you really wanted and who you really were. And certainly not any god, who, if he existed, had made this loneliness, this horror.

No; the only hope was man; his perfectibility, the slow, staggering steps of progress, of human redemption. And in its name he was on the trail of those who embodied evil, that they might be overcome and destroyed.

Paul Michelson realized that he was approaching the edges of insanity.

The trouble was that, unlike most men, he knew that such a state did not exist.

He forced himself to think logically, as if he were back before his class. "'Sanity' is a cultural construct," he mumbled through his ice-caked beard. "It is determined by the degree of acculturation of an individual to a set of communal norms."

He plodded on for a few more steps. It *did* make you feel better. "Storie and McOwen, *The Social Construction of Reality*," he mumbled. The work he assigned to advanced students. The terms, beautiful, stark; shared reality, typification, institutionalization, legitimation, deviance; nihilation. A wonderful yet fragile bridge between the tumbling chaos of mass man and the crystalline abstractions of science.

But even by the norms of my own culture, he thought, plodding along, my behavior is reasonable, logical, and oriented toward a socially acceptable goal; of what more does sanity consist?

Of course he had committed illegalities; yes, crimes. But even folk mores in America sanctioned individual action where authority failed or was corrupt. That was what he had done: acted on a moral premise, with a clearly defined end. His methods might be called unsound. But they were clearly within the zone of sane behavior pertaining in the late twentieth century. No one considered terrorists mad any longer. A certain societal disapproval was mandated, as toward those who violated the norms of grooming; but they were not considered insane, and a certain admiration of their simple and deadly logic was not out of place. Given the widely agreed-upon desirability of a goal, its opponents naturally became historical remnants, and their liquidation was regrettable but no more than that. All progress came that way; vide the manifold revolutionaries of a whole century of human advancement.

No, he thought. I am right. He had been right all along, since that half accident in the forest; and he was not mad, save as his body's dearth of strength was distancing him from reality. He was right; and by this conviction Paul Michelson was warmed as by a flame.

He plodded on, wondering dully from time to time what the old man in front of him was thinking.

After the mill incident a part of him wanted to go on, all through the night, blundering against unseen trees and in danger always of a ravine or sudden drop. Yet although he wanted to he could not. Overtaxed, aged, driven to the edge of exhaustion and beyond, his body could not do it. The energy was just not there. And without that all his will and all his fear could at last drive him no farther and he had dropped to the snow in the dark and for a time simply forgotten to be.

Later, half-frozen, the old man awoke, and moved clumsily about the business of building a fire. His hands would no longer grip the matches and he recalled a story he had read long ago and how it had ended; and so he kept on doggedly until the red-tipped kitchen matches flared at last and the tender dry twigs from the pine trunks caught and the fire flickered and grew through the dead limbs he hacked from surrounding trees. He didn't bother to shield it. He knew that the man who followed him might see, but he didn't care anymore. In some ways he would have welcomed a quick end, like the dog's. In the falling snow, visible as glowing trails above the fire, he struggled into the down bag and lay staring into the flaming heart of the coals.

Then, paradoxically, he could not sleep.

He, the one who hunted, was now the quarry. He had never experienced such a reversal before. Unarmed—by now, with a little thought, the other must understand that—he had no chance to prevail. His only weapons now were his pocketknife and the camp ax, though from the sheer inertia of age he still carried his brother's old rifle.

Halvorsen tried to imagine attacking the other with the ax. But he couldn't. It wasn't that he was afraid to. It was as good an attitude as any to die in (not better; only as good), but he could not picture himself doing it because it was unworthy of him. It meant that he, Racks Halvorsen, had so bungled a pursuit that nothing but his own suicide could end it and probably even that could not retrieve it.

The worst part of it, he thought, is that that's exactly the way it happened.

For he plainly remembered now the fact that he had a hole in that pocket. He'd even complained about it to Alma, and then twice, on successive weeks, refused to take the trousers off so she could fix it. Nor had he sewn it up himself, though like most of the men who spent their winters on leases or in logging camps he could handle needle and thread.

No. He had known. But without thinking he'd dumped cartridges into that very pocket and gone off marching and stalking for days without once taking the time to think. Oh, yes, he thought, I did a lot of thinking. I thought about the old days, about my dad and Prouper and McKittrack. But I didn't *think*.

Well, it was past worrying about now. He had stopped once to run through the inseams and linings of the trousers, to check the cuffs and then the magazine of the rifle, though he knew the search was futile. The round lay somewhere back at Coal Run or Grafton Hollow or on some slope he had trudged so wearily across. It was gone.

So now all there was to do was keep going. Tomorrow and if God granted the next day too. Though he might not. Well, Halvorsen thought, I will leave it now to whatever makes things happen to make happen that which will happen anyway. And he would do his best, which was all he had ever claimed to be able to do.

And thinking that, the old man closed his eyes on the flames.

Some subconscious sense woke him much later. It was black dark and the snow was whiskering his face. The fire was out, and something was moving behind him.

Halvorsen came awake. He felt for the knife in his trousers and slowly, slowly, rolled over inside the bag to face the unseen thing that rustled in the darkness. For a time he stared wide-eyed into blackness like the belly of a mine. Out of it sighed the night wind, freighted still with snow; but aside from that all was quiet.

No. There was something there, and not far from him. He could feel its presence there, could (feel? imagine?) its breathing under the sigh of night. His nostrils moved, but though it was upwind of him he could smell nothing. He snapped the blade open and held it outside the bag and waited, staring sightlessly into the wind, shaken by the invisible beating of his heart.

After a long time brush crackled and he heard the pads of something heavy moving away.

When he awoke again it was still dark, but with a difference. It was not long before dawn. He felt the sharpness in his hand and folded the knife closed and got up quietly, lighting no fire, and packed up in silence and moved stiffly away into the woods, going uphill despite the dark, for he knew the land hereabouts.

Yes, he knew where he was. What he did not know was where he was going. There was nothing ahead of him to go toward. The roads and the towns were behind him. Yet to turn would be to head directly toward his pursuer. So he walked on. When he had gone about a quarter of a mile the hills began to show against the eastern sky and somewhat later the overcast began to lighten. He walked steadily on, very slowly, tasting the foulness in his mouth that came with no food, belching occasionally. He was getting thirsty too now that they had left the river behind (it was not good to eat snow; you lost too much body heat melting it). He kept looking back, but it was not until an hour after dawn, when he was at the top of the first hill of the day, that he saw his pursuer.

He was not far behind. Maybe a mile. Something looked wrong though. Halvorsen squinted back at the thing that jerked and hobbled along, dragging the slow scratch of its passing over the white smoothness. At last he saw. The other was using a crutch. Perhaps from the fall back at the mill. It was easy to break an ankle or sprain a knee in a fall like that, must have been eight, ten feet easy.

The sight encouraged him considerably.

He turned and hitched the useless rifle higher on his back and plodded up over the crest of the hill.

It was an hour or so later, when he was descending the other side, that he recognized the wide valley before him. Hardly even a valley; almost a continuation of the wide broad tops of the two hills, and beyond them, the long dark ridge of the tallest of the three, Selwyn's Hill. Yes. He remembered this land.

Presently, late in the morning, the snow resumed. It

hadn't ever really stopped; only slackened into a translucent gauze over the distance, a wash of white in the air. Now it came down hard, as hard as the day before, as hard as the old man remembered snow ever coming in all his life, and he had to lean forward into the rising wind. The heaviness of it surprised him. There had already been so much. Well, and hadn't he told Mase and Prouper and McKee at the Bear, and Alma too when she came up, that it would be one hell of a cold winter? The way the squirrels had busted their tails, and the way the fuzzy-bear caterpillars looked that fall . . . he remembered one winter now, back when Alma was little, just before the war . . .

The old man walked on down into the valley, staggering cautiously, wearily, vacantly, through the great white carpet of smoothed snow.

Sometime later, near the valley bottom, he paused by a gash in the whiteness. The snow ended sharply in a ten-foot-long patch of dark slate, shaped like a giant's footprint. The bare rock steamed slightly in the cold and a film of water dripped from rock to rock and collected at the heel in a pool the size and shape of a washbasin. The old man smiled and bent to this, falling on all fours to drop his face to the pool. The water was cold, with a slight mineral-oily tang; on its surface colors uncoiled slowly in brilliant snakes. He wiped his face after many swallows and sat up. He studied the tracks around the pool.

"Yes," he said aloud.

They were fair-sized tracks, approaching the pool from uphill. He leaned close above them, examining the edges for frost crystals and the fine piles of kicked-out snow. If there were any, they were already covered by the new fall, and by that alone he saw that the coyote had been here no more than a couple of hours before. Came down most likely for a morning drink. They were big prints. No monster, but respectable. Coyotes were new to the old man. Twenty years before they were as unknown in these woods as penguins. But now, he had heard, they were filtering in, in the endless ebb and change of nature, and he had heard a couple of them howling in the gray light of dawn once back of Lacey Knees Hill.

He hoped this one was finding enough to eat.

Halvorsen recollected himself and looked over his shoulder. The hill he had just come down was cloaked with a good growth of tamarack and behind their branches he could see no movement but a slight disquieting sway. He dipped his face again and drank all the water he could hold, his gums aching with its subterranean cold, and then got up and began walking again.

The valley was broad, long, and well set about with hemlock. Big hemlock. Halvorsen, pausing for rest beside one four-foot-diameter giant, thought this might almost have been virgin woods. It hardly seemed likely, recalling the naked hills of his boyhood. This whole half of the state had been shucked like an ear of corn in less than thirty years. Then the loggers moved on west. But this valley had been abandoned for a long time. The hemlocks might have come back. After the slashing, after the rabbit-teeming thickets of berry and thorn, had come thick stands of—

No, damn it; now he remembered. This *was* old growth timber. He recalled someone on the gas lease telling him about it. They'd cut the white pine out of here in ought-something and then for some reason never came back for the hemlock and the big hardwoods, red oak, maple, gum. Some dispute over who owned the land. Anyway it hadn't ever been cut and then in the twenties the state took all the Kinningmahontawany over for forest lands. And then it had been forgotten.

Dragging his way across the freezing waste, he remembered how this valley had looked in summer, thirty-five years before.

In summer it was a mass of hazy green, seen from the hills. Up close, under the whispering roof of millions of leaves of oak and cherry, basswood and ash, red maple and the deep-ocean blue of the great hemlocks, it was a sibilant and shadowed land. Between the trunks of the old evergreens spread a rustling carpet of fern, nodding over the black spring-dampened earth, so rooted thick a spade was useless to chop through it. In the stands of oak the ancient ferns gave way to mountain laurel, deep green and blue, purpling in fall with tiny redolent flowers.

And in and among the trees living things moved, numerous as the leaves. Mice, shrew, weasels, chipmunks; a hundred species of birds; ten thousand of insects. Silent at the first intervention of a visitor, the forest began gradually to buzz and chatter, click and trill and hum; and from time to time under your feet would come the rocketing flutter of grouse or the slow coil of watching rattler.

And it is all still here, thought Halvorsen, pushing his way slowly through the still blanket of cold that sealed for a time the green within its earth. It looks dead; like it's been dead for years. Yet the spiders were egged, the squirrels holed, woodchucks denned, wasps hived. Did each of them, he wondered, know that it was winter? Did each count the passing sunless days? Surely the deer and the rabbits did, and the deep-coated winter flesh-eaters. But what of the others? Did the new spider in its egg dimly count the days till green came, till leg-uncoiling?

Probably not, the old man thought. But somehow they knew it was coming. If winter lasted through a century's time they would still be found here waiting faithfully. Only the warm-blooded ones might not last; and even then, the old man thought, he would lay a couple bucks on the squirrels' coming through.

The old man crept on, like an ant, over the white undercurve of the valley, beneath the cold-stripped trees. And the course of his slow thoughts and remembrances turned slowly from past to present to green past again, more real, more vivid, than the desolation that surrounded him.

In a way, he thought, he was glad the coyote was out here with him. It made him feel less alone. It seemed like coyotes would be here for a while now.

Like the beaver. He could remember when a beaver, in this part of the east, was as foreign an animal as the coyote was now. Once plentiful, they'd been long gone even when McKittrack began trapping. Then about 1920 some game people brought a few back from the Midwest and now there were beavers again all over Hemlock County. And the bears. The bears had never really left; there had always been a few. But just in his lifetime they had come back to the point that it was no big thing now to see tracks out in his garden in the fall, up on Mortlock, or even to see them shambling around in late-summer daytime, when the blackberries hung sweet and ripe.

He remembered how McKittrack had once shown him how to trap bear. "Your wardens don't let you do this no more, Bill," the old man had said. "But I'll show you how anyway."

His foot slipped at that moment on a loose log or rock

under the snow and he fell. It did not hurt. His thin old body came gradually to rest. It felt so easy there that he rested for a few minutes, enjoying the effortlessness of surrender. But he could not surrender. He was Racks Halvorsen and he had never given up. He tottered to his feet again, tasting oil from the spring. He spat to one side and looked up at the snow-filled sky.

He looked back, and saw the man move slowly out from the trees on the hill behind. A little over a half mile back.

Not much farther to go.

He moved on up the valley, dragging his feet. He felt numb, resigned, like a leaf before the advent of winter; like an old tree as the flames licked about its roots. It was the cold, he thought, that was doing it to him. He didn't know how much longer he could go on.

He was Racks Halvorsen and he had never given up . . .

Through the long afternoon of that day the two men pushed on, apart, yet together; two warm things adrift in a vast cold, steadied only by their wills, plodding slowly through the descending soundlessness of the heaviest snowfall in thirty years. They moved west, away from the river, climbing gradually into a highland long deserted by the affairs of men. The Kinningmahontawany was never much frequented. Once or twice in a season a few parties of hunters would try its edges, but they drew back quickly, after a day or two of the silence, the remoteness.

And this was no normal season. Weather and a persistent rumor kept men from the deep woods that year, kept them close to the roads and the power lines, the comforts of heat and food and ready drink.

So in their slow progress the two men were alone as

they climbed the second of the two gently rising hills of the highland's edge. Beyond that was another, steeper one; and beyond it a hundred square miles of . . . nothing. Of the Wild Area. A hundred square miles of empty land, unpeopled, uncut, unsown, unmetaled; forest and hill; green in summer with a lush verdance, but in this season desolated and wrapped and laid to rest in an ever-thickening shroud of white and silence.

He came back to himself slowly, like the flood of a tide. He had been sitting in the faculty lounge, with Mac and Teresa, and dinner was recently over. They all held drinks. It was warm . . . he was wearing his old Harris tweed jacket, and he felt the liquor tickle his nose as he drank, and . . .

No. He was lying prone on a surprisingly soft bed. Only as he thought about it for a time did it occur to him that what he was lying in was snow. Only at his neck was it cold, slightly compacted with what melting heat was left in his blood.

Suddenly and with great force he sneezed. For the second time. It was the first one that had brought him out of the dream. This sneeze jerked his head out of the snow, and he rolled over slowly and sat up. An inch-thick layer of fresh flakes slid from his back. It was late afternoon by the dimming light, and ten by his watch. He stared at its bland face for several seconds before understanding that it had stopped. He unsnapped the band and dropped it. Four ounces less.

Michelson groped under the snow for his crutch, then for the rifle. As he staggered upright he braced for a wave of pain from the knee, but none came. He bent to probe. It was still swollen, but it hurt less. Perhaps, he thought fuzzily, the cold of the snow helped reduce the edema.

271

He looked around at the woods and groped for where he was.

In the course of the morning they'd come down off the first low hill. Creeping along, they had crossed another during the day, and then descended into a wide valley, drained by a frozen-over creeklet. There had been no sight or sound of man all the day long, save for the dragging tracks of the one he followed, on whom foot by foot he slowly gained.

Now, looking ahead, he saw that he stood at the foot of a third and steeper hill. Not as steep as those he'd climbed three or four days before. But steep enough, towering up against the gray sky in that peculiar plateaued formation so many of the hills hereabouts showed. Steep enough so that, facing it, something in him had failed for a little while, and pitched him unconscious face down before it.

Funny. He couldn't remember hitting the ground.

He looked next for the old man's trail, but couldn't see it. Where were they, the footsteps? Had he lost them? For a moment he wondered whether he might already have caught up with him, already fulfilled his execution. Then he saw the line of half-filled footsteps, a diagonal wavering before him up the face of the hill.

He moved a step forward, into the wind, and then, after a time, another.

And stopped. It was just too steep. He paused, baffled, and remembered why he'd fallen: his strength was unequal to the climb. He stared up at the hill, narrowing his eyes against the blowing snow. But *he* went up it. How had the old man managed *that* superhuman feat?

Slowly his mind understood, and he too turned and began climbing at a shallow diagonal across the face of the rise.

It was slow work. His knee began to throb again. The weight of the rifle oppressed him and he continually had to struggle with the impulse to drop it in the snow and go on without its twenty, no, nearer two hundred pounds.

That made him think though of what he could drop and he stopped and searched his pockets and found three full magazines. He had a full twenty rounds already in the rifle. That would be plenty. He could do without these. He left them in the snow and went on, feeling the difference, a couple of pounds, as if tons had dropped from him.

As he toiled onward up the hill it grew darker. He wondered what time it was. Five? Six? Dusk came early; the hills cut off the sun. Anyway it was not far off.

The snow drove heavily down the hill, whirling into his eyes and nose and mouth.

As the long afternoon drew toward its end he began to climb the next hill, the third one of the day, the tallest one. What was it? Selwyn's Hill, yes. He remembered a Selwyn, lived not far from Raymondsville, many years ago. Maybe the same family. Once, not far from here, there'd been a spur line, a narrow-gauge railroad. Gone now. What had that been for? Oh yes. The pits, or strippings, or whatever they were. He'd been there a few times. Holed up there in a shack one night even. There were lots of scattered, abandoned things back in these hills. Old lumber camps, abandoned mills like Goldman's, the crumbling foundations of power shacks or grain mills from way back. Or a still maybe. He remembered the time in thirty-one he helped Pete Riddick build a still with his uncle. Have to ask Pete, Halvorsen thought, what ever happened to that uncle of his.

Then he remembered: Peter Riddick had mishandled a well shoot once on the Oriskany Sands. And the nitro did not forgive.

The hill was rougher than he remembered it. A lot rougher. He had to zigzag up it. He did the last part of the slope in driving snow on his hands and knees, crawling like an animal. Like a dog, he thought dimly. He coughed. The oily taste seemed to stick in his throat. It was growing dark when he reached the top and looked up to find that it was only a bench. He had another slope to climb yet, maybe more. Hazily he visualized the pits beyond that, and the shed he'd sheltered in years before. He was moving across the lip of the bench in the blowing snow, staggering from tree to tree, when the oily taste stopped him against one of the giant trunks and he leaned there for long minutes, bent over, coughing into the snow. At last the fit passed and he leaned there exhausted, breathing harshly and listening to his heart.

He was thinking of going on again when beyond the roar of the wind he thought he heard a human voice. He lifted his head and listened.

When he heard the cough, some interminable number of steps later, Michelson stopped and listened, leaning on the crutch.

It came again, a minute or so later, carried down by the wind. The old man. He was that close. Standing still, Michelson peered into the driving snow. The flakes made him blink as they pierced his eyes with tiny points of intense cold. He was up there, not far above him at all.

Halvorsen, he said to himself.

"Halvorsen," he muttered.

"Halvorsen!"

* * *

Damn, the old man thought, leaning still weakly against the solid trunk. That sounds real. "What?" he croaked, not very loudly; but he felt the wind seize the single word and fling it away down the hill, into the white chaos that was the storm.

And the word carried to Michelson, faint out of the dimness above him. He couldn't tell, or even guess, how far above him the old man was.

"I'm gaining on you!" he shouted.

Silence, and the shriek of the snow. The old man must not have heard him. He took a step forward. His knee flamed. *"It won't be much longer,"* he screamed into the wind.

Halvorsen pondered. It must be the man behind him. No one else could be out here in the storm, on the deserted hillside, in the dying light. The coyote did not know his name.

Dimly, he realized that he was not thinking very well. "Who are you?" he called back, a bit louder than before.

Michelson heard only the last word. He stopped again—he had taken another step—and blindly searched the seething air.

"What?" he shouted back.

Halvorsen was startled. The other man could hear him, all right. He's damn close, the old man thought, his mind rising toward alertness from lassitude. Must be just under me, over the lip of the bench, couple of hundred feet down, no more. If it wasn't for this snow, I could probably see him.

"Why are you doing this?" he called.

This Michelson heard. *"To stop you!"* he screamed into the moaning wind.

The old man lost that. He could hear something, but couldn't make out the words. When it gusts, he thought, it blows his words away from me. He decided to try again.

"Why are you killing people?"

"To stop you." The words were clear for a moment. *"And I'm not killing just anyone. Only hunters."*

"Why?"

Again something indistinct. The old man clung to the tree, grimacing, then let himself cough for a long time. The wind seemed stronger, perhaps because he was trying to penetrate its howl. Trying to penetrate the other man's words; trying to penetrate to meaning, to the reason for this strange and lonely pursuit. The wind howled. "What?" shouted Halvorsen, hearing with terror the weakness in his own voice.

"My son. Aaron. They killed him."

And even as he screamed this with all his strength into the storm it suddenly occurred to Michelson that the old man could hear him perfectly; he was trying to wind him. He was trying to make him waste his strength by shouting into the storm. The cunning of the old. As he realized the trickery his rage flared up again behind all the fatigue, the confusion, and the pain.

"I'm going to kill you," he screamed.

The wind roared back at him.

When the old man did not reply Michelson bent his head into the press of snow and climbed a few steps straight up toward where the voice had been. The slope was just too great, so he angled back to the diagonal. I can't be more than a hundred feet away, he thought. If it wasn't for this snow I could see him. And all he needed was that one glimpse, just long enough to aim. Then it would be over; and then he could rest for a time, recoup his strength—maybe he could shoot an animal, get something to eat. Then east, to the road. It would be a long way, it would be rough, but he could hole up at the mill and rest for a while; and most important, he would be safe.

It won't be far now, he promised himself. Maybe I won't catch up tonight. It's getting dark too fast. But tomorrow will be the old man's last day.

Or, he thought with sudden, all-accepting insight, it will be mine.

And above him, the old man clung to the tree's solidity, his ice-rigid hands curled like logging hooks into the snow-seamed bark.

His son, he was thinking. The boy was his son.

He fought down another spell of coughing and forced himself to let go of the tree. The wind clawed at his clothes, scratched at his face, sang in the taut sling and moaned in the empty barrel of his rifle. He pushed off from the hemlock and staggered the width of the bench and began to climb step by panting step up the second slope of the hill.

It was almost dark; yet he could see more clearly than ever. Like a cloth torn aside by the wind, the black shroud of confusion that battered at his thoughts had been flayed into strips and whipped away, and now his mind felt slow and ponderous but totally clear. In that instant of seeing, of clarity, all that he had learned in all his life flicked like a sheet of white lightning across his empty mind. He was weak. Yet it was only his body that was weak. His mind was clear and his will was his own. He might not get where he was heading tonight. He might not succeed in what he even now only dimly planned. His body might defeat him. It had suffered much. Yet a defeat by the body—that was no shame.

The shame was in not trying.

Amazing Grace! How sweet the sound . . .

Halvorsen reached the top of the hill, and in the roar of the storm set his face toward the darkness ahead.

EIGHTEEN

IN ALL THAT DARKNESS THAT SURROUNDED HER, PROTECTED her, the only light was the flickering ruby. It guttered and flared before her tranced eyes, responding within its thick glass to currents she could not even feel.

Señor mio . . . me pesa de toda corazon haberos offendido y propongo firmamente nunca mas pecar. . . . Asi como os suplico, asi confio in vuestra divina bondad y misericordia infinita . . . al fin de mi vida. . . .

Her lips moving around words worn smooth as the rosaries of old women, she prayed into the votive flame.

When the priest came out she rose, crossed herself, and took a place far back in the church, hidden by a pillar. The ceremony began. Above her the stained windows were blank, dark as lead-veined walls; it had just turned from evening. The only light came from the altar, the single heartlike flame that meant the Host was present.

It's just like St. Martin's, she thought, twisting her hands in front of her.

It smelled the same: old wood, old incense, stone and brick and plaster damper, colder, but the same. The same age-varnished pews. The few other worshippers were old and wore dark dresses; no different from those in the neighborhood chapels of Hollenbeck or for that matter of Hidalgo del Parral or Cuauhtemoc except for their pallor; and from the back she could not make even that distinction. The whisperings drifting back through the shadowed nave were Italian and Slovak, not the Spanish of her girlhood, but still it was so much the same that she felt for a moment that she herself had not changed either, that she was once again ten years old, dressed all in white for her first communion, gathered with all the other Juanitas and Marias and Claras, nervous, fingering white missals and nosegays of white asters.

Dressed all in white. . . .

She had not expected this. Underneath, she supposed, she thought of all Anglos as Protestants. But there were Catholics here. Many, to judge from the size of St. Rocco's. They were not Mexican. But the smell and the sounds and the feel of the hard wood against her knees were so familiar that as the words droned on and the server lifted the bells to tinkle like breaking icicles, she nodded, lulled and forgetful and a little sleepy, as she had not been truly sleepy since *it* had happened.

"Go in peace," said the priest clearly, turning to face the nearly empty church. "The Mass is ended."

Teresa murmured the response in Spanish, standing up; and then sat again quickly, lowering her eyes as the women shuffled past, some helping others on walkers. As they moved by one seemed familiar. Her head was higher, her cheeks unpowdered and unmasked by age; with a start Teresa recognized Anne Oleksa. She lowered her face as the woman passed, waiting as the steps moved by and their echoes stilled in the dark air.

When she was alone she raised her eyes again to the lamp, glimmering above the deserted altar. No, not deserted. God is there, she thought. Paul would have smiled at that thought. Probably she no longer believed it either. But then, it was not as a matter of belief that she was here.

I just need to think, she told herself.

In the peacefulness she did not even want a cigarette. She was quiescent, at rest, as self-contained as the candle. She would have liked to stay there forever in the luminous darkness, unforced to act or decide. But she could not. I have to make a decision, she thought then, and the guilt and shame and fear crept back. I have to think about what is best and what I can do. I have to think about how I can save myself, and us.

Her bruises ached and she shifted uneasily on the hard wood.

Sweet had hurt her. There was no gentleness in him. He had wrenched what he needed out of her and his hands had left violet marks on her shoulders, the backs of her thighs, her throat. She had tried too late to scream and then been unable to, smothered and frightened of the fist and the knife; and even that had not been the end of it; he wanted things she had never given Paul, that he had never asked for. Remembering them now she clenched her hands in her lap and closed her eyes. He was frightening, violent, a man she had felt from the start was dangerous and whom she had not liked and whom she had not, never in the smallest way, invited or wanted.

When he left in the morning she had lain rigid and almost thoughtless for an hour, the way she had lain beside him all night; and then gotten up somehow, she still did not know how, and taken a shower that lasted till the water turned cold. She had huddled in her room all day, going out only once to the dining room to eat quickly.

For a time she had thought of reporting him. But by the time she finished the shower she knew she would not. Could not. He had told her what he would do to her if she did. That it would do no good, his word would hold in this town against that of any outsider. And she thought, standing under the shower, that it was done anyway, nothing anyone could do would make her feel clean again. Certainly not a trial. She had let him in. They would say it was her fault, that she had led him on. She had known a woman once who said she had been raped. The men laughed or murmured to her from the doorways of the barrio as she passed.

The room phone had rung twice, but she had stared at it and not reached out.

Please help me, she cried silently, squeezing her eyes against the dim light. Forgive me. For that was the worst thing, worse than all the anger and confusion and guilt for herself: the fact that she would never be clean again for Paul.

I do love him, she thought. I know that now, no matter what happens, no matter that it is too late.

For it was Paul they were looking for out there. In the past two days she had accepted that. Maybe knowing she was not immaculate made her able to understand that he might not be either. That night Sweet had told her that the state police had found his car in Grafton Hollow, broken in, and found ammunition matching that which had been used in the murders. Yet even if it were Paul she still loved him, she could forgive him; she knew how much he had missed Aaron, how shocked and distracted he had been. He'd been like a stranger in the lounge, just before he'd left school.

If only I could have reached him then, she thought, he might not have come back to this place. Or if I'd come with him, he would not have killed. For a moment she half smiled in the deserted church, thinking of what could have been. Then she never would have been alone with Sweet; never been forced to yield to that greed and lust, so corrosive of everything good it touched.

Sin. . . .

Hurriedly she crossed herself and got up. In the vestibule, feeling the cold radiating from the bare stone, she wrapped her coat more tightly around her legs and turned to look down the length of the church. The long convergent lines of the pews, the gradually diminishing polychrome vaultings overhead pointed the eye to that distant ruby flickering, alone yet central, lending by its steady pulse shape and meaning to the whole mass of darkness.

Only tonight, she promised and decided then. I will leave tomorrow morning. One last night for Paul. And if *he* came again . . . no, it could not happen a second time; she wouldn't let it. If she did she would lose everything. She felt that deeply now. She would lose it all. Paul—her self-respect—her soul.

For whether you believed or not, you could still lose your soul.

The outer door gave way to stone steps, salted free of snow, and she went down them carefully, for the last of twilight was yielding now to full night. She walked briskly toward the hotel. The streets were empty, most of the business-district windows dark though it was only a little after five, and her footsteps crunched in sibilant echoes from the walls she passed hurrying, head down.

Just tonight—till dawn—and then I can go, she repeated to herself. Despite the reassurance her eyes flicked up every few steps at imagined movements in the shadows. Back at school they'll be wondering where I am. They'll be mad. I don't have tenure yet.

Yes, that was what she had to do. She should have done it days ago. Sunday; then he, it, would not have happened at all and she would have a different life. Her coming here, what she had learned from the doctor and from Mary couldn't help Paul now anyway. He was beyond her help. All she could do was stay loyal to him.

The fear accompanied her like a stalking animal through all the night blocks to the hotel. She wasn't sure what it was she feared. Mrs. Oleksa, the television van, the hostile stares of strangers; but no one saw her, no one even passed on the sidewalk. The town seemed abandoned, sunk in night and time like the wreck of some once-palatial liner.

By eight she was asleep in her room, packed and with the alarm set for an early departure.

"Who is it?"

The knocking stopped; then began again, harder; the door actually vibrated within its jambs. She sat up in bed and then swung her bare feet to the chill floor, watching the wood tremble, too startled to be afraid. For a moment her only thought was that there must be a fire.

"Who is it?"

And still no one answered. She sat for ten seconds, her pulse shaking her body. Then she turned back the covers and went to the door. She hesitated, her hand on the knob; checked the chain, then turned the lock to free it.

The door slammed open, stopping with a jar at the end of five inches of painted chain.

"You," she whispered, but no sound came from her lips.

Bundled in a thick plaid coat Sweet leaned against the door. His forehead was pressed to it, his face shiny with sweat, his eyes closed. At her word he opened them and stared at her motionlessly and fixedly from the dark hallway. She could see the white around his irises.

"Hey, little Teresa. Ralpho here."

"Go away. I do not want to see you here."

"No, you wait, bitch." Against his weight, she had pressed the door an inch toward closing; with one hand he slammed it suddenly taut again against the chain. The chain's metal fixtures came partway out of the wood. "We're going to talk some, you and me."

"I don't want to. You can't come in here again."

"Changing your tune from the other night? Say, how come you don't answer your phone?"

"You hurt me. I did not want that." Their faces were barely a foot apart. He looks so wild, she thought. Something's wrong.

And then she thought, I don't care. I want him to die and burn in Hell. "Go away," she said again, pushing uselessly at the door and glancing around the room for something she could use as a weapon. Ashtray—

"No."

"I will scream this time. I will. You can't come in here anymore. That night was rape. It was wrong, wrong—*go away*!" She did scream that time, screamed it out in his face. He winced.

"Hey, quiet down, babe."

"Get *out*!"

"Listen. I've found out where he is."

The anger-given strength in her legs flowed away suddenly and she leaned against the wall, staring at him. She tried to calm herself. He would say anything to get inside again. He was the Devil. "What do you mean? He's come into town?"

"No."

"Where is he?"

"In the woods."

"Where?"

"Let me in."

"No. You're lying. I'm going to scream and scream until men come." She was taking the breath when his hand snaked under the chain and caught her face. She tried to jerk away but he held her easily. He spoke hurriedly in a guarded voice.

"Listen. A Civil Air Patrol plane caught a glimpse an hour ago. A fire, out in the hills. It couldn't be anyone else. I just found out."

His hand tightened for a moment, half caress, half threat; and then it left her mouth and she could breathe again.

"Well?"

"Where are they?"

"I can tell you, but—come on, damn it, let me in."

"No."

He whispered curses in the corridor, terrible things she trembled to hear. Then his hand came through the space again and there was a flash of steel.

She took the knife. Stag-handled, five inches of curved deadliness. "There. Now you trust me? Christ! Stupid . . . open the door."

Her hand on the chain, she hesitated a moment longer. Lift it and he would come in. And then . . . but they've been found, she told herself; they've been seen; they know where he is. If Sweet touched her again she had the knife.

She slid off the chain and opened the door.

"Fine, at last," said Sweet, grinning at her as he brushed by. He threw his coat on the bed and sat on it, still smiling.

"Now tell me where he is."

"Sure. In the Kinningmahontawany."

"What is that? I do not know what that is."

"A Wild Area. No houses, no people. State owns the land. It's full of game but there's no hunting allowed. Part of my job is to patrol it."

"Is it far?"

"A ways, yeah," he said. "And it's *big*. Just the part in Hemlock County's three hundred square miles. You can't just get in a car and drive out there, if that's what you're thinking."

"I don't know what I'm thinking yet. The—Kinny—"

"Kin ny ma hot nee."

"I have heard of it somewhere—"

Then she remembered. It was the wild place the girl, Mary, had told her about. She stared down at Sweet. He had said it was his job to patrol it. The badge, on the coat. The knife in her hand.

If she was to trust him, she might as well trust him with it all. "You know," she said, "I have heard there are poachers there."

"What?"

"Someone is getting money for taking rich men there, to the Kinna—the Kinningmahontawany. Where you say it is illegal to hunt."

"Are you serious? Who is it?"

"I don't know that. But I think that Aaron must have found that out. It was not an accident. He was killed for that."

"To keep him quiet, you mean? Then—interesting." He sat still for a moment, thinking, then blinked and sniffed. His eyes flicked to her. "Yeah, that would explain the marks on the wrists, too. I'll have to look into that."

"I think you should."

"Later. Well, you coming?"

"What?"

He grinned cynically. "Don't you want to go to him? his murderer you love so much?"

"I do not like the way you say that."

"I don't care what you like. Are you coming or not?"

"I have to think."

"Yeah." He took out a pack and tapped a cigar into his and. "You think. But don't take too long. Want one of ese?"

Yes, she wanted one; suddenly she wanted one desper-ely. She nodded and he sucked one puff from the one had lit and handed it to her. The smoke was raw and tter than her cigarettes. The filter hardly helped. But ere was nicotine in it and she sat down at the far end of e bed with it.

"Why did you come here tonight, warden?"

"Like I said, to get you."

"Why?"

He shrugged. "Because. I'm the game protector for is county. I was supposed to take care of all this. Then e state cops took over. See? They've cut me right out. I hadn't called Sealey myself tonight, he probably ouldn't have told me about the fire even." He looked at r. "Also—maybe I didn't treat you real well the other ght. Didn't feel like going through the romantic crap. ut if I can get up there before any of them—and I think ere's a way I can—well, maybe I can do something for u, to kind of—make up."

"What could you do?"

"Your sweetie, Michelson—he's up there, alone with y grandfather. If one of 'em hasn't shot the other by ow."

287

"I understand that."

"No witnesses to anything."

"No."

"We might be able to let him disappear," drawle
Sweet, looking at her significantly and tapping his ash o
onto the bed.

"You'd do that? You'd help me get him away?"

"I might."

A current of hope bubbled for a moment in her breas
like a spring emerging from long-compressed darknes
But it was still unclear to her. "Why would you do that?

"For kicks."

Sitting there, smoking, he crossed one khakied le
over the other, making the bed creak, and smiled at he
expression. She put the cigar to her lips again an
coughed; then stubbed it out with a sudden, angr
movement. "Don't joke with me!"

"I'm not. As long as he doesn't come back here, what
your friend to me? I'm no fan of Sealey's, I don't ca
whether or not he gets his man. Might enjoy seeing th
troopers look silly. What's the matter? Don't you wa
to help him?"

"Of course I do."

"Well then." He stubbed his out too and got u
stretched, turned to face her.

"What about—what about the old man?"

"Racks? He's my granddad. He's been senile for year
I'll explain it to him."

"You are sure you want to do this?"

"Pretty sure. Sure enough. Well?" He waited, smilin
slightly. He did not look at all nervous now.

"Can we go soon?"

"Pretty soon, yeah. Just a couple of things to take ca
of first. You've decided to go, then?"

"I think I have. Now?"

"Soon, I said."

And still grinning his face came closer and closer, and then she felt his lips rough on hers and his hands on her shoulders and the bed soft under her hips. She didn't bother to struggle this time. Just twisted her head back from his hands, her hair from his searching lips, and looked up to the shadowed, lightless ceiling; the webbed, dusty corners. As his hands found, opened, her teeth bit silence into her lips.

Paul was no longer hers. No matter what happened she had lost him forever, no matter if he escaped for he would have to run, no matter if this last degradation was not of but for him. She knew that finally beyond logic, knew it lay deep in the subtle mechanisms of fate. And as she turned her eyes away from Sweet's straining kiss she began to weep, understanding that in saving him, in giving what she could have been for him, she was losing everything, even him.

But she had made her decision.

NINETEEN

Friday, December Fifth

IT WAS MICHELSON WHO WAS FIRST TO WAKE ON THAT FINAL day.

He woke with the sky overhead a clear and glowing gray and the interlacing needles of the hemlock like black embroidery above his upturned eyes. He stared into the light for a long time, marveling at the smooth melding of each sliding cloud, how they fused to form that high, pale opalescent seal between the earth and the sun.

Gradually he became aware of his body, and of where he was.

He lay almost entombed in a mass of thick needles so heavy he could not move a leg or raise a hand. Here under the close-set lower branches of the ancient tree the snow lay in the thinnest sprinkle over many inches of dried brown. The broad, rough trunk was solid against his back. He was half-sitting, half-lying against it in a sort of circular cave, with the bole as its center, and he was looking up along its vertical axis to the sky. Outside the sloping radii of the lowest boughs he could see nothing but white. The whole little cave was filled with a dry piny smell. It was dim and perfectly still under the tree and he thought suddenly, It's late, I've got to get moving. Yet it was so warm there, wrapped in the boughs he'd clawed down over him the night before, so enclosed, so dimly and pleasantly hidden, that he lay there for more minutes simply resting before at last he was able to force himself into movement.

He emerged into the light headfirst, shoving at the snow with his arms, and looked about. The sudden brightness made him blink. He reached back under the tree for crutch and rifle, dragged them out, and stood up.

With daylight the hillside was a lovely place. The close-set old trees had caught and held tons of snow in sandwiched pyramids that hung motionless and soundless in the still lee of the hill. The day was beginning overcast, windless, and the snow had apparently stopped during the night.

But cold. It was still cold.

Michelson brushed dried needles from his jacket and trousers and stamped his feet. The knee hurt, but not as much as before. Maybe I can do without the crutch now, he thought. He tested the leg gingerly. It hurt when he bent it but seemed better. He decided to try it without the crutch. He opened his coat to check his side next. The pain of the wound had subsided into a dull goad. No new blood showed inside his shirt, but around the clot the skin was tender, pinkish, and hot to his touch. It's infected, he thought. But that would be no trouble with antibiotics, as long as he could get it taken care of soon.

He zipped up his coat and coughed shortly and spat. He thought briefly of hot coffee, but as a monk thinks of women; as a desire so far from possibility of satisfaction that the desire itself arouses no image and so no real response. He was past thinking of food at all.

Floundering across the new snow, he looked for the track. It was gone; snowed under. No matter; he knew the direction. Uphill a little ways more and he felt sure he would pick it up. The old man had been holding to a straight line since they had come over the crest of the ridge last evening. He would find him up ahead, or on the slope of the next hill. And that would be it. He contemplated the end of the chase without glee. He was too tired for that.

He pushed ahead a few steps and stopped. He was very weak and the shortness of his breath bothered him. There just was no more strength left. He went a few more steps, leaned on the rifle for a time, went on a little farther. Once when he staggered to a stop he pulled at the neck of his jacket, pulled out the cotton drawstring that closed it, and put the knotted end into his mouth. He chewed at it. It felt good in his mouth.

He floundered forward, his eyes fixed ahead.

Halvorsen woke a little after that. As the man behind him had, he lay still for some time, staring at whatever his eyes had opened on from the vacuum of unconsciousness.

It happened to be a high rock cliff, of dark slate, buff sandstone, and a reddish rock, maculated with patches of ice where springs ran between the strata. He looked at it for quite a long time, not thinking, not wondering, not even quite being. He just looked.

At last he shook himself and rolled out of the sleeping bag and pulled on his boots. He stood up, buttoning his coat and glancing up and down the length of the pit.

Eighty years before this canyon, this artificial pit, had been part of the hillside. At that time it had probably looked no different from any slope here: wooded, grassed in summer, white in winter; crisscrossed with rabbit tracks, deer trails, perhaps an old trace where Indians had passed.

Fifty years before it had been a shallow trench, filled with machines and men, sheds and company buildings

and bunkhouses and puffing engines. They had come
suddenly and in ten or maybe twelve years had carved
out all of that which they wanted that lay close to the
surface and then blasted and sliced deep into the hill,
down to its rocky roots. Till finally there was no more of
it to be dug out and loaded on the little cars and sent
clanking and rolling down out of the valley to the logging
spurs farther north. That same day the company buildings closed, and the machines were loaded on the little
railcars and they left, and the men left; and a little while
later a few of them came back and took up the rails. And
then nothing remained but the raw, deep slash, half a
mile long and two hundred feet deep.

Now, as the old man looked down its length, it was
much the same as he remembered it from thirty-five
years before. A few more slate slides had come down the
cliffs. Between and among the tumbled rocks that dotted
the level bottom stood a few small hopeless-looking
trees, bare and stripped by winter. At one side stood the
old shack he'd remembered, too dilapidated now even to
sleep in, a mere tumbled heap of silvery-gray weathered
lumber. A little distance away from it was the overhanging boulder the old man had sheltered under through the
last half of the night.

Halvorsen bent stiffly and began to roll up the bag.
Then he stopped. He looked at the bag, and at the pack,
and at the black splotch of charred wood and ash atop
the slanted rock. No. There was no need to roll it up. No
need to pack. He wasn't going anywhere.

But he did it anyway, just because it felt right to pack
up in the morning, and then sat down at the edge of the
boulder and looked back along the floor of the canyon.

He'd entered it the night before well after dark. Lower
down where he'd hit it, it was shallower and the sides
were easy. Up here, deep in the hill, the sides were

clifflike and very high. At both ends the floor was level. The machines and men had scooped the hill out right down to the floor strata. Of course, though level, it was not perfectly smooth. The slides from the cliffs, and the bigger boulders that they had mined around and left, still littered the valley's floor, humping like sleeping animals under the snow. But in the night it had been easy enough to walk, feeling his way along, going slowly.

The old man rubbed his face and looked at the pack speculatively.

He'd dragged himself through the length of the canyon last night, and barely made it, bruised and dizzy from falling in the dark. He trusted his memory of the old cut but the distances were so much longer now. It was like when you were a child, he thought: a cleared half acre was a vast field to you. When you grew up and came back it was only a yard. But when you grew old . . . he'd gone back to his parents' farm again a few years ago. The old house had fallen in and was grown over, long forgotten. After his folks died no one had cared to scratch around in that soil any longer. Funny thing, though. As far as size went . . . it looked pretty much as it had when he was a kid.

He could still see his tracks of the night before. Snowed over pretty heavily, but still plain. They led up to this rock, to where he'd built the fire, using boards from the shed. To where he had worked through most of the night, pausing only once, to search the darkness above when the high hum of an aircraft had crossed and recrossed the pit before fading finally into the distance.

Out in front of him, between the boulder and a slanting rockfall, there were no tracks at all. He bent to catch light along the plane of the surface. It had been snowing still when he'd finished. It had stopped sometime after that, when he'd crawled at last into the bag and lain listening to the distant howling of a coyote until sleep had come.

He judged it was good enough.

The old man sat down on the rock. Waiting, he began to hum. It was an old tune, resurrected from somewhere back in his mind.

Humming, Halvorsen looked down at the valley again. He could see pretty far from the rock. Maybe six hundred, seven hundred yards, to where the cut turned with the curve of the hill. He could see far enough. He looked at the snow again between the rocks. It looked all right.

He rolled under the rock again, and lying there fully dressed looked at the pack. He looked at the far end of the cut. Nothing showed there yet.

Through many dangers, toils, and snares
I have already come . . .

Still watching the far end of the canyon, Halvorsen reached into the pack and took out the pint bottle. The seal broke with a little snap.

'Tis Grace hath brought me safe thus far
And Grace will lead me home.

Michelson was not thinking as he walked. Just walking took too much will and strength and strategy. He would estimate how many steps to the next rock, and then he could rest. Or he would stand for long minutes trying to decide which way was shorter around a clump of trees. He did not think much. But yard by yard, he got on.

After a time it grew easier, a little, and he knew he was off the top and on a slight downhill. He hoped he would catch up with the old man soon. He wasn't sure he could take another climb, no matter how easy.

Without his watch he no longer had much idea of the time. But it was no more than an hour after that when he saw the slanting line ahead. It was straight and cut across the face of a hill. He wondered vaguely what it was for a long time before he reached it. When he did he was still not sure until off down one side of the grade of it he saw the rusting wreck of an overturned railroad car, looking oddly little, toylike. Old. The snow lay gently against its russet metal.

He was on an abandoned railroad bed. On its surface he could make out faintly a lone man's footprints, wind-smoothed, snow-covered, but definitely there.

The old man went a long way in the dark, he thought. I hope he found a warm place to sleep.

Michelson went very slowly up the grade. He stopped to rest often, leaning on the rifle. His knee had loosened and was throbbing again. He wished he had kept the crutch.

Well, he promised himself, it can't be too far now.

As he moved up the cut he saw that it led into a canyon, or valley, in the side of the hill itself. On his left it had been sliced away like a cake, exposing the layers of rock. On his right was at first merely a low bank of rubble, but as he went on it grew into a second and only slightly lower cliff. The grade he walked on widened to become the floor of the canyon. Far above, at the edge of the cliff faces, he could see trees way up at the top.

With each step into the canyon the dragging tracks he followed were plainer. It was windless down here and the overdrift that wiped away prints was less. Ahead of him he could see what seemed at first to be the end of the cut, but as he neared it he saw it was instead a shallow turn, with the cut growing even deeper and broader beyond it.

He turned the corner and stopped for a moment, impressed.

It was bigger than he expected. From where he stood to its far end was nearly half a mile. To either side two sheer verticals of strataed rock faced each other three hundred yards apart. It was narrow for such a deep cut. At the far end, where the pit stopped abruptly, a frozen beard of blue-white ice leapt out of the rock and tapered a hundred feet down the blind face of the cliff. It was an impressive landscape, all in monochrome: the black and somber gray of the rock, silver gray of the few saplings and a tumbled-down shed, the narrow band of gray sky, the white of snow.

Michelson was moving forward once more when he saw the old man.

He seemed to appear from under the earth, from amid the rocks. At this distance he could see little detail, but the old man was limping about, picking things up from around a flattish boulder with a black patch atop it. Apparently he had only just woke up.

Michelson smiled.

The old man had trapped himself. The sides of this cut were far too steep to climb. He could see that it was a dead end. Halvorsen must have remembered this place well enough to come to it in the dark, feeling his way maybe, thinking to shelter in it overnight and get out. But I got here too soon, Michelson thought. I got going before he did for once. He was too tired; he overslept probably. And now I'm here, and it's too late.

In a very few minutes it would all be over.

He moved forward slowly, wading through the deep snow. He still followed the tracks, though he could see that they led straight to where the old man was moving about.

Then he looked up, and over a distance of a quarter mile they regarded each other.

Michelson hesitated, his hand on the rifle sling. It was a long shot. He wasn't that steady anymore and he had only twenty rounds left. I'd better get closer, he thought. A lot closer. He slogged forward again, biting his lips at the grinding pain in his knee. It hurt each time he put his weight on it. He kept his eyes on the old man, smiling as he saw him look up at the sheer rock walls that bound them in.

"You've trapped yourself, Racks," he mumbled, around the ice that clotted his beard.

The old man was moving rapidly around the rock. He still seemed to be picking things out of the snow. Michelson could see all this quite plainly as he plowed forward. At last, when he was still some three hundred yards from the boulder, he saw him straighten and pick up his useless rifle and begin walking away.

"Where are you going?" Michelson whispered, pushing himself along the floor of the ravine. "You can't get out that way."

It seemed the old man realized that, for he stopped after a few steps. Michelson could see his face plainly as he looked back toward his pursuer.

"I'm coming," he murmured, wading steadily through the snow. Except for the knee he could no longer feel anything in his legs. They moved like prostheses, like lifeless things of wood.

The old man turned and he saw his back again. He seemed to be making for the end of the canyon, a little to the side of where the stream fell, magically turned to ice in its outward arch. He did not seem to be going very fast. Not that I am either, Michelson thought. Neither of us could outrun a healthy toddler.

He remembered Aaron as a toddler. A fat child. Fat

and strong. Odd how he had become so thin as he grew. With the memory came a surge of pain, not physical like all his others, but deeper and more wrenching, yet strangely unreal to him; a cry from someone he once had been, but who was now buried deep under layers of cold ash, under the cave-in of a self.

But the cry was not very loud and he smiled again and looked ahead to where the old man hurried and jerked along, trying to flee him, trying to flee his own end.

"Killer," said Michelson softly, moving through the deep snow steadily, painfully, intently; but he said it with a note almost of regret. His breath echoed back harshly from the straight dark walls of rock and puffed out behind him in light-filled clouds of fog that drifted upward in the still, cold air of the pit.

Beyond the black-marked boulder, which Michelson had almost reached, the old man turned his face backward. At a hundred yards Michelson could see him plainly. The patched, old-fashioned red and black coat. The worn wool trousers. The old-style green cap, earflaps down.

And the set old face. He saw no fear in it. Perhaps up close he might have. But from this distance he could see only determination and a set of the mouth that he interpreted as hatred.

He was catching up rapidly now. The other was not far from the dead end of the pit, near a pile of tumbled stone under the waterfall.

Michelson saw where he had spent the night.

It was a few steps ahead of him along the trail. Under the boulder—the black patch, he saw, was the scorch of a dead fire—was a little overhang, a sort of den. Around it the fresh snow was scuffed up and trampled. Beyond that was the trail the old man had just left. To the left of the boulder a slant of large rocks from a collapsed section of the cliff tumbled down almost to it.

Michelson aimed his stagger between the edge of this pile and the overhanging boulder. Not far now, he told himself.

He saw that the old man was starting to climb the rockfall at the far end of the canyon. The fall went up the cliffside for a few yards, maybe thirty feet, but then it stopped and above that the bare rock rose vertical till it met the unexcavated part of the hillside a hundred feet higher up, where the thin trunks of trees stood dark against the gray sky.

Michelson frowned. There was no way out. What was the old man doing?

Halvorsen seemed to reach the same conclusion then, for as Michelson came around the side of the boulder he turned, standing against the far wall, hanging, it seemed, by his hands from some ledge or outcrop of it. He was so plainly visible there, and so close, that Michelson felt the time had come at last. I'll do it quickly, he thought, feeling here at the end a bit of pity. There's no need to make him suffer anymore.

He pulled the sling from around his shoulder and, still walking forward, swung the heavy rifle around in front of him and raised it to his shoulder.

He took one more step, and his leg gave way.

At least that was what he thought in that first startled instant. Or that under the unsullied surface of the snow something had given way when he put his foot on it, something like a breaking stick. For his descending boot had come down on something irregular and hard that resisted just for a moment, and then snapped away.

He looked down just in time to see, beneath the thin covering of new snow, two forks of split green sapling trunks bite together on his lower leg. He saw no more; it happened too rapidly. Carried forward by his eager momentum, off balance in the act of aiming, his body still went on, though his leg remained gripped and immobile in a crushing pressure; and he fell, turning, and with a short choked cry buried his face in the snow.

At the sound of the cry the old man's long-numbed fingers gave way at last and he slid backward and down, the sharp edges of the rocks digging into his unresisting flesh. He came to rest after a few feet, face downward, feeling the icy plane of stone against his haired cheek.

Racks Halvorsen lay against the stone for long minutes, and then, slowly, raised his head.

From his slight elevation at the blind end of the canyon he could see far down it; could see everything with exquisite clarity. He could see each rock-cramped sapling, each fissure and cleft of the dark walls, each detail of what had just happened below him.

The dark figure of the man who had tracked him, and whom he had tracked, so far, lay face downward and arms outstretched. One leg was bent absurdly sideways, with the ankle and lower leg rooted firmly into the ground. Ahead of the outstretched hands was a black line that the old man stared at for a moment before he realized it was the automatic rifle.

Halvorsen lay stretched on the flat surface of the rock, and looked; and did not care. He was past caring. He was half-drunk.

He had lain there in the brightening morning light, the ledge close and comforting above his head, and watched the entrance to the ravine. Lying there, watching the gap, he took a first drink from the bottle that he'd packed all the days, all the miles, saving it for the time when he would have to call on it to push him for the last few yards. It was the first liquor he had tasted for fifteen years and it was syrupy and ice cold in his mouth and warm in his chest and then a ball of flame in his empty belly. Slowly, sipping it, he'd drunk half the pint. Then he had capped the bottle carefully and placed it upright on the rock.

Whoever outlasted this morning would need it, and could find it there.

Yet even with the whiskey's help, he found it hard to get up when he saw the limping figure framed in the entrance to the canyon. And then he had to get his pack and sidestep the trap and decide where he was going. There was really no choice though. It had to be away from the approaching man or he might shoot too soon. So at last he'd decided, tottering off away from the boulder, toward the blind end of the pit.

He found it hard to stay upright enough to walk.

It was not a sudden weakness. He had felt its imminence for days. Now, after the long night of work, there were no more reserves. No more energy in his gaunt and tired bones. No more desire at all in his old and reluctant heart.

Only the transient energy in the few mouthfuls of alcohol, flickering weakly through his veins, kept him upright and moving on. He did not move fast or even at a creep. He moved in a rocking stagger, like a man fighting quicksand. His heart beat in slackening fury at the unendurable, the inhuman agony of walking a hundred feet through deep snow.

With each look backward he could see that his pursuer was gaining. He was overtaking him, and too quickly. Halvorsen saw that he would be close enough to fire long before he reached the trap. He turned his face again toward the far wall and groaned. He tried to take the next step, and the next, just a little faster; but he could not; there was nothing left.

All the same, somehow he had reached the foot of the

ockslide. He might have stood there and waited. It
vould have been as good. But from somewhere far back,
voice decades away, he remembered that for a snare to
vork, the animal had to be distracted from the jaws. Had
) be offered an interesting bait.

He had started to climb the rockslide.

And now after that snare had worked he lay full length
gainst the cold rock and watched the figure below him
egin to stir. He did not care. He was resting and that
`as enough. Rest, a long and undisturbed period of
oing nothing, of not having to care, was all he wanted.
`he liquor-warmth stroked his mind, gentling him to-
`ard sleep, toward nothingness.

In this passive state he groped weakly for his rifle, and
rought it close to him on the flat rock. The heavy, dark
`ood, the use-burnished metal, felt comforting. Each
ontour of the stock was familiar and intimate and
eassuring.

The man below moved one arm feebly and tried to
ush himself up. Halvorsen heard him moan as his
ngers explored the twisted leg. He was not concerned.
`he saplings are right, the old man thought hazily. Just
ie right thickness, split and wedged apart with the ax
nd a lever pole, bent and set with the hand-whittled
`ooden dog. McKittrack had showed him that one these
xty years gone, a set the old trappers used in these
oods before there were such things as iron traps. If it
ould hold a bear, it would hold a man.

The man seemed to be struggling with it. Halvorsen
ould see his face plainly, the hollow eyes, the ragged
e-caked beard, the open mouth. The old man lay and
atched him. Now, he asked himself, what are you going
o do with him?

He lay and considered the matter drowsily. It felt so
amned good just to lie still that he felt averse to even

thinking about walking out. The warmth of the whiskey tingled in his hands and face. He wished he'd brought the bottle up with him instead of leaving it there on the rock. Another sip would sure go down nice, he thought.

Still, he thought, I can probably walk out if I have to. If I can get a little rest first. That was the great thing. He was plain beaten into the ground right now, and that was the truth. His eyes drooped closed. He rolled sideways into a more comfortable position and felt a sharp edge dig into his side.

What was that, in his coat?

Annoyed, he shifted position again, but it was wedged under him, against the rock he lay on. It was hard and sharp and a little storm of tired, petulant fury swept the old man and he reared up and tore the buttons open and pulled it out and had his arm ready to pitch it down the rockslide when his fingers told him what it was.

It was the magazine; the sheet-metal box that went to the other's rifle. He remembered now picking it up at the copse, back along the trail, so many days ago he had lost count. In the excitement and then the fatigue and above all in the absent memory of an old man he had forgotten it was there. He brought it close to his face and squinted. There at the bottom of it, stuck against the wall by the faulty follower, was still the glint of brass.

Halvorsen held it, thinking. Yes, it might fit his rifle.

In fact it definitely would. I'd have to allow for different bullet weight, he thought. The Army-issue ammunition was loaded differently. But the cartridge were the same. He probed speculatively at the magazine. It's wedged in there good, he thought. Something inside it was broken—the spring, most likely—and the follower had dropped back down and been jammed there by a piece of it.

He laid it on the rock beside him and relaxed again.

'll rest for a while up here, he thought. Then I'll walk on
ut of the cut, out of the forest, overland east to the river
nd then to the road. With a cartridge he could get
ood—a deer, or at least a rabbit if he was patient. And
e could set snares now; he had the time, at last. He had
ll the time in the world now.

He felt, at that moment, very patient indeed, and very
ontent. He closed his eyes and lay warm on the rock,
nd relaxed into it; and sleep stole quietly up on him
om behind.

Michelson lay outstretched for long minutes, stunned
y the force of the fall and by the shock of the snapping,
earing thing that had happened in his leg.

And then the pain came.

He dug his hands deep into the unresisting snow. His
hole side felt wrong, and the pain from the destroyed
nee, growing minute by minute, throbbed upward from
in hot dizzying waves. He could hear the rush and
urge in his ears.

With a sudden shove, rejecting the earth with both
ands, he sat up.

He found himself only half-kneeling. His right leg, the
ne in the trap, was bent sideways rather than back. In
lling that leg, held vertical, could not go forward with
e rest of his body; and the already weakened knee was
e point that gave way. He had heard its snapping tear,
sound that made him shudder again as he recalled it.

He explored the leg with his fingers, trying to right it.
he knee moved loosely. It felt unanchored. The
rangeness of it, the pain, made him feel sick.

Like an animal, he began to dig frantically around the
lges of his trap.

The old man had buried the trunks of two small trees
ere, each of them, he saw as he scrabbled away more

305

snow, anchored solidly under the rocks between which he had walked. Each of the trunks had been split lengthwise for several feet and the two halves bent outward. Then, he guessed, the old man had propped something in between the spread forks to keep them open.

That was what he had stepped on, letting the springy wood snap together on his lower leg with terrific force.

The ankle did not hurt much. It was already numb. The pinioning wood gripped it with crushing rigidity against his weak attempts to free it. The pain came from his knee, and it washed over him again and retreated a little and stood there waiting as he beat his fists impotently on the staked-down wood.

It was not the stakes that held him, though. He could see them wobble as he moved. With work he could probably pull them out. What held him fast was the way the trunks had been set with their far ends under the massive weight of the rocks. He could not move the trunks upward. Perhaps he could unwedge the smaller rocks that held them in—he was stronger, even now, than the old man, surely—but with his leg held like this he couldn't reach them.

As he realized this he stopped working at the trap and looked around him. Another wave of pain came in, submerged him, tumbled him over and over along a dark bottom, and then receded and let him struggle up for breath.

The old man, he saw, was still lying up above him. He had changed his position a little, but Michelson couldn't make out what he was doing. He looked around. If he could get his hands on a stout stick, something long to pry with . . . but the old man would have made sure there was nothing like that within reaching distance.

Then he saw the hole in the snow ahead, and looked

from it to the old man, lying motionless now on his ledge.

Watching him, he stretched out his arm toward the hole in the snow. It was a good three feet away. As he'd fallen the rifle had gone flying. He grunted and lay forward again from the kneel, stretching out in the imprint he had made. With his arms fully extended his fingers were still a foot from the gun.

He stared at it. If I still had the crutch, he thought hopelessly. If I still had something, anything, to pull it in with.

He thought of chimps being tested with bananas just outside the bars.

Above him the old man moved slightly. He glanced up at the movement, and as he did so a new and fierce inundation of agony came in and up his leg and left him gasping and biting into the muffling snow.

When it retreated at last he lay there weak and spent and almost at peace. The old man had won. He'd been trapped like an animal, and this was the end. The old man would leave him here and bring back police and they would take him from the pit, if he was still alive by then, and then they would go through their legal charades and finally he would be caged like some vicious beast.

I'm not vicious, Michelson thought, feeling the snow cold against his cheek.

All he had wanted was justice; what was deserved according to a higher concept of law than the law of men. What was human, and more than that—what was humane.

Michelson whimpered softly in pain and fear and rage, and tried to sit up. His hand brushed one of the stakes, and it moved.

He looked at it, gripped it, worried it back and forth.

With a rasping sound it slid up out of the hard-packed snow. He looked at it. It was a little under a foot long.

He flung himself out again, gasping with the pain, and scrabbled in the snow at the extreme of his reach. The stick rattled on something hard under the surface of the snow. He clawed it back. The close rock walls of the pit gave him back his own panting, the scratching of wood on metal, and at last echoed his muffled groan of mingled agony and triumph when he felt the end of the barrel with his gloved fingers.

Pulling the gun in hastily, he stripped one hand naked and dug clotted snow from the muzzle and action. His fingers stuck to the icy metal and he pulled them away, leaving bits of bloody skin. A little cloud of frost smoke surrounded him as he struggled upright in the trap, putting all his weight on the one good leg, and raised the trembling length of the heavy rifle toward the last obstacle between himself and freedom.

Sleep hovered, but it did not descend.

Halvorsen opened his eyes, blinking wearily. His eyeballs felt as if they had been taken out, sandpapered thoroughly, and stuck back in his skull. But he had to do something. What was it? He puzzled at it for some time. His thoughts were like scampering rabbits, and he kept losing their trails. But at last he nodded ponderously.

He couldn't leave the man here, in the trap. Hell, he wouldn't leave an animal in a Y trap. The circulation would go; the paw, no, the leg, would be dead after a day.

Halvorsen grunted sleepily, reluctantly. I'll have to go down there, he thought. Take away his gun, then give him something to pry himself out with. I'll have to guard him good on the way back. Maybe tie his hands with a belt or something. It would be hard. But basically it was the end.

Incuriously, he watched the man below working out one of the stakes. That's all right, he thought. They don't anchor the saplings. Just hold them in position until they're sprung.

Then he saw the man spread-eagle himself, suddenly prostrate on the snow, as if adoring some god or devil instantaneously manifest behind the old man on the vertical rock.

Halvorsen, quite suddenly awake, sat up and reached for his own weapon.

And then for the magazine. His gloves were too bulky and he stripped them off, cursing himself in a hurried whisper for a fool and an old fool, and thrust his fingers hastily inside the metal box. He could feel the curve of the cartridge and—yes, there—the sharp end of the broken spring. He felt his fingernails tear on it, and then something yielded suddenly, bent, and there was a hollow snap as the cartridge came free into his hand.

He reached for the Springfield just as Michelson, triumph in his eyes, stood up before him only thirty yards away.

When the last echoes of the shot had dissipated, thundering and rumbling away over the hills to west and north, east to the river, south, loudest, out of the pit's mouth and down and away unheard over the deserted hills and silent naked woods of the Kinningmahon-tawany, the two men stood for a little time silent, facing each other over the space of snow and rock between them.

To one side of the pit lay a broken piece of wood and metal. Its stock was shattered, its barrel bent almost at a right angle. It lay half-buried where the impact of a bullet had torn it from a man's hand and flung it into the snow.

Beginning to tremble, the old man lowered his own rifle slowly from his shoulder.

Michelson looked at his own hands, not yet ready to believe what had happened.

The two men faced each other for a long time. At last one of them cleared his throat and coughed; and looked down at the other with something like pity, or compassion, or a kind of shared pain; or anyway something deep and ineluctable that they both, for some reason, at last had begun to share.

"What's your name, anyway? It ain't McCoy," said the old man.

"Michelson," he said. "Paul Michelson."

"Oh," said the old man. And then, at last, "I see."

"Do you?"

Halvorsen nodded slowly.

They were still standing erect, facing each other, when the high whine of an engine reached them, distant but perfectly distinct, focused where they stood by the sides of the pit. They both looked upward, toward the high gray clouds.

"Must be a plane," said Halvorsen at last.

"Uh huh."

"They're looking for us. Weather's lifting."

"I guess so," said Michelson. Together they looked toward the top of the hill, the high edge of the pit. The sides were too steep to climb. To get out they would have to retrace their steps, back to the pit's entrance, and then turn and climb one last hill.

"I can't walk," he said.

"I'll help you," said the old man. He slid down from the rock, leaving his rifle there. He held out a hand. "Come on."

And after a moment Michelson nodded too.

TWENTY

THE ROAD WAS A SILVER STREAM BETWEEN TWO BANKS OF JET.
Glass against her cheek, her hair combed by the icy wind
that seeped around it, she stared out through the
passenger-side window into hurtling night.

She felt numb, cold as the glass, motionless at her
heart as the hills.

After finishing with her Sweet had ordered her to get
dressed. At his office she had waited silently in the cab of
the green Game Commission pickup while he busied
himself in back of the building. Once she had heard the
roar of a motor, and the whole truck shivered and
crouched as something heavy crawled up and into the
back.

And now they were on the road.

Beside her, his face lit amber by the dashboard, Sweet
was smoking another cheroot. Its slow fire moved in
jerky circles as he chewed on it. The wheels hummed
over the road, jolting from time to time on hummocks of
ice, rattling her skull against the glass. She thought, He is
driving very fast. But then, they were the only vehicle on
the road. It was four A.M. and for the past hour they had
passed no one.

"Where are we?" she forced herself to say at last, looking out at the looming black-on-black of the ridges.

"Potter County," the warden said shortly. He pointed the cigar off to the left. "Roulette's out that way. We got to take a right pretty soon, go along Cord Creek for a ways, then over to Hefner Creek Road. It's kind of the long way around, but it gets us closer."

"It is a long way."

"Yeah. It is. Another hour at least, if Nichols Hollow's cleared."

"Then what?"

She saw his teeth flash in the dim light as he glanced toward her, reaching out to brush her hair with the tips of his fingers. If not for the confines of the cab she would have jerked away. "Don't worry about it, babe," he drawled. "I'll get us there even if the road don't."

The truck jolted; he pulled his hand back and cursed as they began to skid. She watched his face as he concentrated on the driving. The numbness was ebbing now, like the departure of an anesthesia. She couldn't look at him without a shudder.

I really hate him, Teresa thought. She wondered at it. She had never hated anyone before.

The pickup jolted again as they turned off the main road. The headlights picked up snow-covered oil tanks, piping, a tin-roofed shed, all dark and abandoned-looking, and beyond them a crumbling New Deal concrete bridge. Sweet shifted gears and it all slid past back into night as they reaccelerated along a winding track that dropped sheer on one side to a creek. The truck whined upward, climbing until only the hill was left, to one side, and on the other a drop into a gulf of darkness. A gulf into which she slid, enfolded in the warmth of the cab, lulled by the drone of the engine.

* * *

"Hey," a voice said. A hand was shaking her and she was suddenly cold. "Hey!"

She opened her eyes to find the doors wide and the engine idling. Sweet was standing by her, calf deep in snow. Beyond the glow of the dome light the night pressed in. He reached across her and she tensed. He turned the key and the engine died.

"Are we here?"

"'Here'? We're as far as you can go by truck, that's for sure."

"What do you mean?" She rubbed her face and yawned.

"I mean that roads don't go where we're headed." He grinned at her. "Come on, get out. It'll be dawn soon, and it's a long way yet."

He disappeared behind the pickup and a moment later chains rattled. It was as freezing in the cab now as it was outside and she gathered her nerve and jumped. The snow cushioned her landing, but she seemed to go down and down. Standing knee-deep she looked around, hugging herself.

It was so dark. Only straight above was there a steely glow of eventual daylight. All around them rose the sheer faces of the hills, black dark, like walls of obsidian.

Sweet was swearing from the back of the truck. She hesitated, then plodded clumsily toward the sound. The pink glow of the parking lights showed his snarl as he struggled with the tailgate. At last it crashed down and he reached inside and two metal ramps scraped out. She watched, not speaking, as he climbed up into the bed.

Then there was a whine and a roar, and something massive clawed at the steel of the bed. Metal squealed as it slid down the ramps, then dug into the snow, throwing ruby-glowing clouds of it, oil-smelling, noxious. She started back; she had never seen one of these before. Its

313

engine roared again and then dropped suddenly to a purr and its lights came on and Sweet was walking back from the snowmobile, rubbing his gloved hands and looking at her.

"You ready?"

"We are going on that?"

"Unless you figure on hikin' it, yeah."

"What about the truck?"

"Just leave it. You can leave one of these anywhere." He moved past her toward the cab. The dome light was still on and she watched him grope beneath the seat and pull out a long cloth case.

"What is that?"

"Shotgun," he said, unzipping it. The barrel emerged first. He stripped the canvas off and threw it back under the seat.

"Why are you taking that?"

"You never know, in the Kinningmahontawany," Sweet said. He held the gun muzzle-down along his leg and fed in shells. "People don't go back here much, where we're going. We might run into a bear, or even a cougar." He reached in for the keys and the courtesy light went out. The only sound now in the dark was the purr of the smaller vehicle, the only light the parabolic glisten of its headlight on the snow.

"Let's hit it," he said, taking her arm.

"Where . . . where do I sit?"

"Behind me. Here. You ever been on a motorcycle?"

"No."

"Put your arms around me. It's going to be bumpy, so keep your knees flexed. Be ready for it." He grinned. "Understand?"

She did not bother to answer. Sitting close behind him, hands locked around him, she could feel the hard

314

muscle of his belly under his coat. Her head was against his shoulder blade. The engine beneath her made her whole body vibrate, made her teeth chatter.

"Ready?"

She moved her face twice against his jacket, already shivering.

The seat lurched suddenly, and she was pulled backward. She grabbed for him, feeling the muscles tighten in his back as the machine roared and gathered speed at a frightening rate. The wind bit at her face and she hid it in the rough wool of his shoulder.

Before a shattering noise, behind a flare of white light, they bored upward into the silence of the hills. Holding to him, her whole body shaken by the engine, she almost forgot her fear and hate. Hatred, of the man she held so tightly. Fear, of what she might find at the end of this journey.

Paul, she whispered hopelessly to herself above the shriek of the wind.

"Another," said the old man.

"Can't."

"Another, I said!"

Michelson raged. Panted. And at last, lifted his leg and staggered a step forward. Then he stopped. He couldn't face another. He leaned into the hill, leaned on the old man's shoulder. Halvorsen's arm was around his waist, digging into the wounded side. On the slight wind their breaths mingled in a white plume, luminescent in the morning light, that drifted rapidly up the hill ahead of them as if mocking the cruel slowness of their progress.

"Hurts like hell," Michelson grunted, staring upward. It wasn't much farther to the top, not really. But he was so tired. . . .

"Come on," said Halvorsen, looking into his face. "That plane's gettin' closer. We got to be up there when it comes over."

"'Got to.' What for? So I can stand trial—"

"You'll be alive, mister. We have to walk out of here, you won't be."

Michelson regarded him with hatred and hopelessness and apathy.

He took another step.

Together they struggled slowly upward, past the opening to the pit, toward the bare hillside above its cliff. The high whine was still distant beyond the hills. To Michelson it didn't sound like a plane. A helicopter? Seemed too high-pitched. But the pain in his legs, the lightheadedness of fever and half a bottle of raw whiskey . . . he could be mistaken. Certainly there was something out there, and it was coming nearer, all right.

"There it is," said the old man sometime later. He was panting too. The tall man he half carried was heavy and the energy of the whiskey was almost gone. From time to time the birches detached themselves from the hillside, beginning a slow, stately whirl around them, and he had to blink and wait for them to steady or he knew he would stagger and break and pitch them both into the snow.

If that happened, he could not guarantee that either of them would get up again.

"What?" whispered the man beside him.

"I said: there it is. The top."

A little while later they came slowly out of the tree line at the crest. The summit was almost flat, cut off probably when the pit was being worked, and from the trees to the edge of the pit was bare snow over cruel, frozen earth and rock. Here and there a jagged edge thrust up through the white like teeth in a discarded jawbone, biting skyward.

316

"Where's the plane?"

"I don't know. I thought you saw it."

"I haven't seen anything yet. Let's get away from the trees here," said the old man.

Michelson groaned as his companion stumbled over something beneath the snow. Each time the old man faltered he unthinkingly tried to put weight on the destroyed knee. "Damn it, take it easy."

"Sorry."

Looking at Halvorsen's head, the familiar green floppy-eared cap tucked almost under his arm, he felt a sudden unexpected flash of appreciation, almost tenderness. The old man's skin was white and his cheeks, bearded with half an inch of gray stubble, sagged in flaccid folds. His pale-blue eyes were set, squinting out at the brink toward which step by step they dragged. He trailed me, Michelson thought, all this way; frustrated my every attempt to escape. I tried to kill you, he thought. And now you're carrying me.

"Where are we going?" he asked the old man's down-turned face.

"Out where he can see us."

"Where is he?"

"Over there, sounds like." Halvorsen extended his free arm to the southeast, back over the pit, which was opening now below them as they approached the edge of the cliff. A row of the rocks, set like a fence but wide apart, came up from the snow a few feet back from the edge. "Gettin' louder. Must be just above this overcast."

"It doesn't sound like a plane," said Michelson.

"No, it sure don't," said the old man, a sort of exhausted wonder in his voice.

They collapsed together slowly into the snow a few yards from the edge. Michelson lay motionless thinking: no farther. If no one comes, this is where I'll die. They were well clear of the birches now, well out into the open. As the distant whine rose and fell, slowly but steadily seeming to near, they turned their faces skyward toward the high, smoky ceiling.

"There it is," said Michelson after a few minutes.

"Where?"

"Out there. Coming out of the valley. Way down there."

The old man shaded his eyes. "I don't see nothing."

"Look where I'm pointing."

"Oh. Yeah, I see it. I was lookin' for an airplane."

"It's a snowmobile."

"Sure is."

"Think he'll see us from down there?"

"He better," said Halvorsen. Standing up, he took off the green cap and began to wave it slowly above his head.

"There they are!" Sweet shouted over the drilling whine of the engine.

Teresa lifted her head. Her cheeks were wooden, without feeling at all. Her body too was numb and tremulous with three hours of jolting. The wind blasted into her eyes and a film of water obscured her sight. Then the wind whipped it away and she saw . . . the hill. The slanting cut. And high above it, on the crest, two dots against the snow. One of them was waving.

"It's the pit," Sweet was shouting back at her. "The old strip mine. I figured that's where they were when the plane reported the fire. It's the best place around here to wait out a storm."

But she was only half listening. All her attention was ahead of them, on the orange-red speck that lay beside the smaller one that waved. If he was unmoving—could he be hurt, could he be—

The engine screamed and she clutched at Sweet's coat

again. The snow spewed up behind them in a white mist that blew from the whirling treads, hung in the clear air like powder smoke, then slowly sifted earthward, leaving only a blue haze and a drumming pulse that ebbed out into the empty hills.

"Hold tight now."

Up to now Sweet had avoided climbing hills. He knew the contours here and he had driven the machine fast but levelly through the valleys, along the ridges where he had to, but seldom up or down; a breakdown or spill out here would be no laughing matter. But now he had found them. He had been right. And in a sudden thrill of triumph and power he aimed the blunt skis at the hill. The engine blatted as he shifted and they went up, bumped level as they crossed the old railroad grade.

Then it was the hill itself and behind him Teresa held tight, too frightened to cry out, and he grinned as he gunned it up the bank, leaning forward like a rider urging a horse to a leap. At forty miles an hour his eyes barely registered the dragging footprints that appeared from nowhere, zagging among the trees. He twisted the throttle and the nose rose, up, up, until Teresa felt it coming back and over on top of them and she opened her mouth to scream.

"You're going too fast!"

"I got it," he shouted back above the roar. Somehow the nose held steady and the engine, alternately blipping and blaring, drove them from side to side as he aimed the vehicle between speed-blurred boles so close she could have touched them. And then it dropped, they were on the level again, and then the last trees whipped past and a wide space opened ahead.

"See?" he shouted back. *"All you got to do is trust old Ralpho."*

The machine was sweeping in a curve when she saw

the rock ahead under the snow. Sweet did not. His head was turned, he was waving at the two men who waited for them. But she saw it and when she screamed his head whipped back but too late, and her cry was cut off short as they hit and the machine rose, howling, and turned in the air and came down again into the snow.

Halvorsen was still standing, waving, and Michelson still lying apathetically at his feet, when they saw the speeding machine suddenly leave the ground and roll, shaking off its riders. For a moment it seemed to pause, freed of earth and gravity like a released balloon. Then it plunged suddenly downward and shattered itself, tumbling to a halt in furrowed snow and earth, sending hood and windshield and metal parts skittering across the hilltop.

"Jesus," said the old man. He dropped his arm and began to run through the snow toward the wreck.

And Michelson lay motionless, staring at the second, smaller person who lay full length, arms out. He knew he did not know the other one, the big man. But there was something familiar about this one, something of the already known to the fan of dark hair spread on the snow.

"Teresa?" he muttered.

The old man reached Sweet. He was on his back, just starting to stir. As Halvorsen bent to him he sat up suddenly, shaking himself.

"Ralph. You all right, boy?"

"Yeah. Guess so."

"Come on, get away from that thing. Might catch fire. You know you were goin' way too fast."

"I know. I wanted to get here."

"Took you long enough," said Halvorsen then. But when his grandson looked up he smiled a little.

320

"Well, I'm here now, Racks."

"And I'm mighty glad to see you . . . but who's this?"

The woman was face down. Halvorsen brushed snow from her head and carefully turned her over, cradling her neck. Pretty little thing, he thought. Dark like an Indian. There were white patches on her cheeks. He took off his gloves and turned them inside out and laid the rabbit fur gently against the frostbite. He heard someone behind him then and pointed to the blue bruise on her forehead.

When Sweet said nothing he turned his head. His grandson was walking through the wreckage, kicking pieces of fiberglass aside. As he watched the warden bent and pulled at the side of the seat. When he stood up again he held a short-barreled pump shotgun.

"She still alive?" he asked, coming over to Halvorsen with it.

Teresa moaned. She was conscious first of softness, warmth, against her face, and next of needles of pain as feeling returned. When she put her hand to her head she felt someone holding it. She began to smile; but her eyes opened not to Paul, but to someone unfamiliar, someone old.

"Who are you?" she whispered.

"Racks Halvorsen, ma'am. You took you a heck of a spill there. How's your head?"

"It hurts."

"Eyes look okay. Why don't you try to stand up?"

"I will try." She felt shaky, but it was better standing. She groped for some snow and held it to her forehead and looked around.

"Paul!"

He was gaunt and hairy, his face was pale and bruised and crusted with ice. He stared up with pain in his eyes as she picked her way toward him.

321

"What the hell are you doing here?" were his first words.

"You're hurt!"

"My leg. Did you come up from school? How long have you been here?"

"A few days. I came after you. But I couldn't find you. Where"—she hesitated—"where were you?"

"Doesn't matter . . . hey, you all right?"

She wasn't; she was crying. She had found him at last but too late; he was hurt and in trouble. All her guilt and hurt and worry, all too late. And now he sounded angry with her. It was the last straw and suddenly, at last, it overwhelmed her and she crouched over him and put her hands to her face.

"What's the matter?"

"I was looking for you. I tried to help."

"You should have stayed in West Kittanning, Terry."

Then they were hugging and he was crying too, a little, and cursing at the same time when she knelt on his bad leg.

"Well, at last," said a cold voice. "Mister Michelson. You know most of the state will be out looking for you in about two hours, soon as this overcast lifts."

Michelson looked up. Towering against the gray sky was an unfamiliar man, muscular and tall, in a lumberjack coat. He examined the badge and the gun, then returned to the face. It was handsome, but there was something hard and hidden behind the eyes.

"Who're you?" he grunted.

"Ralph Sweet here. Hemlock County Game Protector."

"Oh." He looked back at Teresa, held her closer, and reached for her hand. But she was looking from him to the warden.

"Ralph—"

"What?"

"You're going to help, aren't you? Like you said?"

Behind Sweet Halvorsen had come up and stood now, hands in his pockets, a worn-looking old man with deep pouches under his distant blue eyes.

"Mr. Sweet is going to help you get out of here," she said rapidly to Michelson. "We are going to leave together."

"What's that?" said the old man slowly.

"Shut up," said Sweet. He glanced around. "Hey. Where's this machine gun he's supposed to have? I don't see it."

"Down there," said the old man, nodding toward the pit edge.

"And where's your rifle?"

"Same place. Say, Ralph—what's she talking about? I been trackin' this guy for days. Now I've got him. He's got to be taken in."

"That's right," said the warden.

"But you promised to help us," Teresa said.

"Yeah. I guess that's right too, isn't it?" drawled Sweet. He felt in his coat pocket and brought out a mashed pack. He offered it around, but no one else moved or spoke. He extracted a cigar slowly, straightened it, and lit it with relish. It was crooked in his mouth. When it was drawing he looked around the hilltop. "So those two things kind of contradict each other, don't they? You know—I don't think we can do both of them. I mean, even a game protector's only human. Which kind of means that not all of us out here are going to be able to make it back."

"Maybe not," said the old man, behind him. "But we can send help. State police ought to be able to fly that helicopter now it's clearin' up."

"That's true," said Sweet, still smiling. He turned to his granddad. "But think about this, Racks. Let's say just you and I came back. Say they never found these two. You know there's a lot of territory around here. You could say you lost the trail. Wouldn't that be—*neater*, sort of?"

Michelson felt Del Rosario squeeze his arm. He glanced at her. She was smiling, but there was some more complex emotion in it too. Damn, he thought. What's going on? What's she got worked out with this guy? The sense of defeat, of resignation and apathy that had possessed him since the old man had lowered his rifle lifted a little. He hardly dared hope, but . . .

"Yes, and we will leave," she was saying now brightly. "I will take care of him. Just tell us which way to go, and we will never come back. I'll make sure he doesn't. I will forgive you and pray for you. You will never feel bad about this, Ralph."

"No, I don't think I will."

"Wait a minute," said Michelson then. "I can't walk."

"No, his leg's about gone," said Halvorsen. He sounded puzzled too. "Ralph, what are you talking about? We can't let him go. He's killed a lot of people, way I understand it. Tried to kill me too."

"I don't plan to let him go," said Sweet.

"Then what are you two talking about?"

"I'm going to leave them here," said Sweet. He brought the muzzle of the shotgun jauntily up from his boot. "But we have to make sure they don't talk to anyone else. About anything."

The three of them looked at him in silence for a time. He stood easily, letting smoke trickle from his mouth. He looked relaxed. Only Teresa, perhaps, saw the fine pallor around his lips.

"Ralph, just what you got in mind here?" said the old man at last.

"To leave 'em," said the warden. He turned suddenly on the old man. "Look. You're just going to have to trust me. You been out of circulation for a long time. Some stuff's been going on around this county you don't know about. Not about the accidents. Before that."

Crouching there before him, listening to the strained reasonableness in his voice, Teresa knew suddenly what he meant.

"What kind of stuff?" the old man was saying. "What have you got yourself involved in, Ralph? Damn, I had a bad feelin' about you. Ever since your pa and ma broke up—"

"You don't need to know. In fact, it would be better if you didn't."

"It is the hunting," she said.

"What do you mean?" said Halvorsen.

Now that she knew, the words came tumbling out. She was talking to Paul, not to the old man, not to Sweet. "It's illegal hunting. Poaching, they call it. Here on the state wildlife preserves. That's it, isn't it, warden? You take rich men here out of season and they give you money to let them shoot animals."

"Ralph?" said the old man.

Sweet shrugged.

Beside her she felt Michelson sit up.

"So you want to—what? Talking about leaving them here, making sure they don't talk to nobody. That sounds like—I don't want to say it," said the old man. He had his grandson's arm now. "Is that it? Is that what you mean? You young son of a bitch. What else have you been doing behind that fancy badge of yours?"

"Forget it," said Sweet. He had stopped smiling. "You wouldn't get it, old man. You don't need money, back in the woods. You don't have to deal with people. Just forget it."

"Sweet," said Michelson.

The warden looked at him expressionlessly. "What, mister murderer?"

"What about my son?"

Beside him, Teresa could feel the tension gathered in his upper body.

"What about him?"

"That's right," said the old man, still staring at his grandson. "The Michelson boy. It was a shotgun slug they found. A twelve-gauge. What have you got in that pump, Ralph?"

Sweet shrugged again. Then, with a smooth, unhurried, almost casual motion, he stepped back from them —from all three of them—and the barrel of the pump came up a little more, so that the old man, too, could find himself in the way with only a small motion of it. "Listen, Racks," he said. His voice now was not jaunty but low and hoarse. "Grandpa. Listen. None of that matters. Believe me. There was no way out of doing it. You'd have done it too if you'd of been me. But there's others on the way, I don't have time to argue. You got to make a decision here. Are you standing with them or me? Because they're staying here—for good."

And Halvorsen, looking not at the gun as the others did but at the insolence and open fear in the eyes above them, thought: Who is that? Is that Alma's little boy? Or a stranger? He turned his head a little as he mused to look around the hillside, lonely, wind-bare; around at the hills. They stretched out for miles under the sky, as they had for all his life. But now one thing was different. At this height, they no longer towered above him. At this height, where he stood after all his years and all his pain, he was as tall as the hills.

Lying in the snow, the pain in his leg cooling away, dropping away, Paul Michelson watched the warden too.

It wasn't the old hunter, he was thinking with still-emerging astonishment. Not old Halvorsen, the man I hoped and tried so many times to kill. That man is standing there now trying to decide whether to die with me. Nor was it the other hunters.

I was logical, Michelson thought. I examined it all and justified it to myself. I was sure I was right in what I did. But I was wrong.

It was too enormous to understand and he was too weary and too cold. His mind fluttered like a wounded bird, beating itself again and again against the icy wall of one fact:

The men he had killed were innocent.

Beside him, her arm around his trembling shoulders, Teresa watched the man she had trusted against all her body's fear and hatred. *I've lost,* she was thinking at that moment. I have lost because of my pride and my foolishness. If I had not wanted this man somewhere in my heart, he could not have taken me. And if I had not wanted him somewhere, even the tiny, hidden, dark wanting that I cannot acknowledge because I know no good woman could have such a thought, I would not have trusted him. I was blind. Blind to trust him, the man I knew so well to be evil, the source of all our evil.

"Well?" demanded Sweet, his voice casual and loud once again. He took a last drag on the cigar and it hissed into the snow at his feet. "How 'bout it, Racks? You going with me, or staying here with them?"

Halvorsen had taken a step toward him as he spoke, and the two men—*odd,* Teresa thought, *they do not look in the least alike*—were almost face-to-face. The old man was looking up at him earnestly. "Ralph," he murmured. "It's not that easy. We got to think about this."

"I did. That's why I brought *her* up here." He met Teresa's eyes for a moment before his went back to his grandfather's. "She and him—they're the only ones who know, now. And he's a murderer. If they disappear it's all neat, it's all solved, it's all wrapped up. State doesn't even have to pay for his trial. This will end it—right here." His voice sharpened. "Well?"

Halvorsen glanced back at the two of them, sitting in the snow not far from the edge. Teresa stared; beside her Michelson tensed too. They had seen his look. It was cowed, guilty; the look of a once-independent man who now was bowing, for the first time in his life, to the lie that others said was the way it had to be.

"Don't," whispered Michelson.

The old man stepped up beside Sweet and turned to face the others. The warden smiled.

"Ralph," said Halvorsen.

"What, Gramps?"

"When we get back I'm goin' to tell the truth. Just like I always done. I recommend you do the same."

And then Halvorsen, behind Sweet, had his arms around him, pinning back his arms. "Get his gun!" he yelled.

"Let go, Racks, dammit!"

The old man did not answer. Teresa stood up, horrified. The warden's hands, with the shotgun in them, were coming up despite the old man's restraining arms, his contorted face.

"Let go. You'll get it too. I mean it!"

"Help me!" said the old man, looking at Teresa and Michelson.

She began to run.

Sweet gave a heave, his shoulders swelling, and broke free. Halvorsen was thrown back for a moment. When he moved forward again the warden was ready this time and the shotgun was free and he swung it suddenly, butt first, and the old man cried out and fell.

"No!" Teresa screamed as Sweet reversed the muzzle toward him.

She was still screaming when she reached him. He swung half around to meet her, beginning to grin. Then he saw the knife.

Or rather could only really catch a dull gleam for an instant as it came around toward him, driven with all a small woman's strength and terror. Instinct tried to pull him back; his feet could not follow, they were sunk deep. Instead he threw himself backward, away from dark, fixed eyes and dilated nostrils. But it was too slow. And unlike a man she did not aim for trunk or gut. He knew that just before the point sliced into his eyes. He cried out and dropped the gun and lashed out, blind, catching something soft with his fist.

Teresa made no sound. His wild swing had caught her arm, knocking the blade off somewhere. She did not bother to look after it. Instead she bent, and then backed away from him, holding the shotgun uncertainly.

"Terry! Over here!"

She moved backward toward Michelson's voice, still holding the gun on Sweet. The warden stood swaying with his hands to his eyes. From beneath them a runnel of blood suddenly poured down one cheek. Behind him the old man lay still in the snow.

"Terry," Michelson said again.

"Stay there, Paul."

Sweet shook his head again, then lifted a bloodstained mask. One eye was closed. The other, bloody, intact, glittering, found her. He took a step forward. She backed toward Michelson, toward the jagged rocks that rimmed the pit.

"Stop," she said to the warden.

Sweet said nothing. He kept coming. Blood and a clear liquid ran down one side of his face. He held out his hands for the gun.

"*Shoot him,* Teresa!"

"*No, no puèdo—*"

Sweet smiled. He stumbled on something beneath the snow, then recovered and came on. When he was five feet away she closed her eyes and jerked at the trigger.

The sound and recoil shocked her. She had never fired a gun. It bucked out of her grasp and struck her painfully in the breast. She dropped it and stepped back, almost falling.

The warden stopped, his face first blank and then surprised. He looked down at his shoulder. A hole had opened in his coat, just above the collarbone, and suddenly it was full of bright blood. When he looked up again his expression had changed. He came the last few feet in a rush, kicked the shotgun aside and reached for her. She twisted away, but stumbled on a hidden rock. The edge was too close to maneuver. He had her shoulder now. His face was close. It was nightmarish; she struggled once again, once more, as she had in a dim room; his breath still stank of cigars. As she thought this her braced feet slid backward in the snow. As she glanced back the canyon opened under her eyes.

"Here! Over here!"

At the shout from behind Sweet's head turned. She swayed dizzily at the edge, held in his arms. Far below she saw the bottom; rock-littered snow; trees, foreshortened by height; the tiny tracks, as if made by ants . . . one leg kicked at air and her throat closed. Then unexpectedly, the warden released her and she half turned and fell across one of the rocks, knocking the breath from her with a plosive whoosh.

Above her she made out dimly two men swaying slowly together at the edge of the pit.

Michelson held the warden to him with all his remaining strength. From the moment that, dragging himself forward by his arms, he had lunged up toward Sweet's neck, he felt the other's strength. It was too great for his. Fresh, rested, they might have been almost a match; Sweet broad and big, Michelson slimmer but taller. But like this, starved, frozen, his leg useless, it could end only one way.

And it was ending now. The choke hold he'd used to distract Sweet from Teresa was effective—a Pittsburgh cop had used it on him once, at an antinuclear demonstration—but he didn't have the strength to hold it. Sweet must have wrestled at one time, or else he thought fast. He had tucked his neck instantly, blocking Michelson's arm, and now he turned and broke free like a bear through spiderwebs.

Michelson grunted over two swift blows to the stomach. He let go and felt the other's hands on him in turn. The grip was inelegant but there was strength behind it, brute force, and in seconds he felt himself being forced backward between the rocks. Sweet's face moved between him and the clouds. Warmth spattered his face. The ruined eye was open, empty, the pupil sliced nearly free and swinging out from the collapsed eyeball as the warden leaned.

Michelson grunted. His back was close to breaking. He raised his good leg and kicked at Sweet's knee and missed, kicking the air. The big man growled. Michelson saw the fist coming but couldn't move. It smashed his skull against the rock and his fingers loosened. When the white flash cleared he felt himself going back, sliding backward, and then snow beneath his back, and he was sliding down—

"Paul!"

It was her voice. The only one left who cared. If he let go, she would be alone—with him.

His failing grip—fingers sliding, clawed, down the close-woven wool of Sweet's coat—found something metallic and hard. His right hand hooked around it and set. His other arm went out, flung wide with precognition of the coming fall. It scrabbled through snow for a grip, tearing fingernails on frozen earth. He kicked again, desperate, no longer his mind at all but his body fighting now, genes that had survived a hundred thousand battles. This time his boot struck bone. Sweet grunted. A scraping sound, then Michelson's breath exploded as the other fell full length on his chest.

They rolled together madly, kicking and striking and biting. His knee was torn abruptly with what would have been unimaginable pain had some filter between his body and his mind passed it. For at that instant, behind and under his upper back, there was nothing. His free arm flew wide once more, grabbing out desperately a Sweet screamed hoarsely next to his ear. But Michelson was not listening.

He had the rock.

His body twisted toward the drop but slid no farther. He sobbed for breath. The hard, uneven face of the stone embossed itself into his fingertips. His left hand was holding his whole weight. And more; his right remained spasmed closed in Sweet's coat. Looking now along it he saw that they lay together past the teeth and on the last slanting declivity before the drop. He held himself from it by his left hand. By his right, as he looked down, he held the warden. Sweet's lower body hung over the edge. His bleeding face was upturned, eyes sealed. His left arm was wrapped around Michelson's right like the ancient welcome of the Romans.

"Paul!"

He felt her fingers on his and looked up. The rock was solid, bedded in frozen earth hard as diamond. It would never move. But beneath four hundred pounds of weight his fingers were bending slowly. As he looked up from them he saw her set her boots against the rock and reach for his wrist.

"Paul, let go of him. I'll pull you up."

"Terry—"

"Let him go! He's dragging you down!"

Michelson stared up at her, mute, in agony yet past feeling it. He was being pulled in two; yet there were things he wanted to say. To explain. Ah, words, he thought. *Ultima ratio* of the intellectual; forgotten artifacts of metaphor, desperately signaling the incommunicable. He knew they were useless. Yet still something unenlightened in him wanted to say that he was sorry. For Aaron, for the old man, for those he had been wrong about in the woods. To say that he would die now; it was demanded, and he wanted to. Or even that he loved her. But here at the end he was amused a little to find that he had no breath to say anything in any other way than the last way he would say, or do, anything at all.

"No!" screamed Sweet suddenly, and began to claw his way up the arm he gripped so desperately, to the shoulder, the waist—

But Michelson had already opened his hand.

* * *

She lay sprawled across the rock for a long time looking down at the scarred grooves in the snow, at the clawed-up dirt. She must have breathed, but she was not aware of breathing. She did not move forward. She only huddled there, pressing herself into the surface of the cold stone until slowly she became cold stone herself.

A long time later she felt a hand on her shoulder, and turned her head.

It was the old man. He looked ill; his hand trembled visibly as it lay on her coat. His mouth moved.

"What?" she said, after a moment.

"They went over?"

"Yes."

"Have you looked yet?"

"I do not want to."

He patted her shoulder again, heavily, and began crawling forward. He went slowly. He looked back at her once, then bent and lay full length, digging in the toes of his old-fashioned laced boots for anchors as he looked down. Then, after a minute or so, he pushed himself back and got up and began brushing the snow from his black and red coat, looking off toward the far hills.

"He is dead?" she whispered.

"They both are."

His voice was empty of shock, empty of sorrow; it was only tired, infinitely tired. She watched him. Standing at the edge of the hill, the wind in his face, he looked at the trees, the hills, the clouds once more; a long, devouring look slowly turning to wonder, a look like a child's. Then he seemed to see her, and went to her and bent clumsily and put his hands on her tear-stained cheeks.

"Come on," the old man said gently. "We'd better be getting back."

THE AFTERIMAGE

THE DEER STOOD RIGID ON THE HILLSIDE, TREE-SHROUDED, tree-gray.

Its square flanks trembled with life. Life was a white smoke at its muzzle, a quiver of lashes over dark liquid eyes. It stood ready for flight or battle, gently wagging the antlers that branched over its high-held head, gazing steadily downhill between the close-set trunks of the great trees it knew more intimately than any man.

The buck had heard the strange far-off sound, and had come curiously out from its covert. Now it was watching the two figures that moved across the valley beneath its hill.

They moved slowly, one a few paces before the other. As it watched one of them fell. The other turned and waited, patient, weary, terrible in its uprightness and its carelessness of cover and the man-smell that came suddenly on the wind.

As the deer watched, trembling with the desire to flee, against the sun-shafted sky between scattered clouds came something that filled the valley with humming thunder. It descended swiftly, hovered near the two figures, who had stopped moving to watch it, and then came to the ground not far from them, blowing the snow up and away from itself in a rolling wave of white.

The stag bounded suddenly into motion. After a hundred leaping yards it stopped, high up the hill, panting in the cold, delicious air. It glanced back. The two figures, the strange thing, were safely out of sight.

It trotted a few steps toward its covert, and then paused, lifting its head as if in thought. It did not understand what the two walking things were, nor did it understand the unnatural thing it had just seen. But from what dimly it knew, what keenly it heard and saw and smelled, it understood suddenly one thing.

The dying time was past.

The season of man was over. Now all there was to fear were natural things: cold, hunger, coyotes. Save for these there stretched now free before it another year. A vast desert of time, time to live, to eat, to duel that strong old one in the next valley. Time to lust and breed and then nuzzle wonderingly at the small ones that staggered steaming from the bodies of its does.

The buck did not understand men. But they did not matter to it. They came; and then they left, back to somewhere it did not care to go to or know or even wonder about.

The men were transient. They did not remain. Only the hills remained, and the seasons' change, the light of day and the dark mercy of night. Only these—these and their perceiver, its own miraculous unique and knowing self—would, it knew, endure forever.

ACKNOWLEDGMENTS

Though novels must be written alone, they are seldom works of the isolated imagination of the author. In this book I am especially indebted to J. M. Zias, for development of the characters during a hike above Cuba, New York, and to Dave Wolf, R. P. Lewis, Marilyn Goldman, and Tony Ardizzone for advice and criticism. Any errors of fact or interpretation are of course my own.

GRAHAM MASTERTON

JOHN FARRIS

THE BEST IN HORROR